Praise for Claire
Medieval Rc

"Claire Delacroix is a shining star o̲ .... ɡ̲ᴄ̲ɴ̲ɪ̲ᴇ̲. C̲ɪ̲ᴇ̲v̲ᴇ̲r̲ɪ̲y̲ original, emotional and fast-paced, full of twists and turns, her books will sweep you off your feet!"
—Julianne Maclean, USA Today bestselling author

"A beguiling medieval romance...readers will devour this rich and compulsively readable tale."
—Publishers' Weekly on **The Rogue**

"When you open a book by Claire Delacroix, you open a treasure chest of words, rare and exquisite!"
—Rendezvous

"An engaging tale of lost love found."
—Booklist on **The Rogue**

"Enthralling and compelling!"
—TheBestReviews on **The Scoundrel**

"A delightful romp through medieval times in a game of cat and mouse...**The Scoundrel** is an enjoyable read, mixed with passion, humor and an unexpected plot that kept me turning the pages."
—Romance Junkies

"[Claire] Delacroix's satisfying tale leaves the reader hungry for the next offering."
—Booklist on **The Warrior**

"**The Beauty Bride** is a book that captures you from the first page...a magical and inspiring story. Four hearts!"
—Pink Heart Reviews

"A lyrical medieval-era romance!"
—Publishers Weekly on **The Beauty Bride**

*"Full of adventure, intrigue, likable characters and an exciting romance, **The Warrior** is medieval romance at its best..Ms. Delacroix has penned another engrossing, impossible-to-put-down tale, a Perfect 10. Don't miss it!"*
—Romance Reviews Today

*"After reading this magnificent book, it's easy to see why Ms. Delacroix is considered one of the best medieval romance authors around. With careful attention to detail and a beautiful writing style, she whisks you to the Middle Ages for a grand romantic adventure...**The Beauty Bride** is a fabulous read!"*
—The Romance Studio

*"What better way to begin a story than by providing the reader with a strong, determined hero out to avenge a wrong with a spirited and equally determined woman by his side? **The Rose Red Bride** is blend of passion, humor, fairy lore and everlasting love. A great read!"*
—FreshFiction.com

"An enchanting historical [romance] that mixed a great tale of the fairy realm with a beautiful, sensual love story...an historical as refreshing as it is gripping!"
—Romance Junkies on **The Rose Red Bride**

"Terrific!"
—The Best Reviews on **The Snow White Bride**

*"**The Snow White Bride** is a gripping story with an emotionally wounded yet wonderfully strong heroine. What a passionate, romantic read!"*
—Vanessa Kelly, one of Booklist's new stars of historical romance

"Another keeper penned by a master storyteller. Don't miss out on this medieval series."
—Writers Unlimited on **The Snow White Bride**

The Warrior's Prize

Claire Delacroix

The Warrior's Prize
Claire Delacroix

Copyright 2014 Deborah A. Cooke.
All Rights Reserved.

Cover by Kim Killion.

❧

Without limiting the rights under copyright preserved above, no part of this book may be reproduced, stored in or introduced into a retrieval system, or transmitted, in any form, or by any means, (electronic, mechanical, photocopying, recording, or otherwise), without the prior written permission of both the copyright holder and the publisher of this book.

This is a work of fiction. Names, characters, places, and incidents either are the product of the author's imagination or are used fictitiously, and any resemblance to actual persons, living or dead, business establishments, events, or locales is entirely coincidental.

The scanning, uploading, and distribution of this book via the Internet or via any other means without the permission of the publisher is illegal and punishable by law. Please purchase only authorized electronic editions, and do not participate in or encourage electronic piracy of copyrighted materials. Your support of the author's rights is appreciated.

❧

Printing History:
Deborah A. Cooke trade paperback edition
December 2014

This work has been published in a simultaneous digital edition.

❧

Dear Reader;

*And so we come to Elizabeth's story, the final book in my True Love Brides series and probably the one most requested by readers. This book is a little bit different from previous linked books I've written: although the majority of events in this book occur after those in **The Frost Maiden's Kiss**, there is some overlap. Elizabeth and Rafael's story begins when they meet, which is right before the climax of Malcolm and Catriona's story. I wanted the book to stand alone, though, so you'll see some of those scenes presented again here, but done a little differently. I had a wonderful time writing Elizabeth's story—and helping Rafael to challenge her expectations—and I hope you enjoy reading it.*

*This brings us to the end of The True Love Brides series, which carried on the stories of the eight siblings at Kinfairlie first introduced in The Jewels of Kinfairlie trilogy. We have, however, only had the stories of seven of the brothers and sisters, a fact which many of you have noticed. It's no spoiler to let you know that Ross is left without a partner or a true love at the end of Elizabeth's story. We haven't heard much from him in recent books. He has been at Inverfyre, completing his training in the service of his uncle, the Hawk of Inverfyre. If you take a peek at the family tree for Ravensmuir and Inverfyre on my website or download it from my online store, you'll see a little bit more of what the Hawk and Aileen have been up to since the telling of their story in **The Warrior**. Married in 1409 (the same year as Elizabeth's birth) they hosted a family gathering at Midsummer after their vows were exchanged. This gathering was where we first met Roland, Catherine and their eight children from Kinfairlie. Roland and the Hawk were cousins and milk-brothers (which meant they shared a wet nurse) so the Hawk's five children with Aileen are second cousins of the family at Kinfairlie we've come to know so well. We're talking a little break from the family now, to give Ross and the other children at Inverfyre a few years to grow up, then I will launch another medieval series set in the Highlands and Inverfyre. Ross won't be the only one to have his story told in that series!*

*In the meantime, I wanted to return to my medieval roots, so to speak, and write a series of linked romances set during the Crusades. My first published book, **The Romance of the Rose**, was set in the 13th century, in France and the Latin Kingdoms, as the heroine went on a pilgrimage and the hero served with the Templars. My upcoming series, The Champions of Saint Euphemia, is set during the twelfth century, when the Latin Kingdoms were diminished by the Muslim leader Saladin. This series of medieval romances follows three knights and a squire, as they leave the*

Holy Land to return home to Europe, having accepted an errand from the Templars. Gaston, the hero of the first book, believed he would be a Templar for the duration of his life: he's served fifteen years with the order when he learns that his older brother has died, making him unexpectedly heir to their family holding. He accepts a request to deliver a package to Paris for the order, believing that doing so is a trifle he can readily fulfill on the way home. Another Templar knight, Wulfgar, is ordered to accompany Gaston to defend the party en route, which was the mission of the Knights Templar. A third knight, Fergus, has completed his term of service and is returning home to Scotland to wed, as previously arranged. Gaston's squire accompanies him, as does the lady Gaston hastily weds before his departure. The small party soon learns that Gaston has been entrusted with a treasure beyond price, and that someone—in their party or in pursuit—will stop at nothing to possess it. Each of these four stories is a medieval romance in itself and features one of the men in the company, but the mission undertaken by the knights evolves over the course of the linked books. Again, there are overlapping story elements, with some key scenes told in several points of view, but the chronology of the adventure begins in Gaston's book and ends with the last book in the series. There is an excerpt from Gaston's book, **The Crusader's Bride**, at the back of this one. **The Crusader's Bride** will be available in May 2015 and there are pre-order links available now at some portals.

I am also working through the Ravensmuir and Kinfairlie books to create audio editions, with the plan of ultimately having audio available for the entire series. It's a time-consuming process, but quite an interesting one. Right now, **The Rogue** and **The Beauty Bride** are available in audio, with **The Rose Red Bride** in production and **The Snow White Bride** and **The Ballad of Rosamunde** to follow. Please check my website for more details if you like audio books.

Until next time, I hope you are well and have plenty of good books to read.

All my best,

Claire

Books by the Author
Claire Delacroix Books

Time Travels:
ONCE UPON A KISS
THE LAST HIGHLANDER
LOVE POTION #9
THE MOONSTONE

Medieval Romances:
ROMANCE OF THE ROSE
HONEYED LIES
UNICORN BRIDE
THE SORCERESS
ROARKE'S FOLLY
PEARL BEYOND PRICE
THE MAGICIAN'S QUEST
UNICORN VENGEANCE
MY LADY'S CHAMPION
ENCHANTED
MY LADY'S DESIRE

The Bride Quest I:
THE PRINCESS
THE DAMSEL
THE HEIRESS

The Bride Quest II (or The Scottish Bride Quest):
THE COUNTESS
THE BEAUTY
THE TEMPTRESS

The Rogues of Ravensmuir:
THE ROGUE
THE SCOUNDREL
THE WARRIOR

The Jewels of Kinfairlie:
THE BEAUTY BRIDE
THE ROSE RED BRIDE
THE SNOW WHITE BRIDE
"The Ballad of Rosamunde"

The True Love Brides
THE RENEGADE'S HEART
THE HIGHLANDER'S CURSE
THE FROST MAIDEN'S KISS

THE WARRIOR'S PRIZE

Short Stories
BEGUILED

Apocalyptic Romances:
The Prometheus Project:
FALLEN
GUARDIAN
REBEL
ABYSS

ಎ

Deborah Cooke Books

Contemporary Romance:
The Coxwells:
THIRD TIME LUCKY
DOUBLE TROUBLE
ONE MORE TIME
ALL OR NOTHING

Paranormal Romance:
Dragonfire:
KISS OF FIRE
KISS OF FURY
KISS OF FATE
WINTER KISS
WHISPER KISS
DARKFIRE KISS
FLASHFIRE
EMBER'S KISS
THE DRAGON LEGION NOVELLAS
("Kiss of Danger", "Kiss of Darkness"
and "Kiss of Destiny")
SERPENT'S KISS
FIRESTORM FOREVER (2015)

Paranormal Young Adult:
The Dragon Diaries:
FLYING BLIND
WINGING IT
BLAZING THE TRAIL

ಎ

The Warrior's Prize

Monday, June 21, 1428

Feast Day of Saint Maine and Saint Eusebius, Bishop of Caesaria.

Claire Delacroix

Chapter One

Ravensmuir, on the east coast of Scotland

Elizabeth had watched the Fae gather for Midsummer's Eve and hasten toward the sister keep of Ravensmuir. She did not trust their actions a whit, and knew she had to go to Ravensmuir to discover the truth. Alexander had changed his thinking about escorting her there once a company of mercenaries traveled toward Malcolm's keep, so Elizabeth had stolen out of Kinfairlie this very morning, with her beloved mare, Demoiselle.

To her surprise, she had met the Earl of Douglas on the road at such an early hour, with his niece Jeanne and a company of men escorting them. Jeanne was richly dressed, as if she meant to attend a coronation, though there was no other destination on the road than Ravensmuir.

Elizabeth recalled the earl's insistence that Malcolm was betrothed to his niece, this Jeanne, and bit her lip. She had heard just days before that Malcolm had taken a bride. All of Kinfairlie was aflutter that Malcolm had wedded the serving maid Catriona, seemingly on impulse, naming the son she had delivered in Ravensmuir as his heir.

Evidently her companions had not yet heard the news, and Elizabeth would not be the one to enlighten them.

They rode in comparative silence, none of them evidently welcoming questions about their plans. Perhaps it was the hour, but Elizabeth was content to be silent.

When the new tower of Ravensmuir came more clearly into view, she could not help but gasp aloud.

"Zounds," the earl muttered beneath his breath. "What a fortification!"

Jeanne straightened in her saddle with evident interest.

Elizabeth surveyed the new structure with awe. Ravensmuir's new keep resembled the lost one in many ways, but was more formidable. While the old keep had been forbidding, perched on the coast like a bird of prey, this one was tall and bold, taking a resolute stance. It reminded Elizabeth of a knight staring down a foe, fairly daring his opponent to strike.

Certainly, this keep would not be readily assailed. Her brother Malcolm had left Scotland to seek his fortune shortly after inheriting the holding of Ravensmuir, shortly after the old keep fell to ruins. He had earned the disapproval of his older brother, Alexander, Laird of Kinfairlie, by selling his blade. It was clear, though, that Malcolm had learned much of defending what he would call his own in his years as a mercenary.

The morning sunlight turned the stone of the high tower to a golden yet rosy hue. The walls were tall and smooth, and a gatehouse had been built to bar the opening in the middle of the old thorn hedge that Elizabeth remembered from childhood. That hedge, planted in a protective arc behind the moat, stopped short of the rocky cliffs at either end. The road was blocked where it passed through the hedge by this gatehouse and its portcullis. The hedge had also grown taller and thicker since last she had visited. Even the gaps at the ends of the hedge, once wide enough that a person could have ridden a horse around the barrier, seemed more narrow than they had been. Elizabeth saw men moving stones there, making the way even more precarious.

The road ran straight toward that gatehouse, as always it had, and across the barren moor. This ensured that none could approach the keep without the laird or his sentry knowing of it. The moor outside the hedge was beaten down more than usual, and Elizabeth could see the mark of many fire pits on the land. There were half a dozen tents there yet, although they were being struck, and the single fire smoked as if it was being extinguished. This must have been where the masons who had rebuilt Ravensmuir had camped. Most, it was clear, were gone, and these men would be departed soon.

"It might be a vision," the earl muttered beneath his breath, clearly surprised by the sight of the new keep. "It might have been built by a sorcerer, to have grown so high and strong in so little time."

Jeanne, her red hair blowing in the breeze, smiled in obvious anticipation. "The laird is rich," she declared with satisfaction. "For no man could order such a construction otherwise."

"A fine new keep," the earl noted with satisfaction. "It will suit you most well to be lady here, my dear."

"Indeed, uncle," Jeanne agreed. "I have always believed it my fate to wed a rich man." She granted Elizabeth another cool smile. "Perhaps I shall drink sweet mead from a golden cup at Ravensmuir." She laughed then, well pleased with the life she believed she rode to claim.

Elizabeth did not comment again, although she was sorely tempted. Jeanne, in her opinion, had been indulged in every possible way for every day of her life. She was pretty and could be pleasant enough when all went according to her plan, but Elizabeth had seen her denied a sweet when they had both been small, and she would never forget the fury of the other noblewoman's tantrum.

What would Jeanne do when she met Catriona?

What would she do if Malcolm denied her?

A wicked part of Elizabeth looked forward to the other woman's first sight of Malcolm's new wife.

Indeed, Jeanne had been waspish when Elizabeth encountered them on the road, noting how Elizabeth's beauty had faded, like that of a rose touched by the frost. It had been unkind of her to say as much aloud, and even the earl had frowned, though Elizabeth knew it to be true.

One day, beauteous Elizabeth, you will come to me. I already grow impatient.

Even in the morning sunlight, the murmured pledge of Finvarra, King of the Fae, made Elizabeth shiver. Indeed, it seemed she could not forget the words, for they echoed in her thoughts repeatedly. Perhaps he had cast some spell that devoured every other notion she might have had, the better to ensure she was haunted by his pledge.

Of all her kin, Elizabeth Lammergeier was the only one who could see the Fae, and so, she was the sole one who spoke with Finvarra, the King of the Fae.

She had wished repeatedly that the gift would abandon her, but to no avail. Even now, the gathering of small Fae, all scampering, flying and racing toward Ravensmuir, was disconcerting, though her companions were oblivious to it. Elizabeth kept her gaze upon her gloved hands, the better to ensure she did not react to the Fae.

She became aware of another horse riding alongside her and assumed it one of the men in the party. She glanced his way and started to find herself confronting Finvarra, King of the Fae, on a steed of deepest pewter.

She might have summoned him with her thoughts, though Elizabeth doubted she had any such power over him.

"Come to visit your brother one last time?" Finvarra asked, his dark eyes gleaming.

Elizabeth caught her breath and averted her gaze, knowing the folly of staring into the depths of his eyes. Jeanne and the earl were unaware that the Fae king rode alongside their party.

Finvarra dropped his voice low. "Or dare I hope you come to me?"

Elizabeth shook her head, even as niece and uncle admired Ravensmuir's proportions.

"Seven years have passed since we paid the tithe to Hell, and it comes due again at Midsummer's Eve," Finvarra informed her. "The Laird of Ravensmuir, his soul as black as a raven's plume, will be our offering."

"Nay!" Elizabeth protested, unable to keep silent. Her mortal companions glanced at her with concern. "He has built a gatehouse too close to the hedge," she said, fabricating a reason for her outburst. "I always liked it without one."

"A maiden's whimsy," the earl said with a shake of his head. "It would hardly be sufficient defense and a prize worth the having must be defended." He patted his niece's hand, clearly meaning her and not the keep.

"Malcolm volunteered to take his comrade's place," Finvarra whispered, stroking his beard as he eyed her with confidence that all should be as he decreed. "He gave his word, and it cannot be broken now."

Elizabeth clutched Demoiselle's reins, knowing she could not let this be.

Finvarra stroked her hand and Elizabeth hastily pulled it away. "You could offer yourself in his stead," he suggested.

Nay, she would not do that. She did not trust the king of the Fae. Likely he would seize them both. She shook her head again, refusing to look into his dark eyes.

This explained why she had seen the Fae converging upon Ravensmuir. They gathered to collect and then surrender their tithe.

Which would be Malcolm, newly home and with a new bride.

Finvarra smiled with infuriating calm. "Until we meet again, my Elizabeth," he murmured, the words making Elizabeth shiver. His figure and his horse shimmered before both disappeared. Elizabeth watched the stardust fall to the ground, glitter one last time, then fade away completely.

What could she do to help Malcolm?

ða

The portcullis was barred against the arriving party, a fact that the earl did not find pleasing.

To make matters worse, Malcolm also did not hasten to admit them to Ravensmuir's bailey. Elizabeth could see a man who must be her brother near the portal to the hall and he spoke to several of the men before sauntering toward the gatehouse. He was too far away for her to see him clearly, but his tabard was the only one that bore the insignia of Ravensmuir. The earl also seemed to recognize Malcolm for his face grew more ruddy as he stared at the approaching warrior. The earl fairly stamped his feet in his stirrups and Jeanne's lips pinched tightly.

By their manner, one would think they controlled Malcolm's holding already.

"It will not be thus when I am lady, Uncle," Jeanne said in an undertone to the earl. "You can rely upon a warm greeting then."

"Of course, my dear," the earl replied. Elizabeth noted that he was particularly avid and scanning the men inside the walls with great interest.

Was it because they were mercenaries? Or did he count their numbers? Elizabeth had never seen so many warriors at close proximity and she was aware that more than one masculine glance lingered upon her.

At least upon her cursedly full breasts.

She felt her color rise a little, though such attention did not usually fluster her as once it had. It was the warriors and their manner, as well as her conviction that men such as these took whatsoever they coveted, without apology, seeing to their own desires above all others.

Strangely enough, she was suddenly glad to be in the earl's party and not arriving at Ravensmuir alone. It was odd to credit Alexander's doubts, but she saw that he had spoken sense in this matter.

The man wearing Ravensmuir's colors came to stand behind the portcullis, his arms folded across his chest as he assessed the newly arrived party. Elizabeth recognized the brother she recalled in his features, though he was an older and more grim Malcolm than she had known. His eyes were narrowed and he was deeply tanned, not to mention that his manner was less than welcoming. Could this hardened warrior truly be the brother who had teased Elizabeth and her sisters so mercilessly all those years ago?

The shadow of death was dark upon him, that much was evident to Elizabeth, so his end must be near. She thought of Finvarra's words and shuddered. What had Malcolm done that could make his soul fit to be a tithe to Hell? Why would he volunteer to take the place of another when he had so much advantage to his hand?

"Malcolm!" the earl declared, his manner so fulsome that Elizabeth distrusted him. "What cause have you to bar the gates? It will be most inconvenient for your masons."

"The last of them pack their goods at this point, and they have little need to access the bailey," Malcolm said, no hint of emotion in his tone, much less that of welcome. "And we have had some trouble these past days."

"Trouble?" the earl asked. Elizabeth would have wagered he knew of it already.

"Aye, an intruder in the hall," Malcolm arched a brow. "But it is of no matter. I bid you welcome, Sir Archibald." He nodded to someone out of view and the portcullis began to rise. It did not creak, as the portcullis at old Ravensmuir had done, but rose smoothly and silently.

Elizabeth noted that it was the same doughty grill of iron she remembered, with the same fierce points on its base, but previously it had been installed at the entry to the keep itself. Malcolm must have salvaged it from the ruins. She looked at the gatehouse as they rode through its portal, wondering how much else had been retrieved from the destroyed keep. She felt a flicker of excitement to see what Malcolm had done.

The Fae were thick on every side in the bailey, though she strove to ignore their presence. It did no good to reveal awareness of them as a mortal, but Elizabeth was shocked by their numbers and variety. Were all the Fae in Scotland gathered at Ravensmuir?

This tithe that Finvarra said would be paid on Midsummer's Eve must be of great import to them. Even Finvarra himself should be at his own court at Knockma in Ireland, not in Scotland. She doubted that the Elphine Queen was pleased to have a visiting monarch, and one inclined to take charge, linger in her court so long.

"Elizabeth!" Malcolm said as she rode through the gates and a smile touched his lips for the first time. He took the reins of Demoiselle, scratching the mare's nose with a familiarity that reassured Elizabeth, and led the steed to Ravensmuir's portal. Demoiselle nuzzled his hair, as she had before his absence, and it seemed the mare did not see any change of import in Malcolm. Jeanne clicked her tongue in disapproval that Malcolm did not so tend her, and the earl counseled her to be silent with a gesture.

The earl and his party trailed behind Elizabeth and Malcolm, but still she heard the earl's sudden intake of breath. And no wonder, for Ravensmuir's bailey was filled with fighting men, all armed, all watching intently. Elizabeth did not doubt that if a man in the earl's party made a move against Malcolm, the offender would be dead in a heartbeat. There was a tension in Ravensmuir's bailey, as well. Was this the nature of these men all the time? Or had the discovery of the intruder made them so wary? It seemed to agitate the Fae, who moved quickly on all sides.

Before the portal to the hall itself, Malcolm reached up to grip Elizabeth's waist and lift her from the saddle. They eyed each other when her feet touched the ground, snared in a sudden awkwardness. Elizabeth did not know what to do. Malcolm was so different, a man now, not a boy, and one accustomed to earning his way with his sword. The death she saw in him was disconcerting, to say the least, and she knew that Finvarra had told her no lie. It was impossible that she should throw her arms around this stern warrior and welcome him home, as she would have done once before.

There was a glint in Malcolm's eyes, though, a hint that he saw her doubts. "You have grown taller," he said, an affection in his tone that made her smile.

"You look more like a warrior," she dared to counter.

Malcolm's lips quirked even as his eyes sparkled with familiar humor. "And you have learned *some* tact. Well done, sister mine."

Elizabeth laughed, unable to help herself. When he teased her, she could see the brother she had known so well. In her younger days, Elizabeth had been known for speaking her mind and had oft been in trouble for it. Malcolm had oft been in trouble, too, making mischief, although truly he had never been able to compete with Alexander as a prankster. Malcolm kissed her brow and Elizabeth did embrace him briefly then, for she recognized the brother she loved behind this stern guise and was glad of his return.

Could she do anything to help him to survive Midsummer's Eve?

"Are you truly wed already?" she whispered and Malcolm pulled back to consider the earl. His eyes narrowed again as two of the earl's party were dispatched, the pair of horses breaking into a gallop as soon as they had passed through the gatehouse.

"What is amiss?" Elizabeth asked quietly, seeing a quickening in Malcolm's manner.

"Do not ask and do not look beside the gatehouse," he advised.

Elizabeth frowned and might have argued but his gaze became intense and she understood she should remain silent. She saw the shadow of death grow more resolute upon her brother's brow, the sight making her spirit quail that he would be lost, just when it seemed every reward was his to claim.

Since Finvarra, the King of the Fae, had declared his intent to claim Elizabeth, she had also been able to see death in the mortal realm. No doubt Finvarra had inflicted this curse upon her to make the mortal realm less appealing than his own, but certainly, the illusion had prompted Elizabeth to decline many potential suitors. More than once, she had met a man and known at a glance that he would be dead and gone within the year. She saw death in a gruesome way, as if those around her had arisen from their graves. It was a glamour of Finvarra's, and Elizabeth knew it, but still she could not shake its power. The sight of rotten flesh hanging from the bones of those who were soon to die had a tendency to influence her behavior at court gatherings and festivities. The smell of festering corpses rising from the man who shared her trencher affected her appetite at the board. Over recent years, Elizabeth had gained a reputation as both a strange maiden and one easily displeased by a man's attentions.

That death shadowed Malcolm was unacceptable. Elizabeth had to save her brother from Finvarra's cruel harvest. What of the comrade Malcolm replaced? Could she compel that man to take his rightful place again? There must be some honor between fighting men!

"Such folly comes to us with age," the earl cried heartily. "I have a gift for you, Malcolm, but left it at my own abode. My runners shall fetch it."

Jeanne's features were pale and her lips so tight that they nigh disappeared.

"It must be a gift of considerable size," Elizabeth murmured.

Malcolm dropped his voice low. "If it exists in truth. Does he suspect that I am wedded?"

Elizabeth shook her head. "I said naught, though Eleanor and Vivienne confided as much when they returned to Kinfairlie."

Malcolm nodded minutely and she guessed that he was glad of this. His gaze met hers again and his smile turned wry. "And I will wager that Alexander does not approve, as he does not approve of any deed I have done since inheriting Ravensmuir."

Elizabeth saw that Malcolm was vexed by Alexander's disapproval. She might have said something but in that moment she saw the ribbon that unfurled from the man her brother had become. It was the pale green of the sea and edged with silver. She followed its course to find it knotted to another ribbon of deepest amethyst edged in gold. The way the ribbons entwined told Elizabeth that her brother had wed well and for love, even if the match was unconventional.

The sight gave her great relief, and she was glad once again of her ability to see these Fae signals. It also renewed her resolve to see Malcolm saved.

"He will," she said with confidence. "For he will see the love between you."

Malcolm touched her cheek and she was aware of the roughness of his finger. "You have more faith in that than I do, Elizabeth," he said softly. "But we shall see soon enough. Come and meet my wife, Catriona. She may have need of your strength on this day."

"Might I meet your companion?" she asked, trying to sound only mildly interested. "The one who traveled home with you? He had the name of one of the archangels, I believe." She frowned, trying to recall.

"Rafael," Malcolm supplied. "Aye, you can meet him, at least under my watchful eye."

"You do not trust your friend?"

"We have been comrades, Elizabeth, in a harsh trade. It is not the same as friendship."

Elizabeth wagered that was true enough, given the situation her brother was in, but held her tongue. Could she convince a hardened mercenary to step forward and do what was right?

She could certainly try.

Malcolm did not seem to notice her sudden silence. He raised his voice to call to the earl. "Pray come into the hall, Sir Archibald. Though it is early, your ride has been long. I would invite you to refresh yourself." He returned to take Jeanne's hand, kissing its back and leading both women into the hall. Jeanne fairly preened at his attention and Elizabeth bit back a smile.

It was petty of her, but Jeanne had been so unpleasant for so long that it would be sweet to witness that maiden's disappointment.

And sweeter yet to know that they would never be kin.

*

An angel had set foot on the earth.

The sight struck Rafael in the heart he had forgotten he possessed, a blow as piercing and sharp as that from an arrow.

He knew she could not truly be divine, but Rafael could conceive of no other explanation for the beauty who approached with Malcolm. She was looking up at Malcolm, as yet unaware of Rafael, which gave him time to stare.

Rafael had never believed that angels were beings of perfect beauty. He had always assumed that having witnessed both good and evil would leave a mark upon them, and this angel looked haunted by a sorrow that had scorched her soul. The combination of beauty and devastation was more alluring to him than he could have believed possible.

It made him think they had seen much of the same in this world.

He wondered whether she had come to judge him, or to smite him. He suspected that no judgment of his soul would be favorable, but did not shirk from the knowledge of all he had done.

He had survived and that had some value.

The strange thing was that even though he expected this woman would scorn him, he did not want to avoid her. She moved so smoothly across the ground that she seemed to float above it, and he was certain a creature so lovely could not tread upon the earth like any other mortal. She wore a kirtle of crimson as red as blood, its hems embroidered with the gold of the sun. A silver circlet graced her brow, her ebony hair bound beneath a veil of finest gold. Her skin was as fair as ivory and Rafael stared, like a man struck to a pillar of salt for daring to gaze upon such magnificence.

To his surprise, Malcolm escorted her directly to Rafael. Only in his comrade's hall could he be in any proximity to such a maiden, clearly nobly born and yet unwed. He knew she was no angel in truth and feared she was the one Malcolm had sworn to marry. Rafael did not want to see this angel weep in disappointment to learn that Malcolm was already wed.

Oddly, her presence made him recall the accusation of Malcolm's wife, Catriona. She had charged him with being a poor comrade and a poor friend for letting Malcolm take his place and pay his debt to the Fae. Theirs was a fair exchange, and Rafael knew it well, a bargain that repaid the debt Malcolm owed to him. But as he watched this angelic being approach, Rafael could not evade the truth of Catriona's words. It was the mark of angels to shine light upon the deeds of men, to not shirk from the acknowledgment of the truth, no matter how unsavory it might be.

Catriona was right: no man of merit would let another die for him. No man who called himself a friend would let that man take a blow for him.

Yet he and Malcolm were partners in arms, comrades, not friends.

"Malcolm, you must not keep your oath," she whispered, her voice as sweet as the honey of Rafael's homeland. Her eyes were a clear green, he saw, a green as clear as the ocean's curl, and her lips both full and rosy. Her words were so close an echo to Rafael's own thoughts that he was startled. "They cannot claim your soul!"

Malcolm glanced quickly down at her, as if he would silence her, then gestured to Rafael. "Elizabeth, this is my comrade, Rafael Rodriguez. Rafael, my sister, Elizabeth."

Rafael nigh swooned with relief that she was not the earl's niece, Jeanne. He bowed low, not daring to touch her hand or step closer. He knew his place in the court of a nobleman—and actually his place was not *in* that court at all. It was in the stables or the bailey or the armory. They exchanged polite greetings.

"Where is Catriona?" Malcolm asked him.

"She tends to Avery," Rafael confessed, referring to the babe that Catriona had delivered just days before, and who now was Malcolm's heir.

When her brother glanced toward the solar, Elizabeth looked fully upon Rafael for the first time. He had braced himself for her disapproval, but her gaze brightened with an awareness that made his own heart leap. She glanced over him and flushed slightly, as if she liked what she saw of him. Rafael dared to be encouraged that she might not condemn him with a glance.

She was even more beautiful at close proximity, and he admired how fearless she was in meeting his gaze after her survey. She was not a fool, for he knew she recognized what he was. Her gaze hardened then as she surveyed him, her disapproval so clear that he wondered whether he had imagined that glimpse of admiration.

She might not be an angel, but she had the audacity of one, which Rafael liked well enough.

"Would you escort my sister to the board while I make Lady Jeanne and the earl welcome?" Malcolm asked and Rafael could only comply dumbly.

The weight of Elizabeth's hand on his arm was like a feather, her touch as cool as a river. He felt the curve of her breast brush against his arm and was aware of no other soul in the hall. She held her head high and did not look directly at him. Rafael caught the scent of her perfume and all within him clenched tightly.

It was not simple lust that fired his blood, though. He was smitten with no more than a glance, just as his hero *Mio Cid* had been. For the moment, he simply savored the mingled sensations of desire, admiration and a keen awareness of the lady, for he expected only trouble from the choice of his errant heart.

Lady Elizabeth was Malcolm's sister, which made her a noblewoman, and no man of property—even Malcolm—would let a man such as Rafael court his sister. It was a strange twist of fortune that allowed him to escort her as he did in this moment, and Rafael was a clever enough man to know that it might never happen again.

This might be the closest he ever stood to her.

This might be the sole time she ever touched him.

He savored every single step. She might speak to him. That would be the sum of it. At best, he might catch a glimpse of her again. Their paths could never be tangled, much less joined. He would never touch her more than he did in this moment—and for the first time ever, Rafael regretted what he had become.

He had had no choice, to his thinking, but still.

"Are you the one my brother replaces on Midsummer's Eve?" Elizabeth asked just before they reached the high table. Her dislike of the notion was more than clear, and again he admired that she was so undaunted. Her gaze locked with his, her disappointment in him evident.

One censorious glance from this maiden and all his life seemed to fall short of the measure, a measure Rafael had not guessed held merit for him. All this she had kindled within him with a look and a single question. He should have been terrified that a virtual stranger could have such power over him.

Still Rafael welcomed the fact she had any curiosity about him. Confirming her guess could only show him poorly in her view, yet she would not have asked if she had been one to avoid the truth. In this moment, he felt ashamed of his own weakness and could not meet her gaze.

"I am," Rafael confessed with reluctance, then continued with a rare honesty, "for he is a better man than I."

If he had expected her to argue his merit, Rafael was doomed to be disappointed.

"Indeed," she said, though her condemnation was less scathing than he had expected.

Did she see that there was hope for him? It was an unexpected and compelling notion. Rafael dared to meet her gaze and his heart skipped that the lady did not turn away from him.

Yet.

Her words were low, but ardently spoken, her clear gaze locked on his own with a resolve that made his heart pound. "I understand that when a man is given a chance, he is a fool not to seize it."

Rafael was shocked that she fairly dared him to do differently. Elizabeth watched him closely, even as she challenged him to change his ways, then she lifted her chin and turned away, taking her place at the board.

It was unthinkable that Rafael should trade places again with Malcolm, that he should decline Malcolm's offer and put that man back in his debt. It was neither reasonable nor fair to break a wager willingly made, but Elizabeth's manner made Rafael feel a new guilt about the bargain he had struck.

How remarkable that a maiden like this, one who should have shunned him on sight, was the one who saw there was promise in him. How like an angel to peer into the secret heart of a man and find a glimmer of light. Suddenly, the land Rafael had come to despise showed such uncommon appeal that he doubted he would leave Scotland any time soon.

No matter how much it snowed, no matter how cold the winters at Ravensmuir, it was worth enduring any physical discomfort to linger near a maiden such as Elizabeth.

Indeed, she might take pity upon his condemned soul.

*

Rafael Rodriguez.

There was a name to light a flame in the heart of a woman devoid of sense, and truly, Malcolm's comrade was a man who might steal that heart with a simmering glance. Elizabeth had never met the like of him. He was dangerous and dashing, so vital and virile that he made the men of her former acquaintance look like mere boys, regardless of their ages. The way Rafael smiled, as if he knew a potent secret or as if he might tempt her to partake of forbidden pleasures, made Elizabeth flush with awareness even though she knew his truth. He was dangerous and certainly wicked, a man who had undoubtedly despoiled many a maiden and broken many a heart.

Then carried on his way, without remorse.

How could a man who sold his blade be possessed of any remorse? Nay, this was a man who took what he desired, perhaps even savored it, then sought a new fleeting pleasure to satisfy him. He would be callous and reckless and readily bored, and certainly not one upon whom a lady should rely.

Unless, of course, she wanted her keep defended and could pay the price.

Elizabeth was sure Rafael's price would be high.

She bit her lip and wondered what it was like to be despoiled.

Then she wondered whether she would ever know the truth of it, or whether Finvarra would seize her before she could experience the pleasure that man and wife could share.

She caught herself, realizing that even a brief encounter with a man who could not possess any morals had put dangerous notions into her thoughts.

Indeed, Elizabeth had not believed her own audacity when she challenged Rafael to be a better man. She had scarce recognized herself, but knew she had done as much for Malcolm's sake. There was little time to be demure about the matter. She had been surprised that Rafael had not replied sharply that she tend to her own business. Instead, this fearsome man had given her an assessing glance, as if he could assess her merit with ease. His look had sent a shiver through her.

Followed by a dangerous and beguiling heat.

Oh, that heat was seductive. It hinted of all the matters Elizabeth yearned to learn, of the reason why Alexander and Eleanor were so quick to retire to their chamber on winter nights, of the sly smiles she saw her sisters grant to their wedded spouses. It was the reason her mind turned to such temptations.

Or he was the cause of that. Elizabeth had never seen a man more likely to live a life of adventure and romance, a man destined to travel far and wide, to make what he would of his life. He could have been the hero in an old tale, stronger, bolder, more reckless and handsome than any of his fellows—and destined to win every prize. Elizabeth wished she could have been immune to Rafael's allure, but evidently she was woman enough to still feel a thrill in his presence.

Was it because he could read her thoughts? Was it because he obviously had expertise in the art she wanted to experience? Elizabeth was certain Rafael knew every nuance of how a man and woman might love. She was certain he would welcome the opportunity to demonstrate them all to her.

Even knowing it would be folly to invite his interest, Elizabeth wondered how a single kiss from Rafael would taste.

She did not doubt that it would change her view of kisses for all the rest of her days. Indeed, she doubted that any reputable man's embrace would stand the comparison.

She would not dare to ask for such a token. Indeed, such curiosity could only lead her to woe. Nay, she had to convince Rafael to make a different choice, and that he had even considered her challenge for a heartbeat had been more of a victory than she had expected.

This was the man who should die in Malcolm's place.

It would only be just.

Elizabeth studied Rafael, telling herself that she merely sought the means to awaken his sense of honor. That she was not certain he possessed one meant—she assured herself—that he required closer scrutiny.

It certainly was not hard to look upon him.

That Rafael was a mercenary was clear. He was as tall and muscled as Malcolm, both a sword and a dagger hanging from scabbards on his belt. There was a quiet ferocity about him, as well, and she knew he was keenly aware of his surroundings. Indeed, he looked like a man who would miss no detail, as well as one who could kill with his bare hands.

He was garbed in black, not a speck of ornamentation on his garb. His chausses were black leather, simply cut and plain. His boots were tall and wrought of black leather, so similar to his chausses that it was difficult to tell where one ended and the other began. Elizabeth also had no doubt that his legs were muscled and flushed a little to catch herself admiring them. On this day, he wore a white chemise of linen, the lace open at his neck to reveal both his golden tan and a tangle of dark hair upon his chest. His tabard was also black and fell to the top of his thighs, and he wore black gloves.

His eyes were darker than a midnight sky and his hair was as black as ebony. It possessed an unruly curl and glinted in the light. His skin was tanned to a deeper gold than that of Malcolm, so rich a hue that it must have been darker in the first place. His eyes were thickly lashed and surprisingly so, giving him a lazy and sensual look, one that was encouraged by the slight smile that curved his lips.

There was a whiff of the greater world about him, of conquest and battle, distant lands and potent kings. That had to explain her unholy fascination with him. Never mind that his voice was deep and his accent exotic. He moved with the lithe grace of a cat, at ease with his body and its power as he strode to the far side of the hall. He leaned back against the wall and crossed his booted legs at the ankles, watching the portal with narrowed eyes. His fingertips were not far from the hilt of his blade and he gave an impression of coiled vigilance.

Elizabeth understood that Rafael was prepared for whatever might occur. He was a fighting man with experiences far beyond her own. She knew of skirmishes and battles, but Rafael lived in the realm of war. He fought weekly, if not daily, dispensing death and capturing the spoils. There was no complacency or comfort in Rafael's life, no moment to be at ease, no leisure. She wondered how deeply or how often he slept. Rafael had lived with death and Elizabeth did not doubt that he had killed others himself.

Indeed, that realization revealed why Rafael, of all men, should be the one to make her heart leap. His familiarity with death had an affinity with her curse to witness it everywhere. When the mortal world seemed colorless and pale in contrast to that of the Fae, when she felt cold and distant from her fellows, it was welcome indeed to be shaken awake by the sight of this man, and warmed by his vitality.

The strange thing was, Elizabeth realized, that she could not see the shadow of death upon him at all. Every man in the hall bore a shadow of lesser or greater degree, but not Rafael.

How could that be?

Chapter Two

Rafael folded his arms across his chest and steadily met Elizabeth's regard, looking so long, lean and dangerous that her heart skipped. He suddenly smiled so hungrily at her that Elizabeth's innards clenched. His confidence in his own allure was outrageous—and undeserved. He was not so finely wrought as that.

Well, he *was* as finely wrought as that, but what snared Elizabeth's attention was that he was different.

Her mouth went dry at the realization that Rafael thought she found him attractive.

How hideous that he was right.

Worse, he savored that knowledge.

Worse again, Elizabeth did not doubt he would try to use it to his own advantage.

And she did not know how to play this game, much less what to say or do. Elizabeth felt maidenly and sheltered, a sense that she intensely disliked.

It was one she was tempted to change.

Aye, there was something about Rafael and his manner that challenged Elizabeth to make her life what she would have it be, just as he had certainly shaped his own. She yearned to be daring and bold, to defy convention—as her aunt Rosamunde had done—and to do all of that with Rafael. It was no small thing to lust for adventure, but in Rafael, Elizabeth had a treacherous sense that she had encountered a man who could fulfill all of her expectations.

If it suited him to do so. There was no telling how long such a man might be intrigued by her, if indeed he was, even now. He might simply be amused by her. That was an irksome notion. Elizabeth knew the right course and believed that only she could sway Rafael to do what was right—if indeed, any other soul could do so. Though she knew little of men, she would have to use

Rafael's interest in her to save her brother from Finvarra.

It was a prospect that made her palms damp.

It also meant Rafael would die, but better him than Malcolm. She reminded herself of the greater good. Indeed, did not all of these men expect to die without warning? Every day they survived must be a victory.

In contrast, Malcolm had left that life. He had a wife, a son, and a home. It was unjust that he should lose all of that, while Rafael survived.

Particularly as it had been Rafael's folly that had gained Finvarra's attention in the first place. Nay, a man of any merit paid his own debts.

Elizabeth straightened with new conviction. It was folly to find any appeal in such a man as Rafael, despite his allure, and she knew it, though her body evidently did not. The man did not even have a ribbon that might be bound to a true love! Perhaps it was knotted securely within himself, as if he was one who adored only himself. Perhaps he was incapable of love. Elizabeth nearly shook her head in disapproval. Rafael had an abundance of God's gifts but wasted them with his choices.

She would appeal to him, solely to save Malcolm, not because she herself found any pleasure in it. Her heart skipped at the prospect, calling her a liar, but Elizabeth was resolved.

She could do this deed.

She *would* do it.

And if she learned something of the passion between man and woman in doing so, she would likely not regret that.

❧

Rafael had not been impressed by the Earl of Douglas when that man had visited Ravensmuir before. He thought the older man showed too much interest in Malcolm's new hall, an interest that smelled of covetousness. He and Malcolm had been in complete agreement with nary a word exchanged between them, and the earl's tour of the building under construction had omitted all of the defensive details built into the walls. Still the earl had demanded Malcolm's pledge to wed his niece, and Malcolm had agreed—believing he would be dead when that debt came due.

Jeanne proved to be like her uncle, only more so. Her gaze had swept over the interior of Ravensmuir's hall in open assessment, and Rafael thought she might have defined its cost within a silver penny or two.

The contrast between her manner and that of Elizabeth was striking, and indeed, the contrast did Jeanne no favors. Rafael knew Malcolm's sister watched him and cast a glance toward her, watching her blush when he caught her staring at him.

It was odd that he should be intrigued by her, for Rafael had no patience with innocence. He favored experience in women, confidence in one's allure and skill abed. Elizabeth possessed none of these traits, though she had a boldness unexpected.

Yet Rafael was curiously tempted by her.

That she might be an angel sent to redeem him had been a foolish impression. Rafael knew that no deity spared concern for his soul, and once away from Elizabeth's side, his wits returned to remind him of that.

Indeed, he doubted he could be redeemed.

Under normal circumstance, that no longer troubled him, but on this day, the realization made him restless.

He considered Elizabeth, seeing that same confidence in her own security that all of Malcolm's siblings shared, and wondered how his life might have been, if he had grown up in such safety. It did not bear consideration, as he had not, and he was what he was, but Rafael found himself wondering.

Even though he was a consummately practical man.

Why had she even come to Ravensmuir? Why had she come alone? Rafael doubted she had left Kinfairlie with the earl and marveled anew that a maiden would ride out at dawn, unescorted, even to travel to her brother's nearby keep.

What madness possessed her guardian to allow it?

Or had she crept out of her home without approval? It was an intriguing notion, and he wondered at her true nature. Perhaps that was the root of it, for he would have found a defiant maiden more intriguing than a demure one.

Rafael watched Elizabeth as Catriona descended the stairs from the solar, the ring on her left hand revealing her identity. Perhaps Elizabeth also recognized the dress that her brother's wife, Eleanor, had given to Catriona. Certainly, Malcolm's new bride carried herself with the pride of the lady of the manor.

There was no doubt that Elizabeth guessed Catriona's role and was pleased by it. Rafael saw the maiden's eyes light in a mischievous anticipation that made him want to smile. Her gaze flicked between Jeanne and Catriona, and he knew she eagerly anticipated Jeanne's reaction to the news that Malcolm was already wedded.

She was not so angelic as that, then. Rafael did smile that this lovely maiden was a little bit wicked herself.

Though he could not blame her, not when it came to women like Jeanne.

He wagered then that she had left Kinfairlie without approval, and perhaps without even her guardian's awareness, and liked that even more.

Perhaps they had more in common than Rafael had initially believed.

Perhaps she was not even so innocent as he had expected.

As Rafael reflected upon this intriguing possibility, Malcolm escorted Catriona to the earl, bowing low before that man. "I am delighted to introduce my wife, Catriona, to you, sir."

The blood left Jeanne's face and her eyes flashed with fury. Rafael watched Elizabeth, though, and savored her impish smile.

And he had thought her enticing before. The look of her now, eyes dancing with devilry, fired his blood and tempted him to taste her.

He would know then the state of her innocence. A kiss would reveal all.

"Welcome, sir, to Ravensmuir," Catriona said, curtseying in her turn.

The earl was clearly surprised and struggled to hide his reaction; Jeanne made no such effort. His considerations about Elizabeth came to a halt then, for Rafael did not trust the earl, not with an army at his back. He eased his dagger from its scabbard, anticipating trouble, and straightened in readiness.

"She was supposed to be dead!" Jeanne cried, just before she jabbed her uncle in the shoulder. "You promised me that she would be removed!"

The earl looked as if he would have preferred to be anywhere else in Christendom than standing before his silent host and hostess.

"Jeanne, I do not understand your meaning," the earl said, his tone making it clear that he lied.

"I fear I do," Malcolm said. "For an intruder tried to kill my wife last night."

The earl took a step back. "How trying for you. I thought Ravensmuir better defended than this." He forced a laugh. "Should I fear for my niece's future within these walls?"

"I think not, for I suspect you know the man in question." Malcolm's voice dropped low. "Perhaps you dispatched him on that errand."

"Nonsense!" The earl was dismissive.

"My wife saw you look upon his corpse and believes you recognized him."

Elizabeth, Rafael noted with a quick glance, was both outraged and fascinated by these tidings. There was much advantage, in Rafael's opinion in a woman showing her thoughts so readily as this.

He liked that she was passionate, as well as loyal to her brother.

The earl glared at Catriona. "Nonsense, and nonsense to serve her own ends, to be sure."

Malcolm shook his head, and Rafael anticipated that he would provoke the earl. "Then he is as anonymous as I feared." He raised his voice to give a command. "There will be no decent burial for that villain, then. Cast his corpse into the sea and let his soul be damned forever." Several of the men in the Sable League nodded and moved, as if to do Malcolm's bidding.

Rafael swallowed a chuckle at the tactic and felt Elizabeth's gaze flick to him.

"You would not do that to Stephen!" Jeanne protested then turned her anger upon her uncle. "You would not let that happen to him, not after all he has done in service to you!"

And so, the truth was out, and it was precisely as Malcolm had believed. Rafael exchanged quick glances with their fellows, for they could not anticipate the earl's reaction. It would not be good, to be sure.

"Jeanne, hold your tongue. You do not help the matter," the earl chided.

"Nor do you, uncle!" Jeanne advanced on Malcolm, flicking a dismissive hand at Catriona. "Will you put her aside to keep your pledge?"

"That I might wed into a family who embraces murder to see their ends achieved?" Malcolm shook his head. "I think not."

Jeanne was livid, and Rafael suspected that this tantrum in having her desire denied revealed her true nature. Malcolm had evaded a dire fate, to be sure, and he appreciated Catriona's serene nature and good sense more than he had thus far.

"You promised me!" Jeanne spat at her uncle. Her face turned crimson in her anger and her voice rose shrewishly, making her even more unattractive. "You said I would be Lady of Ravensmuir. You said this keep would be mine to manage. You said I would be wedded this very day! I rose from bed when it was still dark to do your will. I rode all this way, but it was for *naught!*" She punctuated this last with a stamp of her foot and a covetous glare around the hall. "I want it," she insisted, as if sheer will could make it so, and folded her arms across her chest.

"Yet it shall not be yours," Malcolm said.

Jeanne exhaled, then marched to confront Elizabeth so abruptly that the maiden jumped. She did not recoil, though, her eyes narrowing as she faced Jeanne.

Rafael took no chances. He slipped around the perimeter of the hall, his grip tight on the hilt of his blade. No one would injure Malcolm's sister while he was present.

"Give it to me," Jeanne demanded, her hand outstretched.

Rafael was only a few feet behind Elizabeth, and he guessed by the way her shoulders straightened that she knew it. All of the people he admired most were observant, so he was glad she proved herself to be so as well.

"I do not understand your meaning," she said.

"Give me the herb that will let me see the Fae," Jeanne demanded, her manner far from what one might expect of one asking a favor. "I will drink sweet mead from a golden cup and live in finery and wealth. If my family cannot ensure that it will be so, then I have no qualms in abandoning them for a better life."

Elizabeth immediately pulled a dried herb from her purse, prepared to comply. Did she believe in the same whimsy as Malcolm and Catriona, that the demons he and Malcolm had faced six months before were benign beings called the Fae? Rafael could not believe it.

But her reaction told him that he must.

"Might I have a glass of mulled wine?" Elizabeth asked, as if there was naught unusual in desiring to see these creatures. The wine was brought from the kitchens and poured into a cup, which Catriona heated over the fire. Elizabeth put the herb into it, and the aroma changed, becoming more savory than it had been.

Rafael winced, for it seemed to him to be a waste of good wine. He would not have spoiled it to see the demons again, no matter how affluent they appeared to be.

"Wild thyme," Catriona said, glancing up at Elizabeth.

"Aye. It is said to give mortals the gift of seeing the Fae, for a short time at least."

Catriona shook her head slightly. "That is not a property of it that I know."

"Give it to me!" Jeanne demanded and seized the cup greedily. She drained the cup, then looked about herself warily.

Rafael had not believed that the herb would have any effect, but Jeanne's eyes widened with horror as she stared about herself.

A person could either see the demons in Malcolm's hall as Rafael did, or not. Rafael ignored them routinely, for he sensed that they would be prompted to torment him even more if they knew he could see them. There were dozens in the hall, if not hundreds, of every shape and size, twisted and dark and exuding malice. He would never have imagined that a potion could change what a person could see, but evidently he was mistaken.

There could be no doubt that the scales had been lifted from Jeanne's eyes, not when she squealed with disgust.

"They are *everywhere!*" she cried with disgust. "It is as if the hall is full of vermin!" It was no consolation to Rafael to be proven right, not when every ghoul in the hall targeted Jeanne after she acknowledged her ability to see them. They surrounded her, pinching and biting and striking her on all sides. Indeed, there were so many of them that she could scarcely be seen. Jeanne tried to evade them, to no avail, and he saw half a dozen of them dive under the hem of her skirts. Then she screamed in pain. "It bit me!"

Yet his angel chuckled, savoring the other woman's discomfort.

Rafael moved to one side, the better to see Elizabeth's reaction, and found her eyes sparkling merrily.

She was not so angelic at all.

And that realization made her objective clear. She came to save

Malcolm from his wager with the Fae, not by dissuading her brother from keeping to the terms, but by seeing Rafael sacrificed in Malcolm's stead. Rafael had no intent of dying on Midsummer's Eve not even to please a fetching maiden.

Rafael found it both disappointing and reassuring that Elizabeth was not different from him in the least. She had an agenda and she would see it fulfilled, regardless of the price to others.

He wondered if she, like he, was amenable to making a bargain to see such ends realized.

As Jeanne screamed and fled to the bailey, followed by her uncle, Rafael wondered what Elizabeth might surrender to see her objective achieved.

'Twas time he found out.

ે♣

"Your justice is cruel, *mi piqueño ángel*," Rafael murmured from behind Elizabeth and she jumped, unaware that he stood so close. She spun to find his gaze fixed upon her so intently that her heart skipped a beat.

"I do not understand." She managed to smile, even though she thought she might drown in Rafael's steady gaze. Could he truly read her very thoughts? She could not dispel the notion.

"Do not pretend that is so. You wanted to see Jeanne surprised by the tidings that Malcolm was wedded." That smile curved his lips, giving him a lazy and seductive look. Elizabeth thought of entire days spent abed and knew Rafael would know how to fill those hours well. "You could have warned her on your ride to Ravensmuir."

Elizabeth felt her color rise. "If the reaction of the Fae means Jeanne will never return, I cannot find fault with it," she said, her voice sounding more husky than she knew it to be. "I meant the other part you said, the part I did not understand."

Rafael considered her, his gaze slipping over her features and lingering upon her lips. His smile turned mysterious and he leaned so close that she could not fully draw a breath. "I thought you to be an angel," he murmured, his deep voice making her shiver.

"An angel?" Elizabeth laughed, knowing her voice was higher than usual. "Surely not!"

"Surely so." Rafael held her gaze with conviction.

Elizabeth had no idea what to say, but she could not bear the prospect of him turning away. Again she felt out of her depth, and said the first question that came into her thoughts. "Have you seen many angels in your time?"

Rafael's lazy smile warmed her to her very toes. "Never a one until this day."

It would have been tempting to explore that notion, but Elizabeth tried to return the subject at hand to her quest to see Malcolm saved. "As would be fitting, for a man who had pledged his soul to pay a tithe to Hell."

He shrugged, untroubled. "I thought an angel intervened on my behalf, as unlikely as that might be."

"Unlikely?" she retorted. "Why?"

Rafael lifted a brow, which made him look all the more wicked and alluring. Elizabeth stared at him, her entire body thrumming beneath his attention, and she felt a conviction that they two shared a secret. He dropped his voice to a whisper that made the goose flesh rise on her skin. "Because you are no angel of mercy, it is clear," he murmured.

"Jeanne deserves no mercy! I am glad to see her denied of something she desires."

Rafael feigned astonishment so well that Elizabeth could only laugh. He chuckled in his turn and braced a foot on the dais beside her. His thigh was so close that she could feel the warmth emanating from his skin and stifled the urge to touch him. "A vengeful angel, then."

Elizabeth felt her manner turn mischievous, and she said aloud the words she should have kept to herself. There was something about Rafael that tempted her to do and say what she should not. "Truly, I am more glad that we shall never be kin."

Rafael's eyes sparkled and he seemed to fight a smile. "Perhaps you are an angel of judgment? Or an avenging angel?"

Elizabeth realized that Rafael was teasing her, completely against her expectation, but his manner was seductive as well. Her heart was thundering, and she felt aglow in his attention. This man possessed a dangerous power, to be sure. "It is you who would call me an angel or not. I made no such claim."

"Indeed." His gaze swept over her as surely as a touch. "You would simply tempt me—" this last lingered on his tongue, sounding sinful and wondrous at the same time "—to surrender my own life for that of your brother." Rafael shook his head, apparently rueful. His dancing eyes made her doubt that he was truly so. "So you prove to be mortal, after all, and not so different from all others I have known."

"Because I tempt you?" Elizabeth asked, then flushed furiously at the boldness of the words she had uttered without thinking.

Rafael's smile flashed. "Because you would see your goal achieved, with no care for the price paid by others." He pretended to be disappointed. "I had hoped an angel might intervene on principle alone."

"It is principle to pay your own debts and keep your word!"

"But not stand by your sworn word?" Rafael leaned closer, his manner so intent that Elizabeth could scarce draw a breath. She could smell his skin. When his gaze locked with hers and he smiled slowly, she was certain she blushed to her very toes. Her toes certainly curled in her shoes. "Would you not miss me, my lady Elizabeth," he whispered, and she could not avert her gaze "were I dead and gone by Midsummer morn?"

"Not so much as I would miss my brother," Elizabeth replied, though she was not entirely sure that was true. It was invigorating to talk with Rafael, for it made her feel reckless, as if she flirted with danger, even while she sat in her brother's hall.

"I hear doubt in your voice."

How could he be so perceptive? Elizabeth tried to change the subject slightly. "Have you no remorse? No sense of honor?"

Rafael grinned. "None. Why should I?"

"Because it is a mark of a man of merit, to give his word and keep it, to stand by his friends and do what is right."

"Truly." Rafael yawned. "I am glad that I have known so few of them, then. They sound most tedious." He caught her gaze again, a glimmer of humor in the depths of his eyes.

He *was* teasing her.

"I do not believe you," Elizabeth said, just as she might have argued with one of her brothers—though truly there was a charge to their exchange that she had never felt with one of her siblings. "You would have me think you more wicked than you are."

Rafael eyed her with new interest. Elizabeth sensed that she had said precisely what he wished her to say, though she could not understand his intent. "And how would you know for certain how wicked I am?"

"I cannot, but you would not be my brother's comrade if you were not trustworthy in some matters. I will guess that you speak to me now because you consider my challenge to be a better friend to Malcolm."

"And you would be wrong."

"Yet I am not convinced."

Rafael leaned close and Elizabeth could not catch her breath when he watched her so avidly. "Are all the maidens in this land so bold as this?" he murmured. There was an intimacy in his tone, as if they shared a secret, which made her think of confessions whispered abed. She flushed to an even deeper hue, but kept her chin high.

He would see it as weakness if she backed down now and Elizabeth wanted very much to surprise this cursedly confident man. "I do not understand."

"Catriona was quick to speak her mind to Malcolm when she arrived, though she was but a serving maid at that time. And now I find myself dared by a maiden to die in her brother's stead." His smile broadened so that he looked more hungry and his gaze lingered on her lips. "I thought maidens were to be chaste, sheltered and occupied with embroidery until their wedding day."

Elizabeth could not help but scoff. "I have spent sufficient hours at embroidery to find it as tedious as you say you find men of honor, and there is no wedding day in my near future."

"Whyever not?" Now he looked to be so scandalized that Elizabeth was tempted to laugh. His next words eliminated that reaction, though, as did the daring look in his eye. "Have you been too bold in sharing your favors? How naughty that would be, *mi pequeño ángel!*"

Elizabeth gasped that he would make such a suggestion. "Nay!"

Rather than being affronted by her response, Rafael seemed to be amused. His eyes danced at her reaction, and she knew he would have loved her to slap his face.

Elizabeth straightened, feeling dutiful and disliking it more than usual. "My brother Alexander granted me the right to choose the man I would wed, and I find none fitting."

If anything, that confession seemed to please Rafael even more.

Indeed, he laughed. "Perhaps we share the view that men of honor *are* tedious."

Elizabeth stammered at that, for there was merit to his argument. She did like how unpredictable Rafael was, and how he matched wits with her so well. It was irksome to realize that she found this dangerous mercenary far more intriguing than any solid and reliable suitor presented to her thus far.

Rafael laughed at her discomfiture. "So, being the bold maiden that you are, you came to Malcolm's hall to assess the mercenaries gathered there, to see if another manner of man would suit you better." He leaned down again, his expression making her heart skip. "Should you care to sample one to be certain, I would volunteer."

Elizabeth was shocked. "You dare too much! I came to Malcolm's hall to try to save his soul!" When Rafael did not reply, she continued, daring to scold him. "Surely you could take your rightful place and finish what you alone began."

"Surely I would be churlish to decline Malcolm's offer and to restore the debt between us. It is clear that it troubled him to owe me a boon, and in this, his debt will be repaid."

Elizabeth frowned at this detail she had not known. "How so?"

"I saved Malcolm's life when first we met." Rafael appeared to be insouciant but he watched her reaction so closely that Elizabeth suspected he was not. "Now he has vowed to save mine and all will be even again. The fact is that I would rather be living than dead."

That smile toyed on his lips as he eyed Elizabeth. "But should you wish to try to change my mind, *mi piqueño ángel*, and try to revive my forgotten sense of honor, or even if you should like to assess the merits of a man devoid of merit, I should be delighted to indulge your whim."

He bent over her hand then, brushing his lips across her knuckles so slowly that she shivered to her very marrow. Elizabeth felt warm, as she had not felt warm in years. Indeed, her blood might have been simmering in her veins, a sensation that was most wondrous.

"We might make a bargain of our own," Rafael whispered, his lips moving against her flesh as he held her gaze, and Elizabeth sensed she wagered with the Devil himself. "The question is, of course, what would you offer in exchange for Malcolm's life?"

Elizabeth felt her mouth open in surprise but nary a sound came out. Rafael was taunting her and she knew it, but when his gaze clung to her lips, she licked them without meaning to do so.

He caught his breath and his eyes flashed, then she saw him swallow. If anything, he was even more intent then.

"Is everything an exchange for you?" she demanded breathlessly.

"Everything is an exchange for all men, no matter what they say of it. All favors must be repaid and all gifts must one day be reciprocated."

It was a harsh view of the world, but one Elizabeth supposed was characteristic of a man in his trade.

"People with their wits about them do well to understand the terms of the exchange with complete clarity before making agreement."

"That sounds like a guideline to live by."

"And so it is, and so I share it with you, for it is not only my kind who expect something in exchange for whatsoever they would give."

He was utterly serious and Elizabeth understood that he was warning her, though she did not know from whom or from what.

"Take care in what invitations you offer, my lady," Rafael continued and his gaze burned into hers. "If I choose to accept any exchange you suggest, there is not a man alive who will be able to stop me."

"What of the Fae?"

Rafael's manner turned harsh. "There are no Fae, as you people insist on calling them. It is the dead who haunt Ravensmuir, and a portal to Hell itself that will be opened on Midsummer's Eve." He arched a brow, looking diabolical. "The question is who will enter it willingly. I tell you now that it will not be me." He smiled seductively again. "Unless of course you offer an exchange to me that no man with blood in his veins could refuse."

Elizabeth was shocked, but tried to hide it, wanting to appear less innocent in this man's view than she knew she did.

"Would you trade a seduction for Malcolm's life?" Again, bold words she should never have uttered crossed her lips, shocking Elizabeth. She sensed that she played with fire, but she did not care—she had not felt so vibrantly alive in years. And truly, being

The Warrior's Prize

in Rafael's presence tempted her to take risks she normally would not.

His brows shot up, his interest snared. "There is but one way for you to find out."

With that, Rafael abruptly turned and strode away, abandoning her as if he had lost interest in her company. Elizabeth watched him go, wondering what had possessed her to say such a thing.

Yet he had walked away.

Was she so lacking in allure as that?

The air was cool in his absence and Elizabeth shivered. She felt the heat leave her flesh and saw the mortal world dim around her, as it had since Finvarra's first pledge to make her his own. The Fae danced closer to her, chanting in anticipation of her surrender to Finvarra. One whispered to her of infidelity to the Fae king, but Elizabeth ignored both taunt and Fae determinedly.

What was it about Rafael that dispersed Finvarra's glamour? Why was it that she felt so vital in his presence? Was it because of his trade or his familiarity with death? Was it because there was no shadow of death upon him? Elizabeth nibbled her lip as she watched him and wondered.

"Be wary of Rafael," someone counseled and she jumped to find Catriona close beside her. That woman shook her head with disapproval. "He is not to be trusted in the least. Of all these former comrades of Malcolm's, he is the one who sees solely his own advantage."

Rafael cast a censorious glance in the direction of Malcolm's new wife, again as if he had heard her words though he was too distant to have done so. He then strode out of the hall. With his departure, Elizabeth felt as if another layer of fog had been placed between herself and the mortal realm around her.

Then Catriona curtseyed before her. "I welcome you to Ravensmuir, as well, Elizabeth, but must ask of you a favor. Would you make such a potion for me, as well?"

Elizabeth smiled. "Of course, Catriona. 'Tis why I brought it."

Catriona smiled and urged Elizabeth toward the solar. They were almost of an age, and Elizabeth had a strong sense that she was going to like her brother's new wife. She wanted to see the newly arrived babe, Avery, as well, to verify that he was as healthy and perfect as Eleanor had said.

It would probably be healthy to deny her impulse to pursue Rafael, at least for the moment.

❧

Rafael could think of naught but Elizabeth after he left the hall. He had intended only to provoke her a little, to give her a glimpse of the world beyond what she knew, but her unexpected reactions had left him fascinated. He resolutely stayed away, both from the hall and from her, but still she filled his thoughts.

It was Elizabeth's combination of innocence and boldness that snared his attention, to be sure. Rafael liked that she was keen of wit. He liked that she could surprise him, and undermined his assumptions about maidens of her ilk. He admired that even when he provoked her, expecting her to retreat demurely, she lifted her chin with a sparkle of determination in her eye and challenged him in her turn.

He could become enamored of provoking this maiden, though Rafael knew that to be a dangerous impulse.

Indeed, Elizabeth had a ridiculous trust in her own safety, a trust that all her kin shared. It was a sign of having grown to adulthood in a region of peace, a situation so strange to Rafael that he dreaded the moment she learned the truth of men.

Nay, it was how she would be taught the inevitable lesson that concerned him. Something about this alluring maiden made Rafael feel protective of her. Did she not know that many a man would have accepted her impulsive offer and sampled her fully by now? Most of the men in this hall would have taken her forcibly, if it came to that, seeing that as the price for her uttering her invitation so boldly.

He could not believe that she was such a fool that she failed to understand the price of what she offered. Nay, she simply cared more for Malcolm's survival. Rafael had known few who would sacrifice anything of their own for the welfare of another, and her impulse only increased both his urge to defend her.

And to know more of her.

Was it not angelic to bring out the best in a man? Rafael was amazed to realize that there was any merit lurking in his heart, much less that he could be trusted to defend the innocent.

If he spent much time with Elizabeth, he might forget all he knew to be true!

It did not help his resolve that Rafael could see her in every shadow and when he closed his eyes, he saw again her alluring smile. He was enchanted by the mischief that had danced in her eyes at Jeanne's expense, and plagued by a fleeting sense that they two had more in common than he might ever have imagined.

Rafael had no illusions as to his nature. He knew that in other circumstance, in another hall, he might have acted upon Elizabeth's suggestion. Indeed, he might have accepted her wager so quickly that she had no chance to reconsider it. But Rafael knew that he had been alone in Elizabeth's presence because Malcolm trusted him, and he would not betray his comrade's confidence.

Rafael did not, however, fully trust himself. After all, as Elizabeth had noted twice, he was prepared to let Malcolm die in his stead. He was a poor friend, to be sure, yet he found himself remarkably reluctant to prove himself more so.

With any luck, Elizabeth would be dispatched to Kinfairlie in short order, and the distraction she offered would be removed.

Rafael prayed that he would not be entrusted with the task of escorting her home.

No divinity could be so cruel, even to a sinner like himself.

Chapter Three

Rafael was in the stables when he heard Bertrand and Louis jesting about Elizabeth. He was tending his destrier, Rayo, who was not in need of any tending. He froze at the sound of his comrade's voices, unable to keep himself from listening. It was clear to him that they were unaware of his presence. It seemed deceptive to listen to his fellows thus, but Rafael heard Elizabeth's name and wanted to know what they would say.

What he heard only confirmed his every doubt.

Bertrand whistled. "Were she not Malcolm's sister, I could be tempted by Lady Elizabeth and her charms."

"What man would not be so?" Louis retorted. "Hers is a rare beauty, and an innocence beyond compare."

"Did you see her smile?" Bertrand gave another whistle of admiration.

Louis chuckled. "Indeed. It fairly lit the hall. It was good that she turned that smile upon Rafael, for he is not one to forget his place."

"Nay, nor will he be seduced to be any woman's pet."

Pet? Rafael frowned at this choice of word and listened more closely.

Louis seemed to be surprised. "Do you not believe her to be a maiden?"

"Of course, but that situation will not last." Bertrand spoke with easy confidence, and Rafael trusted his assessment. The youngest son of a baron, Bertrand knew the habits of the aristocrats better than most. "She arrived with the earl, did she not? Doubtless there is some match in the making, for she is not so young as that. Nay, she will be wedded to some nobleman, as befits her rank, but if she is like her brother, she will see her desires fulfilled all the same."

"What is that to mean?"

"That any man who would be seen as fit to take her hand is likely so old as to have one foot in the grave, and be more like to sleep abed than to pleasure his lady."

Louis gave a hoot of laughter. "And a lady so young will want a lover of her own. Once her virginity is claimed, she will have the freedom to do as she will while her husband slumbers."

"Keep your wits about you and she might insist her husband hire men-at-arms, including one or two of her *particular* choice."

"One or two upon whom she can bestow her favor! Who better for a lover and pet than a mercenary, who can come to her defense as well?"

Rafael straightened in distaste at this notion and barely kept from revealing his presence.

Bertrand's next words made him glad he had not done so.

"Perhaps that lover might even dispense of her tedious spouse." Bernard's tone was dour. "Though any man so foolish would be dispatched in short order to the executioner's block."

Now it was Louis who whistled in appreciation. "So, she would be rid of both spouse and lover."

"Plus heir to a holding and some fortune, much like her brother. What better situation for a lady who would shape her our future? This family is not a company of fools."

"Ah, Bertrand, you know too much of noblewomen and their ways."

"I speak only from experience. My own sister rid herself of a spouse in this way and rules that man's holding now in her own right. It was she who saw her lover charged with his crime, too, and she who watched his execution."

"Women can be cruel. 'Tis good for all of us that they seldom have power." Louis frowned, then asked the question in Rafael's mind. "But truly, do you see Lady Elizabeth's heart as so dark?"

"Even if she does not have such a dark plan, taking a lover after she is wed to some baron in his dotage would see her future secure."

"How so?"

"She will have need of a son to prove her merit to any spouse who takes her hand. I would wager Lady Elizabeth is sufficiently clever to ensure that her womb will be fruitful, regardless what her wedded spouse chooses to do or not do."

Louis chuckled anew. "I confess, Bertrand, that your tales make me find greater favor with my hounds. They are not so complicated as noblewomen."

"They have that advantage, at least, though I would like to believe that you do not find the same pleasures with them as I have found with noblewomen."

The pair laughed together, well pleased with Bertrand's jest. "How many supposedly legitimate heirs do you believe you have fathered, then?"

"At least a dozen, over the years."

"Nay! It cannot be so! Not you, so rough and unmannered that no one would guess your lineage!"

"There are ladies who savor a taste of our kind," Bertrand said. "Perhaps it is a yearning for adventure and peril."

"Or paying too much heed to the troubadour's tales."

"I cannot say, but I have no quibbles with sating a lady's desire." Bertrand coughed. "You may be sure that if Lady Elizabeth beckoned to me, I would fall to one knee with all speed and serve her every whim with ardor." Bertrand laughed. "I would fall into her bed, with the merest crook of her finger in invitation, and make her cry with pleasure all the night long."

Louis laughed. "And do you call that witless, then? You would be used by her."

"And she by me. The exchange of pleasure is a fair one, Louis, and understood to come with no pledges from either side. My heart and my life are never part of the wager. To risk either *would* be witless and a folly beside. We must know our places and our prospects. 'Tis as simple as that."

The pair carried on then, their voices fading, though their words gave Rafael much to consider.

Was Bertrand right? Did Elizabeth seek to beguile him so that he could serve her whim and secure her future? Did she think to summon him—or a man like him—to serve her husband by day and herself by night when she was wedded?

Would she demand that he kill her husband to prove his affection, then see him executed for murder?

Rafael found the very notion abhorrent. To be mischievous was one matter, but such scheming was quite another.

On the other hand, Malcolm had been heir to Ravensmuir and

had never given any hint of it in the six years Rafael had known him. That man had kept his assets to himself, until he could act upon them and secure his place in the world. Perhaps he had learned to ensure his own status from his family. Perhaps Elizabeth had learned similar lessons. There were fewer options available to women to ensure that they were secure, but Rafael wondered now if there might be rumors about Elizabeth. There might be a reason she was unwed, if other men in the vicinity knew the tendencies of her kin.

It mattered little, for Rafael would never accept such a role. He was no pet, and he would be no married woman's lover. He would not be the adulterer who was found out and punished, nor would he play the executioner in exchange for a lady's favors abed. He considered himself warned by Bertrand's tale.

Rafael brushed Rayo with new purpose. He knew his place. He knew his prospects. He would not be tempted by a maiden's smile to wish for what could never be his own.

He would give her the benefit of the doubt, rather than assuming her to be so cunning as Bertrand's sister. Lady Elizabeth was young and had only known safety and security.

She did not know what she did in offering him so much.

She wished only to save her brother, which was a noble impulse.

The sooner they two were parted, the better, to Rafael's thinking. He did not doubt that Elizabeth would forget him soon, and that was for the best. Rafael would never be the pawn of any noblewoman, kept as a pet to please her abed in secret.

There were, after all, some pleasures not worth their price.

After entrusting the wild thyme to Catriona, Elizabeth was left with little to do. Rafael was still absent, and she debated the merit of seeking him out. There was not much time left to persuade him to her view, though it would be beyond bold for her to go in search of him.

She rather liked the idea of being beyond bold.

She expected that impulse was Rafael's fault. Indeed, there had been a quickening within her when he spoke to her, and one taste of that excitement was far from sufficient.

Elizabeth was resolved to find him but had no chance to act upon her impulse.

"My lady!" Vera exclaimed from close proximity.

Elizabeth turned to find the older serving maid scowling at her. Elizabeth dropped her gaze, ruing the fact that Vera had known her from birth. No one else could have elicited such a strong response in her.

"I would expect you to know better how to conduct yourself," Vera huffed, her tone chastising. "Consorting with the likes of *Rafael*! Do not imagine that I did not see your conversation with that man. Others might have missed the truth, but I have eyes in my head, that much is for certain." She heaved a sigh. "To think of what your mother would have said, had she had the misfortune to see you in such company!" Vera marched to Elizabeth's side, without taking a breath, and deposited Avery in the younger woman's arms.

He was the perfect distraction. Elizabeth could do naught other than catch the infant close, then naught else but admire him. He was a handsome babe already, his eyes a clear blue and his lips pursing in anticipation of a meal. He shook a small fist at her and Elizabeth smiled as she cuddled him.

She was struck again by that yearning to have a husband and a babe of her own, but as she gazed down at Avery, Elizabeth feared such a fate was not to be hers. She grew no younger and Finvarra's claim, which had seemed dangerous but distant, appeared increasingly close at hand. She had thought the choice would be hers to join him in Fae, and it was, but his curse had ensured that the mortal realm appeared at disadvantage.

Save when she was with Rafael. Elizabeth blinked at the truth in that. How could that be? Why was that so? Why did he, of all men, not appear to be shadowed by death?

"Is he not the most beautiful child that ever you have seen?" Vera cooed.

Elizabeth nearly laughed. "You say that of every child born in our family."

"Avery was not born to our family," Vera corrected. "Though Malcolm claims him as his own. And no wonder, for he is a healthy child and will grow tall and strong."

"You cannot know that," Elizabeth argued, though she hoped it would prove true.

"There is a vigor about this one, to be sure. He has defied death already."

"Eleanor said he was tangled in the cord," Elizabeth said, trying to sound as if she knew more of such matters than she did. She had been allowed in the birthing chamber when Eleanor had delivered Alexander's first son, but since then, Eleanor had decreed that it was no sight for maidens. Elizabeth had been compelled to watch Alexander pace the hall during Eleanor's subsequent deliveries, and leave Vera to tending her.

She wished she had paid closer attention on that one occasion. Once again, she felt sheltered and innocent, a feeling she did not like.

Had Rafael seen babies born? She did not doubt he had. Even Malcolm had been able to aid in Avery's arrival!

Vera shook a finger at her. "You try to change the subject, my lady." Given that Vera had served at Kinfairlie since Alexander's birth, Elizabeth and her siblings were accustomed to that woman's blunt speech—just as Vera was accustomed to her charges, once small and now grown, speaking plainly back to her.

"You were the one to speak of the child first!" Elizabeth protested. "I believe you are the one seeking to change the subject!"

Vera scowled. "If it keeps your thoughts as they should be, then all the better. Do not be casting your glances after men such as these, my lady, not if you wish to have a babe like this and a home to call your own."

"Me?" Elizabeth asked, trying to feign innocence even as she felt a blush rising over her cheeks.

"Aye, you! I saw you speak with that Rafael, and never was there a man with a heart blacker than his. You should know better than to consort with his kind!" Vera listed his faults with gusto. "A mercenary, a warrior, a bloodthirsty man with no mercy in his soul." Vera shuddered at her own summary.

Elizabeth realized that Vera might be the best source of information about Rafael to be found. "Can a man not hope to be forgiven for his sins?"

"Aye, he can, but he must do the hoping himself," the serving maid replied tartly. "You are not such a fool that you should be expecting more from a man than he can rightly give."

"Indeed?" Elizabeth was not ashamed to try to keep Vera talking. She did tend to gather the most interesting gossip and rumors, even at Kinfairlie. If only Moira were here: between the two women, Elizabeth would soon know more of Rafael than he knew of himself. She smiled at her own thought, and Vera jabbed a finger toward her.

"Aha! I know what notions make a maiden smile thus! Use the wits you were born with, Elizabeth Lammergeier. Men such as these offer naught to a woman of any ilk, and less yet to one born so high as yourself. They have no homes and coin passes through their hands like spring rain running through the grass." Vera dropped her voice to a hiss. "You should see how they drink and gamble at night, like the very spawn of Hell come to abide in my lord Malcolm's hall."

"I should like to see that," Elizabeth said, almost purely to see Vera's reaction. "Do you think I might stay here this night?"

"Oh! You should not dream of such a situation! It would be unfitting, unsuitable and deeply wrong!"

"But you linger here."

Vera stood a little taller. "I am here to aid my lord Malcolm's new bride, in service to my lady and the new heir. Never let it be said that I did not endure much to serve my family."

"It shall never be said," Elizabeth agreed.

Vera was not swayed from her lecture. She shook her head and eyed the company. "My lady does not care for them being here, particularly that Rafael, but she strives to show honor to them as my lord's former comrades and guests as is right and good." The older woman huffed. "I need not tell you that they were not invited to his board!"

Elizabeth frowned. "But I thought Malcolm sought his fortune on the Continent."

"That he did and returned here last Christmas Eve with Rafael."

"Then how did his former comrades come to be here? How did they know to seek him here, if they were not invited? Had Malcolm told them of his inheritance?"

"Not he! It was that demon Rafael and no other who sent a missive, telling them of my lord's good fortune. He is behind their arrival here, doubtless for some dark scheme of his own. I bade my lady lock the portal to the solar each night, lest we be robbed by those said to be guests in my lord's hall!"

"Surely old comrades would not do thus!"

Vera dropped her voice low. "Yet a man was killed in this hall, just the other night."

Elizabeth frowned. "I thought it was the earl's man, who had come to kill Catriona. I thought Malcolm's comrades had defended him by killing the intruder. Was that not the import of Jeanne's tantrum?"

Vera waved aside this detail. "Such a deed would never have been attempted by any man, had the hall not been filled with men of this kind. It is Rafael's fault, to be sure." She leaned close to Elizabeth, her eyes bright with conviction. "They cannot be gone soon enough, to my thinking, nor can you be returned soon enough to Kinfairlie, where you can be guarded in safety."

Elizabeth did not want to return to Kinfairlie as yet. It was far more interesting to be at Ravensmuir. She wanted to save Malcolm, and she could hardly convince Rafael to change his course if she were sitting by the fire at Kinfairlie.

With her embroidery.

Elizabeth struggled not to grimace. It was too soon to leave.

"When does Malcolm take you home?" Vera demanded.

"After the midday meal, he said."

"The food cannot come quickly enough. I shall go to the kitchens and see if it can be served earlier than expected." Vera bustled away, leaving Elizabeth rocking Avery. The boy nestled against her, put his fist in his mouth and went to sleep. Elizabeth admired him, unable to avoid concerns of her own future.

"Should you wish one of those of your own, there are many here who would willingly aid in that quest," one of Malcolm's comrades muttered from close beside her. When Elizabeth glanced his way, he grinned at her, revealing that he was missing a tooth or maybe two. Elizabeth could smell the dirt of his garb and stepped away from him on impulse.

She stopped short at the weight of a man's hand on the back of her waist and her eyes widened. Surely she could not be in peril at Ravensmuir!

☙

"A man's sister should be safe in his own hall," Rafael said, and Elizabeth caught her breath in relief. She glanced down to see that his dagger had been drawn from its scabbard, the blade shining in the shadows at his side.

The other mercenary clearly saw it as well, for he bowed and backed away.

Elizabeth found herself liking the fact that Rafael came to her defense and turned to him with a smile of gratitude.

He, however, frowned at her. "Go to the solar," Rafael advised tersely. "Or better yet, return to Kinfairlie."

"Are you concerned for my welfare, then?" Elizabeth asked, trying to keep her tone light. "It seems that would be the choice of a man of honor."

"Or one who chooses always to war against folly."

Elizabeth considered him, sensing that he blamed her for his comrade's behavior. As before, Rafael watched her as intently as a cat watches a mouse it stalks in the night, and his avidity made her pulse race and her voice rise. "I am no fool!"

"Then do not pretend to be one," he replied with resolve. Elizabeth was startled and she knew it showed, for no one spoke to her thus. Rafael's tone softened when he evidently noted her reaction. "You are clever enough to see that it is not solely your welfare at risk, but the camaraderie of the company." He arched a brow. "Should they draw knives to fight over you, they could hardly be expected to defend each other's backs in some later battle."

Elizabeth supposed that made sense. "And do you expect to fight again?"

Rafael smiled as if she had asked a ridiculous question. "One thing that is guaranteed in this life is that there will always be another battle to fight. One never knows the day or the time, but my blade will not rust in its scabbard."

Elizabeth studied Rafael, even as she rocked Avery. He lingered, almost as if he provoked her to demand more of him.

As if he waited for her to ask the right question. The weight of his gaze upon her made her flush again, that heat stealing over her skin from head to toe. Her heart beat more quickly and it seemed she could not draw a full breath. She was achingly aware of her body and of its proximity to Rafael's hard strength. Elizabeth had never felt like this, and she did not want the sensation to end.

"Vera says Catriona dislikes you," she said on impulse. "Why?"

Rafael folded his arms across his chest, his expression changing to amusement. "Can you not guess?"

"Aye, I can guess one reason. Because she does not wish to lose her new spouse so soon as Midsummer's Eve." Rafael nodded at that, still untroubled by her implied charge, and Elizabeth dared to prod him. "My brother has a great deal to live for, with a holding rebuilt, a new wife and son, and it would be a poor friend who let such a wager stand."

"So you have said."

Rafael's calm acceptance of this situation annoyed Elizabeth. "He takes *your* place! It is unjust, regardless of what debt stood between you two before." Elizabeth heard her voice rise in frustration. "How can you not even acknowledge what is right and noble and good?"

"And choose to die in your brother's stead?" Rafael raised his brows. "Indeed, you ask a great deal, my lady."

"I do not believe you are so callous as this," she insisted. "You stepped forward just moments past to defend me."

"For the welfare of the entire Sable League, not of you," he said, much to Elizabeth's disappointment. "Little good comes from a woman distracting the men and creating conflict in the company." Rafael leaned closer before she could protest. "Do not confuse me with a knight in one of the tales you hear before the fire at night, my lady. I have lived as long as I have by choosing for my own advantage and naught else." There was a resolve in his dark eyes, one that left her in no doubt that he had killed and often. Rafael's voice dropped even lower, and a harder tone Elizabeth had never heard before. "I defend what I am paid to defend. It is that simple, *mi piqueño ángel*."

"It is not that simple. It cannot be."

His eyes flashed fire, evidence that her words had found their mark. "Do not pretend to be more witless than you are."

"I only heed your own words," Elizabeth insisted, certain that he responded so vehemently because she had found a truth. "You saved Malcolm when first you met. You admitted it yourself. You must have taken some risk in that."

Rafael chuckled darkly. "And a calculated risk it was." He

gestured to the company. "Virtually all of these men have been saved by me at one time or another. I *like* having debts owed to me, instead of the other way around. In a time of trial, there are many debts I can collect to save my own hide. It is a strategy that ensures my own survival and naught else." He held her gaze for a potent moment, as if he would will her to believe him heartless, then spun away.

"I do not believe you so calculating as that," Elizabeth said, raising her voice so he would hear her. "Malcolm brought you home with him, after all."

"And I will wager that Malcolm calls me comrade, not friend."

Elizabeth was vexed that he spoke the truth, but persisted. "I still believe that you know trust is a more stable currency than mere coin."

"And I have already noted that you are too clever to pretend to be a fool." Rafael pivoted to face her and bowed deeply, his manner mocking. "My lady."

Elizabeth would have liked to have thrown something at the infuriating man. She might have continued the argument, more confident with every exchange that no matter how much she dared, Rafael would treat her with honor.

She also was certain she made progress in changing his mind.

Elizabeth had taken but one step in pursuit when a raven's cry echoed through the hall.

જી

When the raven landed on the windowsill of the great hall in the late afternoon, Rafael knew its arrival was a sign that he should heed. Such a bird was a portent of ill fortune, for all who saw it, and a warning. He considered himself warned, and warned against the allure of Malcolm's fetching sister.

He had only to convince himself to heed his own conclusion. Why had he come back to the hall when he had been determined to avoid her? Why had he stepped forward prepared to defend her against Gustav?

She agitated him, to be certain. She was successful in provoking him, to be sure. When had anyone ever appealed to his sense of justice? When had anyone dared to suggest that his life was worth less than that of his comrade, Malcolm? No matter how vehemently he argued the matter with her, she insisted on believing that there was good in him. It was an attractive notion, but Elizabeth was doomed to disappointment.

After all, he would not willingly take Malcolm's place, no matter how much she entreated him to do so. A bargain was a bargain, no matter how readily a pretty maiden could addle his thinking on the matter.

Most of the men of the Sable League were gathered in the hall. The majority of them honed their blades and polished their weapons, and more than a few of them stole covert glances at Malcolm's pretty sister. Squires sat on the floor, ensuring that armor was in good repair. The mood was quiet but purposeful. It was only a matter of time before the earl demanded vengeance for the insult to his niece—though Rafael believed the greater affront was to his own thwarted ambition to hold the new Ravensmuir.

Vera came bustling back from some quest to the kitchens and Catriona had just descended from the solar. As Rafael watched, Vera reclaimed Avery from Elizabeth's arms, as if the younger woman could not be trusted with such a precious burden. Elizabeth almost smiled at the older woman's protective manner, her gaze flicking to Rafael as if they shared a secret, but he ignored her attention. What did he know of serving women who were protective of the infants in her charge? His life could not have been more different than the one that Avery was already making his own.

Vera took no chances in terms of Elizabeth's welfare, for she shooed the maiden toward Catriona with a dark glance toward the company of men. Rafael assumed then that Vera, who he knew had served long at Kinfairlie, had served there long enough that she had seen Elizabeth come into the world. It was remarkable to imagine any person having such continuity and security in their life, and Rafael felt a new understanding of the confidence Elizabeth showed.

When Vera had ensured sufficient distance was between Elizabeth and the men, she bestowed her venomous glance upon Rafael.

He saluted the older woman, smiling and bowing to her, because the temptation to tease her was irresistible. Vera scowled and spun to march away proudly, exactly as he had anticipated.

Elizabeth giggled, the sound tempting Rafael to consider her in turn.

The bird's cry, at least, kept him from striding to her side.

Malcolm leaped to his feet when the raven appeared. He might have been waiting for its arrival, for he showed no surprise at its presence. Indeed, he walked toward the bird with such obvious expectation that Rafael wondered if Malcolm knew the creature to be tame. He recalled the tales he had heard in this abode of the laird being able to converse with ravens, and wondered if there was any truth in it. Certainly this bird watched Malcolm's approach with interest and without fear.

"God in Heaven!" Vera cried and clutched Avery so close that the infant protested.

The raven tilted its head at her words and surveyed the men in the hall with an eerie intensity, scanning the hall before looking back at Malcolm.

Its presence could have been another sign, to Rafael's thinking, that this hall stood at a portal to Hell.

"Welcome, Melusine," Malcolm said, then made a distinctive whistle. The bird cried out, as if in reply, then took flight anew.

"Trust a Hellhound to have a pet raven," Tristan jested and the other men laughed.

"More than one," Elizabeth contributed, the clear tone of her voice making Rafael look up despite his resolve. His heart leapt at the discovery that she was looking at him, as if she spoke to him alone. "Once there were dozens of them living here."

What would she give to save her brother's soul? It was an intriguing question, but the better one was how much Rafael would take.

What price would change *his* mind?

Was there one?

"Perhaps that explains the name Ravensmuir," Rafael muttered and his closest comrades chuckled.

Meanwhile, Malcolm hastened to the window where the raven had been and peered at the sky. He stiffened suddenly, his gaze fixed on something in the distance. Rafael was immediately on the move, understanding that whatever his comrade saw, it was not good.

"Are the gates secured?" Malcolm asked in an undertone just before Rafael reached his side. Rafael halted beside Malcolm and saw the army approaching, his gaze roving over their ranks as he guessed their numbers.

They carried the earl's colors.

Of course. "He is predictable, at least," Rafael muttered.

"Aye, and Louis stands sentinel," Amaury said to Malcolm. "Why?"

"Who arrives?" Ranulf asked, stepping to Malcolm's other side.

In that same moment, Louis appeared at the portal. "A large party approaches," he said. "A party riding to war. I have locked the portcullis and barred the gates, but we should be prepared."

"Is it the earl?" Reynaud asked, looking up from the blade he honed.

"Of course," Rafael said and the others nodded without surprise. This would be no small battle and something quickened within him at the prospect. It was the waiting that broke the spirit. He was glad to have preparations to make, to have the anticipated battle close at hand.

Rafael exchanged a grim glance with Malcolm. "It is time to open your cellar, Malcolm."

Malcolm nodded agreement at that.

Rafael was well aware of Elizabeth's curiosity but paid it no heed. Instead, at Malcolm's nod, he strode to the trap door in the floor, watched Malcolm unlock it, then they two flung open the door. Rafael jumped down into the damp darkness even before the ladder could be lowered into it. Malcolm held a light as he descended.

The cellar was filled with implements of war. They had stored them here secretly, stacking them in the hidden space after it was completed, while the masons slumbered in their tents, unaware of the activity in the hall. Malcolm had acquired sufficient provisions to defend his keep against any foe. The very sight of this arsenal encouraged Rafael, for he disliked facing any enemy unprepared. He had taken a careful inventory of them during the storage, and he was heartened by the quantities. Here were the weapons he knew how to wield. This was the life he knew.

If war came to Ravensmuir, it was best it came on this day, when so many of Malcolm's comrades were in residence.

He was glad Malcolm had prepared so well for this eventuality, and glad they had ensured the earl never guessed of the existence of the cellar during his visit. Surprise was a potent addition to their arsenal.

Perhaps events would send Elizabeth hastening home to Kinfairlie. It might be best, not only for her safety but for her notions of war. He had no doubt that she had heard tales aplenty in which war was noble and right, in which only the evil died and the good always triumphed. There was no blood in those tales, no suffering and no deceit that went unpunished.

Such tales had naught to do with the reality Rafael knew.

No woman of gentle breeding could look upon these weapons and Rafael's familiarity with them and believe him to be anything other than what he was. He was a killer and a warrior, just as were all of his fellows. There was no honor in slaughter and it needed no fine principle to guide it. Avarice often was the motive, propelling many a man just as it guided the earl. The Sable League would fight on the side they were compensated to defend, and only success would be rewarded. This was the truth of his life: war and death and blood. This was what Rafael knew and what he did. Elizabeth would see the truth of it now. She might well flee to Kinfairlie as a result.

She would see what life had made of him.

Had circumstance made him what he was? It was a strange way to think of his situation, and a view Rafael had not considered before. Rafael had never believed that life had given him any choices, but on this day, he thought of Malcolm and his sister, and had to wonder. Had the circumstances of his life been different, might he have become a different man with a different destiny? Might he have evaded the trade of a mercenary? Might he have been an honorable man, such as the one Elizabeth insisted he must be? Indeed, she knew of no other kind, given the security of her upbringing.

Had it *ever* been possible that he might become the manner of man who could offer for the hand of a noble maiden like Elizabeth?

If so, he had been cheated of it, and cheated of that opportunity before he had uttered his first words. The notion made Rafael angry, as if he had lost something he had never desired before.

And that made him yet more angry, if not impatient with the tumult this maiden stirred within him. Rafael knew his own restless nature. He knew he was not a man to settle with one woman in one place. He would always travel, always win his way with his blade, always make the most of whatever opportunity presented itself in any given moment.

Rafael reminded himself savagely that whether that was his choice or the result of his circumstance, at this point, he was fit for no other life.

He could not dispel his anger, but it would be of use to him in the battle ahead.

Elizabeth watched the men prepare for war, finding herself filled with anticipation and curiosity. This was all new to her, but these warriors saw it as routine. Indeed, Malcolm had anticipated an attack and prepared for it with a thoroughness that she would never have expected.

How strange to anticipate treachery and the shedding of blood in defense of what was rightly one's own. Elizabeth knew she would never have thought that way.

At least not until now.

Not until she saw Malcolm's preparations proven to be prudent.

She supposed that possessing anything of merit could lead another to covet that thing. She supposed that a man of sense would be prepared to defend what he had claimed to his name, be that wife or child or holding. She shivered a little, seeing the merit of having an experienced warrior prepared to defend her. The men who had courted her before would have been soundly defeated by the Sable League—what then would happen to their possessions and kin? Naught good, to be sure.

Nay, it made sense to wed a man who knew how to swing a blade.

The men moved with purpose and efficiency, the entire company on its feet immediately after Malcolm's words. There was no haste in their movements, just a calm acceptance of what had to be done and a steady speed in accomplishing it. She could have believed that they had been awaiting such a sign, or even that they were glad of it.

There was, however, no mistaking their glee when the store of weapons was revealed, nor their familiarity with every item in Malcolm's arsenal. They shouted with joy at the sight of metal balls and sheaves of arrows, of knives and swords and armor Elizabeth could not immediately name. They fingered blades and arrow tips, assessed the strength of bows and nodded appreciation of all that was stored there. Elizabeth could see the anticipation in them, the certainty that they would fight soon and fight hard, the relief that they would have good tools to wage war.

Her brother might have been a complete stranger. Malcolm was intent upon his store of weapons and their distribution, his manner quick, terse and effective. There was no hint that he possessed any sense of humor, much less that he was anything other than a hardened warrior who would kill without remorse.

The difference was less striking in Rafael, though Elizabeth did see a resolve in him that she had not noted before.

There was no mistaking the eagerness in the expressions of every one of them.

They were *glad* to be summoned to war. Elizabeth found that a shock, though in hindsight, she was not certain why. Every man welcomed the opportunity to do what he did best, after all.

The Fae dispersed from proximity to that open cellar with all speed, swinging to the rafters to chatter in disapproval. They had an aversion to steel and shuddered in its very presence, though they did like items that shone. Elizabeth did not doubt they would have stolen all the hoarded weapons for their glimmer, gold and gemstones, had there not been so much iron and steel secreted there.

When the cellar was emptied, the weapons were sorted in the hall. Elizabeth was fascinated by the way the men divided tasks without speaking of it. They had fought together many times, it was clear, and each knew the special skills of all the others. Each gravitated toward certain weapons, and they offered choice items to each other in full understanding of who would wield what with greatest ability. There were boys gathering firewood and others sorting arrows and bows, none of whom had been commanded to do so. One heavy-set mercenary had laid claim to what he called Greek fire and was giving some instruction to another in the mixing of various powders that had also been stored in the cellar. He had a boy cutting lengths of string that he said would be used as fuses.

They began to garb themselves for the fighting, as well. Elizabeth watched covertly as Rafael shed his tabard and chemise.

He donned a padded aketon, lacing it tightly around his torso, then hauled a chain mail shirt over top. The chain mail hung to his knees, and he donned another black tabard atop it, belting it closely. This tabard was shorter than the first and cut full, plus there was a golden emblem stitched upon it, over his heart.

He had no squire, evidently, but tended himself, which she thought curious. She saw Rafael check the knife and sword that rested in his scabbards and then don chain mail grieves that covered his legs and boots. He set out a pair of black leather gloves that would rise to his elbows, a metal gorget to cover his throat and a helmet with more than one dent in it before returning to aid the others.

Did none consider that they might not survive this battle? Elizabeth saw the mortality of all of them, though few bore the mark of one soon to be departed. The shadow upon the brow of one man was much darker and Elizabeth knew that he would not live through the battle to come.

Should she warn him? Elizabeth did not know. Could he evade his death? Or postpone it? She had no idea. She watched the doomed man and judged from his expression that he would not be surprised by any tidings she gave him.

Nor would he change his course

They lived day to day, these men, with no expectation that there would be years left to them. It was sensible in a way, and also made Elizabeth feel sheltered for her conviction that she would always awaken on the morrow and live to a goodly age. The greatest risk for her was the birthing of a child, but so long as she remained unwed and chaste, that risk was both distant and small.

As she watched, Malcolm dipped his finger into the soot on the hearth and drew the outline of the point of land Ravensmuir occupied on the stone floor. The men and Catriona gathered around and Elizabeth pressed close behind them, curious above all.

"Here is the cliff of Ravensmuir, and here the keep," her brother said and the men nodded assent. "The thorn hedge extends from here to here, with the gatehouse at its middle. There is no longer any approach from the sea. If they have any wits, they will assume that we are weakest at the ends of the hedge, and so we must drive them back to the middle."

"There is no real passage there," said the man carrying the

shadow of death.

"They may make one," another mercenary noted. "I saw them carry saws to the ends of the hedge. Louis and his crew fired upon them, but they may see the gap widened."

"We will guard either end of the hedge," Rafael said, "so that no horse can pass that way."

"Rocks," the doomed man said. "The boys can pile them in quantity, so the footing is loose and uneven."

"And fire," Malcolm said. "For the horses dislike it. Set a blaze just inside the bailey and lay the bonfire wide. We will place archers inside of that."

"And slay them one by one if they come through that way," another warrior concluded with satisfaction. "Even the corpses will add to the barrier."

Elizabeth shuddered at this gruesome discussion, readily imagining how effective these plans might be.

"At the gatehouse," Malcolm said, pointing to that place. "We will have the first of the oil. The roof is made of stone, with sufficient space to heat the oil."

One man rubbed his hands together in anticipation. "It is a fine thing to serve a lord who has planned his keep so well."

Elizabeth realized they were enjoying the process of planning the keep's defense. Did they enjoy the warfare as well? She was both horrified and fascinated, then glanced up to find Rafael's gaze upon her. He smiled, as if amused by her reaction, and she felt herself flush crimson.

He must think her naive, or a child, but she had never witnessed preparations like this.

She wondered what else he had witnessed routinely that she had never seen before. That only made her yearn to travel far beyond Kinfairlie and even Scotland, to see the marvels of the world and to sample every experience that could be had. She had always loved tales of adventure, but it was the presence of Rafael that breathed life into those stories, making her realize that they were more than tales—someone had lived those daring adventures.

How she wished to live one of her own!

Chapter Four

Malcolm continued to give instruction, clearly having learned much in his years away. Elizabeth listened avidly. "They will likely attack on horseback, and this will be our advantage. From the gatehouse, Ranulf will throw Greek fire." He must mean the heavy set man who had been mixing powders. Malcolm slid his finger across his sketch. "Archers again on the gatehouse and the roof of the keep itself. We will use the arrow storm to create more confusion."

"Burning arrows," one warrior contributed.

"*Poison* arrows," corrected a woman who could only be a whore. Elizabeth had heard that whores followed warriors, but she had never expected to see one in her brother's hall. That woman granted Catriona an assessing glance. "Have you wolf's bane or belladonna?"

"Wolf's bane," Catriona said and left the party to climb to the solar. Elizabeth guessed that her herbs were there. She folded her arms about herself, not feeling unsafe, but not entirely at ease, either.

Did Rafael have a favorite among the other whores in Malcolm's hall? There were a half a dozen or so of those women, their knowing expressions and easy manner with the men revealing their trade. Elizabeth looked around and found one smirking at her, and hastily dropped her gaze. Just as Jeanne had suddenly seen the Fae that she had not realized surrounded her, Elizabeth felt that the company in Ravensmuir's hall was an alien one indeed.

Catriona appeared to have accepted the presence of this woman and the others of her ilk, although Elizabeth supposed she had no choice. She also seemed to be expected to have a stock of herbs, much as Eleanor did at Kinfairlie. Elizabeth wondered if she should have learned more from Eleanor, as her sister Isabella once had done.

Would any man she wed expect her to have such skills with herbs and potions?

Would any man she wed be so familiar with the art of making war? Elizabeth could not believe it, not of the many suitors she had met at Kinfairlie in recent years. Even those who had fought abroad had gone as knights and she doubted their experience had been the same as that of these men.

They certainly had not been as hardened.

Perhaps they had not fought as long.

"Any who reach the hall can be assaulted from above, or cut down in the entry." Malcolm continued. "Two more fires should be set on either side of the hall itself, in order to drive them toward the cliffs."

"Smoking fires would be best," an older warrior with a lined face mused. "I have a means to encourage that."

"Can they dig beneath the hedge?" asked another.

Malcolm shook his head. "It will take time, for the land is rocky, and such tunnels might collapse upon them."

"What of food?" Rafael asked, hands braced upon his hips. "They might mean to starve us out. It would be simpler."

It was almost dizzying to consider all the ways that a keep could be assaulted.

Elizabeth knew without asking that there was no question of her returning to Kinfairlie when Ravensmuir was surrounded and besieged. Indeed, she was glad of the earl's arrival, on that score at least. She wanted to be of assistance in the defense of her brother's holding.

And above all else, she wanted Malcolm to survive.

Remaining at Ravensmuir was the only way to accomplish all of that, and it promised to be an adventure as well. She straightened, realizing that she had been granted her most heartfelt desire. She felt a ripple of anticipation herself, and a vitality almost forgotten.

Malcolm drummed his fingers on the board. "There is hard sausage. There is a well in the bailey that I do not believe can be readily tainted." He nodded. "But this might be the one advantage that they hold."

The men fell silent for a moment, weighing all the concerns and notions that had been voiced, and Elizabeth thought of another.

"Kinfairlie will be hard pressed to assist," she contributed, seeing that the others were surprised that she had spoken. She addressed Malcolm, though she felt the weight of Rafael's gaze upon her. "Even if Alexander guesses you are besieged, he will have to cut through the earl's army to be of aid." She saw Malcolm's doubt that Alexander would have any such inclination and wished she could have removed his doubts. Alexander might disapprove of Malcolm becoming a mercenary, but he was glad their brother was home. He would not have left him without allies in battle.

Before she could speak, Rafael did. "Then we must provoke them to hasten the battle," that man said boldly. "For I do not intend to starve."

"Nor I!" echoed one man and the others gave a cry of assent. They raised their fists in salute to Malcolm.

"To Ravensmuir!" one cried. "May it stand long beneath Laird Malcolm's hand!"

Malcolm's comrades cheered for him, rising to their feet as one. Elizabeth was awed that these men would fight for her brother, even to the death, and wondered how he could compensate them all so well.

Then she wondered how he would himself survive Midsummer's Eve. Her gaze flew to Rafael, who ignored her so pointedly that she knew their thoughts were as one.

"I thank you all!" Malcolm said. "And can only believe that Providence sent you to my gates."

"I have never been called by so pretty a title," Rafael said, prompting them all to laugh. His gaze slid to Elizabeth again and he smiled, a dangerous hunger in his expression that should have warned her to beware.

She bit her lip, enticed as she knew she should not be.

Did she dare seek him out to argue again?

She glanced at Malcolm and saw death even more vehemently upon him. His skin appeared to be rotting from his bones, to her view, and the side of his face was raw where the skin looked to have been sheared away.

Whether it was his wager with Finvarra or the blades of the assaulting company that would doom him, Elizabeth did not care.

The vision made her choice for her.

Rafael flicked a glance her way, one that seemed even more penetrating than before. His eyes were dark, his manner fierce, and she wanted to match wits with him again.

If not more.

For Malcolm's sake.

What if she did offer the exchange he had already suggested? If she surrendered to Rafael, would he ensure Malcolm's survival? Her maidenhead was a small price to pay for her brother's life, when she considered it thus, and truly, Elizabeth yearned to learn whatsoever Rafael could teach her.

She swallowed, resolute in her choice. All she had to do was find Rafael alone, and then summon the audacity to make her offer.

For Malcolm—for Avery and Catriona—she would do it.

૨੧

No man would sleep within Ravensmuir's walls this night, that much was clear. Rafael took the watch as night descended over the lands of Ravensmuir. He stood in the chamber above the entrance to the hall, that room with its windows built small apurpose, and watched the earl's company make camp.

They did not appear to have any inclination to attack in the night.

They *had* tried to cut down the ends of the hedges before darkness fell and had cut down one bush at each end before being repelled by the Sable League. After they had been beaten back, those new gaps had been filled with rocks and stones. It would be challenging to ride a horse through those spaces, though Rafael expected men would invade on foot. Malcolm had set a watch on the ground and twin bonfires already burned, to ensure none crept through the space in the night.

The attacking forces had erected their tents in the fields, beyond an arrow's range of the gatehouse. Their camp was not so far from the one that had been occupied by the masons these past months, and Rafael expected they made use of some of the same fire pits.

The night was clear with stars shining overhead and a cool breeze came from the sea. It carried the smoke from their fires inland. The horses were tethered behind the tents, and Rafael had counted them before the light completely faded. Though they would not be overly useful for the assault, given the preparations, their numbers were a good indication of how many men followed the earl.

The company at Ravensmuir was sorely outnumbered. Rafael could only hope that the experience of the Sable League gave them an advantage that numbers did not. He had conferred with Malcolm and chosen to remain upon watch alone.

Rafael knew the very moment that he was no longer the sole one in the chamber. The foot tread on the stair was sufficiently quiet to be stealthy, but he heard it all the same. He saw a figure in men's garb from the corner of his eye, but it was one too slender to be any man he knew. Given that the earl had already had a spy in the hall, Rafael took no chances. He spun, pulled his dagger and surprised his guest.

In a heartbeat, he had one hand locked around the arrival's throat, holding that person's head against the wall. His other hand held the blade against the intruder's ribs, its tip near the heart, and he pinned the individual to the wall with his hips. The intruder stilled abruptly, clearing feeling that blade, and gasped.

Only then did he note the alluring scent of his captive's skin.

Elizabeth.

In men's garb. Of course. Malcolm would have had the women change, so that they were not so readily identifiable at a distance.

Her pulse fluttered beneath his hand and he could see that her eyes were wide, even in the darkness. Her skin was softer than silken velvet beneath his hand, and she felt fragile. She had not cried out, though, and did not tremble in fear. She was more stalwart than he might have expected. He felt her take a breath when he lowered the knife and her breast pressed against him in a way that sent a fire of awareness through him.

It was the nature of battle to elevate all within a man to extremes. Perhaps it was the mortal danger, but even the first of preparations made appetites extreme. Rafael knew the men had eaten more than was their wont, some had drunk more, others would be sampling the whores with vigor, perhaps to prove that they were yet alive. The drive for sensation would be greater in victory, more of a fever-pitch, but even in this moment, he could have taken this beguiling maiden without a second thought.

Was she aware of the risk she took?

Rafael wanted to show her, to teach her something of men, even if it tormented him to have only a taste of her before she fled back to the solar where she belonged.

Elizabeth caught her breath and licked her lips, which did little to assist Rafael in controlling his urges. "I could not discern you here in the darkness," she whispered.

Rafael took a deliberate step away from her, knowing it was best. He told himself that he remained close so that they could whisper to each other, though he knew that to be an excuse. His fingers were reluctant to leave the smooth skin of her throat, and she did not pull away from his touch.

Her hair was braided now, an ebony plait hanging down her back.

He sensed her trepidation and wished to reassure her, a gallant urge which seemed foreign to the man he knew himself to be. "It is better to keep the chamber dark, so they cannot see that anyone watches."

"Surely they would assume that someone does?"

"It does not hurt to let them doubt."

Elizabeth smiled then, the curve of her lips drawing his hungry gaze. Had she ever been kissed? "My father always said that surprise was a potent weapon."

"And so it is."

Her skin was soft beneath his hand, her presence alluring and feminine. He watched his fingers stroke her throat gently, just the tips touching her skin. She swallowed again, then tipped her head back, her eyes shining as she watched him.

As if she would invite more.

Rafael realized he had been long without a woman. After all, there had been none at Ravensmuir these past six months, not until the Sable League had arrived with their whores just days before.

That could be the only reasonable explanation for Elizabeth's effect upon him. Rafael was not one to favor innocence, after all. He let his fingertips slide down her throat in a slow caress, daring to let them wander into the slit at the front of her chemise. She should have pulled away. She should have slapped his hand.

But she did not, and Rafael found himself easing closer again.

"You should be abed," he murmured, watching how she closed her eyes. She was responsive to his touch, a discovery that he found most welcome.

"So should you be," she countered, that unexpected mischief lighting her eyes.

"Not on this night," he replied, watching his fingers slide around her ear. She parted her lips and tilted her head, inviting him to touch her more boldly. He was put in mind of a cat and bent closer, his lips but a finger's breadth from her own. She smiled at him, a lazy expression that knotted his innards.

She was Malcolm's maiden sister.

Rafael lifted his hand away abruptly.

What was this he did?

Rafael's tone turned scolding as he stepped away from Elizabeth. "What is in your mind that you are abroad in the keep at night, alone and undefended?" he demanded. "You do not even have an eating knife."

Elizabeth's smile broadened, that cursed confidence making him want to teach her the price of her folly. "I was looking for you, and I knew that you would defend me well."

"Your confidence is undeserved." Rafael returned to the window, feeling both disgruntled and unsettled. He sheathed his dagger and stared out into the night, keenly aware that Elizabeth did not leave.

"I would make a bargain with you, Rafael," she admitted from behind him, her words husky. That she used his name sent a jolt through him, though he was certain he misunderstood her scheme. There was no doubting the sensual promise in her tone, although Rafael doubted she was aware of it.

He knew the bargain he wanted, just as he knew it was folly to desire her.

"You have tried to make a wager with me since we met, and I have declined your invitation to die in Malcolm's stead repeatedly."

"But I have not offered you a reward," Elizabeth said.

Rafael spun to consider her.

Her gaze was steady as she continued, though her words surprised him. "You said every matter is an exchange. What if I offered you a kiss to take Malcolm's place?"

Rafael shook his head. "Then you would offer what I could take freely, whether you offered it or not." He arched a brow. "And a kiss is a fleeting pleasure to offer a man in exchange for his life.

Your price is too low." He let his tone harden. "Return to the safety of your bed, my lady, for that is where a maiden should be when the hall is full of fighting men."

He could see Elizabeth blush, even in the darkness, and he was not truly surprised that she did not leave. Not this one. She would not abandon her purpose so readily as that. Indeed, he wanted to know what she would do.

Would she offer more than a kiss? Rafael clenched his fists, knowing the reply he desired to that question.

Elizabeth took a step closer, letting her fingertips fall upon his arm. She let her fingertips trail over him, mimicking the way he had caressed her, sliding her hand up to his shoulder. Once her fingers touched his neck, she leaned against him slightly, the curve of her breast against his chest.

She looked up and he was certain he had never seen a more alluring sight in all his days. "It is true that you could steal a kiss, but I wager it would not be so sweet as one freely offered." Her gaze locked with his, a dare in her smile. "I believe the best kisses are those mutually savored, not those inflicted or forced."

"But you do not know?"

Elizabeth blushed a little. "Of course not." An impish gleam lit her eyes, tempting his smile. She slid her hand up to his ear, the feel of her fingers in his hair awakening him in a way she surely could not anticipate. "But I would like to find out." She pursed her lips, watching her own fingers on his flesh. "Your skin feels so different from mine," she mused and Rafael reminded himself that he had no interest in innocents.

"I thought we discussed Malcolm's welfare."

She smiled. "I think the best bargains have more than one objective."

Rafael shrugged, striving to appear indifferent. "I will not trade my life for a kiss, no matter how potent it might be."

Elizabeth nodded, unsurprised, then tilted her head to regard him. "But what of more than a kiss?" she asked in a whisper, and he was certain he had heard her incorrectly. She stretched to her toes and touched her lips to the exposed skin of his throat.

A jolt of lust ripped through Rafael from that single point and he seized her upper arms, intent upon putting distance between them. "You jest with me."

"I do not." Elizabeth slid her arms around his waist and leaned against him, the scent of her skin rising to torment Rafael. "It was your suggestion."

He found he could not push her away, not when she watched him with such welcome in those eyes. "And you rejected it, just hours ago."

Her smile was confident. "I was surprised by your suggestion. I had but to think upon it to consider the merit of your scheme." She bit her lip and blushed again even as her voice dropped to an intimate whisper. "In truth, I would like to know what it is like."

"And so you increase your offer from a kiss to the greatest intimacy, so readily as that?"

She colored and looked discomfited. "I meant to offer my all from the outset, but when Alexander took me to the market in York, he said it was wiser to begin with less than one's final price."

Rafael stared at her, uncertain whether to be more shocked that she thought of this as so simple an exchange, or that she had never journeyed farther than York. How small her world was in comparison to his own! But then, what else would he expect, given her status? "This cannot be a bargain that you mean to keep," he managed to say.

Elizabeth's eyes narrowed slightly, as if she were insulted, and again he saw her resolve. "I am not a whimsical young girl or one who promises what she will not do. Make no mistake, Rafael, I will surrender myself to you this night, right here and right now. You may take all I have to offer. I ask only that you fulfill the debt to the Fae on the morrow in Malcolm's stead."

The idea enflamed Rafael as much as her quiet determination. It was a bargain he wanted to take, even as he knew it would be folly to do so.

"You set a trap for me," he complained, recalling Bertrand's words all too readily. "You would have me attempt to dishonor you so that Malcolm could discover us thus and take a penance from my hide."

"Malcolm is with Catriona in the solar," Elizabeth said firmly, revealing that she had planned for this eventuality. Her offer was not wrought of impulse then. She had schemed this seduction, a most interesting revelation. "He believes me to be in the nursery with Avery and Vera."

"Vera, then," Rafael argued, knowing that woman would be all to glad to see him in Malcolm's disfavor.

Elizabeth shook her head. "Vera believes me to be in the solar with Malcolm and Catriona. Not a one of them will seek me out before first light." She stepped away him, which confused him for her resolve was clear. "Which gives us some time."

To Rafael's astonishment, Elizabeth untucked her chemise from the chausses she had been loaned and began to unfasten it. She held his gaze, then tugged the chemise over her head, revealing her bare breasts to his view.

Rafael stared, certain he had never seen such perfect breasts in his life. Her skin was creamy and looked like ivory in the shadows, her nipples dark and tightly beaded. It was the purpose in her expression, though, that could be his undoing, for she clearly intended to do as she vowed.

Rafael inhaled sharply, wanting what she offered more than he had wanted anything in a long time. It could be so readily done, so quickly accomplished, and no one would be the wiser. He could take all she offered and not deliver his part of the wager. Indeed, he could deny that there was a wager and simply claim her maidenhead now.

It would be wrong.

Rafael averted his gaze, knowing what he should do, then realized Elizabeth's ploy. It seemed to be madness because it was. She did not *truly* offer herself to him. She took a risk, but not that much of one. She had insisted repeatedly that he was a man of honor. She meant to prove as much by forcing him to reveal that he would not take advantage of her on this night.

And then she would inveigh upon him to do what was right and take Malcolm's place.

She expected him to deny the prize but, by honor, pay the price.

Rafael smiled and turned to look intently upon her bare flesh. He let all the hunger of his desire fill his expression, hiding naught from her, and took a step closer. He walked like a predator, a man who would have what he wanted, a dangerous mercenary who could not be relied upon to do anything but see to his own satisfaction.

To his pleasure, she noticed the change. He saw how she caught her breath, how she fought the urge to cover her nudity with her hands. He let his gaze rove over her and ensured that his appreciation showed. He would give her a surprise, one that would send her fleeing back to one chamber or another, any place where she would be safely out of his company.

And he would have that kiss.

"I welcome your suggestion and your invitation," he said, keeping his voice low with promise. He crossed the chamber and flicked the portal shut, then turned the key in the lock. Her eyes widened in a most satisfactory way. She would not forget this lesson, to be sure.

"It will not take long, but I would not be disturbed." Rafael lifted the hem of his tabard and his tunic of chain mail as he marched back toward her. Elizabeth's breath came quickly, just as he had anticipated, and she backed into the wall. She did not flee, however, though her alarm was clear.

"Do matters always proceed with such haste?" she demanded with a measure of concern that proved his plan a good one.

Rafael chuckled. "We have not much time. I would make the most of it."

She caught her breath and bit her lip, the sight making him sharply aware of his desire. Rafael had to send her running quickly, lest he lose control of his own impulses, lest this situation proceed too far. He would not be rough, but he would not linger either. He doubted she would find much pleasure in his touch, not with him both garbed and armed. Any maiden of sense would be appalled and flee.

Rafael seized the end of Elizabeth's braid, towering over her as he tore the lace that fastened the end. He cast the lace across the floor as she stared at him in awe, then tugged her hair loose of the plait. He spread her ebony tresses over her shoulders, fighting the urge to slide the silken length of it across his lips. He speared his fingers into her hair and cupped her head in his hand, struck again by how delicately wrought she was.

He tipped her face upward with a gentleness he had not planned, then touched his lips to hers. She shivered, then her lips parted, and Rafael found himself kissing her with all the ardor and admiration he had felt since his first sight of her. He backed her into the wall, trapping her between his body and the stone. He closed his free hand around her bare breast, teasing the nipple to a taut peak even as he kissed her deeply.

It was a sweet and potent kiss, a stolen salute, an embrace he was certain would be cut short. Rafael made the most of the opportunity, certain it would be his sole taste of this enticing woman. He plundered her mouth with possessive ease, knowing his boldness would compel her to halt the embrace in short order. He slanted his mouth across hers and demanded more than she had given, more than she would give. All the while, his fingers teased her nipple, drawing it to a tighter bead, pinching it and caressing it. All the while he crushed her beneath the weight of his body, certain the reality of such passion would terrify her.

But Elizabeth held her ground.

Rafael intensified his amorous assault. Though there would be no more than this kiss, he meant to make it one she remembered. He meant to put his mark upon Elizabeth, to leave her lips swollen and her nipple aching, when she fled back to the solar. He wanted her to think about the folly of what she had suggested, to ensure that she never made another man a similar offer. She would be able to feel his touch all the night long, if he had his way, and it would give her much to think about. He hoped it kept her awake.

He knew that the kiss would keep *him* awake. He suspected, in fact, that he would be haunted by his refusal to accept her terms.

When she still did not push him away, he eased his knee between hers, forcing her thighs to part, and rolled his hips against her. He ensured that Elizabeth felt his erection and swallowed her gasp of surprise even as he anticipated her rejection.

One kiss would be the price of her audacity.

One kiss would be all he would claim from her.

But Rafael's plan was doomed to go awry, just when he was certain it would succeed.

For Elizabeth, instead of fleeing his bold touch, embraced it. She caught her breath and arched against him in silent demand for more. She slid her fingers into his hair to pull him closer as she returned his kiss with an ardor unexpected.

Indeed, she seemed to have a hunger for him that echoed his own for her.

When she emitted a little purr of pleasure, then touched her tongue to his, Rafael knew his strategy had failed.

Given the two options available—that Rafael would accept her offer and seduce her thoroughly or that he would show himself to be a man of honor and retreat—the choice he had made was infinitely preferable to Elizabeth. His kiss fed that newfound heat within her and awakened a desire for more of his touch.

He had moved so quickly to claim her, that he might have been merely awaiting her invitation. She loved that he saw no need for pretense, for honesty between partners was key to Elizabeth's thinking. Rafael was a man who seized opportunity when it was presented.

He had that in common with heroes in tales, to be sure.

Elizabeth *had* been startled when he had locked the door. She liked that they would not be interrupted, though, and savored his quick thinking. She had been surprised that he had come toward her without removing his garb, and indeed, the way he gripped the hem of his tabard and mail coat indicated that he would not. For a moment, she had been taken aback and doubted her choice, but then he had stared down at her as he unfastened her braid. His eyes shone with intensity and desire, his admiration of her not only clear but reassuring. Elizabeth saw the reverence in the way he spread her hair over her shoulders, and knew he was under the same spell as she.

Elizabeth had been surprised when his warm hand had closed over her breast. The sensation was exciting and pleasurable, but could not compare to what he did after that. The way he cupped her breast and teased her nipple, catching it between finger and thumb, made her squirm with a pleasure she could not have anticipated.

She had seen his eyes gleam with satisfaction before his mouth closed over hers.

His kiss was demanding and powerful, exactly as she had always hoped kisses might be, and the way he pinned her against the wall with his body was beyond thrilling. Elizabeth felt trapped, claimed, and utterly feminine. He was all muscled strength, all power and passion, so vital that she ached to sample all life had to offer. The size of his erection made it clear that she was not the only one in desire's thrall and she welcomed that revelation. Her body hummed with new awareness and she wanted to rub herself against him to feel yet more.

Indeed, if this was but the beginning of the pleasures a couple could share, Elizabeth did not understand why married couples ever left their bed at all.

Rafael was staking a claim and Elizabeth knew it well.

She wanted him to know that she was his for the taking.

Elizabeth pushed her hands into the dark silk of Rafael's hair and drew him ever closer, opening her mouth to him and surrendering fully to his touch. He knew this course and could guide her well. She followed his lead, letting him know that she trusted him utterly. She arched her back and pressed her breast more fully into his hand, even as she opened her mouth to invite more of his kiss. Who could have guessed that such pleasure existed? Who could have imagined that she could save Malcolm by experiencing such as this? It seemed too good to be true.

And it was.

Rafael tore his mouth from hers and muttered something she did not understand. It might have been a curse, he said the words so vehemently, and Elizabeth feared he would step away from her. Instead, he surveyed her, his eyes glittering, and his throat working.

He bent his head so quickly to take her other nipple in his mouth that she gasped aloud. He caught her waist in his hands and lifted her before him, his grip tight and sure. The way he kissed her turgid nipple and then suckled her, first gentle and then demanding, made Elizabeth moan with pleasure. She locked her hands into his hair, holding him fast against her, not wanting him to stop.

Rafael muttered another curse against her skin, then his teeth grazed her taut nipple. Elizabeth thought she might faint with pleasure. She whispered his name and found herself abruptly cast toward the portal of the chamber. She looked back at the silhouette that was Rafael even as he cast her borrowed chemise at her.

"I could take you here and now," he said, his tone fierce. "I could claim what you so readily offer and despoil you forever."

Elizabeth heard some warning in his tone. "We have a bargain," she insisted.

"Which proves your thinking to be faulty." Rafael raised a finger and his gaze was hard. "You have no means to ensure that I keep the wager you would make. I could seduce you and still let Malcolm pay my debt on the morrow." He spun back to the window, bracing his hands on the sill. "You have much to learn of strategy, *mi piqueño ángel*. Now find your way to your bed."

That he would dismiss her, like a naughty child and after that potent kiss, was outrageous. "What if I will not go?"

"Then I spoke aright that you would see me condemned."

Elizabeth frowned, her thoughts and her desire churning. "I thought you wanted me."

"You were wrong," Rafael said, his tone harsh. "I meant only to show you the folly of your choice."

Elizabeth could not believe it. "But that kiss..."

"Was a lesson and a warning." Rafael cast a glance over his shoulder at her. "I have no interest in despoiling innocents. You were lucky in that, and may not be so fortunate again."

Elizabeth felt her cheeks burn that she was not woman enough to tempt Rafael. She was mortified that she had nearly surrendered her greatest asset and might have surrendered it for naught at all. She reached for her own chemise, disheartened.

She had only just pulled it over her head when she realized the truth of what Rafael had done.

He had his back to her and he had folded his arms across his chest, his feet braced against the floor as he stared out at the earl's camp and pretended to ignore her. The air fairly crackled between them, though, and Elizabeth smiled with new confidence. It was a sign that he was not so indifferent as he would have her believe.

Indeed, he defended her from himself.

He was protective of her, which was not a sign of indifference.

She donned her chemise, certain of her conclusion. Elizabeth chuckled, watching how his shoulders tightened.

"I see no humor in the situation," he said stiffly.

"I do. For you, Rafael Rodriguez, have much to learn of hiding the fact that you are a man of merit."

He spun to face her but Elizabeth smiled. "The villain that you profess to be would not have denied his own pleasure. He would have seized all that I offered, then broken his word, leaving me soiled and Malcolm condemned." She shook a finger at him. "But you could not do as much. Be warned, Rafael, for I have your measure now." She held his astonished gaze for a potent moment, then turned the key in the lock, flung open the portal and left the chamber.

She heard Rafael swear violently behind her, once again the tone and not the words revealing his vexation, and she wondered if he spoke in Spanish when impassioned.

Elizabeth realized then that she might never know.

Nay, if Rafael took her challenge and surrendered to Finvarra in Malcolm's place the next night, then he would be the one lost forever.

Elizabeth halted then and glanced back, shaken by the realization. If she won her way, then Rafael would die, and against all expectation, Elizabeth would miss him. She might have turned back, but two warriors climbed the stairs to join Rafael in watching the mustered forces beyond Ravensmuir's hedge. Elizabeth bit her lip, fearing she might not have any chance to speak to Rafael alone again.

She had wanted him to take Malcolm's place, for she had believed that to be right, but now, she did not want either of them to die. Could Finvarra be swayed from collecting his promised due?

Tuesday, June 22, 1428

Feast Day of Saint Alban and the Apostle James (the Less).

Midsummer's Eve.

Chapter Five

At the dawn, the drums began.

There was no opportunity for Elizabeth to speak with Rafael once she left the solar with Catriona. Indeed, he seemed to avoid her apurpose and his mood appeared to be grim, although he might have scowled because of the pending battle. Even with the Sable League in his hall, Malcolm's forces were greatly outnumbered by those of the earl.

Elizabeth witnessed the parlay and heard the earl's demand that Malcolm cast aside Catriona to wed Jeanne. She saw Jeanne on the field beyond the hedge, that woman's spurned hand supposedly the reason for the attack. She noted the earl's considerable preparations and understood that Malcolm's refusal to take Jeanne as his bride was only an excuse.

The earl coveted the new Ravensmuir. Clearly he had no concern with claiming it by force.

Malcolm refused to cede his new wife.

Stalemate.

The first arrow was shot over the walls, burning a trail across the morning sky.

"And so it begins," muttered a mercenary in her proximity. Elizabeth realized she had not truly believed there would be a battle. But warfare there was, quickly and in quantity. Once the first volley had been fired, the battle erupted in truth. Arrows fell from the sky like rain and men tried to climb the outside of the gatehouse walls. She winced as the first pot of boiling oil was tipped over the roof and the men below screamed in agony.

As anticipated, other men tried to come around the ends of the hedges, but were sliced down by Malcolm's men. There was smoke and fire on all sides, shouting and screaming, and a chaos beyond Elizabeth's expectation.

When she first saw a man fall and his blood spill, she waited for him to rise unscathed. A part of her mind knew he would not, but she had not believed until that moment that men truly would be slaughtered over the seal of Ravensmuir.

Until she saw that they were.

Elizabeth was shocked by the savagery of it all, by the relentless assault upon her brother's new keep, and by the determination of his comrades to see his holding defended. They fought steadily all the day, with no respite, seeming to need no rest.

There might be none alive to pay Finvarra's tithe this night!

Elizabeth had to do some deed to assist. Otherwise, she knew she would watch Malcolm and Rafael alternatively, fearing over their fates. She carried water, and soothed Avery, and bound wounds in the hall, though she had no particular skill with that task. There was scarcely a moment to sit down, much less to take a reprieve. Her heart thundered all the day long, though, fear and agitation ensuring that she did not want to pause.

Her thoughts spun all the day long. She thought of Malcolm fighting for his home and knew that Catriona feared for his survival. She thought of Rafael and was relieved whenever she caught a glimpse of him. He was always fighting, seemingly tireless, and perhaps invincible.

She saw the warrior with doom on his brow fall in the bailey and not rise again. The others fought on, stepping over his corpse, never missing a strike. There was proof that none of them truly ever expected to survive any battle they joined. When his body was carried into the hall, with respect and regret, she learned that his name had been Reynaud.

Elizabeth paid little heed to the Fae, though they cavorted merrily in Ravensmuir's hall, as if anticipating some great celebration. She knew what that festivity might be and did not feel nearly so thrilled that Malcolm would die to ensure their welfare, even if he survived this day. She did not glimpse Finvarra, though she might have liked to have words with him.

The shadows were growing long when the Fae abruptly abandoned the hall, scurrying along the rafters and leaping out the windows. In the twinkling of an eye, they all vacated the keep, their move prompting Elizabeth to straighten and turn, peering after them. The sun had not quite set and the western sky was streaked with fiery color. Still there were will-o'-the-wisp twinkles in the distant shadows. Still the earl's men beat their war drums.

Yet Elizabeth heard the Fae music, tinkling faintly as it carried to her ears.

Malcolm's reckoning was upon them. She raced to the solar, joining Catriona at the window and clutching that woman's cold hand. In the distance, she saw another army mustering, one wrought of shadows and starlight, one indifferent to the battle waged between the armies of mortal men.

The Fae came, and they came for Malcolm's soul.

ે⚫

Rafael was agitated.

It was not ideal to be in such emotional tumult. He, like so many others, fought most effectively when he was dispassionate and focused. It was best when he was attuned to every movement in his proximity and when his body responded immediately with force. It was most effective to sense the mood of the other side, to anticipate any chance in their tactics or strategy. He should have been filled with the awareness of war and naught else.

But Rafael was snared in a dangerous tumult. His blood was fired by the fleeting taste he had had of Elizabeth. He could fairly feel her lips against his, the soft exhalation of her breath, the cautious caress of her fingertips on his skin. Worse, his mind was in turmoil, her conviction of his true nature leaving his guts churning.

There *was* some honor in his soul, after all. Elizabeth had seen the truth of him. Otherwise, she would not have been a maiden by the time he let her leave.

That realization launched a dozen questions, the most pressing of which was whether he truly could let Malcolm keep that wager in his stead. But a day before, Rafael had known the answer without doubt.

On this day, thanks to a maiden's trust, he wondered.

Otherwise, the day of fighting could have been any one of a thousand from Rafael's past. He hacked and slashed, jabbed and sliced. He was a ferocious opponent and he knew it, a man of considerable skill and a measure of luck.

Thanks to the distractions fed by Elizabeth, however, Rafael did not survive unscathed. A blow came abruptly from one side, a move and a man he had not anticipated. He parried and felt the weight of the blow upon his own sword, making the blade sing in protest and his shoulder ache. He roared and thrust, nicking his opponent's throat before that man's broadsword swept at his guts.

'Twas the same manner of blow that had felled Franz. Rafael leaped backward, evading the sword's bite, but glimpsed a battle axe blade descending toward him. Rafael spun madly, cursing that his own lack of attention was the reason he found himself so beset. The axe glanced off his upper arm, and he was relieved it was not severed, though the pain was so considerable that it might not be saved. He felt the chain mail driven into the wound and gritted his teeth against the agony. Fury saw his attacker felled in short order, then Rafael dove after the first. He kicked that man, slit his throat, then glared about himself.

He caught his breath and felt the warm trickle of blood on his arm. He had near lost an arm, or part of it, and it was his own wretched fault. A quick exploration revealed that the cut was not so deep as he had feared. He would not lose his arm, provided he cleaned the wound later. He wiped his hand across his brow as he scanned the bailey for another foe, as furious with himself as any other.

Elizabeth distracted him. She tore his mind from the task before him, and such a temptation as the one she offered could see him slaughtered. Worse, it could see him maimed. As in so many matters with Rafael, he favored one option or its opposite, with no tolerance of any point in between. He could tolerate a scar, as indeed he had many, but he would be hale or he would be dead. To be maimed and unable to earn his way would be the worst fate of all. Rafael had been hungry and powerless, and he would never be so again.

Another volley of men began to make their way around the far end of the hedge. Reynaud had fallen, and he could see that Gunter was slowing. Rafael strode toward them, avoiding the hail of arrows, determined to sharpen his attention. There was no tolerance in battle for a man to be distracted. Survival depended upon being alert, and Rafael was usually more alert than most. He heard the boiling oil poured from the gatehouse summit, or more accurately, he heard the screams of those who were burned by it. He smelled the many burning fires and leaped into the battle at the end of the hedge with a roar, slashing at the attackers with two blades.

This was his life. This was his destiny. Battle of this violent nature was what Rafael knew best. Rafael came to the aid of his fellows more than once and left more than one warrior dead with nary a scrap of remorse. This was his trade, his skill, his reason to arise each day. It was a grim and gruesome business, but killing was all he knew.

It did pay rather well, no matter what delicate maidens might think of it.

It was the music that alerted Rafael to the demons' return, that cursed music that had enchanted him once before. He cringed at the sound of it, wanting to be mistaken about its source.

But he was not. They came again, those foul fiends, came to collect their wicked toll, just as they had sworn to do. As before, it seemed they could only ascend to the realm of mortals during the night, for the glowing red orb of the sun had touched the horizon when Rafael heard the first notes. Clearly they were of another realm, for it made no difference to their progress that Ravensmuir was at war, its keep besieged, its bailey and field littered with fallen warriors. Perhaps they savored the blood on the field, for the dead had been in their company six months before.

Despite his better judgment, Rafael raised his head to look at the approaching force. Even though the entangled barrier of the hedge, he could see that they were otherworldly and unholy, and the sight of them made the hair stand up on the back of his neck. He was exhausted but the sight of these fiends quickened his blood and made him grip his sword.

Malcolm and his kin insisted that these creatures were the Fae, but Rafael did not believe it. The Fae were mischievous sprites, if they existed. They were nature spirits that could punish a peasant or bring him riches. They had to be comparatively harmless spirits, ones that populated many a tale such as those Catriona told.

Such whimsy had naught to do with this evil force. There were so many walking corpses in this company that Rafael had no doubt of their true identity. The dead rode with their king, as did ghosts, and blood seemed to attract them. This king savored wagers, and the stakes were souls: Rafael knew no other kind than demons who gambled with such terms.

It was fitting, in a way, that the warrior they had called the Hellhound had inherited a holding with a gateway to the inferno.

The music grew louder and even knowing what he did of its treachery, even as exhausted as he was, still he yearned to dance. Rafael was no fool, but this music cast a spell. The music and those who created it were sorcerers, for they could make Rafael's feet itch even though he had learned the high price of surrendering to the dance.

He jabbed his blade into an opponent and strove to ignore the approaching demons. He thought instead of his first arrival at Ravensmuir the Yule before. He would have forgotten that night if it were possible, but it seemed he could no more keep it from his thoughts than steel himself against Elizabeth's allure. The blizzard of that night was so vivid in his mind that he could still feel the bitter cold. Rafael had never been able to shake the cold of his first northern winter—or perhaps it was the memory of that night's events that haunted him. No sooner had he and Malcolm taken refuge in the stables than that infernal music had begun, enticing them toward a golden light that should have filled him with suspicion.

Tempting him to dance.

Instead, Rafael had surrendered to impulse for the first time in years, accepted a beauteous maiden's invitation to dance, and been snared by demons intent upon claiming his soul in exchange. That night had been more intense and vivid than any other Rafael had experienced. The mortal realm had seemed a poor substitute.

It was a mark of exhaustion that he was, even now, tempted to join their ranks in Malcolm's stead. He knew the price was death. Instead the old debt between himself and Malcolm would be repaid, for Rafael had saved Malcolm's life once.

It had been their first meeting, and this would be their final parting. Rafael winced at the truth of it and heard Elizabeth's challenge again.

He did not want to see her disappointment when he failed to intervene for Malcolm.

In a way, it made sense that Rafael had thought her to be an angel at first glimpse. Her beauty was such that no man could fail to notice her, but it was her manner that had snared Rafael's gaze. No

Madonna ever considered the mortal realm with such acceptance of what had been and what would be.

She had challenged him, as he supposed angels were wont to do.

As the music grew louder and the dusk deepened, his opponents were one by one seduced. They began to dance, dropping their blades as they were enchanted by the arriving company. Rafael reluctantly turned to watch the diabolical host approach, his heart sinking.

It was a reckoning come due.

It was a nightmare come to life.

Rafael saw the will-o'-the-wisp burning in the distance, a sparkle of treacherous lights that hinted at targets that did not exist. The eerie host rode across Ravensmuir's fallowed fields, driving dark shadows before them. Their horses were high-stepping and uncommonly fine, their armor glinting in the twilight, and they seemed to breathe fire. There were knights and warriors, damsels and ladies, in this company of demons, all dressed in splendor and riding as if the uneven land posed no obstacle. There were gleaming gems and radiant jewels, gleaming mail and shining weapons. Some of the men on the field were transfixed by their beauty and halted to stare in awe as the company passed over and through their ranks.

Rafael saw only that the new arrivals were numerous, potent, confident, and possessed of a dangerous beauty. The dead trudged behind them, driven to follow this proud aristocracy by some unnatural compulsion that made Rafael shudder.

The music twitched and teased, winding into his thoughts, tempting him to dance again. Rafael stubbornly kept his boots planted against the ground, forcing himself to concentrate on the holes in the fine leather that were the result of his last such adventure. Once he had begun to dance, he had been unable to stop. Exhaustion had prompted him to take the wager, though he reasoned he might have died that night otherwise.

The demon riders formed a half circle outside the gatehouse of Ravensmuir, one that nearly surrounded the troops of the attacking earl. When their horses stood shoulder to shoulder, there was a glimmer on the ground. Rafael caught his breath as frost spread across the bailey, emanating from the feet of the horses and spreading inward with fearsome speed. It grew in white crystals, like ice forming on the surface of a lake in the autumn, spreading and becoming whiter with astonishing speed. In the blink of an eye, the ground was covered with snow, snow that glinted with the light of the stars. The ice traveled up the legs of the dead, and froze them in place. The wind became suddenly colder and more bitter, even as that wild music gained in volume.

Some of the demons dismounted and others who had been on foot slipped through the ranks of the prancing horses. They stepped onto the frosty ground, playing their lutes and reeds, singing and dancing as they progressed. They made no footprints in the snow, and left no mark of their passage. The demons laughed and cavorted through the ranks of the earl's men, their tune becoming faster and more beguiling. More and more of the earl's men cast away their swords and joined the dance.

Could the others see the demons? Rafael did not know, but the horses shied and the men seemed to be confused. They were aware of the demon host on some level, even if they could not discern them. It became colder yet, as cold as the grave, and Rafael felt a damp wind that smelled of rot. Arrows were launched from the gate house that hit only the empty ground as the confusion infected the forces defending Ravensmuir.

Rafael prayed that none of the Sable League joined the dance.

It seemed that some of the men *could* see the otherworldly host. Elizabeth had offered a potion of wild thyme to those men who wished to discern what she called the Fae. Rafael had been skeptical until he saw his bold fellows turn pale and seem to stare at the approaching company in horror, just as Jeanne had done.

He had himself declined the potion, for he had no need of any substance that addled his wits when he stepped on to the battlefield.

Rafael saw his comrade Ranulf fumble in the casting of another volley of Greek fire from the gate tower. It was clear that the arrivals had distracted that man from his task, as little else might have done. There was an explosion bright enough to blind a man and loud enough to deafen one, then smoke and silence.

Rafael was running to the gatehouse when he heard Ranulf's roar of pain. At least that man was not dead, or not dead as yet. Rafael hastened to his comrade's aid, slicing down an opponent fool enough to step into his path. Ranulf began to swear with vigor,

The Warrior's Prize

an encouraging sign that he might survive on his own.

Rafael was a dozen steps from the gatehouse when he spied Malcolm. The Laird of Ravensmuir stared across the lands outside his own gates, a man entranced. Rafael followed Malcolm's gaze and his heart stopped cold.

A king with a long dark beard rode into the circle, as regal and richly appointed as any monarch. He was garbed in silver and black, and his steed was so brilliant a silver that it might have been wrought of precious metal. There were bells woven into its loose mane, for they tinkled as he rode, and the beast's hooves shone. The others stepped back to create a path for their regent, bowing low as he passed them.

Rafael recognized him, though he wished he did not. This was the king who had claimed six months before that the price of departure from the dance was Rafael's soul. This was the king who had accepted Malcolm's soul in exchange and vowed to collect it in six month's time.

On this night.

The King of the Dead—for he could be naught else—dismounted, then offered his hand to a woman, as tall and as beautiful as he, her hair long and dark. Both of them had whirling marks upon their flesh, dark blue tracery that Rafael had noticed six months before. She too dismounted and put her hand in his. They proceeded regally across the frozen ground to the gatehouse and looked up at Malcolm, expectation in their expressions.

Nay, it was hunger.

The avidity of their expressions was yet more evidence of their true nature, in Rafael's mind, for only ghouls and demons had such a lust for blood and bone. How would they kill him? What would they do with his corpse? Rafael's thoughts filled with a thousand gruesome possibilities.

As he watched, a river of starlight flowed from them to Malcolm. It surrounded that warrior, moving independently of the cold wind from the sea, swirling around Malcolm like a swarm of fireflies that would carry him to his doom.

But there was no need for any reminder to Malcolm, much less any sorcery to compel him to do as he had pledged. Malcolm strode to his demise, keeping his vow like the honorable warrior Rafael knew him to be.

Here was the difference between them.

Here was the truth that could only make Elizabeth despise Rafael.

Malcolm descended the staircase of the gatehouse. Rafael called to him, but his comrade either did not hear him or had no power to reply. The portcullis creaked as Malcolm opened it, then he stepped upon the starlit path that led to his doom.

The king smiled with satisfaction, for the ransom he had demanded—one mortal soul—would be paid and paid promptly.

It was then that the fullness of his choice came to Rafael. Malcolm would die, right before Rafael's eyes, leaving his new wife and holding undefended, and it would be Rafael's fault. This was no fair repayment of whatever debt Malcolm owed to Rafael and Rafael found he could not stand aside.

Not now that he had been challenged by Elizabeth and his lost sense of justice awakened anew.

Even as Rafael stepped forward, Catriona cried out in protest. Malcolm's wife fled across the bailey, Elizabeth fast behind her. The women had remained in the relative safety of the keep, but now they abandoned all good plans.

Elizabeth could not be at risk! Rafael raced toward his comrade, intent upon intervening first, but Catriona reached Malcolm before he did. She seized her husband's tabard, but he ignored her. Malcolm stepped onto that circle of snow and Rafael was close enough to see him shudder.

Catriona would have followed without hesitation, but Elizabeth pulled her back. Elizabeth's fingers dropped to the hilt of Catriona's knife. The maiden's eyes flashed in warning, and Catriona seemed to understand. Rafael did not, but then, Catriona oft told tales of the Fae. There was some detail of these fiends, whatever they were called, that he did not yet know.

He watched as Elizabeth, her expression as grim as that of any avenging angel, took a small knife from her own belt and jammed it into the earth before herself. The blade sank into the soil at the very periphery of the uncommon frost. Rafael cringed to see a fine weapon so abused, for the hilt was costly and the blade had clearly been wrought by a skilled smith.

To his amazement, the frost shimmered for a moment, then melted away from the blade. Rafael blinked in surprise, unable to explain this fact.

He watched as Elizabeth fearlessly stepped over the buried blade. She did not falter and she did not shudder when her boot trod on the unholy snow. Indeed, she, like the demonic host, left no footprint or mark of her passage. Rafael understood that this knife offered some protection for her in confronting the demons.

Or some sorcery that countered their own.

She did not intervene out of innocence or ignorance. She stepped forward for the sake of justice and honor.

And he would do the same.

Meanwhile, Catriona plunged her own blade into the soil beside Elizabeth's, then followed her. The starlight swirled around them, one woman with ebony hair and one with golden tresses cropped short. They clasped hands as they faced their foes, as if to draw strength from each other. Rafael had never seen such valor, and he admired them truly. The sparkling light seemed to keep its distance from the two women—just as the frost shrank from the blade—while it surrounded Malcolm closely.

Like a shroud.

Both of these women would be devastated if Malcolm were lost. In contrast, if Rafael died before the morning light, not a soul would mourn his passing.

Elizabeth was right.

Rafael swore thoroughly at the realization of what he must do. He pulled his own dagger from the scabbard, trusting in Elizabeth's greater knowledge of the fiends. He plunged the blade into the soil alongside those of the two women and stepped over it, following them.

Catriona glanced his way in surprise.

"Time 'tis to be a better friend," he said grimly, though that was but a small measure of what drove him. He offered his hand to her, unwilling to look past her and witness Elizabeth's triumph. Her victory would be short-lived, undoubtedly.

Respect lit Catriona's eyes for the first time since they had met, which he supposed was worth some thing.

Perhaps he would not be condemned forever to this Hell he glimpsed.

The music swelled, growing ever louder in volume, and the king placed his hand upon the hilt of his sword. Catriona's cold fingers closed over Rafael's own and they three stepped forward as one.

Rafael felt cold anew, so certain was he that the price of saving Malcolm's soul would be the surrender of his own.

It appeared he would have little time to marvel at that.

❧

Rafael had accepted her challenge!

Elizabeth did not know whether to be pleased at her triumph or to fear that Rafael would be lost. She was surprised that she had the ability to influence his choices, and was thrilled by this proof.

The blood on Rafael's left glove was considerable and she wondered if it was his or that of another man he had felled. The sight of it made her fear for whatever blow Rafael had endured. Had he accepted her dare because he knew himself fatally injured already? But there was no shadow of death upon him, and Elizabeth had to believe that it was his hidden honor responsible for his choice.

How she wished to ask him! But she knew that speaking within the Fae circle would cast her into Finvarra's power forever. There would be more than enough carnage on this night, though she wished she could contrive a way to see both Malcolm and Rafael survive.

What could be done? Elizabeth was quite certain that Finvarra would not fail to collect his due, whatever that king perceived it to be. He watched her now, his gaze so cold that she struggled not to shiver.

After entering the Fae circle, the three of them stood together in silence. Elizabeth yearned to warn Rafael not to eat, drink or speak while in this circle lest he not be allowed to depart it. She knew that he was not as familiar with the Fae as she and Catriona, but dared not speak aloud herself. She willed him to follow their lead and was relieved that he seemed intent upon doing so.

He was not one inclined to readily accept the counsel of others, after all.

The Fae music soared and the earl's men danced with wild abandon. The sun had disappeared and the night sky was full of stars. The moon sailed clear of the horizon, rising quickly. It wasn't quite full and could have been wrought of finest silver. Its light made the frost on the ground glitter but suddenly, with no discernible signal, the entire Fae company seemed to catch their breath as one. The music stopped.

They turned to watch Finvarra, who had been standing motionless before them all.

That king spared a glance about himself, clearly reveling in their attention. He left the Elphine Queen and took a step forward, pulling his sword from its sheath. The hilt was wrought of gold and shone in the moonlight, embellished with a ruby of enormous size that seemed to pulse like a beating heart. The blade itself gleamed, seemingly with a malice of its own. It might have been the finest steel, honed to perfection, but Elizabeth knew the Fae could not abide steel or iron.

Perhaps there was a glamour upon it. Perhaps it was bronze. She could not say, but she did not doubt that it was sharp.

Her brother Malcolm dropped to his knees before the Fae king and bent his head to surrender his neck to the blade. Did he keep his word as a man of honor, or did the Fae compel him to be so compliant? Again, Elizabeth did not know and she watched with horror as Finvarra's blade was lifted high. The Fae company began to shimmer in agitation, as if they could not control their excitement that the tithe would be collected. Catriona's grip on her hand tightened, that woman's fingers icy cold, as the Elphine Queen offered a golden chalice to Malcolm.

Its contents were a rich golden hue, like mead perhaps or Fae ale. Perhaps it was a mercy, and drinking of this draught would ensure that Malcolm felt no pain. Perhaps it would make him forget all the mortals and the life he had known. Again, Elizabeth did not know.

Her heart leaped though, and she hated being so powerless that she could only watch Malcolm be sacrificed. Catriona clutched her hand so tightly that Elizabeth could not feel her fingertips.

Why did Finvarra not even glance toward Rafael?

What could Elizabeth do?

Chapter Six

As the Elphine Queen lifted the goblet to Malcolm's lips, a gnarled old man darted through the company of the Fae. For a moment, Elizabeth did not know whether he was Fae or mortal. He lunged toward Malcolm and the force of impact sent Malcolm falling backward. The old man snatched at Malcolm's chest, his fingers scrabbling against Malcolm's tabard.

"Mine!" he roared and grabbed something. He gave a ferocious tug and Malcolm fell forward, the move allowing Elizabeth to see the chain around his neck. Catriona stiffened beside her.

Then the old man turned upon Catriona, shaking one fist at her while the other locked around some token hung from the chain around Malcolm's neck. "You would not give it to me, you ungrateful wretch of a child, but you gave it to *him*!" The old man shouted at Catriona, even as he tugged so hard that the chain broke.

He laughed then, gleeful to have captured the prize. A jeweled cross glimmered in his hand as he backed away, his malicious gaze locking upon Catriona. He was mortal, then, for no Fae would prize a crucifix, no matter its splendor. The man seemed to be unaware of the Fae regents so close behind him, or at least indifferent to their presence, which was another indication that he was not Fae. They watched him, as still as shadows and as silent.

"Aileen should never have taken you into our house when your whore of mother died," the old man snarled. "She should never have raised you as our own." He spat on the ground, and Elizabeth felt Catriona flinch. "Spawn of a foreigner, you should have died in your first year, just when your blood mother did."

Elizabeth did not understand much of this, but for the moment she did not care. The old man stepped back with his prize and Finvarra nodded at the Elphine Queen, indicating that the sacrifice should continue.

But the old man's manner and his greed gave Elizabeth an idea. "Do you not seek the blackest soul, my lord king?" she cried on impulse.

Finvarra froze, then slowly turned his attention upon her. Her spirit quailed for she had spoken aloud in the Fae circle, surrendering herself to his power, and they both knew it well. Finvarra's gaze burned with some emotion, though Elizabeth could not have named it.

Her heart skipped a beat when he smiled.

Still she continued, for she had made the sacrifice now, and she would see both Rafael and Malcolm saved if it could be done. "Should your tithe not be the most wicked soul you can harvest?"

Finvarra's smile broadened. "Do you not think we chose with care, my Elizabeth?"

She knew he referred to the fact that Malcolm had labored as a mercenary, much as Rafael had done. Her instinct told her that this greedy old man was more wicked than either of them.

"I think that much can change in six months, in our realm," she dared to say, hoping he would not take Rafael instead. He had fought vigorously in defense of Malcolm's holding this day, and he had voluntarily stepped into the circle, after all.

Finvarra looked between Malcolm and Rafael, considering. Elizabeth feared she had accomplished naught at all.

Then to her relief, Finvarra looked down at the old man who caressed the cross he had stolen from Malcolm.

When Finvarra smiled and his eyes lit, Elizabeth's heart nigh stopped. She knew he had chosen and feared the result.

At his gesture, the Elphine Queen offered the cup to the old man. Without hesitation, that man seized the chalice and drank lustily of its contents. Elizabeth nearly wept with relief.

As the man drank his fill, Finvarra's blade descended with terrifying force. He sliced the old man's head from his body in one fell stroke. Catriona jumped beside her, clearly startled at the speed with which that man had been dispatched.

Finvarra seized the man's head, lifting it by the hair so that the golden brew from the chalice fell sparkling to the ground. The expression on the dead man's face was one of astonishment.

"And so the tithe is paid," the king intoned, sparing but a glance at Malcolm and another at Rafael before he turned away. He considered Elizabeth, the glint in his eyes making her blood run cold. "And another debt is made," he added, his words low and silky.

Rafael exhaled in relief, but Elizabeth lifted a finger in warning before he moved. She was already doomed and knew that another violation on her part of the rules by which mortals could escape Fae circles would make no difference. She would not see Rafael sacrificed now!

To her relief, Rafael held his ground, as did Catriona. Praise be that he was an observant man! The Fae court retreated in regal splendor, their quest completed. The four mortals would have to remain as they were for all the night long, until the sun rose in the east, then back out of the circle with care, recalling their course perfectly. Elizabeth could only hope that the other two were cautious.

Malcolm looked to be sleeping, collapsed upon the ground before them. It was disheartening to see her older brother look so vulnerable, but the shadow of death had been pushed back from his brow. It was there, of course, for he was yet mortal, but its darkness had been considerably diminished.

He would have years to savor with Catriona at Ravensmuir.

Because Elizabeth had intervened.

She was awed in hindsight that she had dared to challenge Finvarra, no less that her words had changed his course. The Fae king could have ignored her, claimed her, or destroyed her. On this night, he would have been at the height of his power in the cycle of the year.

But Finvarra had listened to her, just as Rafael had. It was a remarkable thing. There was a power in her words that Elizabeth had never realized. Not once, but twice, she had changed the shape of events by her outspokenness.

She might have been more thrilled with this revelation if she had not feared the price Finvarra might demand of her. Matters were not done between them, and though she feared Finvarra's intent, something had changed within Elizabeth on this night.

She could influence the choices of others, it was clear, and more, she could shape her own future with an ability she had never imagined she possessed.

Finvarra might be surprised when he chose to collect his due of her.

Indeed, she looked forward to challenging his assumptions.

Just as she looked forward to challenging those of Rafael, now that he was not destined to die and had shown a willingness to acknowledge his own honorable nature. This mercenary showed remarkable promise, to Elizabeth's thinking. Perhaps, men of honor were not doomed to be so very tedious, after all. She almost smiled at the idea, but as they stood beneath the moon's light, Rafael showed even greater promise.

Or Elizabeth's Fae gifts revealed more of his truth to her.

ಶೆ

An angel might fearlessly enter this cursed realm, but Rafael was merely a mortal man. Once Malcolm's soul was saved, Rafael yearned to flee the circle and its horrific visions, but he understood from Elizabeth's gesture that he must remain motionless.

Or be condemned to remain in this company forever.

He wanted also to tend the slash in his arm, for it was deep and had bled through the bandage of linen he had hastily wrapped around it. It ached and he knew he had to see the wound washed and stitched.

But it had to wait until the dawn, which was when these apparitions would fade. He recalled that from Midwinter and also from Catriona's tales. He hoped that the delay in treating his own wound, and that of Ranulf, did not lead to dire consequences for either of them.

Any lingering doubt of their location was removed when Rafael's fallen comrade Franz revealed himself.

Just as he had the last time Rafael had stepped into the realm of these demons.

Hell it was for certain, for Franz was both dead and an unrepentant sinner.

Rafael supposed it was a good sign that Ranulf, who had been so recently injured, was not to be found in this company. That man must yet breathe, which was some solace for Rafael having chosen Malcolm over Ranulf.

Though he could have done without seeing Franz again.

The dead had remained after the other demons retreated with their king. Rafael had not immediately noticed the heavy-set mercenary, not until he stood and turned to leer at Rafael. Eventually, Franz lumbered closer and Rafael dreaded whatever might come of his presence. Franz's arm was gone, hacked from his body at the shoulder, and his gaze was as baleful as ever it had been.

It was a little too close of a reminder of what might have befallen Rafael on this day. Had his arm been severed, he would not have been so able to defend himself, and might have died in the same way as Franz.

Franz had been slashed across the torso and even here, his guts spilled forth, just as they had when he had died. Indeed, he carried them in his remaining hand, cradling them close to his body as a woman would carry a babe. Franz looked exactly as he had when Rafael had last seen him—save that he walked, while he had been dead on the ground at that last glimpse.

Any hope that Franz would simply pass Rafael by was destroyed when that mercenary walked straight to him, halted when they were toe to toe, and leered into Rafael's face.

Franz had not come so close to Rafael six months before and the sight of him had not been so vivid. Rafael might have dismissed this as another trick of the demons, an apparition intended to prod him into moving, but Franz looked to have been exhumed.

He also smelled more foul than Rafael could have believed possible. That specter leaned close as if to ensure that Rafael could not miss the full foulness of his state. There were maggots beneath his skin, writhing there, and Rafael could see bone in more than one place on the dead man's body. There was dirt smeared on his skin and blood beneath his nails, the mire of the battlefield upon his boots. Rafael knew Franz was dead, yet that man's corpse stood before him, disgust curling what was left of his lips.

If this was an illusion, it was one well wrought. Rafael, who was seldom troubled by sights of violence, felt his guts churn.

"Better me than you, right?" Franz demanded.

Rafael tightened his lips and did not reply. It had been an easy choice, even knowing that Franz would likely not return from his assignment. Franz had been infinitely more wicked than Rafael, primarily because he had deceived and misled the one woman who had loved him. That, in Rafael's view, had been beyond reprehensible.

If he had to make the choice again, he would make the same one. Better Franz than Rafael himself. He was unrepentant and time—let alone some gruesome vision—would not change that.

Franz had been the greater sinner.

The other mercenary cast his bleeding guts at Rafael's boots and his lip lifted in a sneer. "Flinch," he commanded when Rafael did not move. "Show your cowardice and back away, Rafael Rodriguez. Or shout at me to abandon you." As Franz spoke, blood spurted from his gullet. Rafael was both horrified enough to want to avert his gaze, and sufficiently transfixed that he could not do so.

What if this was *not* an apparition? What if this really were Franz? It was horrifying that a man could become such as this, independent of what he had done in his life. Despite the teachings of the church, Rafael had never put much credence in the notion of divine judgment. He could not have done so and earned his way as he had. Rafael had always believed that once a man died, his perception and existence ended.

What if Hell truly existed and was populated by those who had lived before? What if he were to be judged? What if an eternity with Franz was his future? The notion was more sickening than Franz's state.

"You should say something, or move." Franz's voice dropped to a hiss. "I would give much to have you snared in this place with me." He leaned closer, the smell of him making the bile rise in Rafael's throat. "Not my soul, of course, for it has been claimed, but I would give whatever else I have. Move, coward. Give me an excuse to trap your faithless soul here with mine."

Rafael stubbornly kept his silence, though his gut churned. If he vomited, would that count as movement and see him trapped in this place? Rafael did not wish to find out.

At such proximity, he could see that Franz's eyes were bloodshot, but still beady. "We could talk," that mercenary invited in the cajoling manner that had seduced Ursula, back in the day. "I could remind you of your sins. The list is sufficiently long that you might have forgotten a few, here and there. My memory is excellent, especially now as there is no ale to be had in this realm. I could prompt your memory when you falter."

Rafael could well imagine. His own recollection of his sins was long enough—even if the accounting was not complete, it was sufficient to see him damned.

Franz dropped his voice to a hiss. "We could make a list." He shrugged. "Although it would be too late to repent."

Rafael stared into the distance, striving to ignore his former comrade.

If he survived this night, would it be too late to repent? He had never considered the option before, imagining it to have little appeal, but a certain maiden's kiss made him wonder anew.

Better you than me. On this night, seeing what had become of Franz, Rafael felt new guilt. No man deserved this fate.

Franz circled around Rafael, looking for a fight, trying to provoke one exactly as he had done in life. Truly, this could be none other than Franz. "Would that not be a fitting fate for one who deceived another? Would that not be justice for your *betrayal*?"

Rafael fought the urge to defend himself. He dared not speak aloud!

Franz breathed in his ear. "Yet the dark king chose the old man instead of you. It cannot be that he was a greater sinner. It cannot be that he has more wickedness for which to atone. Oh nay." Franz shook his head. "It must be because you *tricked* one of them. Better him than you, right? I am certain you reasoned that he had less to live for at any rate." His voice became a hiss. "What did you promise the old man, Rafael, to ensure he died instead of you? That pretty cross?" He shook his head, the gesture sending maggots flying. Rafael nearly did flinch when one landed upon his cheek. "My Ursula had a cross just like that. Were you so base as to steal it from her corpse?"

Rafael's heart skipped a beat, though he struggled to keep his features impassive. He *had* noticed the similarity between Catriona's cross and the one he remembered Ursula wearing, but could not explain it. And truly, he could not think straight, much less solve a riddle, with the horror that Franz had become almost touching him.

"You think only of yourself, do you not?" Franz muttered. "I hope you saw some advantage in betraying me. Was it Ursula you coveted above all else?"

Rafael gritted his teeth and remained silent.

Franz whispered in his ear. "You should know that you would not be without company in this place. There are many who know of you here, many who would see a debt repaid." Franz gestured and a corpse lifted his gaze to meet Rafael's, his expression baleful.

With a start, Rafael recognized his deceased uncle, just as he had been when he had tried to defend Rafael from the invaders. That man had died for his decision to put himself in the path of those mercenaries in his determination to save his nephew.

Franz dropped the weight of his one arm across Rafael's shoulders, his manner companionable in death as it had seldom been in life. "One does not expect Hell to be so personal," he murmured. "Virtually all those you can see are here because of you. Proud of yourself and all you have accomplished? It would be much less crowded in Hell without your efforts, to be sure."

As far as Rafael could see, Franz spoke the sickening truth.

"Look at those young girls," Franz continued in his confidential tone, nodding toward a group of young women. His manner was as it had been oft before, when they had entered a town and come upon the local whores, but Rafael knew he had never killed a whore.

Franz, in contrast, had killed a very pretty one in Paris, just to keep her from telling Ursula of his infidelity.

Rafael looked, confident this glance would prove Franz wrong, and his spirit quailed.

They were maidens, too young to be wed, all with dark hair and dark eyes. Their features bore sufficient resemblance that they might have been sisters and with their coloring, they certainly appeared to be his countrywomen. They wept with a vigor that tore his heart, and he counted them, knowing before he was done what the tally would be.

Four maidens, consoling one older woman who might be their mother.

Rafael did not recognize them, he could not have recognized them, but he knew who they had to be. His heart went cold, for these maidens had been the first of his victims.

"They seem to know you, even to mourn you," Franz confided. "Did you slaughter all the young novitiates in a convent somewhere? Was that before or after we met?"

Rafael studied the company of the dead with greater interest, and no small measure of horror. He saw the lay brother who had given him extra food in the kitchen of the monastery, as well as the first knight he had ever killed with his own blade.

Of course, he saw Ibrahim, but he glanced over that man and his bleeding wound.

He saw the first warrior who had taken a blow from him, the first soldier whose throat he had slit, the first peasant sent to defend his lord's holding that Rafael had dispatched to his maker. Once he looked, it was clear the host was seething with those whose lives he had ended, in one way or another. Rafael saw the slaughtered and the fallen, the great teeming hordes of people who had been dispatched by his deeds, his choices and his blade, all of them gathered on the moor outside Ravensmuir's walls in ominous silence.

The dead survived. Hell was real.

And he would be amongst them soon enough.

One after another, they lifted their heads and stared at him, accusation stealing over their rotted faces, then began to shuffle toward him.

What would they do to him?

How would they have reparation?

"What *was* your first battle?" Franz taunted. "Where did you first kill and steal? You were with Rodrigo de Villandrando when we met. You and *L'Écorcheur* were two of a kind, were you not? Two Spanish slaughterers interested only in your personal gain."

Franz shook his head when Rafael did not speak.

"Vermin," Franz declared and spat blood on the ground, a ridiculous accusation coming from him. "Was it Treignac where you learned to kill and pillage with him? Meymac?" Franz clicked his tongue. He stepped around Rafael, his guts trailing over Rafael's boots. "All those innocents, fool enough to own any riches you desired."

It was better to eye the host of the dead than to look at Franz. Was his father in this horrific company? Rafael would not have recognized that man if he was.

Did no souls manage to attain Heaven's tranquility? It seemed all the dead were with this company of demons, all in torment and anguish.

To Rafael's relief, he did not see Ursula. One soul had escaped at least.

"I have hours yet to erode your resistance," Franz reminded

him and Rafael knew his stubborn former comrade would not abandon his quest readily. "You know I like to triumph."

Rafael did.

But Rafael also liked to win, especially over one whose intent was as dark as this. He steeled himself and held his ground, determined to survive this night now that he had evaded the tithe.

Franz pinched Rafael and exhaled in his face. He ran his hand over Rafael, clearly trying to tempt him to move. He put his fingers into the slash on Rafael's arm, and Rafael dared not think of what pestilence he left in the wound. Franz taunted him, making accusations in an attempt to make him speak. Rafael realized all too well what his former comrade did, and though he knew his own guilt, he did not wish to join Franz in this Hell just yet. Worse, the others came to touch Rafael, to poke him and hiss at him, to make accusations and promises of vengeance. The maidens who must be his sisters wept at his feet and the mother he had never known wailed at what he had become.

Rafael struggled to ignore his tormentors, just as he had learned to ignore an empty belly or a wound that could not be tended until the battle was done. He could not understand—not any more than Franz—why the king of the dead had passed him over when he had chosen the darkest mortal heart.

It could not be that Elizabeth was right, and that there was some merit in his being. Rafael knew the full list of his sins, as she did not, and he recognized that Franz was closer to the truth than she. He had never believed in Hell—a man in his occupation could not—and had always been convinced that there was life and then silence.

On this night, Rafael had to consider that he had been mistaken.

And that changed much in his view. Indeed, the question that plagued him on this night, and plagued him as surely as his former comrade, was whether there was any deed he could do to ensure that he never joined Franz in this place.

An eternity of his former comrade's company would be too much for any soul to bear.

꽃

During that long moonlit night, a crimson ribbon grew across the ground. Elizabeth watched it avidly, for it emanated from

Rafael.

Who had possessed no ribbon, or no visible one, before this.

It was one of Elizabeth's gifts, along with the ability to see the Fae, that she often could see the mark of destined matches. Not only did she see ribbons emanating from those she loved, but those ribbons oft became entwined with others, designating that a couple should be happily wed together. She had first seen a ribbon unfurl from her sister, Madeline, and that had been on the arrival of the warrior Rhys FitzHenry at Ravensmuir. His ribbon and that of her sister had twined around each other in a strange fashion, though no others had been able to discern them. Elizabeth had not understood the meaning of what she had seen, not at first, but Madeline and Rhys had been happily wedded these seven years.

Elizabeth had since seen the ribbons of all of her sisters and seen them twist with the ribbons of the men they wed. She had seen Alexander's ribbon knot with Eleanor's and witnessed Isabella's entwine with Murdoch's ribbon. She had seen how tightly knotted the ribbons of Annelise and Gareth were when they had visited Kinfairlie and upon her arrival at Ravensmuir this very week, had seen Malcolm's ribbon securely fashioned to Catriona's.

Elizabeth had seen her own ribbon shredded and broken short by Finvarra years before and had feared that to be an import that she would find no mortal man to love her. But as she stood in the moor outside Ravensmuir's hedge, motionless with Catriona and Rafael as they awaited the dawn, Elizabeth saw her own damaged ribbon become a more vivid blue than it had been. It seemed to heal before her very eyes, and she marveled at the change.

More, the ribbon emanating from Rafael grew steadily and with purpose. It was as red as blood and edged with gold. As the night progressed, the ribbon inched closer to her own with a determination she believed characteristic of that warrior.

His ribbon grew deliberately, not in a rush, as if distrustful of its own abilities, or as if doubtful of the merit of extending itself. Elizabeth watched it transfixed, silently offering the encouragement of her own heart.

The Fae were gone so far as she could see, and the mortals around her seemed to have lost the shadow of doom on their brows. Had Finvarra revoked one of her Fae gifts? It would not have troubled Elizabeth to lose the power to see either death or the Fae, and the sight of Rafael's growing ribbon encouraged her that her own destiny might have changed.

Perhaps there was a chance that she could destroy Finvarra's claim upon her, even though she had spoken aloud in the circle. Perhaps love could conquer all, as it did in all the best tales, and winning Rafael's heart was the key to her every happiness.

Elizabeth did not know, but she ardently wished to find out.

Just before the dawn, the tip of Rafael's ribbon touched the end of her own. Elizabeth felt the contact as surely as a caress upon her hand. Her heart leapt, just as it had when he had claimed her lips with his own, and heat shot through her body, from temples to toes.

Elizabeth caught her breath at the tingling sensation that filled her, and it seemed to her that the sun rose on a world made new. She had lived in chilly shadows since Finvarra had first staked his claim upon her, but as the mist rose from the field of Ravensmuir that morn, burned away by the sun's first light, Elizabeth felt Finvarra's spell lift from her own eyes and a new hope dawn within her.

Because of Rafael.

Wednesday, June 23, 1428

Feast Day of Saint John the Baptist.

Midsummer.

Claire Delacroix

Chapter Seven

Elizabeth's back was to the sea and the east, but she knew when the sun rose. Not only did its rosy light begin to touch Kinfairlie's forest ahead of her, but the last signs of the Fae's presence faded. The frost circle upon the ground melted at the touch of the sun and the lilt of their music, which had faded, was silenced. The earl's men stirred, like men waking from a dream, many of them with new holes in their boots. It seemed that Finvarra claimed no additional prizes on this night beyond the one man's soul that would be the tithe to Hell.

She waited until the last stars of the night were banished from the sky, then she took a deep breath and moved. She walked backward with steady steps, retracing their entry into the Fae circle. Catriona followed her lead, clearly understanding her choice, and Rafael watched before he echoed their moves.

When they reached the edge of the circle, where their knives were plunged into the earth, Elizabeth led the other two in a circle that marked the periphery of the frost circle that had thawed. After they had walked the circle nine times, Elizabeth heard the cry of a bird.

She looked up as three black ravens descended directly toward them. One landed on the corpse of the beheaded man and began to peck at the raw flesh on his neck.

The second scooped up some small item near Ravensmuir's gates and carried it to Malcolm.

The third raven landed on a stone that had appeared where the Elphine Queen's golden chalice had fallen. With the light of day, the glamour had fallen away, revealing the chalice as the rock it truly was. That bird turned its gaze upon Rafael, its manner expectant.

Elizabeth wondered if Rafael would know what to do. He

glanced at her and lifted a brow, even as he reached for the stone. Elizabeth nodded and Rafael picked up the stone formed of the goblet.

Elizabeth paused beside the knives and pulled out her blade. It seemed to shiver in her hand, then looked as always it had. Catriona followed her gesture, then Rafael, who grimaced at the state of the blades. He turned then and hurled the rock across the moor, his eyes narrowing when it made a loud crack upon impact.

Elizabeth felt the air shimmer and change, fairly crackling around them, and knew the night's spell had been erased. She heaved a sigh, knowing they had safely left the Fae court and circle.

Catriona, undoubtedly sensing the same, ran to Malcolm, falling to her knees beside him. He stirred, but did not awaken until she kissed him soundly.

When he reached for his new wife with a smile, Elizabeth exhaled with relief.

It was done.

Malcolm was saved and Rafael had survived. Better yet, Rafael had accepted her challenge, as sure a sign that she was right about him as there could be. Elizabeth spun to Rafael, wanting to share her celebratory mood, but that warrior scowled at her, then pivoted and marched away.

Elizabeth was momentarily astonished.

Then that crimson ribbon trailed behind him, flicking at her as if in invitation. Elizabeth did not need any more excuse than that to follow.

※

There were men, in Rafael's experience, who were perilous to know.

Such individuals had been, to date, men whose position was always besieged in battle, no matter how apparently secure its location. They had been men whose tunnels always collapsed, against all expectation, or men whose gear failed them in the heat of battle in some freak accident. They were men who might have been struck by lightning had they been peasants instead of warriors. They had been men with bad luck, no more than that, some with such cursedly bad fortune that any friendship was doomed to be of short duration.

He had never yet encountered a woman who was perilous to know, but after the night on the moor, tormented by Franz, Rafael began to think that Elizabeth might be of that ilk. He prided himself on his composure, after all, and his pragmatism, yet in less than two days, she had provoked him to impulsively risk his own life in an attempt to save Malcolm. She had addled his wits with her beauty and her challenges. She had tempted him and compelled him to reconsider his perspective of the world.

She had consorted with the dead before his very eyes.

Worse, she was reckless. What else could explain her challenge to the King of the Dead? She might be possessed of angelic beauty, but Elizabeth was one of those individuals who would not survive to old age.

The sooner Rafael put distance between them, the better. Journeying south with all speed would be his best plan. His fellows would certainly be prepared to depart after the night they had endured, to head back to the familiarity of war on the Continent as soon as possible.

Even war was better than facing the dead in Hell.

Rafael followed Elizabeth's lead in stepping back to the mortal realm and threw the stone as her glance indicated he should. He knew she would come after him, undoubtedly flush with success, but Rafael had to tend to Ranulf. That man had spent the night with his injury and though Rafael did not regret choosing to aid Malcolm first, he feared now for the extent of Ranulf's injury. His own would have to wait yet longer.

He was not surprised to hear a maiden's footsteps in determined pursuit.

Nor was Rafael surprised to pivot and discover Elizabeth's face alight with pleasure. He folded his arms across his chest and awaited her, sure there would be no immediate escape. He knew he should not have been surprised by the wave of joy that swept through him, both at the sight of her and the surety that he was her target.

Joy. There was another unreliable emotion that he could have done without, one that Elizabeth inflicted upon him. Still, Rafael held his ground and waited, savoring the sight of her.

"You could have been killed!" she exclaimed by way of greeting, unable to hide her delight that he had not been. Rafael supposed he should have been troubled that she showed no fear of him, but he could not regret a thing when her eyes sparkled so merrily.

"And the notion pleases you so much as that?" he teased.

Elizabeth laughed. "That you thought more of Malcolm than yourself pleases me so much, and you know it well."

Rafael grimaced. "So I have become a man of honor in your view, which surely makes me tedious company."

She laughed again, and he was well pleased with his influence.

"Never that," she said, a flush staining her cheeks. "You could never be tedious, Rafael."

The sound of his name on her lips struck him like a blow once again, reminding him of his place as little else could have done. Rafael sobered, then frowned at her. "And I suppose you are proud of your disregard for your own welfare?"

Her lips set stubbornly, her expression turning mutinous. "You will say again that I am impulsive and foolish."

"Why else would you dare the King of the Dead as you did?" Rafael flung out a hand, realizing she would see that he was concerned for her and not caring a whit for that if his warning changed her course. "You provoked him in his own court, and you are beyond fortunate that he did not take his vengeance immediately."

"You are protective of me."

"I speak only good sense. No one with their wits about them challenges a king when in that man's court. I had thought you more sensible than that."

Elizabeth folded her arms across her chest and arched a brow. "I suspected he would not retaliate then. Finvarra prefers to wait for his moment."

Rafael felt his suspicion rise. "What is this?" Now that he recalled the exchange, it seemed that she had a familiarity with the King of the Dead. How and why?

"The king, Finvarra, pledged years ago that he would have me, that I would come willingly to him."

The notion made Rafael's innards cold. "We all go to the realm of the dead eventually," he said with forced calm, wanting to be sure he understood her. "Though I cannot believe you to be destined for Hell."

"It is Fae, though you are right. He broke my ribbon years past so that I would never find my true love among mortal men."

Before Rafael could ask, Elizabeth smiled at him, her eyes dancing again. "And there is the marvel of it. We changed our destinies last night, Rafael! Your choice and mine changed what might be. Can you not see it?" She gestured skyward and Rafael followed her gesture.

There were ribbons in the air above them, a silvery green one from Elizabeth that did appear to be broken short, and one as red as blood from himself. His was of such generous length that it rippled in the air and swirled around Elizabeth. It also wound around her ribbon like a tendril of smoke, and Rafael's eyes narrowed.

"Do you see the ribbons?" Elizabeth asked with excitement. "They are a Fae sign of destined love, and ours are entangled." She dropped her voice to a confidential whisper. "Like our fates."

Rafael recoiled from the suggestion and the maiden.

What madness was this?

Their fates entwined? Rafael frowned and blinked at the ribbons, then lied, thinking it the easiest way to dissuade her from this notion. "I see only a morning sky. Are you well?"

Elizabeth's confidence faltered then, but she continued. "Yours grew last night, after your choice was made, and I believe it is because my challenge changed your course. Our choices changed our future, just as in an old tale, and now we can be wed in truth."

"Wed?" Rafael laughed aloud, unable to help himself. "I will never wed."

"But the ribbons..."

"Are a sorcery of some kind, and truly, only you can see them," Rafael said firmly. He bowed. "If you will excuse me, I have matters of *this* world to tend."

"What do you mean?"

"Ranulf is wounded."

"So are you."

"I will tend him first." Rafael turned away, heading toward the cluster of his companions from the Sable League.

"You will tend him?"

"It is what I do."

"Then show me..."

Rafael spun to confront her, vexed by her determination. "Do you see any detail of the world around you?" he demanded, hearing his own voice rise. He felt a need to make her understand what she did, though he did not believe she was a fool. She was innocent, no more than that, and it infuriated him that her own choices could see that changed. "Do you note that we stand upon a battlefield, that men have died and others have been wounded in this place?" he demanded, noting that she did not recoil from his harsh tone. "Do you see the price that has been paid for the whimsy of a woman being denied the suitor she desired?"

Elizabeth held her ground, so resolute that he both admired her and feared for her. "Of course I do!"

That she did not balk meant that Rafael had to be more blunt. "Do you recognize what would have happened to you if our forces had been overcome? Indeed, it is uncommon fortune that we triumphed, for we were solely outnumbered. What do you think would have happened if the gatehouse had been overrun, if the earl's forces had gained the hall?"

Elizabeth glared at him, even as the color drained from her face.

Rafael continued, determined to make her see the peril. "Mercenaries would have kicked down the door to the solar, and what would have happened next, *mi piqueño ángel*? They would not have asked for your hand to dance. You would not have been able to run or to hide. They would have held you down and taken what they desired of you, with no consideration of any price to you." The very idea sickened Rafael, but Elizabeth was undaunted.

"I am not so innocent that I do not understand that," she retorted.

"Were you my sister, I would see you locked in the tower of Ravensmuir," Rafael said, hearing the heat in his own tone. "Not only this day but every day until you were wedded to a man who would defend you."

"And doubtless he would do so by locking me into another tower," Elizabeth snapped. "I do not wish to be protected from life nor even from risk. I wish to live and to know that I have done so."

"You only say as much because you have this cursed confidence in your safety, a confidence that is undeserved."

She did not retreat from his anger, but instead took a step closer. Indeed, she poked a finger at his chest. "You are vexed because you know I am right. You know that there is a bond between us, even if you cannot see the ribbons, for we two manage to compel each other to change."

Rafael was horrified. "You do not realize how fortunate you have been, and would cast it all away! You play the fool!"

"It is *not* folly to want to experience more than a locked chamber in a tower," Elizabeth retorted. "I would journey afar and I would love a man with all my heart. I would taste the pleasure to be had abed and I would know both joy and sorrow. I would savor all that can be experienced and take chances, rather than avoid risk. I would choose my fate."

Rafael would have argued with this uncommon view, but Elizabeth clasped his face in her hands, her touch silencing him. Her eyes shone with a resolve he found most beguiling and he found he could not step away.

"And I would do all of this with you, Rafael Rodriguez," she whispered with fervor, then kissed him soundly.

The touch of her lips sent a welcome heat through him, resonating with his need to celebrate Ravensmuir's triumph on this day and reminding him that he had survived both battle and visit to Hell. Rafael could have caught her close, or carried her off to savor her delights in private, but her passion made him want to ensure that she was not disappointed or mistreated. There was a fire between them, to be sure, but it was one he would not encourage.

He knew his place, as lowly as it might be.

૨ૐ

Elizabeth was not truly surprised that Rafael stepped away from her kiss, nor was she astonished that his manner was wary. He could not see the ribbons, after all, and she appreciated his skepticism.

She would simply have to change his thinking.

She did not doubt that it would take some time and persistence to do so, but already she had made encouraging progress.

She smiled at him, knowing that disconcerted him. "And so, again, you protect me from my own impulses. Your deeds speak more loudly than your protests, Rafael."

His lips tightened to a grim line. "You see only what you wish to see."

"I see that we made similar choices, both more concerned for Malcolm than ourselves. I think that bodes well for our future together."

"I see that we have no future together," he replied tersely.

"Indeed?" Elizabeth did not abandon the notion. "I would wager..."

Rafael interrupted her sharply, his temper showing yet again that she had struck close to the truth. "No need is there to wager! You are defiant for its own sake, as is the way of so many maidens long indulged." Elizabeth might have argued, but he leaned closer. "Believe as you would, but I have no time for maidens who make trouble simply for their own amusement."

"You misunderstand me. I do not willfully make trouble..."

"Indeed you do." Rafael was disdainful. "What is the difference between you and Jeanne Douglas, who would send men to their deaths because the man she desired to wed married another?" The comparison insulted Elizabeth, as she did not doubt Rafael intended. "Secure yourself in Ravensmuir's solar, as is fitting for a maiden of your lineage. Find your embroidery, my lady, that you may yet be chaste on your nuptial night, for on this day, in this hall, there will be much celebrating of a most earthly kind."

Elizabeth refused to be daunted for she discerned the root of his protest. "Once more, you would see me defended, as a knight should protect his lady."

Something flickered in his dark eyes. "I tell you again: I am *not* a hero in one of your tales."

"But you could be."

"I will never wed," Rafael repeated with force. "That was long ago resolved. But should you wish to be despoiled and abandoned this day, I will not decline your offer."

Elizabeth caught her breath.

"Wed one of your countrymen," he counseled in a softer tone of voice. "Choose a man whose assumptions are much as your own, bear him children and be happy." Rafael held her gaze, as if to be certain she knew he made no jest, then he spun on his heel and strode to his companions.

Sadly for this warrior, Elizabeth was not so prepared to abandon him or this quest. She trusted the ribbons, and she believed he was the sole one who could keep her from Finvarra's grasp. The fog that had enveloped her since Finvarra's pledge to claim her was banished in Rafael's presence, which could be no small sign either.

Never mind how vital she felt when she was with him.

She watched him stride away, considering what he had confessed to her, seeking a clue for her quest. She needed to learn more of how Rafael had been betrayed, and when he had been helpless and hungry. Therein lay the key to his conviction that he could never wed. She eyed the floating ribbon, considered how much he had already responded to her, and knew that she was right.

The real challenge would lie in convincing Rafael.

❧

Rafael was resolved. He would leave Ravensmuir and Scotland without delay, *and* he would take a dark-haired whore on his route south. He would ride a dozen of them to break Elizabeth's spell, two dozen if necessary, and he would see his ability to fight with dispassion restored. He would leave this land behind, and all the madness it had conjured in his mind, and his life would be as it had been for decades.

A part of him prayed it would be that simple.

Another part of him marveled that he prayed at all.

Rafael knew Elizabeth followed him, as stubborn as her brother could be, but did not alter his course. There was gruesome labor to be done, the aftermath of war, and if Elizabeth did not care for the view, that was not his concern. One of the Sable League had fallen, but there were more pressing matters than Reynaud's final rest. The living must be tended before the dead.

He had to see Ranulf first.

"And so my turn is come to endure your torment," Ranulf said when he spied Rafael approaching.

Rafael frowned. "I apologize for the delay but I had to attend to Malcolm last night..."

"I know it and I would never blame you for it. He might have died, while I merely lost all the blood in my heart." That Ranulf made a jest was a marvel, for he had endured the pain all the night long. There was sweat on his brow and his usually ruddy face was yet more red. He was breathing heavily and held his right hand in his left. The bundle of cloth wrapped around his hand was wet with blood. "Your injury waits to be tended as well," he said, nodding at the blood on Rafael's arm.

"It can wait a little longer." Rafael noted Ranulf's pallor and had to acknowledge that he had lost a goodly measure of blood. "At least you tried to halt the bleeding," he said and untied the cloth that had been knotted around his injured hand. He could see Ranulf's thumb and the tips of just two fingers protruding from the cloth.

Had Rafael not enjoyed the companionship of Franz, rotted and dead, the night before, he would have said his worst nightmare was before him. Ranulf was maimed, perhaps not so much that he would have to surrender his trade, but the injury would hamper him for the rest of his days.

"I tried to bind it, as you oft advise," Amaury said and Rafael knew the other man shared his discouragement.

"You did well," Rafael acknowledged, even as he made to open the cloth. He schooled his own expression, knowing that Ranulf would watch closely for his response. He was relieved though, that the injury wasn't worse.

At least Ranulf still had the majority of his hand. It was good, too, that the thumb had not been lost. The men gathered around him tried to hide their reactions to the sight revealed, but Rafael felt the ripple of shock pass through them.

Maimed. It was a poor portent for Ranulf's future, no matter how he considered it.

Ranulf's index finger dangled from his hand, attached solely by a bit of flesh, while his middle finger was cut short. Two digits were completely gone, the stump that remained looking like no more than a pulpy mass. Rafael could see the white of the bone in Ranulf's hand, and he noted how Ranulf shook with the shock of his injury. Damage to the face or the hands tended to elicit the most violent reactions, even if the injury was less critical.

"You are fortunate," Rafael said, speaking more heartily than the injury deserved. Ranulf exhaled in relief at this verdict. "You might have lost your entire hand." If that had been the case, the injury would have been much more likely to have ultimately killed Ranulf.

Even this could fester and put his life in peril.

Even this would keep him from fighting so well.

"Strange then that I do not feel so fortunate," Ranulf managed to say.

"Ungrateful wretch," Tristan growled playfully. "Dame Fortune will turn her back upon you now!"

"Indeed, it would have been much worse if you had lost your hand. How then would you have pleased the ladies?" quipped Louis.

"Or even yourself," Gunter teased gruffly and the men laughed. Rafael was keenly aware of Elizabeth's presence as she hovered several steps away, and felt awkward with the earthy talk of his fellows.

Still, talk would not hurt her, and it might convince her of Rafael's argument as his own words had not.

Ranulf managed a smile. "You give little credit to a man's quick thinking," he retorted. "Much less his inventiveness."

"Or what skills he might have with his left hand," added Bertrand.

"Who yet has *eau-de-vie*?" Rafael demanded of his fellows, interrupting their jests.

Two flagons were shoved at him and Rafael took them both. The one with the least in it he gave to Ranulf. "Drink it all," he instructed.

"You owe me now," Giorgio teased Ranulf behind Rafael. "I was saving that for Guilia."

"God forbid that I should have to answer to your whore for the loss of one of her pleasures," Ranulf retorted, his voice weaker than Rafael would have preferred.

He removed the small pouch that was always fastened to his belt. It was wrought of leather, folded cleverly so that it both held a few implements and created a clean surface when it was unfurled. Anticipating him, Louis cast down his cloak to cover the ground beside Ranulf. As always, Rafael deliberately did not recall how he had gained this expertise or this small pouch.

He had paid for it, that was for certain.

Amaury had brought a bucket of water and crouched beside it, intent as usual in learning as much as he could from Rafael. Watching another was how Rafael had learned what skill he had in the treating of wounds, but he always explained to Amaury what he knew in addition.

There might come a time when he had need of such service and was unable to tend to himself.

111

"The flesh must be closed so the wound can heal," Rafael said and Amaury nodded.

"Why the *eau-de-vie*?" Elizabeth asked, moving closer. The men froze for a moment and Ranulf averted his gaze.

"This is not a view fit for a lady," that man said gruffly.

"Nonsense," Elizabeth replied, her tone firm. "I often aid Eleanor in tending illness and injuries at Kinfairlie. I know to make possets and poultices, and one day, I might be wed to a man who defends our holding. I would like to know this skill."

Rafael felt his comrade's surprise, but in truth, he did not expect her to linger long. He moved the cloth so she could see the damage fully, heard her catch her breath, and was certain she would flee.

Instead, she eased closer to get a better look. Rafael felt surprise slide through the ranks of his companions and felt no small measure of it himself.

"You did not answer me," she chided, her hand landing upon his shoulder with an ease undeserved. Rafael felt his neck heat, for he knew his fellows had noted the gesture.

"I do not know. I was taught to rinse the wound and all that would come in contact with it." Rafael shrugged. "As the tactic works, I do not question it."

Elizabeth eyed him, consideration in her gaze. "Taught by whom?"

"It is not of import," Rafael said tightly.

She pursed her lips, clearly thinking otherwise, and her gaze was knowing. He had to learn to control his tone in her presence, for she took ridiculous encouragement from his shows of temper. "Must it be *eau-de-vie*?"

"I was taught that it was best."

Elizabeth nodded understanding.

Ranulf's hand had been washed as best as the men could manage and Rafael inspected it before he nodded approval. He opened his pouch, then chose a needle and linen thread.

"Praise be for our secret weapon," Bertrand said with satisfaction. "I feared you might be lost upon that field last night, and then woe should come upon us all."

"We would all be dead twice over without Rafael's skills," agreed Tristan.

Rafael bristled, guessing that Elizabeth would make more of this talk than it merited.

Gunter held fast to Ranulf's shoulders and watched. Rafael cut off Ranulf's finger, severing the last bit of flesh, and put the finger aside.

"Can it be joined anew?" Elizabeth asked.

Rafael shook his head, wishing it might be otherwise. He threaded the needle and set it on his opened pouch. He lifted the second flagon of *eau-de-vie* and liberally doused both needle and thread.

Elizabeth folded her arms across her chest, her brow furrowed in concentration. Rafael knew she would not endure the next part.

He met Ranulf's worried gaze. "This will hurt," he warned his fellow, knowing that was not the half of it. Ranulf would feel as if his hand was being burned off, but Rafael had learned this trick long before and though he did not understand it, he trusted its effectiveness.

"Pain is better than death," Ranulf said, his voice shaking as if he did not quite believe it. He lifted his injured hand, his arm shaking, then averted his face and closed his eyes. With his free hand, he gripped Gunter. "Do what you must."

"Hold him fast," Rafael advised the others and they did as he requested. Ranulf took a breath, bracing himself, and squeezed his eyes shut.

Rafael spilled the *eau-de-vie* over the open wound.

Ranulf roared in pain and seemed to rise from the ground in his agony. The wound might have boiled, for fresh red blood spilled from it with vigor. Gunter held fast to Ranulf's shoulders and the others gripped his legs. That mercenary swore thoroughly, and Rafael wondered whether Elizabeth had ever heard such language. When he glanced her way, she had flushed and was biting her lip, but still watching.

"I am sorry, my lady," Ranulf said, his voice weak.

"I completely understand," Elizabeth said with a smile.

Ranulf held out his shaking hand again and strove to remain still. The blood was vivid red, but its flow had slowed again.

Rafael stitched the wound shut as neatly as he could manage. The flow of blood lessened again, but Ranulf shook mightily in his pain. As the needle bit into his skin time and again, the fresh pricks in his flesh began to bleed. The large man moaned, but he did not withdraw his hand. He shook, sweat running down his brow. Rafael worked as quickly as he could, then cleaned the hand again with the liquor.

Ranulf groaned then passed out in truth, his large form splayed across the ground. Rafael wrapped the finger securely in clean linen, and knotted the bandage. He cleaned the debris and washed his needle. Elizabeth was still beside him and he knew how best to send her fleeing.

Time it was that the lady faced a challenge herself.

"If you would," Rafael said with a slight bow and handed her the needle. Elizabeth accepted it from him, confusion in her expression. "I would not have your lessons in embroidery prove to have been a waste of your time," he said and understanding made her lips part.

Rafael removed his tabard and cast it aside, then pulled his mail shirt over his head. His padded aketon was heavy with the blood he had shed and he wondered if it would be salvageable. He removed it as well, then winced that the bandage he had hastily wrapped around his wound was completely red. Elizabeth paled at the sight, then flushed as he unknotted the bandage. He winced as he pulled the cloth from the wound, for the blood had dried there. He saw Elizabeth's gaze flick to the wound, an angry gash upon his upper arm that already ached mightily, and watched her swallow with discomfiture.

Here would be the test of her mettle.

Rafael handed her the flask of *eau-de-vie*.

"Show me what you have learned," he said in soft challenge. He thought she would take the dare, but he did not believe she would finish tending his wound. Indeed, he might have a strange scar to prompt his memory of this day.

Elizabeth glared at him. She took the flask from his grip with a quick gesture, but not so quick that he did not see her hands shaking.

She *was* fetching when she was annoyed, even with her lips drawn taut. Her eyes flashed as she took a deep breath, then touched his elbow with her fingertips. There was steel in her posture when she flicked a glance to his face.

"This will hurt," she advised, then spilled a ferocious quantity of *eau-de-vie* into the wound.

It took all within Rafael to keep from bellowing at the pain. His comrades, curse them, laughed.

Chapter Eight

War was Rafael's world, and it was one Elizabeth did not understand in the least.

Nor did she wish to know more of battle. The fighting and the killing was abhorrent to her, but she was fascinated by the way his fellows had turned to Rafael for aid when one of them had been injured.

They trusted him, and it seemed to Elizabeth that men of such pragmatism would only trust another who had proven himself worthy of their confidence. Healing, also, could be the domain of women, and Elizabeth had to believe that any woman who matched her path to that of Rafael would have need of such skills.

She had witnessed the making of possets for coughs and chills and fevers, had heard the arrival of babes, had witnessed the treating of wounds in the kitchen, and had learned how best to rock a child whose new teeth gave it woe.

Stitching of wounds was new to her, though, and she would seize this chance to learn.

Elizabeth had guessed that Rafael would challenge her. She had seen the light in his eyes when he had turned and had braced herself to do whatever he asked.

Surprising Rafael was a feat she would never tire of doing.

The *eau-de-vie* had shocked him fully. For a moment, Rafael had paled so much that Elizabeth had feared he might pass out, just as his companion had. But he inhaled sharply and narrowed his eyes, wavering only slightly on his feet. His jaw was clenched and his teeth bared, a sure sign of the agony he endured.

His expression turned wary again. Elizabeth knew he thought she could not do this, and Elizabeth was determined to prove him wrong.

No matter how her bile rose.

She threaded the needle.

"Ensure the wound is clean before you secure it," he advised tightly. How had he stood all the night, then argued with her this morning, with this injury? She supposed he must have endured worse in his time.

No wonder he thought her a sheltered innocent. Just the sight of his flesh cut open so cruelly was nigh enough to make her retch.

"How?" she asked.

"Rinse your hand, then put your fingers into the wound. It is too deep to see clearly. You have to feel it."

Elizabeth looked into his eyes, half thinking he made a jest. But nay, Rafael was deadly serious, his manner like that of Eleanor when she gave instruction.

Elizabeth took a deep breath and pried open the wound. She tried not to think of it as Rafael's arm, though it was hard to do as much with him glaring down at her and the heat of his flesh beneath her hands. He flinched when she slid her fingertips into the warmth of the cut, then exhaled shakily.

"Any debris will hide at the deepest point of the wound," he said, and she heard the strain in his voice.

She nodded and felt with care, easing something that looked like a shard of metal from the depths of the wound. She placed it on his discarded aketon and Gunter examined it closely. "From the blade in question, no doubt," that man said. "You had best check again."

Rafael closed his eyes and tipped his head back as Elizabeth did just that. She found no more shards and lifted her needle. "*Eau-de-vie* again," Rafael whispered. "'Tis a cursedly expensive wound."

The men laughed though he did not. Elizabeth winced in sympathy as the liquor made the open flesh more red, then rinsed the needle and thread and began to stitch.

"What would you have done without my embroidery needle?" she teased and his nostrils flared. "It seems a location you would have trouble reaching."

"He would have had an ugly scar," one of the men confided.

"My stitches would be poor indeed," agreed another.

"Take more flesh," Rafael advised, and she realized that he was watching her efforts. "So, it does not tear so readily before it heals."

"You will have a scar, to be sure," she said and he tried to smile, though it looked like more of a grimace.

"Simply another for my collection."

It was true that there were a number of marks upon Rafael's skin. Elizabeth did not want to be caught staring at his body, so she stitched quickly and with care. She wanted to finish it soon, but also to do a good job. She was keenly aware of the way he watched her, his gaze like a weight upon her. When she had closed the whole wound, he cleared his throat.

"A little more, *mi piqueño ángel*." His husky tone sent a thrill to her, his voice pitched so that it seemed only she was to hear him. "If it tears, it will be much worse."

"I could stitch it again."

"I will not be in your vicinity."

She lifted her gaze to his, not having considered that he would leave so quickly as this. She saw his conviction, though, and her heart chilled at its portent. Aware that the other men would hear any protest she made, Elizabeth did as Rafael instructed, then knotted the thread. She admired the neatness of her stitches for a moment, then, without thinking, bent to bite the thread, just as she oft did with her embroidery.

Her lips were on Rafael's skin when she heard him inhale sharply. His flesh was warm against her mouth and the scent of the *eau-de-vie* filled her nostrils. She glanced up only to be snared by the intensity of his dark eyes. He did not blink, his gaze burning into hers as it had when he had kissed her.

Her heart skipped. Her mouth went dry. She could not move.

He was not so immune to her charms as he would have her think.

He was leaving to protect her from his impulses.

Elizabeth smiled against his skin, her confidence restored. For she, she was not immune to Rafael in the least. Never had a man prompted such a reaction within her. The ribbons convinced her that she was right to place her trust in him.

On impulse, Elizabeth pressed her lips against him fully, holding his gaze as she kissed the end of his wound. His nostrils flared then pinched shut, his eyes blazing. She thought he might swear and turn away, but she could not look away from his potent gaze.

It seemed the entire world fell away and there was naught for

Elizabeth but Rafael. He bent a little closer, looking dangerous and determined, and her heart skipped as she wondered what he would say.

But she was not to know.

A hand fell on the back of Elizabeth's waist in that moment and she started to find Malcolm behind her. "The stitches are not nearly so fine on any of your other scars," her brother said to Rafael, his tone so resolute that Elizabeth straightened at the warning she heard there.

She saw how Malcolm met Rafael's gaze, some accusation in his expression. Rafael actually appeared to be discomfited, which Elizabeth thought telling. "I thank you, my lady," he said gruffly to her. "The angle was such that I could not have done it myself."

"Indeed," Malcolm said, clearly unconvinced.

"He wanted a pretty scar for a change," one of the men jested, and they laughed.

Save Malcolm and Rafael, who continued to eye each other.

Elizabeth wanted to dismiss the tension between the two of them. "Will your comrade's hand be saved?" she asked Rafael, indicating the man who had passed out.

Rafael shrugged and grimaced, his eyes narrowed as he considered his companion. "I have done my best."

"Now the matter is in God's hands," said a grey-haired man in the company.

"Rafael's best is better than most can do, Gunter," Malcolm said and that warrior nodded agreement. "We have been blessed indeed by Rafael's expertise."

"You speak aright," the first man conceded. "The Sable League would be far smaller, without your gift with strategy and Rafael's talent for healing."

An awkward silence fell over the men then, and Elizabeth realized they were thinking of Malcolm no longer fighting with them. Again she spoke to cover the silence. "How was he injured?"

"Ranulf has a skill with Greek fire," Gunter said. "He must have cut the fuse too short, thus the explosive ignited when he had not thrown it far."

"Did he see the arrival of the Fae?" she asked. Again she felt rather than saw the change in their manner. They might have closed ranks against her and their expressions turned impassive.

"Demons," Rafael corrected softly.

"They are not demons," Elizabeth said with some impatience. "They are Fae, beings other than us who live amongst us and have powers beyond our own."

Rafael's eyes narrowed. "They are wicked."

"They have not our sense of morality," Elizabeth said. "Though I am not certain that makes them wicked. They do keep their pledges."

He considered her for a moment, then turned away. Elizabeth watched him, hungry for his attention, but knowing he would not give it again before Malcolm.

One of the men cleared his throat. "I know only that I saw naught last eve that I would confess to seeing."

The others nodded and this time Malcolm filled the silence. "I thought we would see Reynaud buried on the morrow, in the morning, if that is amenable to all of you." The men nodded agreement. "Catriona wished him laid in what passes for our chapel. The earl's men will be taken back to his lands and a few mercenaries in his employ buried here on this day, but Catriona believed you might all appreciate more time to say farewell to Reynaud. We shall bury him at first light."

"A marked grave?" one man asked, glancing up.

Were they accustomed to their fellows being laid to rest with less dignity than that? By their manner, Elizabeth guessed so.

Rafael was right that she had many assumptions that were not shared by his kind.

She would simply have to learn.

She looked up in time to see Malcolm's fleeting smile. "Aye, for so befits a friend of the Laird of Ravensmuir. If you all think it acceptable, he could be laid to rest beneath the floor of the new chapel."

"That would be a fine tribute, Malcolm," Gunter said, and he seemed to Elizabeth to be overcome with emotion.

"Not too near the altar," Amaury jested and poked Gunter in the shoulder. "We would not see all those laid to rest at Ravensmuir condemned because of the company they would keep."

The men chuckled together, but Elizabeth was aware that something had changed in their manner. They were pleased by Malcolm's offer.

Perhaps their assumptions were not so different, after all. Circumstance shaped much in their lives, but not perhaps their desires.

"We all have labor this morn," Malcolm said. "But there will be a hot meal in the hall at midday, and with the slightest smile from Dame Fortune, a fresh delivery of both bread and ale from Kinfairlie as well."

One man shook a finger at Malcolm. "You fare well at this task of lordship for one so new to its demands," he teased.

"It is my lady wife who considered such practicalities. She has a talent for inventories and planning, it appears, which suits me very well." Malcolm smiled down at Elizabeth. "And so it is a happy day when a man and a woman bind their lives together, each shouldering half of the burden in seeing their duties done. Come along, Elizabeth. I shall have to lend my aid to Alexander in finding you such a happy match."

There was no question of denying Malcolm and Elizabeth saw from the line of his mouth that he would tolerate no argument from her. The mercenaries bowed to her, all save Rafael who simply watched, and Elizabeth took Malcolm's elbow as he led her away.

"You wanted me away from them," she charged quietly. "Why? They are your guests."

"And Alexander has not only arrived, but fears for your virtue, which is his obligation as your oldest brother and guardian," Malcolm said mildly.

Irritation surged through Elizabeth. "They are simply men."

"Aye, they are simply men," Malcolm agreed. "Men accustomed to taking what they desire. Men who plan for the next hour of their lives and no more. Men who have no roots, who would forget their histories, who have learned to ensure their own survival, comfort and pleasure first." He glanced down at her. "They are not evil men, Elizabeth, but neither are they men who have the same expectations as you." He raised his brows. "Much less those of Alexander."

Elizabeth felt her lips tighten. "Alexander bade me choose my own spouse."

Malcolm laughed. "He did," he admitted, his eyes sparkling. "But not from that company."

Elizabeth halted to confront her brother, folding her arms across her chest. "What if I told you that I see my ribbon entwined with that of Rafael?"

Malcolm sobered. "Then you would have my condolences, for you would be doomed to live your life alone. I have never met a man so sure of his place in the world as Rafael." He tapped a finger on her arm. "And I would wager all of Ravensmuir that if you told him of your admiration for him and desire to wed him, that he would decline the honor without hesitation."

Elizabeth felt her cheeks heat beneath Malcolm's knowing regard.

He shook his head and spoke gently. "The key, Elizabeth, in waging war is to recognize when a battle cannot be won, and to retreat without squandering one's resources to no good end." He raised that finger when she might have protested. "I would ask for your assistance on this morn where triumph *can* be won."

"What do you mean?"

"The hall needs to be set to rights before the meal, and Catriona is nigh overwhelmed."

Elizabeth frowned. "But all was orderly there last evening..."

"Yet during the night, a miracle occurred."

"I do not understand."

"You will soon enough." Malcolm smiled mysteriously, then ushered Elizabeth toward the hall.

Such was her curiosity that she went.

When Elizabeth walked away with Malcolm, Rafael knew he should have been glad to see her go. Instead, the company of his fellows seemed lacking.

He was tempted to turn and watch her progress across the bailey.

Rafael was still amazed that Elizabeth had taken his dare and tended to his wound. He was still shaken by the kiss she had granted to him, touching her lips to his wound. There had been a moment of potent intimacy there, a moment in which he could have been persuaded that she was the woman for him, a heartbeat in which he might have believed she was right about their entwined fates.

Nay, it had been a moment in which he had yearned that she

might be right. It would suit him well to have such a woman as this at his side. Though Rafael had never imagined he might have such an opportunity, though he knew better than to hope for what could not be readily gained, Elizabeth made him wish he were another man. She was not readily daunted or frightened, this maiden, and he found his admiration for her only grew with each exchange.

The spell she cast was a potent one indeed.

Rafael lifted the flask and shook it, revealing that there was still some *eau-de-vie* within it. It would not go to waste, to be sure. Rafael took a mouthful himself then passed it around. The others each took a swig in turn, and the liquor restored their usual manner.

In the silence, he knew they all thought of Ranulf being maimed and Reynaud being dead. Ranulf stirred a little, and Amaury gave him the last of the *eau-de-vie*.

"And so we live to fight another day," Gunter said grimly, then nodded to the others. "The Sable League rides from the battlefield again."

There was a grunt of satisfaction at that. "Anyone else in need of tending?" Rafael asked, but they shook their heads in unison.

"Scratches and nicks," Tristan said.

"Naught a cup of ale will not mend," agreed Louis.

"Or another such pleasure," Giorgio said heartily. They nudged him as one, for he was the sole one of the party whose whore had not only traveled with them but had accepted only his attentions.

Bertrand claimed the last of the *eau-de-vie* then shoved a hand through his dark hair. "So, only Reynaud does not rise to fight again."

They crossed themselves as one, then silently divided the labor before them. Bertrand, Tristan and Giorgio went to Reynaud, then carried his corpse to the tent being raised over the place where Catriona would have her chapel built. The canopy would protect the bodies from the sun while the graves were dug. Several of the boys were already digging in spots indicated by Malcolm. The horses had to be tended and then weapons would have to be cleaned and sharpened, in preparation for another day.

There was labor aplenty to be done, and Rafael was not the sole man who would want to wash the mire of battle from his skin. One of the squires confided that there were tubs filled behind the stables, and though he would not have the first water, bathing would still be welcome.

Then Rafael would tend to his steed. His most costly possession and his most loyal one would be skittish. It was the nature of horses to distrust the smell of blood, and it was a healthy impulse, to be sure. Rayo tolerated battle better when he was in the midst of it, likely because he could see. Being tethered in a stall while a battle waged always left the destrier troubled.

And truly, tending Rayo would settle Rafael just as much as it did the destrier. Elizabeth had vexed him because he was exhausted, no more than that.

He knew the nightmares would come when he eventually did sleep.

They always did after a battle. It was one fact upon which he could rely.

Rafael would have to become drunk if he meant to sleep dreamlessly this night, and it was easy to resolve to do as much.

Indeed, that might convince Elizabeth that he was not the man she believed him to be. Rafael could not think of a single tale in which a knight showed his valor by becoming drunk beyond belief in his patron's hall. Indeed, such a lack of grace was oft the mark of a villain destined to die.

His was the perfect plan, in more ways than one.

܀

The bath water was cold and it was not very clean, but Rafael scrubbed himself down thoroughly all the same. At least there was soap, given that they were at Ravensmuir, and he had a clean chemise in his pack.

As usual, his birthmark was noted and commented upon. The strange thing was that after his experience of the night before Rafael could not make his usual jest. He had a port wine mark on his buttock that looked like an open hand, though it was a little larger than a man's hand. He usually jested that it was the Devil's hand upon him, just to frighten the squires, but on this day, he could not utter the words.

He had seen the King of the Dead, after all, and visited Hell itself. It was much tougher to be skeptical of judgment and the wages of sin when he had spent the night with Franz.

He rubbed himself down and dressed in clean chausses and that chemise, tugging on his boots before he strode back to the stables. His hair was wet but he did not care.

All was bustling in the stables, just as he had anticipated. The squires worked steadily, along with the other warriors from the Sable League who had already joined them. The horses had been brushed down the night before, and they were in their stalls. Most were dozing or nosing in their hay, stamping their feet and swishing their tales. At the sight of Rafael, one of the squires came running.

"A number of the steeds have been injured," the boy said, his tone breathless. "And there is no ostler at Ravensmuir. Could you aid them?"

"Of course." Indeed, Rafael welcomed the task.

Once again, his skills were of use, for a cut upon the flesh of a horse was not that different from one upon a man's skin. To his relief, none of the steeds had broken a limb in the battle, and none had been killed. There were a variety of scratches and cuts to be tended, and he noticed that several of the squires had sustained greater injuries. He spent the morning busily occupied and it was welcome labor.

There was a comfort to be had in the familiar sounds and activities. This was his life and always would be. He heard the crude jests being made by his comrades and their tales of their deeds in the battle the day before. Two of the men had kindled a fire in the old blacksmith's workshop, and the sound of hammer upon steel echoed through the air. There were hilts to be repaired and nicks in blades to be smoothed, dints in shields and helms to be hammered out, and more than one horse was in need of a new shoe. The squires mucked the stables and fetched water and food for the horses, as well.

Two of them assisted Rafael, watching his ministrations with interest and fetching whatsoever he needed with great speed. When they began to whisper, his heart sank at their words.

"They say it was the Fae we saw last eve," the one squire whispered to the other, his awe more than clear. He was blond, this Hans, and his eyes were both wide and a clear blue. He always seemed to be astonished in Rafael's view.

"Rafael said they were demons," dark-haired Xavier murmured, flicking a glance at Rafael. Rafael had made a poultice of herbs for this particular horse and indicated that the boy should hold the soaked cloth in place while Rafael bound it with a length of linen. He deliberately did not reply to the comment, though he thought of Elizabeth's assertion that they were not demons.

What else could they be? He recalled Ibrahim's tales and wondered if that man might have been right about something.

"But they are gone!" Hans continued, waving a hand. He was charged with holding the steed's reins and his abrupt move made the stallion toss his head and stamp. Rafael gave him a stern look and he sobered, taking care to hold the horse's head still. "Vanished," Hans whispered. "Into the very air."

"Are they?" Rafael murmured, for he had glimpsed small winged creatures in the rafters of the stables.

"What do you mean, sir?"

Xavier answered. "We could only see them because of Lady Elizabeth's potion," he said, his tone implying that Hans was a fool. "It is evident that its powers faded with the light of the moon and that they are cloaked from our view."

"If indeed they were present at all," Rafael said firmly. A number of small brown demons swung from cobwebs that hung from the rafters, squealing with glee as they frolicked in the stables, unobserved by the other men. It suited Rafael well to let these Fae or demons believe that he could not see them either.

A man who meant to survive, in his experience, did not reveal all he knew.

"But surely they were, Rafael!" said Xavier. "We saw them."

"You *thought* you saw them," Rafael replied, shaking his head. "It could well be that Lady Elizabeth's potion gave you visions of what was not truly there to be seen. If you knew much of herbs and apothecary's brews, you would know that to be possible."

The boys exchanged glances of disappointment. Rafael stood and patted the steed's rump, well pleased with its patience, then glanced toward his own mount. "The smith will have labor for you," he said kindly to the boys. "If you hasten, you will have your duties complete by the time the midday meal is served in the hall." Their gazes lit and they hastened to the far end of the stall to help with the repairs to the armor.

It was only when Rafael went to Rayo that he realized that he was nigh at the last stall in the stables. They must have moved the steeds around to better accommodate the wounded horses and men, but he shivered to see that Rayo was now in the last stall but one. It had been the back wall of that very last stall that had gaped open the previous Midwinter's Eve, spilling the light of another realm into the cold night of this one.

That stall was where it had begun.

Rafael shuddered again and concentrated on practical matters. He paused to admire Elizabeth's mare, a black steed of remarkable size with flashing eyes, and ensured that she was well enough. She was skittish, probably, like Rayo, a reaction to the scent of blood. He doubted he could reassure her much, so continued to his own steed, which would welcome his presence.

Rayo was so dark a hue of chestnut that he oft was considered to be black, save for a streak of white upon his brow. He was a magnificent destrier, and Rafael had oft wondered if there was a trickle of the blood of the legendary horses bred at Ravensmuir in his veins. The stallion nickered at the sight of Rafael, as if to reassure his warrior that he was uninjured. Rafael ran his hands over the horse, making sure that no small wound had been missed. His touch settled the creature and he felt the anxiety ease from Rayo.

Even as he checked the horse, Rafael realized how distant the sounds of his fellows had become. The corridor alongside the stalls seemed to have stretched longer, and the men and boys at the far end seemed both smaller than they should have been and fainter. It was as if they faded from sight, or were being lost in a fog. It could have been that the corridor stretched to three times its length, an odd sensation that Rafael recalled from six months before.

The hair prickled on the back of his neck.

Was it his imagination that he could hear the faint strains of that cursed music even now? Rafael shivered at the chill the air had taken, fearing he knew who was afoot.

The mortals were not alone in the stables, and the small creatures in the rafters were not the sum of their company. Rafael caught his breath as some being swept past him in icy splendor. He glimpsed a hem edged in silvery fur trailing across his boot. He felt a flutter of wings behind him and heard the shrill cries of small beings swinging from cobwebs high above. Rafael gave no sign that he had noticed, though gooseflesh rose on his skin.

Instead, he indulged both himself and Rayo by getting the brush and grooming the beast. Rayo blew out his lips and stamped a foot, adjusting his stance and bowing his head. He was clearly pleased by the attention, though his ears flicked more than they should have done.

So, he was aware of the demons passing, as well. There was a faint rustle of silken garments behind Rafael as the otherworldly company proceeded through the stables, undoubtedly returning to that gap in the wall in the adjacent stall. He knew that he and Malcolm had barricaded it, but he supposed that beings of this kind found that to be no obstacle. They danced and cavorted as they walked, their chatter filled with jubilation that the tithe had been paid.

Where had they been since leaving the moor? Since sunrise? Rafael did not know and refused to speculate upon it.

Indeed, he did not dare look up. He strove to pretend that he was oblivious to their presence, murmuring to Rayo as if he could not explain the beast's agitation. It was wiser, in his experience, to let a foe believe that he was unobserved or that his scheme was undetected.

And Rafael had no doubt that these beings, whether called demons or Fae, were his foes. He had seen the king slice down that beggar who had snatched at Catriona's crucifix, had seen that there was no mercy in that regal countenance when the loss of a mortal life would be his gain. Rafael's ears pricked when he heard the deep tones of that very king, though he hid his awareness with steady brushing.

Elizabeth had spoken out when she should have not have done so. The king had not taken a toll from her for that choice, but Rafael wondered if that left Elizabeth in the dark king's debt.

He listened keenly, hoping to learn more of this king's plan for a certain outspoken maiden. Her fate was not his concern, of course, nor was it his responsibility, but maybe he could ensure that Malcolm saw her defended.

It sounded like an excuse even to Rafael himself, but still he listened.

ès

Elizabeth could make no sense of Malcolm's manner. She might have thought he made an excuse to keep her from Rafael's side, if he had not seemed to be hugging a secret to himself.

As he had done when he was a boy. The glimpse of his mischievous nature was utterly seductive to Elizabeth and very welcome.

But it made no sense that Catriona had need of her aid. She had seen just the day before that Ravensmuir's new hall was sparsely furnished. Two trestle tables had been set before the two massive hearths, and only one hearth had yet seen a blaze kindled within it. The walls had been bare of tapestries and the floor, though strewn with fresh rushes, had been vast and empty.

When Elizabeth stepped into the hall, though, she immediately saw that all had changed. On this morn, there was an enormous pile of furnishings in the midst of the floor. Chairs and tables and tapestries were jumbled together, with crockery pots and metal ewers and cups and plates jumbled in between. There were heavy iron pots that belonged in a kitchen, spits for the fireplaces, and countless other household items. Indeed, the pile was so large and so chaotic that Elizabeth could scarce make sense of it, much less its appearance.

"But where did it come from?" she demanded of Malcolm.

By way of answer, he showed her a wooden box that was more than familiar. The lid was inlaid with wood of different colors to make a bird, its wings outspread and of various hues.

A lammergeier.

Elizabeth's lips parted in astonishment and recognition. "That is Grandfather's box!" she said with delight. "But it was lost in the caverns, when Uncle Tynan died. How is it that you have it again?"

"This morn, it was returned to me," Malcolm said, gesturing to the mound of goods. "Along with all of this." He tapped the box. "To my relief, the old deeds are still within it."

Elizabeth would not have believed it if she had not seen it with her own eyes. "That is a miracle."

"Never mind all of this."

Could it all be from the caverns?

Who had brought it to the hall? Elizabeth scanned the rafters, seeking some sign of Darg, the mischievous spriggan, but she could not see a single Fae. And truly, she could not believe that Darg, given that creature's greed, would have willingly surrendered so much. Catriona was tugging pots from the pile and dispatching them to the kitchens. A few tapestries had been worked free and rolled neatly, but Elizabeth could see that she was indeed overwhelmed by this unexpected task set before her.

Alexander had arrived this morn, as well, it was clear, for he was already at work on the pile. As Elizabeth watched, he extricated a familiar chair from the mound and set it aright, surveying it with satisfaction.

"Do you remember this one?" he demanded of Malcolm. The chair was wood and could be folded. When unfolded, the left leg crossed beneath the seat to make the right armrest and the right leg crossed to make the left armrest, the two making an X beneath the leather seat. The red leather on its seat, back and arms, was worn smooth with use. "Tynan kept it in his solar, and Rosamunde favored it."

"I do indeed," Malcolm said, running a hand over the leather. "It has fared well in the caverns of Ravensmuir."

Elizabeth's gaze roved over the collected furnishings. "They are all from the destroyed keep," she said, recognizing more of them the longer she looked. "But how did they come to be in the hall?"

Her brothers exchanged a glance. "I believe it to be a gift from Uncle Tynan," Malcolm said.

"Nay, from his ghost," Alexander said firmly, showing a belief in the otherworldly that was uncharacteristic of him. "And perhaps a sign that he is finally at peace." He smiled at Malcolm, and Elizabeth liked the approval in his eyes. Somehow, the rift between her brothers had been repaired. "And why should he not be? His chosen heir has returned, rebuilt the keep, wed well and already has a son."

The babe Avery cried out then and Catriona turned to the stairs. Vera, the maid so long in the employ of Kinfairlie, stood at the top of the stairs, rocking the wailing infant.

"There is so much to do," Catriona said, looking between her son and the disruption of the hall.

"Go," Malcolm said, giving his wife a kiss on the temple. "Elizabeth is here to help set matters to rights. She will direct this task in your stead."

Elizabeth nodded agreement and Catriona smiled her relief. Elizabeth began to sort the furnishings closest to hand and direct the placement of those that were presented to her. Though the hall was different than the old one, the rooms were similar in function. She could recall what had been where and dispatch each item appropriately.

It was good to have a task to occupy her, and Malcolm invited her opinion on many items before they were sent to other parts of the keep. Alexander brought many familiar pieces to their attention, and Elizabeth found her thoughts filled with happy memories of times at Ravensmuir. They worked steadily, and she reasoned that Catriona could move all later to her taste, but for the moment, the hall needed to be cleared so the midday meal could be served.

Ruari, the man at arms from Kinfairlie, added his assistance, and eventually, Malcolm's comrades returned from settling their steeds and cleaning their weapons. It was satisfying indeed to see Ravensmuir's furnishings take their places in Malcolm's new hall, and Elizabeth knew that all must be hungry.

Even though she was busy, Elizabeth could not help but notice that Rafael did not come to assist in the task.

Would he share the midday meal?

Or did he mean to slip away from Ravensmuir unobserved? He had confessed his intent to leave. Elizabeth had to know for certain whether he lingered—and do so without either of her brothers realizing that she had gone in pursuit of Rafael.

She would have to choose her moment well.

Chapter Nine

"He has a fine enough steed, this one who escaped us," the king of the dead murmured, and Rafael saw a ringed hand reach past him to stroke Rayo's rump. A shudder ran over the destrier's flesh and he tossed his head. The king chuckled. "Loyal, too. I could tame them both to my hand." His fingers slid over Rafael's arm in turn and Rafael froze for a heartbeat in shock before he carried on.

He shuddered elaborately. "It is already cold in this cursed country," he muttered to Rayo, well aware that the king listened to his words. "We shall be gone to warmer climes soon enough, my old friend."

"And a pity that is," the king whispered. "By the time he returns, the portal will likely be closed forever."

Rafael's ears pricked at these tidings. It would suit him well for the portal to Hell at Ravensmuir be closed, for he would be confident in Malcolm's future safety.

Never mind that of Elizabeth. Could this king retaliate if there was no portal? Rafael thought not, though truly he had no good notion of the king's powers.

"Are you resolved it must be so?" demanded a woman with a sultry voice. Her fingers slid over Rafael's other arm and he glimpsed the blue whorls drawn on her flesh. "I am *so* fond of mortal men."

"Then abduct several before our worlds are parted," the king replied. "There is naught that can be done to halt the change, not now, for all is in motion."

"You did not have to do it."

"I did not do it," the king replied, then sighed. "The world changes, my lady. Men change and that can only cause change for us."

"We could battle them as once we did before..."

"We lost then, and we were much stronger in those days. Truth be told, they were weaker then, as well. They believed in us. They could see us, and they feared us."

"I could make them fear us again!"

The king laughed lightly and Rafael felt him shake his head. "It is not a question of will, my lady. If it were, we could all do as much. Look at them!"

Rafael glanced through his lashes as the king gestured back to the rest of the mortal men. He caught a glimpse of the lady who was the king's companion and was struck by her dark beauty. Like the king, she had hair as black as midnight, and like his beard, it flowed down to her knees. There seemed to be starlight snared in her eyes and in her garments, and her gown glimmered as she moved, reminding him of dewdrops snared on cobwebs in moonlight. She was lovely enough to make any man yearn to touch her, but he did not trust her appearance to be her truth. There was something cold in her gaze, a lack of remorse or conscience that he found also in the king's manner.

Rafael bent over his task with renewed vigor.

"They cannot even discern us, much less see us," the king said, as if amused by the lack of perception shown by mortals. "Even this one, so recently escaped from our grasp, is oblivious." He blew then, an icy exhalation that slid under the collar of Rafael's shirt with a will of its own.

Rafael slapped the back of his neck, spun around and stared about himself, giving every indication that he could not see the aristocratic pair before him. He frowned and shook his head, turning back to the steed.

"You could take him for the next tithe," the queen suggested. "I could savor him for those seven years until it was time to pay what is due."

"There will be no more tithes," the king declared.

"You did not say as much before!" the queen retorted, her dark eyes flashing. "I would not have let you take that one..."

"I did not know myself, not until my blade sheared the head from the body of that thief last eve." He pulled his blade from his scabbard. There was only a small increment of blade below the hilt, as if it had been broken off in the taking of that mortal man's life.

"It dissolved at the touch of his blood," the king said, his manner matter-of-fact, as if such occurrences were familiar to him. The queen in contrast took a step back in dismay. "It is the sign I have both awaited and feared. It is as it has been foretold. The time of our visits to this realm comes to an end, and there will not be another tithe due."

The queen was clearly upset by these tidings, for her voice rose. "How can that be? I know of no such sorcery!"

The king smiled sadly. "It is more than familiar to me. Do you not recall my wife, Una?" Rafael was startled, for he had thought this regal woman to be the king's wife.

"What of her? Surely she is content to remain in Ireland and leave us to our merrymaking."

So, the King of the Dead was unfaithful to his wife. Rafael could not find a shred of surprise within himself at that.

Yet, this king coveted Elizabeth. It was clear that he wished her as a mistress, not a bride, which was an outrageous indignity for a lady of her birth and beauty. Rafael found himself bristling on Elizabeth's behalf.

The king continued. "I fear Una has invoked a great reckoning to ensure that I linger at her side alone." The king grimaced even as his companion laughed.

"She will not see that readily done. Has she not tried before?"

"But not with such ardor as this."

"*She* has compelled the portals to begin closing?" The queen's astonishment was clear, and Rafael guessed she had thought herself more powerful than this Una.

"I see her hand in this, though I do not know the details. Who can say what she has wagered to see this done?"

The queen was not reassured by this in the least. "But how long until the portals close? How much time have I to choose a mortal to keep as my own?"

"You need not have one."

"I like their vigor and their fear."

The king inhaled deeply then exhaled slowly, as if he could smell the future or its truth was in the very air. "In seven years, all portals between the worlds will be gone, and all will be sealed forever on one side or the other, regardless of their kind."

"That is clear if there is not another tithe to be paid," the queen snapped.

In seven years, if this king did not take vengeance upon Elizabeth, she would be safe. It seemed overlong to Rafael's thinking.

The king straightened but did not give any other sign he had heard the queen. "I sense that the portals at Kinfairlie and Ravensmuir will close soon, for they seem less welcoming than once they did. Less tangible."

That was better news, to Rafael's thinking. A part of him wished to ensure Elizabeth's safety though he knew it was not his responsibility and doing as much would only encourage her expectations. If the portals would be closed soon, he could leave without much guilt.

"This is why you sense Una's influence," the queen guessed.

Rafael understood that this king had fancied mortal women in this vicinity before, that perhaps Una knew of the king's plan for Elizabeth and did not find it appealing.

The king looked around himself warily, and Rafael gave keen attention to the course of the brush over Rayo's rump. He could fairly feel the king surveying him. "Certainly, much has changed in this abode," the king murmured.

"Change, I am told, is everywhere," the queen said, her tone dismissive. "I see no reason why Kinfairlie and Ravensmuir should change sooner than other places. I like to cross through these portals!"

"Did you never hear the old tale of Kinfairlie?" the king asked, taking the queen's elbow and guiding her toward the last stall. Rafael could see the golden light emanating from that gap in the wall, but he narrowed his eyes and ignored its gleam. He listened intently. "They still tell it in that hall, for the women favor the notion of a maiden being stolen away by a lover of our kind, one who leaves naught but a red, red rose wrought of ice in exchange for his bride."

The queen laughed. "I remember it well, but I thought it merely a tale."

"A tale with its roots in truth," the king replied.

"What do you mean?"

The king raised a hand. "It is of no import to you any longer." When the queen might have argued that, he shook a finger at her. "What is of import is that these mortals neither fully believe the tale, nor know the rest of it."

"The rest?" The lady laughed lightly, clearly thinking the king but recounted a tale to amuse her. "What more can there be?"

The king chuckled, even as they two progressed regally into that last stall. "I shall tell you all of it sometime. For the moment, you only need know that I, too, have not only a red, red rose that will prove itself to be made of ice, but that I have chosen the maiden who I will claim in exchange for it. Further, I shall do so before the portal to Kinfairlie closes forever, regardless of my wife's ploys. Her scheme will only see my prize sealed in Fae with me forevermore."

Rafael froze, knowing with terrible certainty who that maiden would be.

Just as surely as he knew the responsibility to defend her was not his own.

"And then, I suppose, you will leave my court and return to your own in Ireland, just as Una desires."

"Of course, for I will have collected what I came to find." The king chuckled. "Though Una will not be pleased to see herself outwitted."

Rafael glanced up at the king's dark tone, for it filled him with foreboding. He saw the king step back into the corridor, his gaze sharp, and feared his curiosity would be observed. His heart skipped, but the king was looking down the length of the stables, past Rafael. A smile of satisfaction curved his lips at whatever he saw.

"One last glimpse," he murmured. "For the moment."

"She might not be willingly captured," the queen said, her tone waspish.

"On the contrary," the king purred. "She will choose my court, and she will choose it soon."

"I do not believe it!"

"Then let us make a small wager..." In the blink of an eye, the king and queen were gone. The music faded steadily and the demons in the rafters scampered down to the last stall with remarkable haste. It was clear they feared to be left behind.

The golden light diminished, then was extinguished abruptly. A door might have been closed, for Rafael could not hear the music any longer. It even felt warmer in the stables than it had.

But Rafael did not care for their departure, for he had followed the king's gaze.

Elizabeth was striding toward him, her eyes alight and her rosy lips curved in a smile. Her cheeks were flushed and her smile broadened at the sight of him.

Rafael could not believe she would choose that other realm over this one, whether she called it Fae or Hell. He could not believe that she would be the one to place the rose that was the bride price on the threshold. He could not believe that the dark king was right.

That should have reassured him. It should have given him the confidence to leave Ravensmuir and Scotland, convinced that she would live long and be well.

But he knew that she owed that monarch a boon, for she had broken the rules of his court, and that the dark king had some hold over her besides. It was from her home, Kinfairlie, where maidens were said to choose suitors from this dark realm and trade their futures for a red, red rose wrought of ice.

Elizabeth was not his concern, but in that moment, Rafael wished she might be.

That was the peril of encountering an angel: it made a man wish for what he could not claim as his own.

Rafael watched Elizabeth duck into the stall where her mare was tethered, unable to shake his fear that she would be lost. He heard her murmur to the magnificent mare, clearly of the fabled lineage of Ravensmuir's black destriers. The beast had been bestowed upon her as a gift, if not an entitlement, while he had paid for Rayo with hard coin, earned by his own sweat and blood.

Elizabeth was a nobleman's daughter, raised in privilege and advantage, a childhood as different from his own as could be.

There was the key to it all. Rafael realized then that it was no accident that it had been Franz who haunted him, or that Franz had reminded him of Ursula.

Ursula, too, had been a nobleman's daughter. Ursula had believed herself in love with Franz and had been convinced that he loved her. Against her father's express permission, Ursula had left the life she had known to follow the Sable League and be with her beloved.

It was like a tale told by a troubadour, save that Franz had been no gallant hero. He had been what he was, a mercenary and a rough man of war, a man of simple pleasures and robust appetites. Perhaps he had loved Ursula, but he had been incapable of making her happy.

Instead, Franz had destroyed her.

Rafael frowned as he brushed down Rayo with new vigor. He would never forget how the light had died in Ursula's eyes, how she had come to realize that their rough circumstances were not a situation to be endured for the moment, but would be the fact of her entire life. He recalled her dismay when Franz had gone to the whores after she conceived his child. He saw again her despair when Franz arrived late and drunk at the tent after she had struggled for two days in childbirth, then passed out beside her. Rafael recalled her slow and silent tears, and though it had been said that Ursula died in the birthing of her child, Rafael knew she had died of a broken heart.

She had lost the will to survive, when Franz showed his truth and her babe died, both in the same night.

The choice between himself and Franz had been an easy one, after Ursula's demise.

Better you than me, indeed.

Rafael would not see Elizabeth so destroyed. He would not do the same disservice to this alluring woman. He would not see Elizabeth lose her spirit and her hope, much less see her caught in the mire of war and battle camps. It would be better, far better, that she thought him indifferent to her, better to do her heart a minor injury now so that she could choose another man after he was gone. He would not leave her pining for his return, or hoping for what could never be. He knew he could not frighten her, but she was not slow of wit. He would persuade her, holding back no ugly truth that might aid his cause.

It would be for the greater good, if not the honorable choice, to ruin her regard for him. It was only a matter of time, after all, before she turned from him in disgust. They had naught in common, after all, this bold daughter of a nobleman and he a mercenary of no lineage.

Save an ability to see these demons she called the Fae, but Rafael thought that no real endorsement.

Why not hasten the process of eliminating her interest in him?

He was certain he could manage the deed on this day.

And the sooner Rafael left Ravensmuir, the better for both of them.

※

Rafael's expression changed as Elizabeth approached, and she knew he tried to hide his thoughts from her. She had glimpsed his surprise and pleasure that she stepped into the corridor and knew that to be the truth of his reaction. It was interesting that she had thought him utterly inscrutable just a day before, but now she saw the nuances of change in his expression.

Her understanding of him could only improve with time.

She spoke to Demoiselle, reassured that the mare was both well-tended and seemingly content. The horse nibbled at Elizabeth's braid, then returned to her feed with satisfaction.

When she left the stall, Rafael was out of sight, although she could hear that he was brushing down a steed. She walked toward him, not hiding the sound of her progress, and paused at the end of the stall to watch Rafael tend a large chestnut stallion.

Since it was a destrier, she assumed it was Rafael's own warhorse. Rafael's hair was still damp on his collar and he had changed his garb after bathing. His sword was gone, only the dagger in his belt, and his boots were buffed to a shine again. His chemise looked brilliantly white against his skin and he had pushed up the sleeves. The lace at the neck was untied, as if he had dressed in haste, and he wore a dark tabard with that same bit of gold embroidery over his heart.

His expression was wary when he glanced up at her, but she did not care. He might have doubts of his own merit, but Elizabeth knew she would prove him to be mistaken. He returned to the task of brushing his steed, and she knew it was no accident he turned his back upon her.

Nor was she deterred.

Even if she had not seen the ribbons entangled overhead, she would have known there was a bond between they two that could not be denied. Since meeting Rafael, Elizabeth felt fully alive for the first time in years. The world seemed filled with color and heat, as it had not since Finvarra had beckoned to her.

If winning the love of Rafael was the way to break the Fae

king's hold over her, Elizabeth was doubly determined to succeed. It would be like an old tale, one in which mortal love triumphed over all obstacles, as if she and Rafael were destined to twine their lives together. The notion thrilled her as much as his kiss had done.

"I thought you might have departed already," she said when he did not speak. His destrier was not so dark as the stallions of Ravensmuir, with a white blaze on his brow. She stoked his rump and he nickered.

"You should pretend that I have, for I will be gone soon enough." The horse, to Elizabeth's thinking, was already brushed down thoroughly and in no need of further attention. Its coat gleamed even now and it nosed at the bucket of feed, swishing its tail in contentment. Still Rafael brushed it.

"Do you not mean to remain in service to Malcolm?"

Rafael shook his head. "It is not my nature to remain in one place."

"But I heard that some of the others would stay."

"It will not last," he said, his tone pragmatic. "We are too accustomed to journeying all the time. Ranulf may stay, for he has lost part of his hand." He straightened as if to consider this. "It will not be easy for him to earn his way with such an injury."

"Will you not linger to ensure his wound heals?"

Rafael shot a glance at her. "I am certain there are other healers in this land."

"What of your own injury? Should you not rest to see it healed?"

"I never have so catered to a wound yet, and they have all healed." He frowned, considering the horse, then bent to check the beast's hooves. They looked to be in fine condition and the shoes were perfect.

"He is a fine steed," Elizabeth ventured to say.

"Not of the ilk of the destriers of Ravensmuir, but Rayo is a fine stallion." Rafael stood and patted the horse's rump, murmuring to him as he passed to the other side and checked the other hooves. "He has served me well."

"Rayo," Elizabeth echoed, trying to say the name as Rafael did. "Is that in your mother tongue?"

"It is Castilian," Rafael acknowledged. "For 'lightning.'"

Elizabeth smiled. "He is so fast as that, then?"

Rafael nodded, his pride in his horse undisguised. Elizabeth knew then that they had something in common, for she was mightily fond of horses.

"Then you know of the destriers of Ravensmuir?"

Rafael shot a glance at her. "*All* know of them. I was surprised to find that they were not here."

"Malcolm brought them to Kinfairlie before he departed, so they could be stabled there. My mare, Demoiselle, is of the lineage."

"I thought as much."

So, he had noted her steed. Elizabeth felt ridiculously pleased. "She has born three foals now, all fine stallions."

"So your brother continues to breed them at Kinfairlie?" There was suspicion in his tone that Elizabeth could not explain.

"Alexander manages the pedigree in Malcolm's stead."

"Perhaps he means to keep them."

"He keeps them in trust and breeds as he believes Malcolm would."

"But Malcolm is returned to Ravensmuir and has not his legacy of the steeds."

Elizabeth bit her lip, feeling caught between her brothers. "I believe Alexander awaits Malcolm's request."

Rafael met her gaze over the back of his destrier, a smile tugging at the corner of his mouth. "So, a man must *request* the return of what is legally his own? How odd that the Laird of Kinfairlie rode out the first week after our arrival to return Ravensmuir's seal to Malcolm. I thought it might have burned his hand to hold it so long as he had. And yet, the horses, of far greater value, remain at Kinfairlie." He held her gaze for a moment, then returned to his labor.

Elizabeth frowned, disliking the sense that Alexander had been unfair, in Rafael's view. "They have been estranged," she began, wanting to defend both brothers.

Rafael responded so quickly that Elizabeth sensed she had once again responded exactly as he had wished. "Aye, because Alexander knows what Malcolm has become and does not approve," he said. "So, he returned the lesser of Malcolm's legacy, the seal and ring that would make this barren piece of land his own, but kept the horses, which surely generate much revenue. It is a telling choice."

"Perhaps he but waits for the stable to be restored."

"The stable was the sole building that stood on this holding when we arrived."

Elizabeth found she could not argue with that, for it was true. "I must ask him of this."

"Are you bold as that?"

"Of course! They are both my brothers, and they are both good men."

Rafael considered her for so long that Elizabeth thought he might argue her conclusion. To her surprise, he asked a question that was utterly unrelated. "Tell me of these Fae."

"I thought you believed them to be demons."

"I might be mistaken. And of all those in this place, you seem to have the greatest experience of their nature."

Elizabeth was encouraged that he would heed her words. "They are from another realm, one that is both similar to ours and different. They are linked to the land and sometimes said to live beneath it. They witness the cycle of life and death, but are immortal themselves. They have a joy that is unrivaled among mortals, and are known to sing and dance and make merry."

"But you said they kept their sworn word?"

"It is one thing they seem to hold holy. They are mischievous though and fond of riddles. They will make bargains that include tricks by which the wager can be undone, oft in ways mortals do not anticipate."

"They sound like barons I have served," Rafael muttered and she caught a glint of humor in his eyes.

"There are portals between the realms at certain places, oft places they have been strong before mortals claimed the land."

Rafael glanced up at that. "Like Ravensmuir?" There was no real question in his voice.

"Through the caverns below the old keep," Elizabeth agreed. "And through a high window in Kinfairlie's tower. I know of no other portals in this vicinity, though there may be more."

"And the dark king?"

"His name is Finvarra. He is king of a large group of Fae, the *Daoine Sidhe*, in Ireland and his court is there, beneath a hill."

"Then he is lost?"

"The Fae can travel long distances more quickly than we. He had a fascination with my aunt Rosamunde and journeyed to Kinfairlie in pursuit of her." Elizabeth shivered. "He lingers, I believe, because he has vowed to entice me to join him in his realm."

Rafael eyed her then, his expression inscrutable. "Will you accept his invitation?"

"Would you stay to defend me if I said I was tempted?"

He shook his head. "I will not linger in this cursed land, not for any price. My fate lies abroad."

"Why did you think them demons?"

"Because the dead were thick in their company. I thought that to be a vision of Hell." Rafael pursed his lips. "Perhaps they are djinn."

Elizabeth tried out the word and he corrected her pronunciation. "What are djinn?"

"The Moors speak of them. In their understanding of the world, men were wrought of earth."

"Like Adam."

"And angels were wrought of air." Rafael flicked another potent glance at her. "But there are also djinn, wrought of smoke. They are mortal beings of this world, but ones that have greater powers than ours and do not always reveal themselves. They like a riddle, as well, and are fond of a jest at the expense of mortals." He ran a hand over the horse. "And there are tales of them stealing beautiful mortal maidens for their own pleasure."

Elizabeth found her cheeks heating. "How do you know what tales the Moors tell?"

"Because I have known Moors, it is clear."

"Have you journeyed to their lands?" Elizabeth could scarce imagine the marvels he might have seen there.

"I have. In fetters." Rafael held her gaze steadily and she knew her shock showed. "Because I was sold to a Moor as a boy."

"Did they set you free?"

Rafael chuckled. "I escaped, and before you ask, there is only one reliable way for a slave to escape his owner." He lifted that brow again. "He was the first man I killed, but not the last."

Elizabeth blinked. "But you had justification, to be sure..."

"And you seek to find the gold in the dross, no matter what you are told."

"I see the good in you!"

"And you ignore the evil."

"You could confide the tale..."

"I will not." Rafael came around the horse and confronted her, his hands braced on his hips as he looked down at her. "Your brother, the Laird of Kinfairlie, knows what a mercenary does, which is why he disapproves of Malcolm's choices. He knows we called Malcolm the Hellhound for his savagery in battle. He knows our truth. He knows *my* truth. And like most men, who would never sell their blade but are willing to hire warriors to serve their own needs, he does not approve of killing for material gain. You should take heed of this in making your own choices."

"What is that to mean?"

"That you disregard much in your determination to see your curiosity fulfilled." He lifted his head, as if hearing some distant sound. "Do your brothers know that you have sought me out?"

"Of course not. Either of them would have stopped me."

"And you give no credit to their opinion in this, even though it is based on more knowledge than your own?" Rafael shook his head, his manner disapproving. "You are not so stubborn as to refuse to learn from the experience of others."

Elizabeth felt herself flush yet again, but she lifted her chin. "I would trust my own observation before my brother's assumptions. That is the mark of a person with their wits about them. I know that I feel different with you, and I will not discard my own knowledge of that, much less ignore it."

Rafael spared her a knowing glance. "You feel differently because you have never met a man like me. Your own instincts recognize the danger of this situation."

"I am in no danger," Elizabeth insisted.

"Are you not?" Rafael asked, his tone silky. He moved so quickly that she had no chance to evade him. In the blink of an eye, he had caught her around the waist and lifted her to the very tips of her toes. His arm was locked around her so tightly that Elizabeth feared she would not be able to take a breath. He drew her into the stall and backed her against the wall, crushing her between it and his hard strength, then leaned down so closely that their noses nearly touched.

The Warrior's Prize

Elizabeth was enraptured. If this was danger, she wanted only more of it! This was how fated lovers embraced, she was certain of it, as if neither could ever be sated with the touch of the other, as if no kiss could endure long enough.

She was convinced that he would kiss her again, but Rafael only smiled, his gaze simmering. He looked hard and masculine and driven, his hair disheveled and his eyes darker than midnight. He looked like a dangerous rogue, one who had stolen her heart and was welcome to all else she possessed.

"In no danger," Rafael murmured as if the idea were amusing, then shook his head. "I could take everything you have to offer," he continued, his voice a low growl that made Elizabeth's heart skip. "I could claim your maidenhead and leave you soiled."

"I would not be *soiled*," Elizabeth whispered, outraged by the choice of word.

Rafael continued as if she had not spoken. "In this place, in this moment, there is not a man who could stop me. Then I would leave, precisely as planned, and your belly might round with child by the Yule, with no man to stand by you. Where would you be then, *mi piqueño ángel*? Who would wed you? Who would deign to save you from your own impetuous choice?"

"You would not do that to me," she whispered, her voice so husky that she scarce recognized it.

Rafael arched a brow, which made him look wicked indeed. "Of course, I would. And your brothers know it well."

"You could wed me," she insisted. "I believe you would treat me with honor."

"Your brother would never permit it."

"I would insist!"

He shook his head. "But I would not. I will *never* wed. They will be compelled to find a spouse who will take you with another man's seed taken root, and how would such a man treat his wife?"

Elizabeth braced her hands on his shoulders, disliking his words, but Rafael did not fall silent.

"He might well beat you, given that you would be a sinner and a whore, one too beholden to him to protest his use of his property." Rafael's gaze burned into hers. "For that is what a wife is, a man's *property*, and he may do as he wishes with whatsoever he owns."

"Nay!" Elizabeth protested. She pushed at his shoulders to no avail. He held her captive, proving his own words. "No man of merit would do as much."

Rafael laughed, though it was not a merry sound. "Men *do* as much. I see it all the time. It would be better for you, perhaps, for your spouse to know that you were soiled before the nuptials, for a man disappointed can be vengeful indeed."

Elizabeth felt her eyes narrow. "What do you mean?"

"That if he thought you a maiden, but discovered otherwise on his wedding night, matters could go very badly for you, indeed. Is that the future you desire? Would you discard the wisdom of your brothers so readily as that, given that they—and I—have seen more of the shadows in the hearts of men?"

"You would not be such a knave to me!"

"I *am* such a knave," Rafael insisted, though Elizabeth did not believe him. "I know what you want of me, and should you desire, I will give it to you here and now. I will not linger over the task, and I will not linger in Scotland." His gaze burned. "You are warned of my intent. Tell me, *mi piqueño ángel*, what do you want now?"

Rafael was challenging her again, daring her to defy his expectation.

"You are not so much older than me," she said. "You must have yearned to taste all the world had to offer, and been impatient to be rid of your innocence."

"I was never innocent!" Rafael said hotly. "Before I could speak, my mother and my four older sisters died because of me. There was blood on my hands before I could walk."

Elizabeth was startled by this confession, but she did not believe than an infant could be so guilty. "I think you take more responsibility than is due," she said with fervor. "I think you judge yourself more harshly than any other man would do." She held his gaze, smiled with confidence, then twined her arms around his neck. She saw his surprise, but gave him no time to protest. "And I say a man's deeds are a better measure than his words. In this, you are trying to frighten me, but I am not afraid." She spoke with conviction, then stretched to touch her lips to his.

The kiss did not begin so smoothly as the others, though Elizabeth was pleased that Rafael could not seem to hold himself back. He angled his mouth over hers, kissing her with a hunger that made her heart pound, then tore himself away from her all too soon.

He looked riled and infuriated, his eyes snapping with fury.

"You cannot deny the bond between us," she whispered, reaching for him with one hand.

"I do deny it," Rafael said with a vehemence that told her he was also stirred. "I *will* deny it, for you will not compel me to make a choice that will end in woe for both of us."

"That is only because you are afraid," she taunted, confident she named the matter right.

Rafael stepped back, his fury more than clear. "I am *prudent*," he retorted with heat and glared at her.

Elizabeth smiled. "Afraid," she murmured.

"I fear no one and no thing," Rafael insisted. "Particularly a woman who is no fool but would pursue folly with a passion undeserved. Your trust is misplaced."

With that, he spun on his heel and stalked from the stall, clearly seething as he left her behind. She watched his fists clench and knew she made yet more progress. There was a power between them and Elizabeth savored the fact that they both were aware of it. Indeed, it could not be denied. Rafael fought their destiny, but he would lose the battle.

To their mutual reward.

It was always thus, in the best tales.

Elizabeth thought no further before she realized she was not as alone as she had believed.

Chapter Ten

Finvarra winced.

It was inconvenient, this bond betwixt the maiden whom Finvarra desired most and this mercenary. Their paths should never have crossed and, worse, Elizabeth's abilities to see what should have been discerned only by the Fae worked against Finvarra. Those ribbons convinced her of the warrior's merit when the common sense so favored by mortals would have induced her to avert her gaze.

Still, all was not lost as yet.

Finvarra opened the portal enough to pass through it himself and smiled to find Elizabeth alone and gazing after Rafael. He stepped up behind her, eyeing her perfect proportions, the gleaming ebony of her hair, the lusciousness of her curves. It would take him eternity to tire of her charms, Finvarra was certain.

"He is easy to look upon, for a mortal," he murmured from behind Elizabeth.

She spun to face him, evidently not surprised by his presence, and Finvarra smiled that she was so aware of him. That could only be a good sign.

"Have you come to collect your boon?" she demanded.

Finvarra replied mildly, taking note of her high color, her sparkling eyes and her softened lips. "I spoke of the mortal you watched."

"You did not seek me out to discuss Rafael."

"Did I not?" Finvarra waited for her curiosity to be kindled, then turned away. "I suppose you must know best."

Elizabeth, to his delight, seized his sleeve. "What do you know of him?"

"Little of import, especially as he is determined to leave this land forever."

"What if he does not leave?" she asked. "Or does not leave forever?"

"Then it may be of more import. We shall have to see." Finvarra eased toward the portal to the Fae realm in the end stall, ensuring that Elizabeth saw it. She would know what it was with a single glimpse.

He heard her catch her breath and knew she had spied it. He smiled.

"You know more of men and their secrets than any I know," she said. "Will you tell me what you can see of Rafael and his future?"

"Do you truly wish to be even more deeply in my debt?" Finvarra asked lightly, but he saw how the query troubled her.

She frowned. "What will you have of me? I know you will demand some compensation for my making a plea for my brother in your court. Why did you let me leave?"

"You could have stayed."

"I did not expect to have a choice."

But given it, she had chosen Rafael.

"There is no rush to settle any balance between us, Elizabeth," Finvarra said smoothly. He acted as if he dropped the present he would give to her, as if it slipped from his sleeve without him noting as much. He knew it caught the light as it dropped and felt the sharpening of her attention. He pivoted before the portal and regarded her with a smile. "Let us say that we shall do so when you seek me out."

Defiance flashed in her eyes, but she did not speak her thought aloud. Still, he could fairly hear her response, so ardently did she think of her determination to never seek him out.

His gift would ensure otherwise.

He extended a hand to her in his most regal manner. "I bid you farewell, beauteous Elizabeth, at least until such time as you willingly enter my court and beg an audience with me."

She looked from his hand to his eyes, clearly suspecting a trick. She found none, not as yet, so stepped forward and took his hand. She bent and barely touched her lips to his ring as she curtseyed, then stepped back so that she concealed the dropped trinket from his view with her skirts. "Until then, sir," she said, standing straight in her confidence that she had had the better of their exchange.

Finvarra bit back a smile of triumph, then swept through the portal to the Fae court. He waved a hand, casting a fistful of starlight in his own wake, and hid the portal from most mortal eyes.

Elizabeth, he knew, could still discern it.

The time until she chose to come to him would pass quickly, Finvarra knew. For an immortal, six months of earthly time was but a blink of an eye. Una would have her vengeance and see the portals closed, but Finvarra would have the fairest mortal maiden he had ever seen to entertain his desires through all eternity.

The prospect made his step light.

※

Elizabeth had seen the small circle slip from Finvarra's belt and drop to the thick straw on the floor of the stall. She had not discerned it on his belt earlier, but then his garb was so richly adorned and so alight with precious threads that it could have easily been overlooked in the midst of such splendor.

It was about the size of her palm, as brilliant a silver as the full moon, and had been bound to his belt by a red silken cord. The knot loosed as she watched, as if it had a will of its own, and the disk fell to the ground as quickly as a drop of rain.

Finvarra did not appear to notice its loss. He strolled to the portal that could only lead to the realm of the Fae, and even when he turned to face her again, his gaze did not fall to the gleaming circle on the ground. Perhaps the angle of the light meant that it did not shine from his perspective. Either way, Elizabeth wanted very much to examine it more closely. She ensured it was hidden beneath her skirts when she kissed his proffered hand, and fairly itched to examine her prize as he departed.

Only when he was gone and the portal sealed did she flick aside her skirts and consider the token.

It was circular, bounded in silver shaped cleverly to look like a twisted vine. The vine looped on one side where it was adorned with several silver leaves. This made an excellent handle for picking it up, and indeed, the red cord was knotted to this loop. On the back side, the silver leaves twisted about each other to make an impenetrable surface. The disk itself was bright and clear, and Elizabeth gasped when she realized it was a mirror.

She had seen mirrors that were made of polished bronze, of

course, and she had heard of ones wrought of silvered glass. These were such rich prizes that she had never seen one herself. This one offered so perfect a reflection that she knew it must be the product of some Fae sorcery. To look into it was like looking into a millpond with a surface as smooth as glass, and to do so on a sunny day. It seemed to not only reflect but illuminate, and Elizabeth saw more of her own features than ever before. She noted the sparkle in her eyes and the ruddy fullness of her own lips, then touched her mouth and shivered in recollection of Rafael's kiss.

She caressed her own lip with one fingertip, recalling the pleasure he had awakened in her, and knew there had to be a way to compel him to agree with her and accept their fate.

Elizabeth doubted it would be a way her brothers would like.

Of course. She would ask Rosamunde when she returned to Kinfairlie. Her aunt had never been conventional and had often pursued her own path, in defiance of what the man in the family thought best.

Rosamunde, Elizabeth was certain, would provide the best advice in this matter.

Knowing that, she was no longer so reluctant to return to Kinfairlie, where Rosamunde had recently arrived as a guest.

Perhaps she could say something before she left Ravensmuir to ensure that Rafael not only thought of her but remained.

❧

Elizabeth was reckless, defiant and utterly irresistible.

It had taken all within Rafael to break her beguiling kiss and step away from the temptation she offered. He knew his agitation had showed, and he had guessed from her triumphant smile that she knew its import.

And she declared that he was afraid.

Afraid!

Rafael was not afraid. He had never been afraid. He did not fear some delightful demoiselle, however determined to be rid of her maidenhead she might be, however vengeful her brothers might be. He did not fear the King of the Dead claiming Elizabeth forever, or her being trapped in the realm of these Fae after the portals closed forevermore. The choice of whether to surrender or not was Elizabeth's alone. He was not afraid to love another soul, or to try to live as most men, or even to abandon the sole trade he knew.

Afraid. Whosoever could imagine that a man like Rafael Rodriguez was afraid? Only a young woman who knew naught of the world and its ways!

He fumed as he presented himself for the midday meal in the hall. He sat at the end of the table with his comrades and drank his ale. They had served the meat, and he was aware that the lady herself watched him from the high table. Her brothers had taken note of her interest as well.

Rafael showed interest only in his ale. He *would* become drunk. He would be a besotted mercenary and show his true measure—even though that was not his measure. The fact was that he seldom drank in excess, but he thought recent events justified the change. He did not wish to spend another night in the company of Franz. He would prove that the brother Alexander's expectations of him were justified, and that would eliminate Elizabeth's interest in him.

It would be best for both of them.

"Another ale!" he roared.

Afraid.

"A song!" called someone from the back of the hall when the platters of venison stew had been licked clean and the trenchers of bread cast to the dogs. The hall was warm and the men there appeared to be filled with contentment. Rafael found his fingers drumming, and knew himself to be alone in his impatience to leave the hall. He refused to so much as glance to the high table, where Elizabeth sat on one side of her brother, Malcolm. His new wife, Catriona sat on Malcolm's left, and Alexander, Laird of Kinfairlie, sat beside Catriona.

He drank heartily of the ale, hoping it would dull his agitation, but it only seemed to increase his restlessness.

"A tale, indeed," Tristan echoed, raising his cup. The Sable League added their voices to the appeal, though Rafael wished the party from Kinfairlie would simply depart as quickly as possible.

They did not seem inclined to go. In fact, Rafael sensed a new harmony between Malcolm and his brother. Perhaps the older brother would return the horses to Ravensmuir's stable. Perhaps all would end well for his comrade.

It was clearly time Rafael rode south. He tried to discuss destinations with his fellows, but they waved off such serious discussions and called for more ale.

It seemed that all would celebrate the triumph of the night before. Rafael surveyed the hall, seeking one person so restless as he and could not spy a one.

Not for the first time, Rafael was aware that he was different from those who surrounded him. It was more than his coloring, more than his heritage, more than his mother tongue, his perspective and his experience. He did not fit, even amongst a company of mercenaries. He did not share their ease with peaceful times, their enjoyment of a tale, their ability to savor the moment.

Rafael was always watching the portal, listening for attack, prepared to fight. He was always so prepared to depart that he never unpacked his saddlebags. He could be gone in a trio of heartbeats, with no regret for what he left behind. It was his way, and always would be. Indeed, he had been six months at Ravensmuir, and still his gear was packed, his saddle alongside his steed, his blade honed.

It was past time to leave.

He quaffed another cup of ale.

Rafael did not wait well. That, too, was different about him.

As he watched, Malcolm shrugged, for he was not one to recount tales. The Laird of Ravensmuir glanced at his wife, who could tell a story well enough, but the babe cried from the solar in that moment and Catriona excused herself to nurse her son.

"We must have a tale!" Elizabeth entreated, and Rafael stared into his cup lest he inadvertently catch her gaze. He knew she looked toward him, and guessed that she wished to linger at Ravensmuir so she could speak to him again.

Or perhaps she thought to change his mind that he—*he!*—could be the hero of one of these tales she favored. Rafael had never heard such nonsense in all his days. Heroes in tales were valiant and noble and honorable.

Yet he had treated this lady with honor, despite his yearnings to do otherwise.

Indeed, Rafael burned with the vehemence of his desire for Elizabeth. He knew he had done aright in denying her but in this moment, the choice felt all wrong.

He had need of a woman, 'twas clear. The warmth of a whore's thighs would clear his thoughts. He had been unnaturally chaste at

Ravensmuir and should ride to the nearest burg to ensure his satisfaction.

Then continue south from there.

"I have a tale," Alexander said, rising to his feet. "I think it a most fitting one for this day, when Malcolm is returned to his home, after venturing far abroad, and here has defended what he has inherited to be his own."

"Where are his horses?" Rafael muttered, but no one paid him any heed.

The company roared approval at Alexander's suggestion and the ale was passed around again. Cups were filled, and the men turned their attention to Alexander. The Laird of Kinfairlie cleared his throat, then began to sing.

He had a remarkably fine voice, to Rafael's surprise, though the tale he recounted made the mercenary frown. It was familiar, in some ways at least.

> *"A king there was, named Charlemagne,*
> *Who rode to fight the Moors in Spain.*
> *Men from far and wide pledged to his hand,*
> *And that of his nephew, brave Roland.*
> *They rode to war, ten thousand men,*
> *Slew countless Moors before going home again.*
> *Their packs were heavy with tribute gained,*
> *Their purses never would be empty again.*
> *Seven years they fought and glad they were*
> *To return home with riches and cheer.*
> *They sang as they rode through the pass,*
> *Their hearts were merry at Roncesvaux.*
> *But at Roncesvaux they were betrayed:*
> *An enemy force in hiding laid*
> *The trap was sprung on the mighty host.*
> *And valiant Roland bore the cost."*

"Treachery and betrayal," Ranulf said with gusto. "'Tis the meat of every good tale."

"I thought winning the love of a fine woman was the merit of every good tale," Tristan countered and Ranulf shrugged agreement.

"There is that to be sure." Ranulf scanned the hall, clearly in search of a willing wench to hear his views. "For the love of a good woman is the greatest prize a man can win."

Giorgio drew Guilia into his lap and she teased Ranulf. "Save your fine words for the moment there is a wench to hear them."

They laughed together, as Alexander continued his song. Rafael had another cup of ale to dull the sound of the merriment he did not feel. This tale always irked him and on this day, his reaction was precisely as it always had been.

> *"The die was cast the month before*
> *With a treaty and a wager sworn.*
> *So fierce were Charlemagne's men of war,*
> *And so great their success, year after year,*
> *That the Moorish king proposed a truce*
> *Bargained with whoever Charlemagne trusted most.*
> *One man there was in Charlemagne's host,*
> *Who he admired more than most.*
> *One knight so skilled as to be the best,*
> *One warrior more valiant than all the rest.*
> *One man both fair of face and strong,*
> *One man whose loyalty was their bond.*
> *His nephew Roland was that man,*
> *A knight renowned through every land.*
> *The French king asked his beloved Roland*
> *Who said instead to send Ganelon*
> *That knight had wed Roland's mother*
> *And was known for his tact of manner.*
> *The king saw the merit of the choice*
> *And sent Ganelon to the Moorish court."*

"The right choice must be made when negotiating a treaty," Amaury said. "I would guess this Ganelon spoke the language of the Moors."

"As Rafael does," Tristan agreed and Rafael fairly felt Elizabeth's gaze lock upon him.

"I do not speak it so well as that," he protested.

"You speak it more than any of us," Bertrand countered. "I would choose you to negotiate a treaty on our behalf."

They saluted Rafael and raised their cups high to toast him. He knew the rest of the company, including Elizabeth, watched with curiosity. She whispered to Malcolm who confided some detail to her. Rafael studied the bottom of his cup.

Alexander continued to sing.

> *"But Ganelon did not trust Roland.*
> *Nor did he trust the Moorish man.*
> *He believed his step-son did him ill*
> *And meant for him to be killed,*
> *By this foreign king who claimed he'd treat*
> *And so Ganelon, his allies did cheat.*
> *He told the Moor how best to attack*
> *To ensure Charlemagne would never come back.*
> *He knew the rear guard was led by Roland*
> *And told the Moor to kill that man.*
> *He took a payment of coin and gold*
> *And to no man his betrayal told.*
> *So, Charlemagne believed all at peace*
> *And confident in the treat, led his men east."*

Rafael had heard this *chanson* in many versions over the years, but the version he knew to be the truth was solely told in Spain. That he alone knew of it in this company again marked him as a stranger, an outsider and a foreigner.

It was yet another hint that he did not belong in this foul land.

Much less in Malcolm's court.

It was yet another reminder to be gone as soon as possible.

The ale, he had to admit, was not bad.

Alexander, refreshed by a cup of ale himself, sang.

> *"The company, ten thousand strong*
> *Had fought fierce battles overlong.*
> *They thought of little but home fires*
> *And so it was they were took unawares.*
> *The force rode late for the king did see*
> *The hills and plains of his own country.*
> *The men were threaded through the pass,*
> *Stretched out thin, Roland at the last.*

> *The hour was late, the night falling chill*
> *The silence to Roland seemed to bode ill.*
> *He shivered and looked back to find*
> *Shadows approaching from behind.*
> *Knights there were on steeds so fine,*
> *Their banners red and gold did fly.*
> *A thousand trumpets were blown as one*
> *Their armor lit by the last of the sun."*

There was, to be sure, a cruel beauty in the trappings of war. The pennants and banners, the majestic destriers, the caparisons and gleaming armor, and helms catching the morning sun. It was all so familiar to Rafael, as was the aftermath of battle, with its blood and mud and mire. The song sent a thrill through Rafael, reminding him of all the times he had mustered before a battle, all the days he had admired the finery of his fellows, all the times he had faced a foe with his heart in his throat, wondering who would die in the battle ahead.

He cast a glance at the high table, seeing how Elizabeth was rapt in listening to her brother. Aye, people like this maiden believed war was all glory and honor. They knew naught of the dirt, much less the futility of it all.

The thought compelled Rafael to refill his cup of ale and drain it quickly.

> *"Wise Oliver stood beside Roland,*
> *Awed by the Moors upon the land.*
> *That knight climbed a hill beside the road,*
> *The better to see the numbers of their foe.*
> *He could not count them nor could see*
> *The end of their ranks. "Twas a sea*
> *Of knights on horseback fully armed*
> *Come to fight on mountain scree.*
> *He feared they could not win this day*
> *And to Roland Oliver did say*
> *'Blow your horn and do it now;*
> *Summon the king to fight this foe!'*
> *But Roland laughed and refused the plea*
> *For he thought it would be cowardly.*

> *The rear guard was his to defend,*
> *And so he turned to face the fiends.*
> *'My duty it is to fight for my king*
> *And I will hear my sword sing*
> *As it slices through Moorish skulls*
> *And brings victory, as God wills.'"*

That was the manner of leadership that saw men dead, and for no good end. The folly of Roland was clear to Rafael as it was not to those at the high table. Dying foolishly had never been his own aspiration.

Indeed, he would prefer not to die at all.

A memory stirred at that, the presence of those demons and the portal to Hell a little too close for comfort, and Rafael took refuge in the ale. On this night, it would be worth the price to sleep dreamlessly, even if his own hide was at risk.

❧

Elizabeth clutched her hands together in her lap as Alexander sang. *The Song of Roland* was a thrilling one, and she never tired of hearing it. On this day, though, she was struck by the references to warfare, and wondered if it was all too familiar to Rafael.

He drank ale with a gusto unexpected, more even than his fellows, and she wondered if he were a drunkard. He otherwise seemed to be in such control of his impulses, that she would never have expected as much. When she caught Malcolm's frown of surprise, she knew that something was different about Rafael on this day.

Was it possible that he was as agitated as she?

> *"A hundred thousand Moors were there,*
> *A force more fearsome ne'er did appear!*
> *The rear guard eyed the gathering foe*
> *And more than one quailed in fear, just so.*
> *'Fear not,' brave Roland then did cry*
> *'For Durendal cannot be denied.*
> *My blade will run with Moorish blood*
> *And a blow will be delivered for God.*
> *We will cut down those who lie and cheat*

*We will defend our king from such deceit.
My blade will slash, and it will sing,
And soon we will ride home again.'
Wise Oliver advised his friend
To blow his horn to call the king again.
More forces then would they be
And more assured their victory.
But Roland laughed at such prudence
He swore to offer all for the king's trust.
He mounted his steed, he gave his sign
Ten thousand men rode forth aligned.
From all those throats broke the king's own cry
For they rode to war calling 'Mountjoy!'"*

The company cheered at this and echoed the battle cry. "Mountjoy!"

*"The first Moor taunted them indeed
For he told them of Ganelon's deed.
'What manner of men betray each other?
What kind of knight deceives his brother?
For God's will, you all shall die.
And we shall take your bounty as our prize.'
Roland struck the first blow that night
For he cut down this dark Moor with might.
He sliced his helmet and split his head
With one blow, he struck that man dead
His blade cut the Moor to the spine
For Durendal could not be denied.
The Moors bellowed, their voices brash
The two armies met with a mighty clash.
The blood did flow in quantity,
The full moon shone on death indeed.
Oliver, Roland and Archbishop Turpin
Fought with vigor to the end.
And when back to back fought they three
They knew there was no place to flee.
Oliver begged Roland again to blow
A mighty bellow upon his horn.*

> *Archbishop Turpin did agree,*
> *Though they would not survive, they three.*
> *'Twould be best to call the king*
> *That he might avenge the loss there had been.*
> *Roland did cede to them in this,*
> *And lifted his horn to his lips.*
> *He blew so hard and with such force,*
> *That his temples burst and he was lost.*
> *In giving this last battle cry*
> *So the king's most valiant warrior did die."*

Elizabeth watched as Rafael spat into the rushes. "A fool," that warrior said as he rose to his feet. "He was no champion, but a fool who led others to their demise! That is no hero worthy of a tale!" Rafael sat down with a scowl then and beckoned for the ale.

His fellows withheld it.

Alexander and Malcolm exchanged a glance, and Alexander began to sing again.

> *"The summons echoed through the hills*
> *For thirty leagues, its sound did peal!*
> *Charlemagne knew the sound of Oliphaunt*
> *The horn Roland carried on his belt.*
> *He turned the entire company*
> *The host racing back to the melée.*
> *They found the rear guard, slaughtered all,*
> *And Roland, brave Roland, also fallen.*
> *Angels gathered around the dead,*
> *A trio cradled Roland's head.*
> *Charlemagne watched the heavenly host*
> *Gather the nephew he loved the most.*
> *Brave Roland was carried to heaven high*
> *The earth itself sending forth a cry*
> *For there would be no knight again*
> *So prepared to fight for king and men."*

There was fulsome applause from the company, and Alexander took a sip of ale himself before he bowed in acknowledgment. "And so it was that our father was named Roland," he said. "It was a tribute to a bold hero and a name to ensure his own valor during his life."

"It is a noble name, indeed," Elizabeth agreed. "And a wondrous tale."

The company began to applaud again, all except for Rafael. That man stood again, his manner as intense as Elizabeth had ever seen it, and raised his voice. "It *might* be a wondrous tale," he said and the company fell silent. "If it were true."

"It *is* true!" Alexander protested. "I have heard it told many a time."

Rafael strode down the middle of the hall, his confidence such that he held every gaze. He smiled ever so slightly, which gave him a dangerous and predatory look. Elizabeth could not help but admire the sight of him.

Her destined love.

Rafael's eyes narrowed as he considered Alexander. "A lie does not become true, no matter how many times it is repeated."

"But all know this tale," Alexander said with a smile. The company applauded at his invitation, showing their approval of his version.

Rafael folded his arms across his chest. "But truth is dependent upon where a man stands."

Glances of confusion were exchanged, even as some of the mercenaries shook their heads in amusement. Clearly they knew what Rafael meant.

"But what is the difference?" Elizabeth demanded. Rafael turned a simmering look upon her, one that made her think every soul in the hall would guess how he had kissed her.

To her delight, he answered her.

"It means that one man's just war is another man's abomination. On this side of the mountains that divide the lands of the French king from that of the Castile, Roland's tale is told thus. This is the truth known by those who trace their lineage to Charlemagne." Rafael turned to gesture to all the company. "Unlike every other person gathered here, I came of age on the other side of those mountains."

"In Castile," Elizabeth breathed. There was a land of mystery and romance, for it was the southern reaches of Castile that had once been held by the Moors, and it was said that those cities were filled with marvels and riches. She clasped her hands together in her lap, convinced yet again that Rafael was the one man who had tasted adventure.

He inclined his head slightly in her direction. "And there, in the lands where Charlemagne marched his troops, we tell a different tale of the Battle of Roncesvaux. I was born in Pamplona, in the Kingdom of Navarre to the north of Castile, and there we tell of the Frankish king Charlemagne destroying the walls of the city, pillaging it and slaughtering the residents."

Elizabeth caught her breath.

"We tell of the great Frankish king turning tail after the damage was done, after his coffers were filled with stolen coin, and fleeing into the mountains with his blood price." His voice dropped low. "And we tell of the valiant men who bewailed their fellow townspeople and their kin, who crept into the mountain passes they knew as well as the lines on their own palms, and took vengeance for that unprovoked assault."

Elizabeth lifted her fingers to her lips.

"Charlemagne did not fight the Moors at Roncesvaux," Rafael concluded in disdain, as the company sat silent. He tapped a finger on his own chest. "He fought *us*, the residents of Pamplona, the Christians of the Kingdom of Navarre. He slaughtered other Christians to defend his theft of their gold."

Elizabeth was shocked. "This cannot be true!"

"It is." Rafael lifted his cup of ale and drained it, his eyes narrowing as he eyed Elizabeth. The entire assembly was rapt, but he looked only at Elizabeth. "I assure you that there could not have been four hundred thousand men in the attacking force. Perhaps it was only four hundred."

"For Rafael himself is known to be worth a thousand men in battle," one of the other mercenaries contributed. The rest of the Sable League toasted to that truth and drank heartily.

"But they were more worthy of becoming heroes in a tale than this Roland, for they defended both justice and truth."

Elizabeth could only find herself in agreement.

Indeed, that he valued those traits told her that her instinct about Rafael was right.

"I am not from these parts," Rafael said softly, his words carrying all the same. "I am not like you people and your kind.

Indeed, so great is the difference that some of you cannot distinguish my kind from infidels and enemies." He paused to empty his cup. "And yet the king you hail as the champion of all you hold dear was worse than a mercenary. He attacked without justification, stole, looted and fled to safety." Rafael almost smiled. "Perhaps my kind merely has need of better troubadours."

His gaze bored into Elizabeth's for a long moment, then he put down the cup with a flourish, pivoted and left the hall.

Elizabeth started to rise, but Alexander's hand landed on her arm. His gaze was more serious than she had seen him in a while. "He gives you fair warning, Elizabeth. Let him go."

"I see the ribbons," she said through her teeth.

"You are deceived as to his merit," Alexander said, giving no credence to her observations. There was steel in his tone when he continued. "We will return to Kinfairlie immediately."

"Alexander, I must protest," Elizabeth began but her brother gave her a quelling look.

When she fell into mutinous silence, Alexander nodded to Malcolm and raised his voice. "I thank you, Catriona and Malcolm, for this hospitality on this day, and I salute your match. Let us gather this Saturday to come, so that all of Kinfairlie can see your vows exchanged before our priest, Father Malachy."

"I should like that," Catriona said at Malcolm's glance her way.

"Then it shall be done," the new Laird of Ravensmuir said, his grip fast on his wife's hand. "But it shall be done here, at Ravensmuir." He nodded to Alexander. "I look forward to welcoming you all."

The company applauded the notion of another celebration, especially one so soon to come. Elizabeth watched her brothers shake hands and was discontent that Rafael had departed. Perhaps she would see him in the stables, when they went to saddle the horses. Perhaps she would have one last chance to speak to him this day.

But Alexander must have guessed her intent, for Elizabeth left the hall of Ravensmuir to find Demoiselle saddled and waiting in the bailey, alongside Uriel, Alexander's mount. Both steeds were stamping with impatience to be gone. It was mid-afternoon when they took their departure of Ravensmuir, but no matter how intently she looked, Elizabeth could not catch another glimpse of Rafael.

Saturday it would be, then, unless she managed to visit Ravensmuir before. At least she would have time to seek Rosamunde's advice.

❧

Alexander turned a stern eye upon Elizabeth as soon as they had ridden from Ravensmuir's gates. Truly, he was as predictable as the daily progress of the sun in his opinions, though Elizabeth was not so interested in another of his lectures.

"What seized your wits that you would be so close to such men?" Alexander began. "Have you no care for your reputation? It is not fitting for a maiden like yourself to speak with men-of-war. You must have a concern not only for your virtue, but for the perception of your virtue..."

Elizabeth interrupted her oldest brother's tirade, knowing it was well intended, if tedious. She had seen her own ribbon and she trusted its import enough to be bold. Indeed, she had best see matters arranged as quickly as possible. "You told me to choose a suitor, that it would be my decision which man I would wed."

"Aye." Alexander was wary.

"Then you should know that I have chosen Rafael Rodriguez." Elizabeth gave her brother a confident smile.

"Who?"

"Malcolm's comrade. The one who arrived with him at the Yule. The one who challenged your tale in the hall at midday."

Alexander stared at her in astonishment. "You cannot mean this!"

"I do. He is valiant, for he entered the Fae circle by his own choice to aid Malcolm, though he could easily have paid with his own life. He will see me well defended, given his experience of war." Elizabeth lifted her chin, well aware that Alexander was mustering an argument. "He is honorable, and he will suit me very well as a spouse."

Alexander appeared to be at a loss for words, so great was his amazement. "But he is a mercenary!" he finally sputtered. "And born of distant lands. He undoubtedly will return to his trade, and possibly also to his homeland." He flung out a hand. "You could be abandoned in some rough camp wrought by war-faring men, and should he be killed—as surely such men must all be in time—you will be alone and undefended, as well as far from home."

"I believe I will love him, and that love will be my comfort."

Alexander scoffed. "I believe you are smitten with the look of him, and the tale you have wrought of him in your heart, not his dark truth." He ran a hand through his hair. "Perhaps his kind has no need of better troubadours!"

"But still I have chosen." Elizabeth heard her tone become firm.

"And I forbid your choice." Alexander glowered down at her. "It will not be so, Elizabeth. There is no need to look stubborn, for I will not permit you to wed this man or another of his ilk."

How was it that men invited her decision, then discarded the choices she made? She was not willful, defiant or a fool. She understood Rafael's nature, as her brother and even Rafael himself did not. Elizabeth fixed Alexander with a look. "I *will* be determined, for I have made a choice and you would discard it, despite your pledge to stand by my decision."

"This is not the choice I anticipated..."

"Malcolm fought alongside Rafael, for he was a mercenary as well. You cannot hold Rafael's trade against him any more than you would hold that of Malcolm against him."

"Does this Rafael mean to surrender his trade?"

Sadly, Elizabeth did not know. "I believe he can be convinced..." she began but Alexander sighed.

He put his hand upon hers and his tone softened. "I can see that he would have an appeal, Elizabeth, for you have met few men of his ilk. But Rafael is not the man for you, for he could not make you happy, or secure your future." Alexander's tone turned consoling. "Rafael will be gone soon enough, Elizabeth. Do not make yourself unhappy by convincing yourself that he means more than he must."

"He kissed me."

Alexander bristled. "Did he?"

"After I invited him to do so," Elizabeth amended hastily and her brother scowled at her. She dared not confess how much she would have surrendered willingly to Rafael. Instead she blushed furiously, which prompted Alexander to frown.

"Do not tempt him, or any other man, with more than would be wise for you to offer, Elizabeth, for most men will partake of any feast you present, and do so without remorse. Such is the nature of these men."

"He stepped away," she admitted, wanting Alexander to understand that Rafael was more honorable than he believed.

"Then he is not so fool as to see both of you condemned, and this is fortunate for you." Alexander cast her a determined glance. "Elizabeth, heed my counsel in this. A man who thinks only of his own pleasure and advantage will claim you and forget you within a day, while you, having been so sampled, will carry the shadow of that one interval for the remainder of your days and nights."

"It might be wondrous..."

"It could not be worth it." Alexander smiled gently. "Your lawful husband is more likely to make your nuptial night wondrous, for he will have bound himself to you for a lifetime. A wise woman does not scatter her pearls before swine."

"Rafael is not swine."

"Use your wits, Elizabeth," Alexander concluded firmly. "A moment's consideration and you will see that this is a poor choice of the many available to you. I have given you time and the chance to make your own decision of which man to wed. Do not betray such a gift with folly." He shook his head. "And to think that I was skeptical when they said you spoke with him alone in the stables. It is clear that you must be more closely supervised until he departs."

Elizabeth bristled at the notion. "He wanted to speak of you," she said, once again taking satisfaction in surprising her brother.

"Me?"

"As a fighting man, he had hoped to see the legendary stallions of Ravensmuir on his arrival there and was disappointed that they were at Kinfairlie. He asked why that were so, when you had surrendered the seal to Ravensmuir to Malcolm so quickly after his return, but not the steeds." Elizabeth shrugged. "I confess I had no good answer, for Rafael spoke aright that the stables were the sole building in good repair at that estate."

Alexander gritted his teeth. "He thinks I mean to cheat Malcolm of his legacy!"

"I had that impression, to be sure."

Alexander's eyes narrowed. "And this is the price of courtesy! I knew Malcolm had much to manage while the keep was rebuilt, as well as few in his service, and thought to spare him any trouble."

"Perhaps it is time to restore what is his own, since you two are allied again," Elizabeth dared to suggest.

Alexander seized upon this notion with welcome enthusiasm. "Indeed, there is more than the horses that he requires. I will enlist Eleanor's assistance in this, for she is most sensible. We shall take Malcolm and Catriona a wedding gift that will leave no doubt of my pleasure in seeing him home again."

The rest of the ride back to Kinfairlie was occupied with Alexander making lists and Elizabeth adding suggestions. She was glad to have been of some influence in this, and could not wait to see Rafael's expression when the horses were returned.

Saturday could not arrive with sufficient speed for her.

※

In the quiet of the night, Rafael was not alone. He was wrapped in his cloak and leaning against the wall, unable to sleep despite the ale he had imbibed. The Sable League slumbered in Malcolm's hall on all sides, but that was not the company he dreaded.

Nay, Franz came to him.

If anything, he looked worse than he had the night before. Franz picked up a cup and settled his rotting carcass beside Rafael, casting a heavy arm over Rafael's shoulders. Rafael was certain he felt maggots writhing against his flesh, but he pretended to be oblivious to his former comrade's presence.

He had to be a ghost, a harmless specter.

Franz did not appear so harmless. "Interesting that they recounted a tale of a man betrayed," that phantom murmured, his tone companionable. "It is as if they recognize the darkness in your heart on sight." He leered at Rafael. "Which of them will you betray first? Malcolm, or his sister, Elizabeth?" The specter chortled. "Better you than me, if the Hellhound discovers you have taken his sister's maidenhood." Franz dropped his voice to a whisper. "What if the wench lies to force your hand?" He then chuckled to himself at the prospect.

Rafael closed his eyes and willed Franz to silence.

Or back to Hell.

The specter did not comply, though truly Rafael had not expected otherwise.

Thursday, June 24, 1428

Feast Day of the martyrs Saint Agoard and Saint Agilbert, and Saint Germoc.

Claire Delacroix

Chapter Eleven

It truly was intolerable.

Elizabeth had waited years to meet a man who could capture her heart for all time and had told herself that her patience would be rewarded. She had been certain that she was destined to love a man at ease with adventure, a man who lived at least as boldly as her aunt Rosamunde, a man whose life was worthy of a jongleur's tale and one who would set her very blood afire with a glance. Hers would be a match that filled the hearts of maidens with hope. Hers would be a life so wondrous that it would scarce be believed when recounted. The dream had burned brightly in her heart, warding off the chill of Finvarra's kiss, making it impossible for her to compromise.

Now she had met Rafael, exactly as she had always anticipated, a man who heeded her words and thrilled her with his kiss, a man who had *developed* a ribbon to entwine with her own after they had met, and that man treated her like a child unworthy of his attention. The situation was most vexing.

Elizabeth felt cheated and there was no evading the truth of it. She had been patient. She had trusted in her future, and in those who pledged to love her. She had trusted in destiny and kismet and love, but it seemed her future was not to be as she had dreamed.

This made her defiant.

It was beyond belief that she, who loved a tale more than any of her siblings, should be so unfortunate as to be consigned to a mundane life. Elizabeth paced the chamber that was now her own throughout that night, her annoyance only rising with every step.

She had ridden across the breadth of England in pursuit of Madeline, when her oldest sister had been carried off by Rhys. There was a tale worth recounting to one's children!

She had raced to the Highlands to assist Vivienne when Eric

had been locked in a battle for his survival against his own brother. Elizabeth ground her teeth that she had merely participated in that fine tale of love conquering all obstacles.

She had accompanied the group from Kinfairlie who journeyed to Tivotdale on Twelfth Night, pretending to be vagabonds and entertainers that they might rescue Alexander's stolen bride, Eleanor. That had been an adventure, to be sure!

Her other sisters had been equally fortunate in their matches, though Elizabeth had not been part of their tales. Isabella had saved her beloved, Murdoch, from the clutches of the Elphine Queen, that Fae seductress who would have kept him captive forever. Even gentle Annelise had healed Garrett and helped him to reclaim his birthright!

It was beyond belief that Annelise, of all of her sisters, had experienced more adventure in her courtship than Elizabeth would.

The list continued with irksome consistency. Malcolm had been besieged by the Earl of Douglas and saved by Catriona, his wife of only a few days. Rosamunde had recounted to them her adventures in the realm of the Fae and told of Padraig's valor in saving her from Finvarra's lust.

It seemed that Elizabeth alone of all her kin was to live without adventure.

There had been no opportunity to speak with her aunt the night before, for the telling of tales had run late. Rosamunde had retired with Padraig all too early. Still, the adventure that Rosamunde had lived and breathed was an inspiration.

Elizabeth cast a glance across her chamber to the trunk where she had hidden the mirror that Finvarra had dropped. There was something uncanny about that treasure, to be sure, and Elizabeth did not trust it. Although she had hidden it away—both from her own gaze and that of others—an awareness of it seemed to gnaw at her thoughts, as a mouse will nibble a crust of bread. She was sorely tempted to peer deeply into it, but she guessed that doing as much would be dangerous indeed.

Like looking into the depths of Finvarra's dark eyes.

Had he truly dropped it by accident? Or had he schemed for her to claim it, for some nefarious purpose of his own?

Elizabeth shivered. She had no doubt that there would be adventure of a kind if she surrendered to the Fae king, but she was certain it would offer little pleasure to her. He tried to beguile her, no more than that, to tempt her to imprison herself.

She suspected that if ever she went to him, she would be lost to the mortal realm forever. That was one thing if there was no man for her to love, but so long as Rafael walked the earth, Elizabeth wanted to discover if there could be more between them. She sighed, knowing that one day she would be compelled to pay her debt to Finvarra. Perhaps she would go to him when she was an ancient crone and her beloved was gone.

Assuming that she ever won a beloved.

She sighed and noted that the sun was rising.

The funeral for the fallen mercenary at Ravensmuir would be held before noon. Malcolm had said as much.

Elizabeth decided immediately that she would attend. With any fortune at all, her family would linger abed this morning after their late night and she would be able to evade Alexander's watchful eye.

After all, there was no telling how long Rafael might remain in Scotland, but he would stay for the funeral of his comrade at least. This might be her last chance to speak to him and plead her case.

Elizabeth would do so in no uncertain terms.

*

The mist was still clinging to the ground when Father Malachy saddled his palfrey. She was a more humble creature than the destriers of Ravensmuir, but she was a sturdy mare and a patient one. She was a dapple, with darker spots on her rump and her face, and dark socks, aptly named Soot. Soot was not inclined to high spirits or tantrums, and both endured what had to be done and welcomed life's pleasures. Her temperament suited the priest well.

Father Malachy smiled as he patted Soot's rump. She nickered and rolled the bit beneath her tongue, a routine protest that she made whenever she was saddled. There was no heat in it, just a gentle reminder to him that she would rather be without it. Doubtless she would rather be grazing in the pastures or nosing in her feed. Father Malachy felt no guilt. The journey was not so far to Ravensmuir, though it was early, and she would be well-tended in the stable there while he said a prayer for that lost mercenary.

He wished he had been present to offer last rites, but on the other hand, doubted there would have been any opportunity to administer them. Such was the way of war, and Father Malachy was blessed to be far from it most of the time.

He took a deep breath, welcoming the tang of the sea in the air, and guessed that the day would be fine once the mist burned off. The sky was clearing, and he could already feel that the sun would be warm. From a purely practical standpoint, it would be good to see the rest of the dead at Ravensmuir buried on this day, since the weather was turning yet warmer.

He was leading Soot to the mounting block when someone called to him.

"Father Malachy!"

The priest turned to find Lady Elizabeth striding toward him, leading her own mount by the reins. Demoiselle was a magnificent mare, at least half again the size of Soot, as black as ebony and high-stepping, as well. That mare's nostrils flared as she walked, and she fought the bit with a passion Soot had never shown. Lady Elizabeth did not even appear to notice, so accustomed was she to this horse.

"Might I ride with you to Ravensmuir?" Lady Elizabeth wore a dark kirtle and nary a jewel upon her person. Her veil was dark and her circlet plain, her gloves dark, and her cloak the plainest one he believed she owned.

He blinked, realizing she had dressed for a funeral.

At the same time, he was amazed to see the difference in her manner despite her somber garb. There was color in her cheeks and a sparkle in her eyes. She had been wan for so long that he had feared her fatally ill. Though she still was too slender to his thinking, on this day, it appeared that Lady Elizabeth made a recovery.

"I am not certain that you should do so," he said with care, though he was inclined to grant her any whim when she appeared to be finally in better health.

"Indeed? I thought that one of Malcolm's comrades was to be laid to rest on this day."

"Indeed, he is."

"Does Alexander mean to attend, then?" The lady demurely dropped her gaze when she referred to her oldest brother.

Father Malachy fought an almost-forgotten awareness of her mischievous nature, for her lightheartedness had been in absence in recent years. Again, he was heartened, though he wondered what jest she might make in this.

He chose his words with care, wanting to be diplomatic. "Nay, he does not."

There was no mistaking the twinkle in Elizabeth's eyes when she glanced up. God in Heaven, but she was a fetching maiden! "Surely, a man who died in the defense of Ravensmuir should be remembered with honor?"

When she put it that way, Father Malachy could hardly argue, but he had to defend the Laird of Kinfairlie. "Do not make mischief, Lady Elizabeth," he counseled softly. "The Laird reconciled with his brother only yesterday. It will take time for him to embrace Malcolm's former fellows, if indeed he ever does."

"I understand completely," the lady agreed, far too readily to set the priest's mind at ease. "And indeed, I think of diplomacy not of mischief."

"Indeed?"

"Indeed." She was resolute in a way he also recalled. "I believe someone should be there to represent Kinfairlie, for we all do welcome the defense of Ravensmuir and the sacrifices made in so doing." She stood taller, that twinkle replaced with an air of command that suited her well. "And so I shall see our family duty served, Father, in my brother's stead."

Father Malachy hesitated.

"No one can find fault in my accompanying a priest to a funeral at my brother's holding," the lady pointed out, and again, her way of expressing the situation did sound most innocent.

Father Malachy considered her, standing so regally before him with her magnificent steed, and could not help but smile with pride. She had grown into quite a woman, and she would make some fortunate man a formidable wife.

"Your foresight does you credit, Lady Elizabeth," he said with a bow. "We shall ride forth together to Ravensmuir, and return to Kinfairlie by midday."

He caught a glimpse of her triumphant smile.

Lady Elizabeth had a scheme, Father Malachy would wager. For his part, though, it was enough to see her so restored as to have conjured one.

Thursday dawned a fine summer morning, and the priest came early from Kinfairlie to bless the dead. Lady Elizabeth accompanied him, her garb so severe that she resembled a sorrowful angel even more than before. The sight of her made Rafael's heart leap, but he resolutely kept his distance.

It would have taken a less observant man than he to fail to note the quick glance that Catriona and Malcolm exchanged, never mind the way that Catriona hastened to draw her husband's sister to her side. Rafael saw the flash of Elizabeth's eyes and knew that it had not been her intent to be so vigilantly defended.

As much as he might have wished to have one more moment of her companionship, he knew better than to tease himself with what could not ever be. He stood in the company of his fellows, reminding himself of what he was and what he would always be, as the priest conducted the service.

Reynaud was buried on that point of land where they had all prayed with Malcolm's wife just days before, beneath what would be the floor of the new chapel, just as Malcolm had promised. Several of the men in the Sable League were visibly affected by this honor shown to their comrade, though Rafael would never have believed before he saw it that Gunter could shed a tear.

Rafael watched the roil of the sea as the priest gave his final blessings. He strove to avoid his awareness that the water in the sunlight was the same clear green as Elizabeth's eyes. It sparkled in the sunlight with much the same vigor, and he knew the sea was as unpredictable yet constant as the maiden who tormented him.

It seemed Elizabeth would haunt him, whether he was in her company or not.

He told himself that was better than a foolish choice on her part casting a shadow over the rest of her days.

When the priest was done and Reynaud was buried, Catriona placed a flower on the freshly turned earth. The entire company stood together in the wind for a long silent moment. Doubtless they all considered that they would be fortunate indeed to be so well remembered. Doubtless none of them were in a hurry to leave Reynaud alone.

"A man must have a tribute," Amaury said abruptly, breaking the silence.

"Reynaud has had a fine tribute in this," Gunter noted. "To rest within a new chapel in a holding claimed by a comrade is a finer end than most of us can hope to see." There was a murmur of agreement to this.

"I meant some words to mark his passing," Amaury said. "The blessing is all well and good, but this might have been the first time Reynaud heard it."

They laughed together, clearly discomfited by the truth in this statement in the presence of the women and the priest. To Rafael's surprise, Elizabeth stepped forward.

"What did he like best?" she asked. "If he favored ale, you might salute his memory with a drink."

Rafael bit back a smile, for Reynaud's pleasures had been earthy ones. Elizabeth's innocence was revealed in her suggestion, and he was tempted—if only for a moment—to do as she desired. Aye, he would relish granting her that education.

Louis shoved a hand through his hair. "Not enough whores in these parts for that," he muttered, his words sufficiently low that Elizabeth was not intended to hear them.

Rafael could not help but chuckle, along with his fellows. Catriona averted her gaze and laid claim to Elizabeth's elbow, clearly intending to lead the younger woman back to the keep. Malcolm frowned, and Elizabeth's cheeks flushed.

She lifted her chin, undaunted, her gaze flying to meet his own. "What of tales? Did he have a favored one?"

The men's expressions lit as one. They turned in unison to Rafael, and Amaury wagged a finger at him. "There is one, and you must be the teller."

Rafael frowned. The last thing he wished to do was tell a tale, particularly that one, particularly as he knew that Elizabeth favored tales. He did not want to draw her eye more than he had. On the other hand, that anticipation that lit her features made him want to please her. The woman could have been a siren, sent to lure him into dangerous temptation. He did not have to look to know that Malcolm disapproved.

"I dislike telling tales and you all know it well," he said gruffly.

"But still you told the one he loved the best," Ranulf insisted. "Tell it again, in Reynaud's memory!"

They all entreated Rafael, though he was resolute.

"Only a heartless mercenary would fail to honor a fallen

comrade," Elizabeth said softly in challenge.

Again, she provoked him.

Again, her ploy was successful. It would only be a tale, after all, and she might find a lesson about the nature of men in it.

"Far be it from me to confirm to all and sundry that my heart is gone in truth," Rafael said. He stood up then and braced his hands on his hips, avoiding Elizabeth's shining gaze. "Once, there was a king," he began and his comrades applauded heartily.

Elizabeth's smile could have illuminated the darkest hall.

Rafael ignored her. "Once there was a king," he repeated, raising his voice. "A king in distant Persia, a king who loved his wife most ardently. She was beautiful and he was content to put all other women aside to honor his lady wife. His brother, too, had wed well, or so the brothers believed, and they alone in all their kingdom were men faithful to their wives. And so it might have continued if dreadful tidings had not come to their ears."

He granted a hard look to Elizabeth, though she needed no encouragement from him to pay close attention to the tale. "An advisor to the king reported that his brother's wife had a lover, another man in the court. The king did not believe this tale and attributed it to jealousy of the lady's privilege in his court, but he chose to investigate the matter. To his dismay, he discovered not only his brother's wife in the arms of her lover, but his own wife in the act of loving another man."

"Whore," said Gunter.

"Harlot," agreed Tristan.

Guilia lifted her chin and gave Giorgio a hard look. He caught her hand in his and pulled her closer to his side, which clearly pleased her.

"The king was devastated by this betrayal of his trust and his love, as was his brother. Both women were executed in the public square for their infidelity, for this was what their law decreed should be done with women who did not honor their marital vows."

Elizabeth caught her breath.

Rafael considered the ground. "I confess that the king was so dismayed that he might have taken to warfare, never again pledging himself to take a wife, but there was the matter of his desires. He was a young and vigorous man, and his needs were considerable. He chose then to love, but not to trust. And so he charged his Grand

The Warrior's Prize

Vizier—for this is what these Persians called the man in closest service to the king--to find him a new bride each and every day. He would wed a virgin every day, savor her that night, then have her executed the morning after the wedding. In this way, he reasoned, he would never be betrayed by a woman again."

Rafael heard Elizabeth gasp but he ignored her. Perhaps his tale would teach her something of the nature of men. "And so it was done, as the king decreed. The stones in the public square turned red from the blood of so many executed wives. In fact, in a matter of months, he had wedded and executed so many virgins that there were few left to be found in all of his kingdom. He commanded the Grand Vizier to search beyond his borders for new brides, but the Grand Vizier believed this to be unlikely to earn the favor of his neighboring kings.

"They argued as they seldom did, for the Grand Vizier thought the king's course to be most unwise. The Grand Vizier feared that his life would be the next to be sacrificed, and so it was that he was saddened when he returned to his own home that night.

"It happened that the Grand Vizier had a beautiful daughter of his own, the joy of his life. She was yet unmarried, for he had not found a man he believe to be worthy of her. Her name was Scheherazade."

"Scheherazade."

Rafael heard Elizabeth repeat the name in a whisper. He glanced up and that he had her complete attention, a sight that gave him more pleasure than it should have done. He frowned, stared at the ground and continued his tale.

"Scheherazade saw immediately that her father was troubled and drew the entire tale from him in short order. She served his meal to him and ensured his comfort, all the while thinking about what she had learned. In fact, she lay awake all of that night, wondering what she could do to help her father, and by the dawn, she knew.

"Scheherazade dared not tell her father of her plan, for she knew he would forbid it, but held her tongue until he was gone to the palace. She followed on fleet feet, coming into the audience hall just as the king demanded of his Grand Vizier which maiden he should wed on this day. Before her father could reply, Scheherazade stepped forward and offered herself as the king's new bride. Once the king has set his gaze upon her, he was captivated and Scheherazade's father could not contest his lord and master's desire.

"And so the pair were wed, with great feasting and merriment, and so Scheherazade was adorned and taken to the king's bed that night. He claimed her maidenhead, then slumbered with his head on her shoulder. Scheherazade knew that with the dawn, her life would end. When her new husband stirred, she took his head into her lap and stroked his brow. She offered to tell him a story, and the king, intrigued, agreed."

"This is the good part," Ranulf said, giving Gunter a nudge.

"A scheming piece of work she was to be sure," that man agreed.

"She knew what was best for him better than he knew himself," Louis said. "I should be glad of a woman so gifted."

"You should be glad of a woman at all," Amaury teased and once again the comrades laughed together.

"But what story did she tell?" Elizabeth demanded.

Rafael smiled. "She told the story of the fisherman and the djinn." The men applauded this announcement, their anticipation clear. "Once, said Scheherazade, there was a fisherman of humble means. He had a boat and he sailed out to fish each and every day. Each and every day, he cast his net four times and four times only. Each and every night, he returned to the harbor and sold what he had caught. It was a hard life and as he grew older, he wondered how long he might continue with it."

"Fishing is not the sole trade that leaves a man with such a question," Ranulf muttered and his fellows nodded agreement.

Rafael raised his voice to continue, ignoring them and their doubts. "One day, he sailed out as always he did, but the first time he cast his net, he caught only a dead goat. This was troubling, but he cast his net again, refusing to be discouraged. The second time, the net held only an old pot filled with mud when he hauled it back into the boat. He could not believe his ill fortune, but cast his net a third time. The third time, the net held only broken pottery shards when he pulled it into the boat. The fisherman was worried indeed, for he feared his family would have naught to eat that night. He said a prayer and cast his net one more time. This time, it was heavy when he began to haul it in, and he was encouraged that he might have made up all with this catch. To his surprise, though, there were no fish in his net, only a large copper jar.

"He pulled the jar into the boat with some effort, seeing that the cork was sealed into the top with wax. He noted the mark of Solomon cast into the copper and pressed into the wax, and was heartened that he could sell the copper jar. That ancient king had been known for his wisdom and his riches, and so the fisherman hoped there might be something additional inside the jar that he could sell, as well. He broke the wax seal with his knife and removed the cork. Smoke erupted from the jar in such volume that he was momentarily blinded. The smoke gathered itself and he was confronted by a massive djinn."

The men chuckled and nodded in anticipation, while Elizabeth lifted one hand to her lips, rapt.

"The djinn was black and red, larger than a house, wrought of smoke and fury. The fisherman was terrified by the sight of this being and cowered in the bottom of his boat. The djinn seized the fisherman, telling him to choose how he would die. It proved that the djinn believed he had been released only for Solomon to kill him, so he assumed the fisherman was a minion of that great king. The fisherman told the djinn that Solomon had been dead for many centuries, hoping this would spare his life, but the djinn still told him to choose the method of his own execution. The fisherman, intent upon surviving as long as possible, asked why the djinn demanded this of someone who had never done him any harm."

Rafael smiled. "Scheherazade paused her tale at that point because the sky was lightening in the east outside the window's of the king's palace. She pointed this out to her new husband, reminding him that the day was beginning. The king wished to linger to hear the end of the tale, but his servants were at the portal. His morning meal and his bath were prepared, the Grand Vizier awaited him, there was a court of justice to be held on his day. And so the king reluctantly left his new wife, burning with curiosity as to why the djinn would so punish one who had done him a favor. He decided before he had finished his bath that he would permit Scheherazade to live another day, that she might complete her tale."

The men laughed uproariously at this, and Elizabeth smiled with satisfaction.

"And so it was that in the evening, king and wife feasted again, and retired to the king's chamber again, and coupled with enthusiasm again. When he was sated, the king put his head in Scheherazade's lap and commanded her to finish her tale.

"Scheherazade reminded the king that the fisherman has asked the djinn why he must die. The djinn confided that he had been confined for many centuries. The king, it must be said, asked why the djinn still believed that Solomon lived, if he knew it had been so long, and Scheherazade gently reminded him that Solomon had been said to live for centuries and that many of his fellows had thought the great king might be immortal. The king nodded, much enamored of this notion of kings and their longevity."

"So he would be," Gunter muttered.

"No man of wealth and power imagines he will die," agreed Bertrand.

Rafael cleared his throat for silence. "Scheherazade continued with her tale and the djinn's explanation for his demand. For the first century of his confinement, the djinn confessed that he had been determined to reward whosoever might release him by granting that individual great wealth. When he was not freed, his anger grew, so in the second century of his confinement, the djinn decided that he would grant his liberator wealth beyond belief, riches beyond expectation, yet still no one freed him. In the third century of his confinement, the djinn decided he would grant three wishes to whosoever set him free, giving that person his heart's desire. He reasoned that there were those who did not find allure in riches. Still he was not freed. In the fourth century of his confinement, the djinn became bitter. He resolved that he would kill whoever set him free, and that his gift would be allowing the liberator to choose the method of his death. Again, he asked the fisherman for his choice of how he would die.

"The fisherman did not wish to die, but fortunately, he was a man of some wit. He distracted the djinn by indicating the copper jar. He said he could not truly believe that the djinn had been trapped in a container so very small, and insisted that he was being deceived by the djinn. This suggestion infuriated the djinn, who immediately dived back into the jar, showing that he did indeed fit inside. The fisherman was quick to put the stopper back in place, imprisoning the djinn once again."

"He was quick-witted indeed!" Tristan said with approval and the men applauded the fisherman's cleverness.

"The djinn begged for release, but the fisherman vowed to throw the jar back into the sea instead. When the djinn entreated the fisherman to show him mercy, the fisherman scolded him, for he did not think it fitting that the djinn asked a favor only to reward the fisherman with death. To prove his point, he began to tell the djinn the story of the *Wise Man Named Duban*."

Ranulf began to chuckle, the other men joining in his merriment. Rafael spared a glance to Elizabeth, seeing that she was mystified by their laughter.

"But the sky was brightening in the east by this time, and Scheherazade brought the hour to the attention of her husband, the king. She had had less time to tell him tales that night, for he had loved her more slowly and thoroughly. The king did not regret the duration of their lovemaking, but still he was vexed to not hear the end of the tale. And so it was that again the king let Scheherazade survive the day, because he so wished to know the tale of the *Wise Man Named Duban*."

Elizabeth laughed and clapped her hands at this, her eyes sparkling in a way that reminded Rafael all too well of how sweetly she could kiss.

Aye, there was a lesson in this tale, for a woman with her wits about her could beguile a man and distract him from his true objective.

"I will wager she did not finish that tale on the next night either," Elizabeth said.

"She did not, nor on the next or the next. Each tale led to another, each new tale tucked inside the previous, and each morning, the king could not bear to see his wife executed lest he not hear the end of the tale. And so it was that a thousand and one nights passed before Scheherazade's tale of the fisherman and the djinn came to its ending."

"Did it end well?" Elizabeth asked.

"It ended with the fisherman's son made treasurer of the king of the realm, and his daughters married to the princes of the realm. The king applauded his wife's tale with enthusiasm, for he was well pleased." Elizabeth might have said something, but Rafael lifted a finger. "But the tale was done."

Elizabeth raised her hands to her lips, fearing the king's

decision on this day.

"It seemed to all that the end of Scheherazade's life must come, for her tale was finished and the sun was rising yet again. But the king looked upon his bride, and he thought of the three sons she had borne him in the years of telling her tale, and he could not imagine coming to his bed the following night and not finding her there. He could not think of what he would tell his sons about their mother, and he could not believe that there would be any good lesson for them in his doing such a deed. And so it was that he chose to let Scheherazade live."

"Because he loved her," Elizabeth said with undisguised satisfaction.

"Because she entertained him and bore him sons," Rafael insisted.

"He had his sons by the time the tale was ended," Elizabeth countered. "And he could have paid anyone to tell him tales, had he wished merely to be entertained." Rafael was dismayed to find her argument made sense. "He *loved* her, and in her faithfulness, she changed his view of women and earned his trust." She eyed him and lifted her chin. "I will wager that the tale ends by declaring that they lived happily ever after."

"'And if I am not mistaken, they live happily still,'" Ranulf contributed, which was the customary ending to the tale.

"It is but a tale," Rafael said with heat. "Such whimsy does not occur in the life we know so well."

"But it can," Elizabeth replied, conviction in her tone. She folded her arms across her chest, daring him yet again. "A person has only to believe it is possible for it to be so."

"And therein lies the key," Rafael replied. "For I do not believe it, and so it will not be true for me." He bowed to her with elaborate formality. "I hope that your conviction will similarly grant you the result you desire, my lady."

ૅ☙

Rafael was more stubborn and infuriating than Elizabeth could believe.

How could he not see that his own tale buttressed her argument?

How could he refuse to pursue happiness with her?

There was some detail in his past, she would wager, some incident that had shaped his expectations. If she could find the root, she could undermine his conviction in its truth.

"Do not attribute more kindness to Rafael than he deserves," Catriona advised quietly as they two walked to Ravensmuir together. Vera bustled ahead with Avery and Father Malachy. Ruari trailed behind the pair of them, and Malcolm had lingered behind to chat with his former comrades.

"You saw him choose to aid Malcolm," Elizabeth said.

"I did," Catriona admitted. "But there is a hardness in him and his kind that is beyond your experience."

"But not yours?"

Catriona averted her gaze just as Malcolm joined them. His gaze brightened as he noted his wife's mood and he cast a glance at Elizabeth that was almost accusatory as he took Catriona's elbow. "What have I missed?"

"Elizabeth's defense of Rafael," Catriona said with a smile for her husband.

"You cannot blame him for being wary of baring his soul or speaking intimately to another," Elizabeth said, feeling defensive of the absent man. "Not given his childhood."

"His childhood?" Malcolm echoed. "What do you know of Rafael's childhood?"

"That his mother and and all of his sisters died when he was an infant." Elizabeth shook her head in sympathy. "Anyone who lost their family so young would be challenged to trust in any other person, never mind that he was sold into slavery to a Moor as a child."

Malcolm choked, his shocked reaction drawing Elizabeth's gaze. "He told you this?"

Elizabeth nodded.

"Is it true?" Catriona asked her husband.

"I have no idea," Malcolm admitted, granting Elizabeth a wary glance himself. "But if he has told you more in a matter of days than he has admitted to me in six years, I cannot blame him for being leery of your company."

Catriona eyed Elizabeth, a smile curving her lips. "Perhaps you have enchanted him."

Elizabeth smiled herself, seeing evidence to support her beliefs in this. She knew she had to speak to Rafael again before she left Ravensmuir this day.

She looked back and saw Rafael glance up, as if he sensed her scrutiny. He folded his arms across his chest as he returned her stare. He looked aloof and indifferent, but Elizabeth was not fooled.

Afraid. Aye, Rafael was afraid and she thought she knew why.

Chapter Twelve

Malcolm escorted the women back toward the keep, but still the men lingered near the fresh grave on the point. Rafael doubted he was the sole one thinking that it could have been any of them fallen in that fight. He cast a glance over the company, two dozen mercenaries and yet more squires to service them, and noted the consideration in their expressions.

There was, perhaps, only one foe they could not defeat.

The wind was relentless and cold in this place, more than sufficient to make Rafael shiver, even on a summer's day. Ranulf had stood for the mass, appearing to be as robust as ever, but he sat down on a stone now and ran a hand over his eyes. He looked pale and strained, and his vigor had deserted him again. Rafael checked his skin, but was relieved to find that it remained cool.

It was the loss of blood that had weakened him, but given that there was no fire beneath his flesh, he would be hale again in time.

"Will I die, sorcerer?" Ranulf asked, his tone teasing.

"Of course," Rafael replied. "But not of this injury."

They chuckled together, the other men sitting or leaning nearby.

Rafael looked back at the new keep and narrowed his eyes as he found Lady Elizabeth openly watching him. His heart skipped but he kept his expression impassive. "I suppose it is time to leave," he said with apparent idleness. "To seek new battles and patrons."

He expected a chorus of assent, for they were all inclined to move frequently, but Ranulf shook his head. "Not me."

"What do you mean?" Tristan asked, though Rafael was not surprised by this choice.

"I mean to remain," Ranulf continued. "I asked Malcolm last night and he agreed that I could stay. I will serve as a man-at-arms when he has need of one, but build myself a little cottage over there. He intends to have a village and my abode will be the first within it."

Rafael shook his head. Though he understood the reason for this choice, he doubted that such a life would satisfy his comrade for long. "You cannot mean to completely abandon the life we have led."

"I can and do. I had thought of it before." Ranulf lifted his bandaged hand. "But this only increases my conviction."

"Then who will fight with Greek fire?" Bertrand asked.

Ranulf shrugged. "My days with such explosives are done. One of you will have to learn of it before you depart."

Rafael surveyed his fellows, again expecting to hear of impatience to be gone.

Tristan spared a glance to the new grave. "It could have been any of us," he murmured.

"Or all of us," Amaury agreed. "Reynaud simply ran out of luck. He did not err, and his competence was never in doubt."

"It is a timely warning," Tristan agreed. He looked at Rafael. "I mean to remain, as well. I grow no younger, after all."

"And I will remain here as well," Amaury agreed, before Rafael could protest. "The hunting is good. It reminds me of home in that, but I am not welcome there. I will train Malcolm's hounds, if he will have me, and also serve as man-at-arms as necessary."

"His uncle at Inverfyre breeds falcons," Tristan supplied to Amaury's obvious delight. "To train falcons again is my greatest dream. I remember hunting days with my father's court and would ride forth thus again."

"I thought you bastard-born," Amaury said to Tristan.

"And so I am, but my father kept me in his household."

"If he had acknowledged you, you would not be here."

"Indeed, if he had acknowledged me, he might not have lost all he held dear." Tristan shrugged. "He had a son by his young wife in his dotage, so cast me out then. He fell ill, she claimed the regency, but knew naught of war. His neighbors attacked, killing man, wife and child before claiming his keep." Tristan's gaze was cool. "I could have defended him and his holding, and I would have done so, but he deemed my lineage insufficient to suffer my presence in his hall once I grew to manhood. In the end, the loss was his."

Rafael would guess that the old lord had feared his bastard son, for Tristan was a ruthless opponent. His heart was loyal but well hidden from casual view. His father might have been the first to underestimate his determination to defend those he cared about, but he had not been the last.

Still, these tidings defied belief. "All three of you mean to stay?" Rafael asked, only to have Ranulf, Amaury and Tristan nod.

"You will not see me lingering in these lands," Giorgio said and Rafael was momentarily relieved. "Guilia is with child," that mercenary admitted then and the woman in question blushed. Rafael blinked, for he had never imagined anything could make Guilia blush. "She would return home, or as near to it as we can manage." Giorgio spoke gruffly, then grimaced comically. "She would be *wedded*."

The men hooted and laughed, teasing Giorgio, whose color rose.

He raised a hand finally to silence them, his good nature restored. "And so it shall be done. It *is* my son she bears," he said as the other men teased him. "And truly, my taste for other women has dimmed since I took Guilia to bed." He smiled at Guilia and she blushed crimson, blinking back tears as she took his large hand in her smaller one.

"I thank you, Giorgio," she said, her voice even more husky than usual.

That mercenary nodded and spoke gently. "A woman needs familiarity in her time. We will travel south with you, Rafael, but I will not return to fighting, at least not as yet."

"Ever," Guilia insisted, but Giorgio's gaze slid to meet Rafael's in silent warning.

Rafael understood. Giorgio did not know how else he would feed his new family. This companion would join him in battle, once he was wedded and saw his new wife safely settled in some abode in territories more familiar to her.

It was a timely reminder of how few choices men of his ilk truly had. It was rare for one to make the leap to both security and respectability as Malcolm had, but that man had rare advantages in both his family and the holding that had come to his name.

Rafael reviewed the company, calculating their power. Even if Ranulf, Amaury and Tristan remained at Kinfairlie, they would still offer a formidable force. He had no doubt they could find employ on the Continent. Most warlords would not even notice that there were four fewer in their company than previously, and the repute of the Sable League was impressive.

Then Bertrand shrugged. "I, too, find I have little taste for our former life. Malcolm could do with a few blades pledged to his service, and I think mine will be another of them."

"As will be mine," Gunter agreed. "I like it here."

"What is this?" Rafael asked in dismay.

"I like seeing that one of us has gained a reward," Gunter said gruffly. "It does a heart good after so many years of battle to witness peace and prosperity, especially come to one of our own."

The others nodded agreement, and for a moment, Rafael feared he would ride out alone. "Surely this cannot be so. Surely you have not all become soft and complacent."

"Peace is the trouble," Gunter said. "The Continent is thick with it, my friend. There is little labor to be had for a fighting man in these times."

"There is no such thing as peace, not so long as men draw breath," Rafael argued, for he knew that to be true.

"Why else do you think we traveled this far?" Louis asked, his manner more cheerful than the situation deserved. "No curiosity would have been sufficient to tempt us away from well-paid labor, to be sure."

Amaury laughed and clapped Rafael on the shoulder. "Do not overestimate your appeal, my old friend. We did not miss you so much as that."

Rafael frowned, not liking the direction of this conversation in the least. "There *must* be fighting. The King of France cannot have allied with the King of England."

"But they both run short of coin," Gunter said with a grim shake of his head. "Work that will not be paid is worse than no work at all."

"A man could die in such labor, with no compensation at all," Amaury agreed, and all of them looked again at Reynaud's grave. "'Tis an unholy bargain."

"Rodrigo sits at the right hand of Charles VI," confided Bertrand, to Rafael's relief. That was good news. "Your old comrade will find you labor, to be sure, though it is less clear he will be able to compensate you."

"I trust him with my life," Rafael said. "And have done so many times. Who of you will ride south with me?" There was no chorus of agreement, but instead, the men looked from one to the other.

"I will remain here," Ranulf said, waving his bandaged hand at the keep of Ravensmuir. "Who knows? I might find a wench to have me and become wedded like Giorgio."

Remaining at Ravensmuir was precisely what Rafael did not wish to do. He tried to convince his comrades to depart. "'Tis fiercely cold here in winter," he reminded them. "I feared my very blood would freeze."

"As cold as Bavaria, then?" Louis asked with a wince.

"Colder," Rafael affirmed, turning his attention upon the one close comrade who had not indicated a desire to remain. He gestured to the sea. "With a wind fit to turn your skin blue."

The men shivered, their gazes flicking between the grave, the sea and the keep.

Their silence convinced Rafael that he was building consensus. "I say we head south again, for Rodrigo will ensure our employment," he suggested. "If the prospect of payment is low, we will insist upon being paid in advance. Our repute is sufficient that it will be done. Malcolm is hale enough here, and we have need of adventures anew." He winked at his fellows. "Not to mention more material rewards. If barons do not honor their debts, we shall take what we are owed from the spoils. So it has been before, and so it shall be again!"

To his dismay, there was no rousing agreement from his closest fellows. The others in the Sable League nodded agreement, but even their enthusiasm was less than Rafael might have hoped.

A lack of enthusiasm could see a man dead in their trade.

Ranulf grimaced. "I have tired of the life, truth be told. A man could become accustomed to awakening in the same hall each morning, and knowing where he will be laid to rest. From this point forward, I will raise a blade solely in defense of my own home."

There was assent that time, at least one from the men Rafael knew best. To Rafael's disappointment, Louis added his voice to that of Bertrand, Tristan, Gunter and Amaury.

Rafael straightened with purpose and eyed the rest of the company. There were still fifteen of them to ride out, even after the deaths of Reynaud and Nigel, the victim of the earl's spy. and despite six men staying at Ravensmuir in Malcolm's service.

"I will not remain," he said. "I would ride south this very day."

"I would stay until Malcolm's nuptials are celebrated," Guilia said, entreating Giorgio's agreement with a glance.

That mercenary grinned. "A couple more days, Rafael," he said. "On Sunday, we shall ride out."

Though Rafael chafed at another delay, he did not want to leave without Giorgio. It would not be wise for a foreign mercenary to travel the length of England alone with a pregnant woman. He might be beset at night, and though Guilia was strong, it would be best for all of them to wait a few days more.

Much as he wished otherwise.

Rafael raised his voice to address the remainder of the company. "Come with me to France, where we shall find labor and riches anew!" The bulk of the Sable League cheered and stamped their feet with enthusiasm. Rafael shook a finger at his fellows who had chosen to stay. "And you will all regret your choice when you hear of the fortunes I have won."

It could not be so difficult to hold to his resolve for three more days.

Could it?

ða

Rafael did not see Elizabeth in the shadows of the entry to Ravensmuir's hall. She stood utterly still and her dark garb blended with the shadows so well that he jumped when she spoke.

She noted as much, of course, and took a pleasure in his reaction that irked him.

"I like that you told a tale of a man redeemed by love," she said, speaking quickly as if she feared to be interrupted. Rafael saw that the horses were being led from the stables for her and Father Malachy, who spoke with Malcolm in the bailey.

"He was no mere man but the King of Persia.," Rafael replied, guessing what she would suggest. "A mercenary has naught in common with a king."

"Except fear," she replied smoothly. "You both share a fear of trusting another. His distrust was rooted in betrayal, as must yours be."

"No one has betrayed me."

"Perhaps you did not give any soul an opportunity, for circumstance betrayed you before you took your first step."

He surveyed her, knowing she would not abandon this argument readily. "One or two admissions and you believe you know all of my secrets."

She smiled. "I know more of them than my brother, and he has fought by your side for six years." Her eyes widened, her confidence infuriating. "Yet you and I have spoken only a few times, over a few days."

"You make much of little," Rafael said, ensuring that his tone was dismissive. In truth, he was alarmed, for he had not realized she had learned so much of him.

"I see truth you would disguise," she replied. "I see that your fear is rooted in your experience, for much has been taken from you and you have seen more taken from others." She regarded him steadily, looking mysterious and wise. "But if you refuse to care for anything, then you have naught to lose. Your King of Persia did not care for the loss of his wives, not until he came to love Scheherazade. That love would make him vulnerable."

Rafael smiled down at her, disguising the fact that she had named a potent truth. To be sure, hearing this notion uttered aloud did make his heart race, as if in fear. How could a man face his days, knowing himself responsible for a marvel like Elizabeth? "Indeed, you can spin a fanciful tale yourself, my lady," he said, as if her words had less impact than they did. Rafael gestured to the portal, for her mare was there, and Elizabeth put her hand upon his arm as if she would allow herself to be escorted there with nary another word.

He knew she would not fall silent so readily, no less that she would not be biddable.

Indeed, Elizabeth's spirit was the key to his admiration of her. Even in this moment, he awaited her inevitable challenge with no small anticipation. It was curious that in this lady's presence, he felt more keenly alive than ever he had.

"But think of this, Rafael," Elizabeth murmured as they stepped into the sunlight together and he loved the sound of his name upon her lips. "What then is the point of having lived a life? Would you die at the end of your days knowing that you had been as a seed in the wind, risking your life for whatever cause paid the best, but leaving no other mark in the world of your presence?" She shook her head. "Indeed, you must put little value upon your life to risk it so routinely and for matters not of your own concern." Her grip tightened slightly on his arm and her voice dropped to an intimate tone. "I think your life worth far more that you appear to."

Rafael did not know what to say to that. All his life, he had been discarded like a worthless creature, and he had scarce dared to expect much for himself beyond survival. Ibrahim had told Rafael repeatedly that he would have been sold, if he had been worth a single coin, if there had been even one interested buyer.

Elizabeth paused out of earshot of the others and met his gaze. Rafael saw that she was not unaware of the tumult she awakened within him. "Would you pass from this life without having loved another? Would you pass from this life without having achieved any goal that could be linked with your name?" She gestured to the keep. "Even if Malcolm had died, he would have left a rebuilt holding, a wife with a title, a son with a legacy. His life would have achieved much. What will be your legacy?"

Rafael thought of all those souls in Hell, the souls of those he had killed and knew that this was his sole legacy. He had taken people from this mortal realm, no more than that. It was startling to consider that administering death was his only achievement.

"What then is the point of awakening each day?" Elizabeth smiled as Rafael eyed her in dismay. "Indeed, sir, you might as well take up a needle and learn to embroider, locked in a high tower alone."

Their gazes locked for a potent moment and Rafael knew Elizabeth was aware she had found a mark.

Did she guess that she challenged all he believed to be true?

Elizabeth then moved away from him, put her hand in Malcolm's and stepped into the ostler's grip to mount her mare. Demoiselle stamped and snorted at even her slight weight in the saddle, but Elizabeth controlled the horse with such mastery that Rafael was again impressed. She spared him one last simmering glance, as if to dare him to be the measure of man she could love, then turned the horse adroitly. She touched her heels to the beast's side, without waiting for Father Malachy, and sent the mare galloping toward Kinfairlie.

Rafael found himself watching Elizabeth until she was out of sight.

And still he looked after her yet more.

Was she right that he held the key to changing his own future? He scarce dared to believe it, but Rafael did know one thing in truth: he did not want the dead in Hell to be the only mark of his having been in the world.

And having seen that Hell existed, he did fear to be judged.

Perhaps his little angel truly had lifted the scales from his eyes.

She certainly had made him wonder: if he could leave whatever legacy he desired to survive after his days were ended, what would it be?

૨૦

Elizabeth was in her chamber alone that evening, unable to suppress her agitation. She had a feeling that she had made a difference on this day in talking to Rafael, that she had convinced him to change his course, though he had not declared any such thing aloud. She was restless, wanting to see into her own future, but knowing she must be patient.

Patience was elusive on this night, to be sure. She extinguished her lantern, hoping the darkness would soothe her, but found herself pacing the floor instead. She found her thoughts turning yet again to the mirror that Finvarra had dropped. It was a curious thing but even though she was resolved to simply keep it, she could not stop thinking about it.

She had even dreamed of the mirror the night before, of it casting a radiance across Kinfairlie like moonlight. She had awakened with a desire to see whether it truly could cast such a light. Though she had ignored the urge that morning, for she had needed to hasten to catch Father Malachy, on this night, she could not deny her curiosity. She had tucked it into the bottom of the one trunk that was solely her own the night before, wanting to ensure that it was safely stored and also that no one in her family had a glimpse of it.

It was strange how she felt a need to guard it jealously, no less to keep it secret.

Elizabeth opened the trunk and dug into it, knowing exactly where to find the hidden prize. She was before the trunk where her kirtles were stored, her fingers just on the cool frame of the mirror, when there was a single rap on the portal. Elizabeth pushed the mirror deeper into her stored garments, dropped the lid of the trunk, then turned to face the portal. She did not doubt that she looked guilty of some trick, with her hands folded behind herself and her expression carefully neutral, but she had little time to compose herself.

Rosamunde opened the door, her gaze sweeping over the chamber, then lingering on Elizabeth. "I thought you might be awake," she said, then closed the portal and leaned back against it. She carried a lantern and its light diminished the shadows in the room. "Do I interrupt something?"

"Of course not." Elizabeth fought the urge to squirm beneath her aunt's perceptive gaze.

Her aunt was still dressed for the evening meal, her red hair braided and coiled beneath a gossamer veil of pale gold, secured in place by a golden circlet. Her kirtle was deepest blue, hemmed with rich golden embroidery, and had long sleeves with cuffs that trailed to the floor. Around her waist was bound a girdle, once again of gold, but studded with gems that Elizabeth knew must be of great value. There was a plain gold ring upon one of Rosamunde's fingers, though she wore no other jewelry.

Elizabeth felt plain in comparison, for she had not changed from the simple garb she had donned for Reynaud's funeral.

Rosamunde pursed her lips, considering, then appeared to accept this claim. "How large this room appears now that you no longer share it with four sisters and a maid," she said, smiling easily as she walked around the room. "Do you not find it lonely?"

Elizabeth shrugged and folded her arms around herself. "It is sometimes a relief to not have to share every thought and every frippery." She could readily imagine that Isabella would have stolen that mirror while Elizabeth was at Ravensmuir this day, for Isabella had always had an uncanny ability to find any treasure, no matter how well it was hidden.

Rosamunde chuckled and sat on a stool to consider her niece. "Indeed. I can well imagine that." Again, she studied Elizabeth. "I thought we might talk, while others prepare for bed."

"Of what?"

"They said you had fallen ill," Rosamunde said with care.

"That you had faded like a maiden snared in a dream. I came back to Kinfairlie because of Alexander's concern."

Elizabeth was surprised by this and touched that her aunt had traveled so far in her concern. She moved a stool and sat beside her aunt, feeling loved by her kin. She supposed that Rafael had never had such a sensation and felt a pang of sympathy for him.

"I did not know he had written to you of me."

Rosamunde smiled. "He wrote of many things, he always does, but I was concerned by what he did not confide."

"How so?"

"He did not send news of your nuptials." Elizabeth glanced up to find her aunt watching her closely. "Why do you not wed, Elizabeth?"

Elizabeth heaved a sigh, knowing this to be her opportunity to seek advice, but fearing that her aunt had become conventional in her own marriage. She certainly looked more like a noblewoman in these days, and Elizabeth could not help but wonder how deep the change in Rosamunde was.

"I have not met a man I wished to wed," Elizabeth confessed. "Until now."

"Which is why you do not look so ill as I expected, given Alexander's concern. Indeed, you look exactly as I recall. Is this the influence of love?"

Elizabeth felt herself flush. "Perhaps."

Rosamunde smiled. "And who is the fortunate man?"

Elizabeth saw no reason to hide the truth. "Malcolm's comrade, Rafael Rodriguez."

Rosamunde's brows rose. "A mercenary and a Spaniard." She shook her head and smiled. "Alexander cannot be pleased by this!"

"He is not," Elizabeth admitted, reassured by her aunt's wicked smile. The entire tale spilled from her lips, then, for she knew that Rosamunde had been held captive by Finvarra in the realm of the Fae. She trusted Rosamunde not only with the details of the night at Ravensmuir, but of the ribbons she had seen with Rafael, and his refusal to accept all she offered.

By the time she had confessed all of this, her aunt was the one pacing the floor of the chamber. "He does indeed seem to have honor in his soul," she said, though her tone did not ring with the optimism Elizabeth had hoped to hear. "But you must recognize, Elizabeth, that his concerns have merit. You may not be pleased with the results of your choice once it is made, for you may not see all of the truth."

"I trust the ribbons." Elizabeth did not add that she did not trust Finvarra.

"Where will you live?"

"Wherever he lives." She had not thought of traveling to Europe with Rafael, but the notion had an appeal. She did not expect that Finvarra could pursue her there.

Rosamunde considered her, her fingers tapping on her own elbow. "It seems that this Rafael believes you to have expectations he cannot hope to fulfill. Perhaps he does not wish to see you disappointed."

"Perhaps he is wrong about my expectations. Perhaps he sees those of Alexander."

"Perhaps so," Rosamunde agreed. She perched beside Elizabeth and took her niece's hand within her own. "I have lived with much risk in my time, Elizabeth, but the greatest peril is that of love. There is no pain greater than a love that is not returned, or the rejection of the man you adore beyond all others."

Elizabeth swallowed and nodded, knowing her aunt spoke of Tynan, the former Laird of Ravensmuir, who had rejected her.

"So, know that I grant this counsel as one who has misplaced her love, survived heartbreak and found love again. I would not surrender my memories of Tynan or our time together, however ill-fated it proved to be. Those days and nights are yet precious to me. But I have a happiness now with Padraig beyond all of that, a contentment unexpected and a confidence in his affection that fills my life with pleasure and satisfaction." She pressed Elizabeth's hands. "I understand the allure of what might not be gained. I understand the desire to risk all in pursuit of a goal. But I tell you, Elizabeth, that if you pursue this man with no regard to any cost to yourself, your every sacrifice might still be insufficient to win his heart." She smiled. "And if it is not, then I entreat you to come to me for solace, for I will understand why you made the choice you did and I will know the pain you are enduring."

A lump rose in Elizabeth's throat. "I will."

"Good." Rosamunde kissed Elizabeth's cheek, then nodded.

"And now, you must think of what you will say and what you will do." Her gaze was clear as she held Elizabeth's regard. "If you could say one thing to Rafael to change his thinking of you and your expectations, what would it be?"

"Because all rides upon that one opportunity?"

"Because you cannot know how many chances you will have," Rosamunde said. "When you take a risk, wager all in your first opportunity, for there may never be the chance to try again."

There was the counsel Elizabeth had sought. She nodded, her thoughts churning as she strove to identify what she would say. The mirror was forgotten for the moment, Rosamunde's counsel banishing the thought of it.

Rosamunde stood, then paused beside Elizabeth before walking away. "Perhaps you should strive to make your similarities clear to him, rather than your differences. He will see the disparity in your upbringing, but what draws you to him? In what sphere are you the same?"

Elizabeth knew the reply immediately. It was in the lust for adventure and experience that she and Rafael were of one mind. She had erred in letting him believe that she would meet him abed to force him to offer for her hand. There was no trickery in this: Elizabeth wanted to sample passion, and she wanted to do it first with him.

She had to make it clear to Rafael that her desire was solely to know what such pleasure was like, that she, like he, desired only to experience all that could be savored. She did believe that there was honor in him, and she did believe that he would not abandon her after they were intimate, but that was not the reason she would meet him abed.

Elizabeth would risk all, in the hope of gaining his love, but even if she failed, she would *know*.

And that might be sufficient to keep her warm at night.

Claire Delacroix

Saturday, June 26, 1428

Feast Day of Saint Hilarius, Bishop of Poitiers, and the martyrs, Saint John and Saint Paul.

Chapter Thirteen

Elizabeth's challenge burned in Rafael's thoughts for the days before the wedding. *Afraid.* It was an astonishing word to have associated with himself, and yet there was a resonance in her charge that hinted at truth.

Love made the king vulnerable. There was the root of the matter. A man who prized any possession, be it wife, child or holding, could have his prize stripped from him. Worse, it could be used against him. Wives were captured, children tormented, holdings stolen. Rafael had seen many a man broken by such a loss and had resolved long ago that it would not happen to him.

What would be your legacy? There was the most potent truth of it. Rafael did not want those souls in Hell to be his legacy. As ever, Elizabeth had found a way to make him reconsider his choices.

But to change his life was no small thing to expect, and it would not be readily done. What options had he? What skills? What opportunities?

The questions haunted Rafael, and he labored hard, as if to outrun them and their implications. He hunted with vigor, riding out with Amaury both days and bringing back so many carcasses that Catriona cried for relief in the kitchens. He tended wounds and polished armor, honed blades and brushed steeds. He worked until he ached to his marrow, and then he worked yet more.

He did not sleep overly well, for Franz seemed determined to keep him company at night. He cursed the fact that he had to remain at Ravensmuir until Sunday, then was heartened that he would have one last glimpse of his angel.

Rafael knew that Elizabeth was not afraid of him, not even of his anger. Indeed, when she provoked his temper, she seemed to see it as a mark of her power over him. Rafael suspected she was right in that, for never had there been a woman who could stir his responses as adeptly as she.

He was resolved to be composed and implacable on the day of the weddings, lest she take encouragement from his manner. Aye, he had to be polite and indifferent. She did not need to know that she had put him in turmoil, not until he had decided upon his course.

Rafael was tempted, sorely tempted, to give Elizabeth what she wanted of him, but he knew that could only lead them both to ruin. First, any seduction would be an insult to his host and comrade to despoil that man's sister. Secondly, he could not wed Elizabeth honestly, not without a holding. Thirdly, even if he had possessed the ability and the inclination to wed her, Rafael knew such a match would be doomed. She believed him to be some gallant knight, and the only result of time they spent together would be her disappointment. She would end like Ursula, and of all the sins he had committed, the destruction of Elizabeth's hope would be the worst.

That would be a rejection of all Rafael held to be good and right.

He was so concerned with the notion of his legacy that Rafael barely noticed the other change in his thinking: for the first time in all his days, he was concerned about his right to wed.

꽈

Rafael was prepared when the party came from Kinfairlie, or so he thought. He donned his best garb, black velvet and white linen, a black tabard worked with a line of gold upon the hem and a black cloak lined with shimmering gold. His boots gleamed and the gold rings on his fingers shone. He stood with his fellows as the party arrived from Kinfairlie, content to lose himself within the company. He anticipated that all of Malcolm's family would come from Kinfairlie, prepared to be entertained and fed richly. He also anticipated that the brother Alexander would not have fully surrendered his disdain, though he would eat and drink at Malcolm's board. Rafael expected that Malcolm's trade would cast a long shadow over his family's view of him, and his relationship with them.

But Rafael was due to be surprised.

The Laird and Lady of Kinfairlie rode at the head of the

procession, the coats of their black destriers gleaming in the sun. The lady was fair, like Catriona, her hair coiled up beneath her veil. A pair of squires rode before them on palfreys with the banner of Kinfairlie held high. Another noble pair rode behind them, the woman's hair red of hue and the man swarthy. There were children aplenty, and truly Rafael did not trouble to count them. They were richly garbed and as fair as the Lady of Kinfairlie, carried by servants riding palfreys.

Elizabeth rode her mare alongside Alexander and Eleanor, and Rafael again was proud to note how well she rode. She made it look effortless to manage the very large mare, but Rafael knew Demoiselle was not such a complacent mount as that. The three black steeds were each as wondrous as the next, their trappings black and silver, their necks arched and manes braided. To see them together was a marvel. Truly, Rafael had never seen their ilk, and he acknowledged that the tales of the steeds of Ravensmuir were based in fact.

Elizabeth herself was dressed in green and silver, the hue of her kirtle making her eyes shine like emeralds. Her gaze leaped immediately to him, lingering in a way that revealed he had not disappeared into the company as readily as he had hoped, but Rafael determinedly turned his attention to the rest of the party.

His heart skipped, though, his awareness of Elizabeth as keen as ever. He would never forget her, that was for certain. He wondered then if the knotted ribbons between them were a cruel jest of the King of the Dead, a ploy to see her destroyed in this realm for daring to speak aloud in his court. Elizabeth, of course, would believe the ribbons to be a reliable sign of the course she should take, and it was clear she would heed no warnings. What if the dark king wished only to see her ruined, so that she had no choice but to choose to enter his realm forever?

The notion made a fearsome sense. If these beings were djinn, such trickery was most characteristic.

And if these beings were djinn, not demons, then Ravensmuir was no portal to Hell. Indeed, Hell might not truly exist. He could return to his conviction that he would never be judged, that there was only life and oblivion and naught in between save the smoky illusion of the djinns.

Save for the companionship of Franz. That could have been a

gift from the dark king, an illusion sent to trouble him. Rafael realized he wanted to see that dark-bearded king defeated more than he had desired anything in a long time.

Nigh as much as he desired Elizabeth. He could not possess her himself, not for any duration at least, but perhaps he could thwart the dark king's scheme to claim her.

It would be worth a try.

The arriving party seemed numerous indeed, and Rafael had a moment to think that they would eat Malcolm's larder bare. But then, behind all the relations and servants and children came wagons of meat, bread and ale. Alexander offered all to Malcolm with grace, and Rafael was astonished.

His lady wife, Eleanor, had brought seed for Ravensmuir's fields, which lay fallow, so that the keep could be well provisioned for the winter ahead. Rafael was stunned by the generosity of this wedding gift.

Indeed, he had never known people to aid each other like this, to offer practical gifts of considerable expense simply to be of assistance. Rafael was awed by their generosity, so awed that he did not see Elizabeth bring her mare to his side.

"You look surprised," she said, a laugh in her voice. "I confess I would never have imagined it possible for you to be so."

Rafael glanced up at her dancing eyes and could not hide his amazement. He gestured to the wagons, fairly groaning beneath the weight of provisions brought from Kinfairlie. "Such generosity," he murmured. "I thought your brother disapproved of Malcolm."

"And so he does, but he would have Malcolm remain and restore Ravensmuir. The task will not be readily done." Her chin set with a resolve Rafael began to associate with her. "We are kin, Rafael, and there is no bond stronger than blood. We disagree and disapprove, but always we are family, and always we defend and aid each other."

Rafael let his gaze rove over the provisions again, feeling the lack in his own life. He had no kin. He had no family. There was no one upon whom he could rely. He had comrades, to be sure, but if they were better compensated to betray him, most would do so. He had accepted that truth long ago and knew that he could rely solely upon himself.

But Malcolm had gained more than a keep, a wife and a son.

He had returned to family, where he would never be alone again.

For the first time, Rafael felt envy for his former comrade.

He realized Elizabeth was watching him closely. She leaned down from the saddle to whisper to him, her eyes bright. "Is there no one upon whom you can rely?" Her question was gentle, as if she felt compassion for him, and Rafael bristled.

"I have need of no one at my back," he insisted, knowing that while it might be true in this moment, that might not be the case forever.

"But do you not feel the lack of a family?"

"A man cannot miss what he has never known."

Elizabeth bit her lip and eyed him for a moment, an unexpected compassion in her clear gaze. She straightened then at the sound of hoof beats. Her features lit and she pointed across the moor. "Look!" she whispered, awe in her voice.

Rafael looked and was awed in his turn. Alexander had turned back and pointed to the road between the two sister estates. Rafael saw the dust rising on the road and guessed what gift Alexander brought.

The legendary steeds of Ravensmuir, the great black destriers that had been bred at this estate for generations, were returning to the stables where they belonged.

There had been a time when Rafael had believed these horses must be a fable, for their repute seemed too great. And Malcolm, when they had met, had ridden a good steed but not a spectacular one. When he had learned of Malcolm's origins, he had taken this of confirmation that the Ravensmuir horses were not so wondrous as was oft told.

But on their arrival at Ravensmuir, Malcolm had confessed that he could not have risked one of his family's horses in war. Now, as Rafael watched the great hooves of the returning herd pound the road, he understood why. Their manes and tails were braided and they had been brushed until they were glossy. They arched their necks, even as they ran, such joy and confidence in their stride that no man who ever admired a horse could have averted his gaze.

Indeed, he had never seen a sight so magnificent. Rafael took a step forward in his admiration and heard the curse fall from his lips. "Zounds!" He barely recognized his own voice, so filled was it with marvel. He was glad to still be at Ravensmuir, glad he had lingered the extra days, glad he had the chance to see these creatures with his own eyes.

Elizabeth laughed beside him. Her mare was small compared to these stallions, and as they tossed their heads, nostrils flaring and dark eyes flashing, Rafael recognized that the mare had not their temper either. The mare stamped, restless to run as well, but Elizabeth held her in place. It was one thing to see Alexander's fine mount, but quite another to see dozens of these beasts racing toward Ravensmuir.

They were ridden by ostlers and squires, young men who laughed with such delight as they brought the horses to a milling halt that Rafael guessed they seldom had ridden their charges at full gallop. They halted before Ravensmuir's gates, the horses snorting and stamping in their impatience to run yet more, their harness gleaming in the sun.

Malcolm was clearly close to being overwhelmed with emotion by the sight of them, and he walked through the herd, touching one and then another, stroking a nose and patting a rump. Rafael realized that he would know many of these individual steeds, for he had been gone six or seven years. By the way he was bitten and nudged, they recalled him as well. It was a joyous reunion and a noisy one, and to Rafael's relief, there was much to be done in seeing the steeds settled in the stables again.

That Malcolm had such wealth to his hand was wondrous.

His comrade's future at Ravensmuir was secured.

But that was not all the joy that would come to Malcolm on this day. But moments later, Rafael saw wonder light his comrade's features as the cries of birds filled the air.

Malcolm turned and raised his hands as ravens soared out of the blue sky. They might have been conjured from the very air, so suddenly did they appear. They circled the new tower of Ravensmuir, as if to inspect it, then settled on the roof, so unruffled that they might always have been there.

One swooped low over Malcolm and gave a cry that made that man laugh aloud.

"It is a sign," Elizabeth said, her eyes bright with unshed tears. She looked radiant in her pleasure, and once again, Rafael thought of angels touching down to earth. He could have watched her all the day and night.

"How so?"

"The presence of the ravens is believed to be an endorsement of the Laird of Ravensmuir," she confessed. "Malcolm left when the ravens abandoned the holding, for he felt they had judged him and found him lacking."

It was such a whimsical notion that Rafael did not know what to say.

Though he knew what it was to feel that one's efforts had fallen short.

"But now they are returned, and the horses are back, and all will be well," she concluded.

"I apologize that I thought ill of Alexander's intent," Rafael said formally, for he had misjudged the man.

"I am not." Elizabeth laughed again at his glance of surprise. "Why else do you think the steeds returned?" Her eyes sparkled with such vigor that Rafael could not avert his gaze. She leaned toward him as if they had conspired together and laughed so that he was tempted to join her. "We contrived this together."

"How can this be?"

"I told Alexander that you wondered at his intent, and he was so insulted that he called for the horses to be prepared to journey on this day." She was so merry that Rafael was transfixed. "It is your doing, Rafael, that they are here, and I hope you are glad of what you have wrought."

It was enticing to imagine as much, but Rafael did not fully believe any credit was his.

"I say it is your doing," he retorted, unable to keep himself from smiling at her. "And I thank you, for I am glad to have seen their splendor with my own eyes."

"It is what we have in common," Elizabeth confided, her words startling Rafael. "I would see all the marvels of the world and seek both adventure and passion. I would stand witness to all the fables made truth, to all the riches and all the poverty, just to know that it exists." A knowing glint lit her eyes. "For truly, what merit is a life lived sheltered? I fear such a life would feel longer than it was and I for one have no desire to endure it." She wrinkled her nose. "I would rather have a palace of memories when I die than a perfected embroidery stitch." Her smile turned wicked then, the sight making his heart clench, then she walked the horse away from him, her head held eye.

She was clearly confident that she had snared his attention, and Rafael, even knowing as much, could not keep from watching her go.

What could he give her in return for the gift of understanding she granted to him? Not what she asked of him, for that would be ignoble, but there had to be some other gift that would demonstrate his esteem.

Something she would remember, even treasure, after he was gone.

Rafael bit back a smile, for he had an inkling what that perfect gift might be. It was one he would enjoy delivering, to be certain, and one that would shape Elizabeth's expectations for the rest of her days and nights.

୨ଈ

That conversation was a fine beginning to Elizabeth's view. She liked when Rafael eyed her with such intensity, and she liked even better when he slowly smiled, as if he might devour her in one bite.

Nay, he would make a feast of it, ensuring that she knew she was being claimed. Elizabeth shivered in delight at the notion. She liked how his gaze burned into hers, how he was becoming less mysterious to her with every exchange, how his very presence made her heart skip and all seem bright around her. She felt so vital with him that she had no doubt of her choice.

This would be the night. She had only to contrive their meeting.

The wedding vows were exchanged and the mass celebrated, the midday meal served with ceremony and the wine from Kinfairlie consumed. It was a fine day and the company was reluctant to leave the board and the camaraderie to be found there. Elizabeth was glad to see Malcolm so pleased. There was a lull in the conversation, a moment when some soul would call for a tale, and Elizabeth seized the moment to draw Rafael's eye back to herself.

She rose to her feet and raised her voice. "Rafael Rodriguez, when last we sat at this board, we heard the *Song of Roland*, and you declared Charlemagne to be no hero as you knew heroes to be. Would you tell us of a hero you admire?"

The men broke into applause at this notion. In this, Elizabeth knew she would discern more of Rafael's truth, for whatsoever a man admired revealed his secret heart.

As she had expected, Rafael took his time before he replied. He finished his cup of wine, then swept to his feet and bowed to her. "I am no teller of tales, nor am I a troubadour, but I cannot deny a lady her request."

"You told a fine tale the other day," Elizabeth reminded him.

Rafael's smile flashed, making him look dangerous and unpredictable. "Perhaps I was inspired by the curiosity of a beautiful maiden," he said.

The company cheered again and Rafael strolled down the length of the hall to halt before her. He was so handsome and virile, his gaze so steady upon her, that once again Elizabeth's toes curled in her slippers. He offered his hand and she placed hers within it, feeling almost dizzy when he kissed the back of her fingers.

Then he spun to face the company, his short cloak flaring out around him, his steps measured. He pivoted to face her and smiled at her so that her heart fluttered. "In Spain, my lady Elizabeth, we tell of the greatest hero of all, one Rodrigo Diaz de Vívar."

"Rodrigo Diaz de Vívar," Elizabeth whispered, finding the words exotic on her tongue.

"*El Cid!*" roared one of the mercenaries and a group of them thumped their fists on the board in approval. Elizabeth glanced to the Sable League in confusion for she did not know this tale.

Rafael inclined his head to them. "*Mío Cid,*" he corrected. "*Il Campeador.*"

"What does that mean?" Elizabeth asked after she repeated both phrases.

Rafael smiled. "They say he was called *Mío Cid,* by the Moors, for they so admired his skills at making war that even in defeat, they acknowledged his valor. There were Moors also serving in his armies for the same reason. *Sidi* is their word for champion, but all the men of Castile I have ever known have called him *Mío Cid*, my lord or champion, a variant of the Moorish. *Il Campeador* is the Castilian for *the champion*, and is the title used by troubadours." He lifted a brow and Elizabeth nodded that she understood, impatient for him to continue.

"I like tales of champions," she said with a smile. "Particularly of those men who have chosen to be champions."

Rafael inclined his head, then paced in front of the high table. His voice was rich and carried over the hall easily. "Rodrigo was born in Vívar, a town near Burgos, in the years when the Moors held much of the southern lands known as Andalusia. He was raised in the court of the Castilian king, Ferdinand I, and later in the court of Ferdinand's son, Sancho. It was there he learned to treat women with dignity and honor, regardless of their status, and all his life, he cleaved to that principle."

Elizabeth counted one trait that Rafael shared with his hero, for he had been most gracious to her.

"In those days, the land was divided and the lords at war. There were Christian kingdoms in Iberia, mighty Castile as well as neighboring Léon and Galicia. All were unified under the hand of Ferdinand I, but upon his death, his territories were divided between his three sons, as was oft the practice. Sancho ascended to the throne of Castile; Alfonso was granted the throne of Léon and Garcia was given the crown of Galicia. From that moment, each brother was consumed with the desire to claim what had been granted to his brethren, and to unify his father's kingdom, but under his own hand. At the same time, these kings also made war against the cities held by the Moors, hoping to conquer again the territories and claim the wealth rumored to be within their walls, for war has need of coin to see it funded."

This, Elizabeth realized, was where Rafael had learned that aristocratic brothers did not assist each other. Perhaps he had expected Alexander to besiege Ravensmuir and claim the new keep for his own, as well as keep the horses at Kinfairlie. She was glad his assumption had been challenged.

"Rodrigo knew that his future would be one of war, and he strove to become the best warrior of his comrades. He was made royal standard-bearer for Sancho on that king's ascent to the throne, but soon Rodrigo showed his military prowess. He led so many campaigns against the other two kings and their forces and was victorious so often that he became famous for his success. His victories made Sancho more powerful and Castile ever larger, so Rodrigo was well-rewarded for his triumphs. He had riches and homes, servants and more horses than a man could ever ride. He rose ever higher in the ranks of Sancho's army, serving the king at court with his own hand when he was not at war. And so it was in Sancho's court that he met the woman who captured his heart. It is said that when Rodrigo saw Doña Ximena for the first time, he was struck with a love that would burn through all his days and nights."

Rafael clenched his fist and pounded his chest in a gesture that thrilled Elizabeth. "No other woman would suffice. No other woman could command his love. Because Rodrigo had every advantage to his hand, even though he was not so nobly born as she, her father consented that she should wed this knight. They were wedded, and her family was convinced that her future could not be better assured. Of course, it was not."

Rafael paused to clear his throat. The hall was rapt. One of the mercenaries passed him a cup of wine and he sipped of it before continuing. "King Sancho died young, suddenly and without a son. And so it was that the kingdom of Castile was bequeathed to Sancho's brother, King Alfonso of Léon, the very king whom Rodrigo had defeated so soundly so many times. Alfonso did not take kindly to having the man who had conquered his armies so often within his own court. And so it was that Alfonso exiled *Mío Cid* forever from the unified kingdom of Castile and Léon."

Elizabeth gasped at this, but Rafael slanted her a simmering glance. She had no time to draw a conclusion from this before Rafael presented one to her. "And here we see that a man can fight with valor and serve his lord with honor, yet be cheated of all he would hold dear. His wealth was seized by the new king, the portal of his own house locked against him, and no one would speak to him in his home. His wife and daughters even had been sent to a monastery by the king, so he was denied the sight of his beloved as well."

And this was how Rafael came to believe that fortune was fleeting. Elizabeth locked her hands together in her lap.

"*Mío Cid* was not one to admit defeat, however. He had a week of grace to leave Burgos, the city where kings kept the high court of Castile, and he used every moment of it. He could have disappeared into the hills and lived like a brigand, but it was not within him to retreat from a battle. Instead, *Mío Cid* resolved that he would make himself a kingdom, where his fate could not be turned by one man's whim or another, where his beloved wife and his daughters could be safe forevermore. He would earn a fortune to ensure his daughters had fine dowries, and he would see them wedded to men of honor and valor. And to do this, he would leave Castile and his wife behind, in order to build the future he desired for his own."

Elizabeth recognized that Rodrigo had sold his blade to see to the security of those reliant upon him. That was a noble objective, and she wondered if Rafael had a similarly noble goal.

Rafael spoke with ferocity as he eyed Alexander. "Rodrigo became a mercenary and an outlaw by choice, because the alternative made his heart bleed. He had a wife and two daughters. He would not see them abandoned, impoverished or despoiled. He would not see them trapped under the thumb of a king who despised their father." Alexander nodded in understanding of this inclination, though Elizabeth could see her brother still did not approve.

"And so, *Mío Cid* summoned the men who had served him. And he raised his voice before them, pledging that he would share with them whatever riches they gained, that he would see them treated with dignity, that he would request their blades be sworn to his service. He offered them the choice to follow him or nay. And so it was that the entire town of Burgos rang with the chorus of their agreement, and King Alfonso in his palace wondered at the noise. The king was said to have come to the window in time to see the finest flower of chivalry ride through the gates of the town, the best of his army leaving his service to follow *Mío Cid*."

The mercenaries grinned at this, nodding approval of the men's choice to follow such a leader.

"*Mío Cid* camped across the river from Burgos for three days and three nights, calling for men to join him. He sent out runners to all of Castile and León, extending his offer to all valiant warriors. Knights rode to his banner, his camp swelling a little more each day. Townspeople crept out at night to bring provisions to the camp, for all the town believed that the greatest warrior of all had been disserved but they were afraid to defy the king in daylight. Two hundred knights were pledged to Rodrigo before even he left Burgos. On the morning of the fourth day, the hills echoed with the thunder of hoof beats as *Mío Cid's* army rode away from Burgos and toward the border of Castile. He went first to the monastery where his wife and daughters were staying, and told Doña Ximena of his plan. She wept that they would be so parted, but took him and his men to the chapel to pray for their success. He left all his coin with his lady wife, that she would have riches whatever his fate. When he left, she stood proudly to watch him go, tears running down her lovely face, and the pain of parting for *Mío Cid* was like that of having his nails pulled from fingers. Three hundred knights followed him, even knowing that, for they knew he would share whatever spoils they gained."

There it was again, the notion that a woman's love could be the anchor to a warrior's life, and the conviction that a wife should be both honored and defended. Elizabeth smiled with her surety that Rafael would treat her well.

"They took Casteion immediately, for the townspeople surrendered to *Mío Cid* rather than battle against the famous warrior. Here he gained three thousand marks in tribute, plus herds to feed his army. He freed the Moors in that town, for he did not wish them to speak ill of him, dispersed the coin to his knights, and rode on. So it was at Alcocer and other towns, so it was that he rode from victory to victory, his wealth ever growing, his grace undiminished, his generosity well-known. The Moors he freed often joined his forces, those men who had joined him as foot soldiers rose to become knights in their own right, all sworn to his hand saw their fortunes increase. Mío Cid regained all he had lost and more, and better, this time no man could take it from him."

Rafael wagged a finger at the company. "And here he showed his mettle, for he was not a man to keep all riches for himself, or to forget alliances. Still he believed himself to be the vassal of King Alfonso, for that man was king of Castile. He sent tribute to that king, fine warhorses and gifts of gold and treasure, and Alfonso marveled at this." Rafael raised his brows. "He accepted the gifts, but did not relinquish his edict against *Mío Cid*."

Rafael paused, no doubt to emphasize the faithlessness of this king. Elizabeth could only agree.

"So *Mío Cid* continued for three years, taking Xerica, Onda, Almenar, Murviedro, Cebola, Peña Cadiella...so many cities that I cannot recall all of their names. Always he sent tribute to Alfonso of Castile, the king he still considered to be his liege lord, but gained no reprieve from that king. And so it was that *Mío Cid* came to the city of Valencia, with ten thousand knights sworn to his service, and laid siege to that town of marvels and riches."

"Have you been there?" Elizabeth asked.

Rafael nodded, prompting her desire to see the city herself. "Of course. It is as beauteous as it is reputed to be. It was built first by the Romans, called Valentia in honor of valor of the soldiers who first claimed that territory. The Moors call it *Medina bu-Tarab*, which means City of Joy." His lips tightened even as Elizabeth tried the exotic name on her tongue. "Though it was no place of joy for me."

She blinked, but Rafael had spun away. He paced the floor, as the company waited, and continued tersely. "It was a siege, as a siege always will be, the roads secured so well that naught went in and naught went out. They lacked grain in the city, and had no bread, though there was wine and fruit to be sure. It was believed that the King of the Moors in Morocco would send aid, but he did not. He heard the cries of his brethren, there was no doubt of that for messengers did escape, but so fearful was he of *Mío Cid,* that he did not reply." Rafael examined the toe of his boot. "During war is when the true measure of a man can be seen, as well as the strength of any alliance."

Again, Elizabeth saw how Rafael had gained his expectation that others could not be trusted or relied upon. How lonely his life must have been! No wonder he was so wary of making bonds with others.

"The city fell to *Mío Cid,* and surely the inhabitants feared he would be vengeful as a reward for their defiance. But Rodrigo was a fair man to his dying day. His goal had been to have a kingdom of his own, and in Valencia, he established one. Again, he freed the Moors who had surrendered with the town. He dispensed the spoils amongst his knights and granted coin even to the Moors, for he did not wish them to starve. He bade them choose, whether to remain or to leave, for he would rule Valencia from that day forward. He elevated a priest to be bishop of Valencia, so that all could receive the sacraments, and converted nine mosques to churches."

This was Rafael's notion of responsible leadership. Elizabeth approved heartily of it.

"Valencia was attacked soon afterward, by the King of Seville, but even though that king rode with thirty thousand warriors, he was defeated, and his coin swelled the treasury of *Mío Cid's* new kingdom. He sent for his beloved wife and his daughters, and they arrived in triumph, Doña Ximena joyously embracing her beloved husband and champion before the entire town. In Valentia he made his home and defended it from all who would steal or taint it. From Valentia, he saw his daughters well-wed with fine dowries, to men who would honor them well. In Valentia, he ruled until he died and he died in its defense, leaving Doña Ximena to rule in his stead."

Rafael turned to face the high table, his stance proud. Elizabeth's heart pounded. Here was a fine example of marriage, in her view, for Rafael's hero had treated his wife as his equal partner and Rafael saw this to be good.

This warrior would suit her well as spouse, indeed.

"And this is a hero to hold high, in my estimation," Rafael concluded in a ringing voice. "He was a man both lethal in war and fair to those he vanquished, a fearless man who made his life as he would have it be."

Elizabeth did not miss the quick piercing glance Rafael sent her way as he said the word "fearless."

She stood up, undaunted by his stern manner. "He was a man loyal to those he held within his heart," she said and saw Rafael start. "A man who treated women with honor and a man who labored as a mercenary only after Dame Fortune turned against him." She saw Rafael's surprise at what she had taken of this tale. "He was a man who treated his wife as his partner and confidante, a man who kept his word, and a man who was kind to those beneath his hand who had less advantage." She lifted her cup. "I salute your champion, *Mío Cid*, and you for the telling of his tale, Rafael Rodriguez."

The company roared agreement and lifted their cups to drink Elizabeth's toast. Alexander passed a hand over his brow, but Elizabeth had eyes only for Rafael.

A heat lit in his eyes then, a fire that made her heart pound. He drank her toast, then strode down the length of the hall toward her to bow low in front of her. Elizabeth offered her hand boldly and Rafael claimed it, his warm fingers closing over her own. His eyes gleamed, his smile made her heart thunder, then he kissed the back of her hand slowly.

That dangerous smile lifted the corner of his mouth, and his gaze locked so firmly upon her that Elizabeth was certain her dream would come true.

Claire Delacroix

Chapter Fourteen

It was only a matter of time before Elizabeth sought him out. Rafael was content to wait, content to savor his anticipation. He felt young in a way he could scarce recall feeling before, both drawn to Elizabeth and wanting to make the fascination between them last as long as possible. She was beguiling and confident in a way that was alien to him, certain of her safety and trusting fully in those around her, all because of her childhood. He watched her dance, regretting that his experience had been so different.

Rafael would have liked to have been able to court this maiden of life and fire. He doubted he would have the opportunity, though. He expected that by the time he returned to Scotland—if indeed, he ever did—she would be wedded with children of her own, her merriment likely sacrificed to duty and the company of a dour man.

His gift of this night would ensure that she knew what best to demand of her legal spouse, and would warm her nights forevermore.

He had no doubt that he would recall this evening for all his days and nights. So he took heed of every detail, committing each and every one to memory.

He filled his memory palace with this night.

And this beguiling maiden.

Rafael let Elizabeth choose the moment they next spoke, for she would judge it best.

The lutenists struck the tune and the family from Kinfairlie led the dancing. Like most of the mercenaries, Rafael sat back. He savored the wine that had been poured, and the sight of Elizabeth as she danced. She was light on her feet, graceful and merry, a vision to entice any man. He lost track of her in the crowd for a single moment, and then she abruptly dropped to the bench beside him, her cheeks flushed and her eyes filled with expectation. His heart leaped, though he kept his expression guarded.

"Dance with me," she demanded, clearly anticipating his agreement despite his manner. She was not readily fooled when it came to his mood, and he liked that she was so perceptive. It was startling that he did not mind her seeing his secrets so readily.

"I will not."

"You are a vexing man," she charged, though her tone was filled with laughter.

Despite himself, Rafael was cajoled into matching her mood. "And yet you continue to seek me out," he teased. "Perhaps I am not sufficiently vexing to deter you." He frowned at her. "Perhaps I should try harder."

She only laughed at him. "Perhaps you could never be so vexing as that," she said and he hoped it was so. "It is my destiny to love you."

Rafael's fine mood was banished. "That cannot be. There is no destiny, only choices made and circumstances shaped."

She eyed him. "As *Mío Cid* shaped his life."

"Indeed."

Elizabeth leaned closer to whisper. "I liked your tale well. It persuaded me that we do see matters the same way."

"Indeed?" Rafael watched her, wondering at her conviction. He supposed he would never cease to marvel at her confidence.

"Indeed." Her expression turned wicked then, the way her eyes shone stealing his breath away. "I would learn of passion, Rafael, no matter the price." She spoke with a vigor he knew was inappropriate, but which he admired greatly.

Rafael flicked a glance at the high table but neither of Elizabeth's brothers had noted her location. "We have argued of this already..." he said, wanting her to be utterly clear about her desires.

"We can be lovers this night without marital vows between us," she declared, interrupting him.

Rafael blinked at this unconventional suggestion, but a study of the lady revealed that she made no jest. This was far more than he had intended to propose to her.

"Why would you risk this?" he murmured.

The set of Elizabeth's lips became stubborn. "Because I would *know*. Regardless of what comes after this, I would have tasted true passion." She shrugged. "Perhaps it would make it easier to bear whatever my fate might be, for I doubt adventure will be part of it."

Rafael found himself dismayed that he had been successful in convincing her that they had no future together, though it was a sign that she heeded his counsel. It was best to be pragmatic, even if he did not mean to take all she offered. His gift to her would introduce her to the passion of which she was capable, without indulging his own. This, he was certain, was a fitting legacy of his days at Ravensmuir, for her expectations of men abed would be shaped.

And shaped well.

"You say you will not ever wed, after all," she continued. "And since we are destined to love only each other, that means I shall be alone once you leave. I do not doubt that will be soon." She granted him a demanding look.

"On the morrow," he admitted and she wrinkled her nose.

"Then it must be tonight. At least the memory of passion might keep me warm at night in future."

"Even while laboring at your embroidery, locked in a tower?" Rafael could not resist the urge to tease her.

Elizabeth laughed. "Maybe even that." Devilry danced in her eyes. "How shall I know unless you show me? No man of honor will trouble himself, for we have agreed that they are tedious." She grimaced. "I expect he would save such pleasure for his mistress, rather than insult his lady with pleasure abed."

Her gaze slid to his, temptation in her eyes. Rafael let his gaze drop to her lips, recalling the sweet honey of her kisses, as well. Were they not in the hall, he might have reminded her of the vigor of passion and its demands, the way it could catch up a man and a woman and lead them far beyond any intentions.

But Elizabeth licked her lips languorously as he watched, as if to invite his touch, and the sight sent a jolt through Rafael. She leaned against him, her breast crushed against his arm, her expression knowing. She seduced him apurpose, confident that he would treat her with honor, and Rafael could not pull away—much less ignore the temptation she offered—once he had felt the turgid peak of her nipple.

She was aroused, perhaps as aroused as he.

But she did not realize he would take no more than his due.

Rafael met her gaze, knowing his own was simmering.

"Or perhaps Finvarra will claim compensation for my speaking in his court," she murmured, then shook her head. "Though I cannot imagine that I would learn much of passion in his court."

"Do you make this scheme to loosen his hold upon you?" Rafael asked, but Elizabeth shook her head.

Then her smile was mischievous again. "Only mortal men hold chastity in such high esteem," she confided in a whisper and Rafael nearly laughed at that. "Finvarra would welcome me chaste or sampled." Her eyes danced. "But I would make him wait until I am an old crone for that."

Rafael's heart clenched as he recalled the dark king's plan to hasten her choice, and he parted his lips to warn her.

But Elizabeth put her fingers over his mouth to silence him, leaning ever closer. "I would know of passion now," she insisted in a whisper. "Because I am cursedly impatient." Her voice turned husky. "Show me, Rafael. Show me this very night."

It was the invitation he desired above all others. Rafael leaned down, letting his lips brush her temple and hearing her quick intake of breath. She was so responsive that he knew their night would be a memory to savor, even if he was not fully sated himself. "How can I decline?" he murmured and felt her shiver. "Where shall we meet?"

She flushed in her pleasure, a most bewitching sight. "In the stables, here at Ravensmuir."

"Nay, there are too many ostlers and squires there." Rafael took her hand in his, lifted it and pressed a kiss to her palm. She quivered, her eyes wide with desire. "And they will seek you out to return to Kinfairlie."

"Then it shall be there," Elizabeth countered with resolve. "Have you been to Kinfairlie?" Rafael shook his head. "The wall is broken to rubble behind the tower, on the side nearest to the sea. The fields are rough, so no one comes that way. I could meet you there, by the old twisted tree."

Rafael nodded, knowing precisely where he would take her after they met. "At midnight, then," he vowed, then kissed her hand again. Her flesh was soft against his lips, the scent of her skin enough to torment him.

He looked up at her, half wondering if she set a trap for him.

Nay, she would not do so but Alexander might. Rafael would evade it, to be sure, for he was more wily than the Laird of Kinfairlie.

"I will not linger," he warned her. "Do not be late, *mi piqueño ángel.*"

Elizabeth's smile turned seductive and Rafael felt his very blood heat. "Oh, I shall not be. Upon that, sir, you can rely."

❧

Rafael sought out Malcolm after his conversation with Elizabeth, knowing that he had to make his plans clear to his comrade.

"I know the others plan to leave on the morrow. Are you certain you will not remain?" Malcolm asked.

Rafael smiled. "Do not jest with me. You and your brother will be gladdened to see such mercenaries departed from your hall and your lands."

Malcolm shook his head. "I make no jest. You are less a mercenary than a friend, Rafael." His gaze sobered. "I would not see you return to that trade for lack of choices."

Rafael was startled by these words. "And what is that to mean?"

"That I have need of a seneschal to defend my borders and my hall, and I can think of no man more deserving of the post."

Catriona leaned around Malcolm, evidently having overheard the conversation. "And I would not have you leave because of our disagreements in the past."

Rafael shook his head hastily, not wanting Malcolm to know that he was sorely tempted. "It is my nature to wage war," he said. "And there will not be sufficient of it upon your borders, not now, for me to win the tribute I desire."

Malcolm frowned. "So, you will depart as soon as the morrow?"

"With first light."

"You will always be welcome at our board," Catriona said.

"And should you change your thinking, you know I would welcome you in my hall," Malcolm said.

"I thank you, but as I said, I would depart."

"You may not find passage readily across the Channel," Malcolm warned. "We were charged double on our return home because they did not trust the look of you, and only then because I vouched for you."

"I will see it done." Rafael watched the company, his gaze landing unerringly upon Elizabeth, and felt the need to warn his friend. "I would not turn my back upon the Earl of Douglas, and I do not hold the seal to a keep he desires. Do not trust too readily, Malcolm, not when every treasure has come to your hand." He gestured to the hall that had been so rapidly constructed and felt again that pang of envy for what his comrade had won. "Ravensmuir was always your destiny. Guard it and all your treasures with vigor."

Malcolm smiled and the pair shook hands heartily.

Friend. It was a remarkable thing to be called a friend, and Rafael knew he would savor Malcolm's salute forever.

&

The spriggan Darg, like many beings of advanced age—and, it must be said, like many of not such advanced age—was a creature of habit. After its unwilling participation in the escape of Rosamunde from Finvarra's captivity, Darg had returned to Ravensmuir. Though the keep was ruined and the once-grand caverns beneath the earth had crumbled, there were still many tunnels sufficiently wide to allow for the passage of one small spriggan.

A spriggan, in its most common form, can be fitted into the palm of a human hand. Darg, like many spriggans, was dark all over, as if covered by the gnarled bark of a tree. Darg's nose was pointed, like a teasel, and it possessed the small beady eyes characteristic of spriggans. It was more than beady eyes and quick fingers that this particular kind of Fae had in common with its fellows, but also a lust for gold and treasure.

Darg had originally hidden itself in the caverns beneath Ravensmuir when the forebears of Malcolm and his siblings had traded in religious relics. In those days, the tunnels had been heaped with riches—silver, gold, reliquaries and plunder from churches. It had been such a rich hoard that Darg had never memorized its entirety.

At least not before it had been stolen away.

The treasure had not truly been stolen—it had been retrieved by its rightful owner and sold. But Darg, as was typical of a spriggan, believed all treasures it perceived and coveted to be its own, so in Darg's mind, the spoils had been stolen.

Furthermore, they had been stolen by the woman who had been the bane of Darg's existence for years, one Rosamunde.

If Darg had known that Rosamunde visited the new keep of Ravensmuir, the spriggan might have stirred itself to visit the hall, simply to look upon that old foe. A wary peace had been established between the two, thanks to Darg's assistance in retrieving Rosamunde from Finvarra's court, but the spriggan still could have roused itself to ire.

As it was, Darg slept deeply after that adventure.

As the company made merry in the new hall of Ravensmuir, Darg slept on a mound of golden coins that it had discovered some six months before. Just when the spriggan had become convinced that all treasures of merit had been removed from Ravensmuir's tunnels, a mortal had deposited a considerable quantity of gold in one.

He had buried his treasure in a tunnel that opened to the sea, tucked around a turn of the passageway and out of the wind. Darg had watched the man in question as he hid it, his manner furtive, and had investigated immediately after his departure. The coins had been buried in sacks of velvet, but Darg exhumed them all, tossing aside the velvet after spilling the coins into a gleaming and highly satisfactory pile.

The spriggan had seen finer hoards and certainly more varied ones, but a mound of gold several times its height was not to be spurned. The spriggan had carved itself a nest in the pile and burrowed in to sleep.

It did not sleep so deeply though that it did not hear the approach of an intruder. The spriggan's eyes flew open, then narrowed in suspicion. Clearly, some thief came to plunder Darg's newly gained prize.

ð

Perfect!

Elizabeth's ploy was working better than she could have hoped. Rafael had agreed.

And he had done so with that promising heat in his eyes. This would be a night beyond all others! She was impatient for the celebrations to be completed, but knew she must give no sign of her scheme. Indeed, she dared not even acknowledge Rafael again, for Alexander might take note.

Elizabeth danced and she made merry. She spoke to the guests and held Avery while Catriona and Malcolm danced. She laughed at the tales told and sipped of the ale, all the while tapping her toe for time to pass.

It was when she returned from the garderobe that she fairly tripped over Alexander and Malcolm conferring in the shadows. Having encountered these two scheming just so many times in their youth, Elizabeth instinctively hid in the shadows and listened without remorse.

"You should know that I have had a missive from the earl," Alexander said softly. "He wishes to treat with you."

Malcolm snorted. "He was defeated and his men fled the field. I need not make any concession to him."

Alexander inhaled sharply in his disapproval. "He is most determined to make an alliance with our family..."

"And hide one of his spies within my walls again," Malcolm said with disdain.

"*And* ensure that this week's events are not repeated," Alexander corrected sternly. "You must realize, Malcolm, that Ravensmuir's location is strategic. In rebuilding it and doing that so well, you have rekindled an old covetousness in the earl. He yearned to hold Ravensmuir before, and now it is even more alluring."

"I will fight to the death in defense of what is mine own..." Malcolm began hotly, but Alexander interrupted him.

"And what then?" he asked softly. "Would you see Catriona assaulted when she made her way alone to pray in the new chapel? Would you see Avery injured by a stranger when he rides to hunt? There are a thousand ways to strike at a man without mustering an army outside of his gates."

Elizabeth sensed that Malcolm was unhappy with these tidings, even without seeing his features clearly. "Then what?" he demanded with frustration. "I should betroth Avery to some viper of the earl's line like Jeanne, and that before he even utters his first word?"

"Nay, of course not." Alexander cleared his throat. "Though it *was* suggested."

Malcolm made a sound of disgust.

"They want a match," Alexander continued. "I mean to write to Ross and discover his circumstance. Consider that it might be good for us to have an ally inside the earl's family."

"I doubt Ross will wed for our convenience."

"He might be smitten by one of the women the earl proposes for a match. He might have some alluring nieces or cousins." Alexander shrugged when Malcolm's skepticism was clear. "Or richly rewarded for his compliance by the earl. I mean only to *ask*."

"I dislike it, even so. Why would you put this burden upon him?"

Alexander did not reply for a moment, and Elizabeth eased closer to ensure she did not miss his words. "Because I gave my promise to Elizabeth that she could choose the man she would wed."

"And so?" Malcolm asked, his lack of understanding clear.

"And so my hand could be forced very easily," Alexander said tightly. "It would not be the first time that a marriage was conspired by abduction and rape, and I would not see matters come to that."

Malcolm frowned. "He is that determined?"

Alexander nodded.

Malcolm cleared his throat. "You know that she favors Rafael. You could see her wedded in short order..."

Alexander gave a short bark of a laugh. "I endeavor to ensure her happiness, Malcolm, not guarantee her misery and demise. She will wed no mercenary while I draw breath, upon that you may be certain." He drummed his fingers on his own elbow. "Nay, there must be another solution."

"Write then to Ross," Malcolm said, his voice tight. "Perhaps there will be success in that."

"Perhaps."

Malcolm lowered his voice. "And until this is resolved, do not let Elizabeth leave the keep alone."

The brothers nodded, then moved back into the throng of celebrants, leaving Elizabeth with more to consider. If they were right, and the earl meant to ensure that some cousin or nephew allied to him despoiled her, thus compelling her to wed that man, Elizabeth could see only one solution.

She must be rid of her maidenhead herself, to diminish her own appeal.

Which meant that her night with Rafael must be a consummation of their relationship. There could be no half-measures and no delay. If she was to be compelled to wed any man, it would be Rafael, the man of her choice.

Elizabeth was then more impatient to depart Ravensmuir and for midnight to come. Finally, the party from Kinfairlie took their leave, amidst many affectionate embraces and promises to visit the following week. The sun was dropping to the horizon, setting the western sky afire. Elizabeth looked over the company for Rafael, but could not spy him anywhere.

Perhaps he had gone to Kinfairlie already.

Perhaps he chose a place for their assignation.

Or made preparations.

She hugged herself in anticipation.

In her heart, Elizabeth still believed that such intimacy would only go another step in earning Rafael's trust, and be another stone in the foundation of their future together. She believed that they would be man and wife one day, but even if they were not to be so, they would be lovers true.

Rafael would be her first and her only lover.

No one would ever be able to change her choice.

※

Rafael left the hall after his conversation with Malcolm, determined to be prepared to depart with the dawn. He strode from the hall to the stable, fetched his saddlebags, then crept to the lip of Ravensmuir's cliffs. All were in the hall, the sounds of their merriment carrying over the land. The sentinels looked inland, guarding against a return of the earl and his men, though Rafael did not believe he would be back so soon as this.

Rafael scanned the coast as he walked south toward Kinfairlie, wanting to be certain none saw his destination. When he was content that no one watched, Rafael suddenly ducked down below the lip of rocks. He crept along the coast to the path he had discovered months before, then followed its course down toward the sea.

The cliffs had not crumbled here, as they had where the old keep of Ravensmuir had fallen into the sea. The drop to the water was less than where the old keep had stood, the land gradually sloping down to the fens to the south of Kinfairlie. When Rafael had learned of the trade of Malcolm's forebears and the caverns beneath the old keep, he had explored the shore. Sure enough, he had found caves etched in the rocks, with tunnels stretching behind them into dark caverns. Rafael had chosen one that seemed to end in a blocked tunnel—or one with a passage too small for any man— and had buried his plunder there. Out of sight and out of the wind, he had believed his riches as safely secured as in any treasury.

At least until he returned on this eve to pack them.

He halted just inside the cave to stare. The coins, which had been counted and secured into velvet bags when he left them, were now mounded against one wall in glorious disarray, their richness displayed to any man who might stumble upon them. He had been robbed! Rafael fell upon the coins and counted them with fear.

Yet the sum was the same as he had left. He counted twice to be certain, then could not make sense of it. He pushed through the jewelry and other trinkets he had collected and could not identify a single item that was missing. Even the copper jar he had taken from Ibrahim was still there, though he shook his head at the sight of it. It was too easy to recall the old man's conviction in the unseen, never mind his certainty that those beings wrought of smoke were to be feared. His conviction was not unlike that of Elizabeth in the Fae.

Rafael had been able to see the djinn as well, though he had never given any hint of his abilities. They had preferred to be overlooked, and he had seen them exact punishment from any fool enough to admit to seeing them.

Ibrahim had been convinced at a glimpse that the copper vessel was a trap for a djinn, just like the one in the tale he liked most to recount. Amongst all of his possessions, Ibrahim had treasured this one the most, for he had been certain that one day, he would have to defend himself from the djinn's mischief. He had paid a ridiculous price for it, making it impossible to sell the vessel at a profit.

As a boy newly liberated, Rafael had taken the vessel as his own, but had never been able to sell it either. It had been cursedly inconvenient, practically a millstone upon his back, but he had not been able to abandon it.

Rafael rolled his eyes at the folly that could be passed from one man to another, even as he began to count and secure his coins in their velvet sacks again. This time, he should leave the unwieldy copper jar behind, he decided.

In that same moment that he realized he was not alone.

Something muttered in the cavern.

Something small and dark, sharp-faced and sharper-tongued. Something that was not large enough to be a man or even a child, something with skin that looked to be made of weathered bark.

Fae.

Or djinn.

If there was a difference, in truth.

"Another thief has come to despoil, the gold I win by blood and toil. Cursed vermin on every side, these mortals I cannot abide!"

Rafael strove to keep his expression composed. He would not reveal that he could hear this creature, for surprise was the best tool. Instead, he moved closer to the djinn trap, which was nothing more than a large copper vessel knotted into a net with a cork that could be bound securely in place. He nudged it with his elbow, seemingly making an inadvertent move, noting that the cork was as it should be. The opening was skyward, the interior hidden by the rope. There was something uncanny about that rope, Rafael had always felt as much, for it seemed to singe his fingers. Ibrahim had confided once that only the use of a certain word would allow any knot within it to be untied.

Rafael had always thought that to be nonsense, but now he wondered.

"They smell, they sneak, they steal my prize, mortals and their greed I do despise."

Rafael saw the small figure march into view, small enough that he could hold it in one hand—if he had possessed any desire of so doing. It glared at him and stamped, muttering all the while, then seized a single gold coin. It evidently was convinced he could not discern it and gripped the coin, intent upon carrying it away.

Rafael chose to test his notion. He rummaged in the pile of gold coins, as if seeking something in particular, and the creature paused to watch him closely.

"It cannot be gone," he whispered. "Not the greatest prize I possess!"

The creature put down the coin, edging closer in it curiosity. Rafael sent coins scattering in apparent desperation, digging into the pile with increasing frenzy. The creature drew ever more near.

"Aha, here it is!" Rafael said with apparent joy. He sat back to admire a ring set with a stone of red glass. It had virtually no value, but it shone brightly and was so large that it would have been worth a king's ransom had it been a genuine stone.

"The ruby that is the marvel of my collection." Rafael smiled at the stone, turning it so that it caught the light, breathed on it and shone it against his sleeve. He felt the creature's keen attention. Indeed, it was almost at his elbow, its greedy little fingers twitching in anticipation of snatching his prize.

Rafael sighed. "One day I shall meet the lady worthy of wearing this priceless ruby upon her finger." He shook his head. "But not yet, I fear." He stood, then feigned a slip, gasping as the ring fell into the djinn trap. He pretended then that he could not see where it had fallen, and turned in place, apparently seeking it on the ground.

The small dark creature leaped past him and dove into the copper jar, fingers outstretched. As soon as it was inside, Rafael moved like lightning to jam the cork into the neck of the bottle and bind it down. The rope seemed to tie itself more tightly than he ever could have done.

The small creature screamed. *"A curse, a curse, and a foul lie! Deceived I am and left to die."* It kicked the jar with vigor, then glared at Rafael.

He shook the jar and smiled. "So, you *are* the same as djinn," he murmured to his captive. "This is good to know."

The creature raged. *"You cannot see me, this I know..."*

"Because I did not reveal that I could see you before you were trapped?" Rafael clicked his tongue. "A man who means to survive does not reveal all he knows. I am glad to see that the djinn trap is of use after all. I have carried it for many years." He set the trap aside and rapidly packed his gold away. The creature must have kicked against the copper, for it rang dully, but it could not escape.

"It burns it does, this trap for djinn, and I should not be kept herein."

"It was wrought by a man who knew far more of your kind than me," Rafael said mildly. "That is what I was told of it, and though I never believed the tale, it must be true. There is but one way to escape it." The creature was silent as it awaited some clue. Rafael smiled. "For me to release you, of course."

"I wager freedom will not be won, not quickly from a fiend like this one."

"He told me the way to do it. It is perhaps the only lesson of merit he granted to me." The creature hissed, clearly dissatisfied. "I will release you readily, but you must grant me three wishes in exchange."

The creature stamped and swore. It paced and kicked, then, its fury spent for the moment, spoke in sulky tones. *"I make no vows to mortal men, for they forget their pledges in the end."*

"Fair enough," Rafael agreed easily. "Indeed, I understand your wariness more than most." He packed the last of the gold coins into his saddlebags and secured the buckle, then dug in the soft sand of the cavern floor. When Rafael lowered the djinn trap into the hole, its occupant bellowed in fury.

"What is this that you would do? What harm have I ever done to you?"

"I cannot loose you, not without the exchange made, for you might take vengeance upon me for the insult," Rafael replied, his tone reasonable. "And I leave for distant shores in the morning." He shrugged. "Why not sleep a while?" Seemingly oblivious to the Fae's fury, he buried the djinn trap so that only the barest tip of the cork was visible. The creature shouted, but its cries were so muffled that any soul who stumbled to this place would think them the echo of the wind.

Rafael hefted his saddlebags and slipped out the cavern. He paused to ensure that there was no one watching and returned to the stables.

He was amazed to discover that Ibrahim had been right about the vessel.

He thought of the tales he had heard from Ibrahim, the ones he had thought merely tales until he had arrived at Ravensmuir. He considered that he might request this djinn's favors.

But the djinn in question had need of some time to consider the alternative to granting Rafael his will.

And Rafael had to teach a maiden about pleasure.

He smiled in anticipation as he swung into Rayo's saddle and rode the destrier across the darkened moor. His heart was pounding, his desire raging, and the promise of his little angel's pleasure was all he could yearn for, and more.

ả

The bells in Kinfairlie's chapel tolled midnight.

Elizabeth slipped from her pallet and donned her kirtle, hastily lacing the sides. She seized her boots and swung her thickest cloak over her shoulders, drew up the hood, then crept down the stairs.

The hall was utterly silent. Even the children must be sleeping in the solar, for all Elizabeth heard was the rhythm of sleep.

In the great hall, there was snoring, which was a perfect sound to cover her footsteps. She donned her boots and crossed the hall quietly. She wanted to run, but she moved with care. She made her way through the kitchens and out the back door of the keep. She hastened through the kitchen gardens, then over the small broken stone wall at the back side of the keep. There were only fields here and empty land, with the sea in the distance. Up the coast, she could see the dark silhouette of Ravensmuir.

And a horse racing toward her.

Elizabeth's heart skipped with anticipation. She left the tumbled stone of the fence behind, and stood beside the twisted tree even as Rafael rode toward her. His cloak blew behind him as Rayo galloped closer, the golden lining gleaming. He halted the horse some distance away, then walked the beast quietly over the last distance.

No one would hear.

She saw the wariness in his manner again, the way he scanned her surroundings as if he thought they might be observed. Rafael's smile flashed when he was alongside her and Elizabeth's heart raced.

"So, you are a bold maiden indeed," he whispered. "I thought I might arrive to learn you had chosen to stay in your chamber."

"I do not issue dares that I will not keep," she said, feeling wild and unfettered.

Rafael chuckled. He bent and caught her around the waist in one smooth gesture, lifting her before him. He pulled her across his lap and turned the horse at the same time, then bent to capture her lips beneath his own. The wind was in Elizabeth's hair, the solid strength of Rafael at her back and his mouth locked upon hers. His gloved fingers were in her hair, his cape flaring behind them as Rayo cantered back the way he had come. She could smell the sea and the heat of Rafael's skin and Elizabeth returned his, amazed at her own boldness.

This night she would gamble and she dared not imagine that she would not win.

This was what it meant to be alive.

Sunday, June 27, 1428

Feast Day of Saint Cyril of Alexandria.

Claire Delacroix

Chapter Fifteen

Rafael took Elizabeth to the cavern, leaving Rayo tethered to graze upon the cliff. Both Ravensmuir and Kinfairlie were distant and dark, and the wind would have stolen any sounds they made. He dismounted then lifted her down, stealing another kiss before he took her by the hand and led her down the hidden path. She did not falter or hesitate, her eyes shining when the cavern was revealed. Around the corner had been the hiding place for his treasure, but Rafael would remain by the opening, where all they could see was the expanse of the ocean.

"We might be alone in all of Christendom," Elizabeth said, as if there could be naught better.

Again, Rafael was amazed by her. None of her protectors knew of her location. No one would see them in this place and none would hear her if she changed her mind and called for aid. Yet Elizabeth came with him willingly, trustingly, and Rafael was humbled by that.

Such confidence. Such innocence.

Such trust.

He would not betray her.

Rafael removed his cloak and cast it upon the stone. Elizabeth watched, then followed suit, unfurling her own cloak atop his. Hers was of fine wool, dyed to the vibrant hue of a sapphire, and was lined with silver fur. It was thick and luxurious as befit her status. His was thick and woolen, faded slightly from wear, serviceable but unadorned. The contrast made the differences in their status so clear that Rafael faltered.

Again, Elizabeth seemed to read his thoughts. She came to him, her fingers landing upon the bit of embroidery on his tabard. "Why is your insignia so small?"

Rafael could only utter the truth. "I have no insignia, for I am no knight."

Elizabeth frowned slightly and he wondered if she reconsidered her choice. "Did you not earn your spurs under the tutelage of an uncle?"

Rafael smiled at her assumptions. "I earned what is mine with the weight of my blade." He touched the golden embroidery on his tabard, their fingers entwining over his heart. "This is but a token for good fortune, granted to me by a lady who was quick with a needle."

Something flashed in those wondrous eyes, an emotion quickly disguised. Was she jealous? Rafael sorely hoped so. "Had she stitched one of your wounds?"

"Nay, only one woman has done that." He bent and touched his lips to her fingertips.

She smiled then, well pleased, and the sight sent heat through him. Her finger returned to encircle the emblem. "What is it meant to represent?"

"It is a pomegranate, for that is what I requested of her."

"An apple of Granada," Elizabeth mused and he was surprised she knew of it. "I have never seen one, though I have heard of them." She glanced up at him. "In tales of valor."

Of course. Rafael smiled down at her, snared by the welcome in her eyes.

"They grace the insignia of more than one knight I know, perhaps because the juice of the fruit is as red as blood," Rafael admitted. He wanted her to understand more of him. "The fruit, like so many other things in life, is both tart and sweet." He gave her an intent look. "There is a seed secreted within each bead of that juice, a reminder that all joys have their price."

Elizabeth bit her lip as she considered him. "That is a harsh way to look at life."

"But a true one."

"When will you cease your trade?" she asked quietly, her gaze searching his.

"Never." He might regret that truth, but Rafael feared it was unassailable.

She shook her head, impatient with his reply. "Do not be ridiculous. At some point you will halt, if only because you are killed while waging war. But *Mío Cid* rode out to secure a haven for his wife and daughters and to ensure their futures. What goal have you in your trade? Why did you begin it?"

"To survive."

"But you have done that," she insisted. "Why would you willingly abandon it?"

"I will not. It is what I am and what I do. I know no other life."

"But Malcolm..."

Rafael interrupted her, wanting to be sure she understood the obstacles before him. "Had the benefit of not just a legacy, but training for his future responsibilities in assuming that legacy. He had need of coin and naught else." He smiled, a little rueful to admit the truth. "I have coin, and naught else. And so I continue, as we all continue, until we fight no more. We have war in our blood, like hounds who have had a taste of the kill, and its allure cannot be forgotten."

Even as he said as much, Rafael hoped it could be otherwise. He knew though that if he gave Elizabeth any hope of his eventual return, she would cling to it, along with her conviction of destiny's promise. He would not give her false hope. He concluded with greater emphasis than had been his intention. "It is the way of the world, *mi piqueño ángel*."

Of course, Elizabeth was not deterred. He saw in her eyes that he had not shaken her conviction a whit.

He realized it would have shaken him if he had.

"What does that mean?" she whispered, those eyes alight. "You always say that, but I do not know what it means."

"*Mi piqueño ángel?*" he asked and she nodded. "It means 'my little angel.'"

Elizabeth smiled then, well pleased, and touched her lips to his again. "But I am not an angel," she murmured against his mouth. "Nor am I so little."

And she was not his. The truth struck Rafael to his marrow.

It was time to give the lady his gift. It would be a kind of homage to her.

Rafael doffed his gloves and framed her face in his hands, bending to kiss her thoroughly. She stretched to her toes and wound her arms around his neck, returning his embrace with ardor. An understanding of the tenderness and passion that could exist between a woman and a man, an expectation of what she could demand of the man who would wed her, an understanding of her due would be his gift.

It was not much, but it was all that Rafael Rodriguez had to give to a woman of Elizabeth's ilk.

Perhaps she would remember him kindly.

He knew he would never forget her.

🙵

Elizabeth was nigh overwhelmed with pleasure. Something in her manner had enflamed Rafael for he kissed her with more vigor than ever he had before. She thought he might consume her whole, and she did not care if he did. His mouth locked upon hers, his tongue slipped between her teeth and Elizabeth opened her mouth to him in complete capitulation.

He would show her the way.

He groaned at her capitulation, a wondrous sound, and swept her into his arms, depositing her gently on the pair of cloaks. He did not break his kiss but unlaced her kirtle, jerking the lace free on either side. Elizabeth regretted that she had worn anything other than her chemise, for she wanted to feel his hands upon her.

She moaned when the weight of his hand closed over her breast, and cried out in pleasure when he pinched her nipple as he had once before.

"Does it hurt?" he murmured into her ear and Elizabeth shook her head.

"It is wondrous, a sting and a tingle together. Do not halt!"

He chuckled and rolled the peak of her nipple between his finger and thumb, watching her with bright eyes as she arched her back and gasped with pleasure. He claimed her lips again, that enticing fire in his embrace, his kiss rough and possessive and demanding. That he could lose some control in his desire for her was exciting beyond compare.

When he lifted his head, Elizabeth tugged her loosened kirtle over her head, and cast it aside, then untied the lace of her chemise. He watched her avidly, smiling that roguish smile, then his hand slid beneath the hem of her chemise. His palm was warm upon her thigh, his expression dangerous as he eased his hand ever higher. Elizabeth felt herself flush. She felt the heat gather in her belly and the moisture between her thighs. She yearned for something she could not name.

Then Rafael's fingers slid between her thighs, proving that he knew what she wanted. He touched her in that most intimate place, caressing her with a surety that made Elizabeth gasp and writhe. She felt a tempest rising beneath her skin but he was relentless, driving her ever higher. He kissed her with fervor again, then traced a line of kisses down her throat, his whiskers grazing her skin in a way she found most exciting. She locked her fingers into the thickness of his hair, then cried out when he closed his mouth over her taut nipple.

He suckled and kissed it, running his tongue and his teeth across it so that it ached from his attentions. His fingers still moved against her, teasing her to ride this storm that he conjured. Elizabeth was lost in his embrace, unable to believe the power of sensation, uncertain she would survive this sweet torment.

She felt wanton that she was nearly nude and he was yet fully dressed, and could imagine him seducing her like this in some corner of a hall or in a chamber that they shared. His fingers eased inside her and she moaned from the depths of her being at the pleasure he conjured. He did not relent but caressed her as if determined to bring her very blood to a boil. He paused and she opened her eyes, unable to catch her breath as her heart raced. She smiled back at him, knowing she was flushed and pleased, thinking this was the sum of it.

For it was fine indeed.

"It is wondrous," she managed to whisper.

But Rafael cast her a wicked smile. "It has yet begun," he murmured.

He lifted the hem of her chemise, baring her belly to his view, and traced another path of burning kisses ever lower. Elizabeth gasped when his mouth closed over her, then she sighed at the touch of his mischievous tongue. He gripped her buttocks and lifted her to his embrace, tormenting her with pleasure so that she knew not what to do. That storm built with savage fury and she cried out for something she could not name. She writhed like a harlot, greedy for his touch and yearning for all that he could give.

The crescendo came suddenly as if she had been cast from the cliff toward the sea far below. Elizabeth heard herself shout with pleasure as a tumult shot through her veins.

She opened her eyes long moments later, heated and panting, only to find Rafael watching her with mingled satisfaction and amusement.

"I thank you," she said, hearing that her voice was uneven. "Why do wedded couples ever leave the solar?"

Rafael laughed. "Not all are as passionate as you."

There was no criticism in his tone, though Elizabeth knew this could not be the sum of lovemaking. He was still fully dressed, after all. She reached for him, claiming his hand. "And that cannot be all of it," she whispered in awe. "For you have not had your pleasure."

"My pleasure is in witnessing yours," Rafael said with force, then reached for her again. She understood then that he did not mean to possess her, and her heart swelled at his gallantry.

Indeed, his choice only convinced her of the merit of her own.

"But I would see you fully," she whispered, letting her hand fall to his belt. "I would see how a man is wrought."

He hesitated, yet another sign of his scheme, and Elizabeth knew she had not long to overwhelm his objections. She cast off her chemise, baring herself fully to his view, and took advantage of his surprise. She unfastened the buckle of his belt and laid it aside with care, then pushed him to his back. Rafael braced himself on his elbows, as if he would stop her, but Elizabeth quickly removed his boots.

"Elizabeth," he growled in warning and though she liked the sound well, she saw that he began to sit up.

On impulse, she put her hand on his erection, feeling its size through his chausses and tightened her fingers around his strength. Rafael caught his breath and froze, his eyes glittering. "You used your mouth to grant pleasure," she whispered. "What if I use mine?"

His eyes flashed like lightning and Elizabeth understood that her suggestion would please him well. "No lady does as much," he began to protest, but Elizabeth's fingers were busy on his laces. She tugged his chausses over his hips and touched him tentatively, smiling when she was rewarded by his moan of pleasure.

"Temptress," he whispered as he fell back against the cloak, and Elizabeth knew he was hers to claim.

ቈ

Rafael never could have imagined Elizabeth possessed such audacity.

All the same, he could not resist her touch, much less her delight in what she did. She learned far too quickly for him to evade her touch, and he certainly could not contain his response. He pulled her away in the last moment and spilled his seed on his own chemise. When he was gasping in the aftermath, her cursed fingers were busy, pulling the chemise over his head.

"I would see all of you," she insisted and he did not have it in him to fight her.

When he was nude and she was nude and she cast herself across his chest, triumph sparkling in her eyes, he could not resist her. He speared his fingers into her hair, liking that she had left it loose for the night, and spread the ebony tresses over her shoulders.

She arched a brow, tracing circles on his chest with her fingertips. "I suppose that there is more pleasure than can be shared."

He could not suppress his smile. "I suppose you know that I do not mean to show that to you."

She bit her lip, looking so impish that he considered himself warned. "I suppose you have guessed that I do not mean to leave you a choice."

"I cannot wed..."

"I do not care," Elizabeth retorted and claimed his lips in a kiss as potent and commanding as the ones he had given her. Truly, she learned too quickly, for her fingers were in his hair, her hands holding him captive to her kiss, her mouth demanding and enticing. Rafael found his hands locking into her hair, holding her fast as their kiss turned incendiary. He was barely aware that she cast a leg over him, but then he felt her bare breasts pressed against his chest. Her knees locked around his waist and her softness touched his erection, sending a jolt through him. She lowered her hips and rubbed herself against him, making him moan.

He rolled her to her back then, for he could do naught else. He took command of their kiss, his hands roving over her silken skin, for that was his only chance to save her chastity. He eased a hand between them, though he did not want to break the contact, and would have caressed her to grant her pleasure. He would have denied his own need, but Elizabeth gripped his buttocks and drew him closer, so that the sweet wet heat of her was right against him. Rafael bared his teeth and closed his eyes, putting his brow on her shoulder as he fought for control.

Elizabeth rolled her hips in invitation.

And he could not decline. He eased inside her, shaking at the effort of maintaining control for a little longer. She gasped and gripped his hair, nibbling at his ear as he buried himself in her sweetness. He feared it was too much for him, but Elizabeth surprised him anew.

"All of you," she demanded with ferocity, locking her legs around his waist. "Show me all of you."

And Rafael could only comply. He drew back, bracing his weight on his elbows so he could watch her as he claimed her. There was no fear in her expression and if she felt pain, she hid it well. Indeed, she smiled at him, as beguiling a temptress as there had ever been, and when he began to move, her eyes lit with pleasure. She gripped his shoulders, gripping his skin with her nails, which only inflamed him more.

"Do we find pleasure together?" she asked, her cheeks flushing more with every moment.

"If Fortune smiles upon us," he said with a smile, then caressed her with a fingertip.

"That is not Fortune," she whispered with a laugh, even as she writhed beneath his touch. "Unless you have changed your name, Rafael Rodriguez."

"Not me," he said, loving how responsive she was to his touch. He drove her higher and higher, her movements fueling his own passion, until they were moving together with such a smooth rhythm of mutual pleasure that they could have been meeting abed for decades. They smiled at each other, so attuned each to the other that Rafael had never known the like.

He pushed her higher and higher, waiting for her to find her pleasure first. When Elizabeth cried out, her body tightening convulsively around him and her fingers digging into his shoulders, Rafael could not hold back. He buried his face in her neck, inhaled deeply of her potent perfume, and welcomed his own release with a roar. Elizabeth laughed lightly and kissed his neck, drawing him more securely into her embrace as he dozed.

This was how it felt to be a champion.

And the sensation was wondrous indeed.
It did not, however, last.

❧

Elizabeth was dozing when the eastern sky first began to lighten. It was yet an hour until the dawn, maybe two, but Rafael was wide awake. He was taut with the import of what he had done.

He had taken what was not his to take.

And he must make the matter come aright.

Rafael would ride out this very morning, a new objective to his days. He could not offer for Elizabeth's hand as a man-at-arms in service to Malcolm but perhaps, like *Mío Cid*, he could win a holding, then return to court her in truth. Perhaps he could have a future like her past, and one with such a glorious woman at his side.

For the gift Elizabeth gave to him was hope, and it was pungent to a man who had never tasted of it before.

Rafael knew the odds were long against him. He knew it likely that he would fail. He doubted he could manage to succeed in such an endeavor before Finvarra tried to seize Elizabeth. But there was merit in the striving. He dared not give her false hope. He dared not encourage her to wait for him, for that would be too cruel should he fail and not return. He had to trust in her conviction that Finvarra would not prompt her choice and believe in his own inevitable success.

Maybe even in destiny.

For Rafael Rodriguez, for the first time in all his days, would ride to war with a purpose and a goal. And he would leave a legacy of merit, should the fates be truly on his side.

Rafael held Elizabeth against his side, unwilling to disturb her well-earned slumber even as his resolve built. Her hair was free of its braid, unfurled across the silver fur of the cloak. He stroked his fingers through the silken length of it, wanting to touch her, and had an idea. He would have a talisman of this moment, a mark of the pledge he made to himself to ensure the lady was honored.

But she could not know what he did, for she would understand the gesture's meaning.

Rafael separated one hair from the rest and plucked it free. Elizabeth stirred slightly, her lashes fluttering. Rafael claimed a second hair and she grimaced a little, then yawned. The third hair he claimed with haste, winding them together and tucking them into his purse just before her eyes opened.

Elizabeth smiled at him, stretching languidly, nude and beautiful. She was sated, he could see, and he loved the sight of her. He yearned to remain with her, but the sooner he departed, the sooner he might return. Hope lit in her eyes when she ran a hand over his bare chest, only to be replaced by disappointment when he handed her chemise to her.

"Morning comes," he whispered, unable to deny himself one sweet kiss. "It is time to ensure that you are found in your own chamber at first light."

She did not suggest that they be found together.

Indeed, Elizabeth looked vulnerable and uncertain as never she had in his experience. Rafael could not resist the opportunity to reassure her. He pushed his fingers into her hair and cupped her nape, looked into her eyes, then kissed her with sweet ardor. Her lips clung to his, her hands landing on his shoulders, and he drank deeply of her sweetness.

He broke the kiss suddenly, for he would not be tempted again, then rolled away from her. Rafael stood, then seized his own chemise and drew it over his head. He was well aware of the watchful silence behind him.

"That seems a farewell embrace," Elizabeth said, her words husky.

Rafael kept his back to her and bowed his head. "I warned you already that men of honor are most tedious."

She caught her breath and he glanced back to see that hope had lit in her eyes once again. He held her gaze, because he could do naught else, and though he did not wish to give her false hope, Rafael hoped that this time, Elizabeth could truly read his thoughts. They stared at each other for a long potent moment, then moved as one to dress and depart.

※

Elizabeth had no regrets, save that something had changed in Rafael's manner.

He seemed distant after that last kiss, and even that kiss had been tinged with a sadness that Elizabeth associated with partings. She saw a new resolve in him, but feared to ask its import.

She guessed he still meant to leave.

She did not wish to hear him say as much.

She hoped he would ask Alexander for her hand in the morning, but now that her innocence was lost, all of Rafael's protests echoed in her thoughts, feeding her doubts.

She did not want him to feel compelled to wed her, for she wanted a life with her to be a choice made freely. She did not want him to be bound to her against his will. She ached to know his intent, but she knew he did not wish to confide it in her.

And for once, Elizabeth was afraid to provoke Rafael for more.

She curled against him as he rode to Kinfairlie, hoping this would not be the last she saw of him. His arm was tightly wrapped around her, his manner grim, and they reached the crumbled border wall all too soon for her taste. The sky was smeared pink and she could hear a woman in Kinfairlie's village shouting at some child to see the goats milked and quickly. She feared now to be caught, for she would not see Rafael chastised by Alexander, not for what Elizabeth herself had done.

She had compelled him to claim her. She had made her choice and used her own power over Rafael to make him do as he did not wish.

She wondered only now at the price of her choice.

He halted Rayo by the twisted tree and swung out of the saddle, gripping her waist to lift her to the ground. For a poignant moment she was in the circle of his arms and could see the regret in his eyes.

"I do not regret it," she whispered with fervor. "No matter the price."

"Nor do I," Rafael said, his finger sliding up her cheek. "Nor can I. I hope only that the price is not too high."

"I will pay it," she said, feeling defiant again.

Rafael smiled. "And I would protect what is precious," he murmured, his gaze trailing over her as if he would memorize the sight of her. She knew she looked to have been savored, that her hair was unbound and her garb askew, but his slow smile was filled with admiration. "Be well, *mi pequeño ángel*, for if there is no goodness left to defend, then the carnage of men has no point." He held her gaze, then turned away.

That was the moment Elizabeth knew for certain that he meant to leave her.

She choked back a sob, determined not to beg or entreat him, then walked steadily to Kinfairlie's portal. She heard hoof beats behind her, but did not look back.

Elizabeth had gambled her all, and she feared she had lost.

On the threshold, though, she wondered. What had Rafael meant about a man of honor?

Did he call himself one?

Elizabeth spun, but he was far up the coast, his destrier racing north in haste to be gone.

Or in haste to embark on a quest.

Elizabeth smiled then, her heart aflame with new hope, and willed Rafael to succeed.

❧

Rafael returned to the cavern, after he had taken Elizabeth back to Kinfairlie, burning with his new purpose. He cast his saddlebags at the floor of the cavern and dug in the dirt with his bare hands. In moments, the djinn trap was revealed, its occupant as displeased at it had been earlier.

"You have a choice in this moment," Rafael said briskly. "For I can release you before I depart, or leave you in captivity."

The small djinn was defiant. *"A price you will ask, that much is true, but I know not that I would give aught to you."*

Rafael squatted down beside the trap and spoke so that his determination would be heard clearly. "The price of your freedom is simple: you must grant three wishes to whoever sets you free."

"Three wishes to you, worse, wishes three, this price is far too high for me."

Rafael straightened. "Then you may remain there. I do not care."

"Aiiiiiiiii!" The creature screamed, and whatever it did made the copper vessel shake. Rafael watched with interest, wondering if the djinn trap would hold. The bottle trembled and rattled, but the cork did not budge.

The creature swore and there was a clunk, as if it kicked its prison. It was not surprised to have failed, so Rafael assumed it had tried the feat before, without success. *"A wicked trap wrought of a spell. Some sorcerer learned his craft in Hell!"*

Rafael chuckled at that, for he had believed these creatures to be of Hell's making. "You will surrender three wishes to whoever sets you free," he insisted. "Whether it is the lady Elizabeth or me." He realized he had been listening to the creature too much for its curious habit of rhyming its speech was echoed in his own.

"Elizabeth? The maiden born of Kinfairlie? What has she to do with thee?"

"You know her?"

The creature fell into a silence that could only be called stubborn. Rafael knew he would not hear that story soon.

He had not time to wait.

He buried the coin around the djinn trap, surrounding the vessel with gold. The coins clinked, which was much to the creature's interest.

"You plan to depart but leave your hoard? Why would you leave your treasure stored?"

"It is for the lady Elizabeth," Rafael informed the djinn. "Finvarra would..."

"Say not his name, least not so loud!" the creature cried.

Rafael leaned closer. "That one would snare her in his realm," he confided. "And trap her there when the portals close between our worlds. Should she free you, you will grant her three wishes and aid her to survive his scheme."

"You cannot trust one such as he," the creature whispered. *"A trick he has for everything."*

"Then she will have great need of you, and you would be wise to not disappoint my hope." The creature again fell silent. Rafael threatened it with its own rhythm of speech. "Do not play games with me, even dead I will find thee. I will take payment from your hide, and show you torment none can abide."

The small djinn hissed. *"I like neither wager nor debt, I stay here rather than take your bet."*

"Then we are agreed," Rafael said easily. He buried the djinn trap once again. "Perhaps by the time someone comes, you will have changed your mind."

He heard the creature scream again. He heard it bellow and he saw a slight vibration as the jar shook only a little from its efforts.

He had no doubt that time would feed the djinn's compliance.

He returned to Ravensmuir, his saddlebags empty, more than ready to be gone. The sooner he departed, the sooner he might return.

While he waited for his companions, Rafael sat in Rayo's stall and braided the three long ebony hairs from Elizabeth. He coiled the finished braid around his wrist and bound it there, vowing that he would not remove it until he was by her side again.

Nay, until her hand was securely within his own.

※

Elizabeth rose from bed when the bells began to peal from Kinfairlie's chapel, calling the townspeople to the earliest mass of the day. The village was sleepy and quiet all the same, unusually so, but there had been much merriment at Ravensmuir the day before. Many would sleep late after those revels and go later to mass.

The hall was silent, but Elizabeth's heart thundered with that newfound hope. A man of honor. Rafael had never referred to himself as one before—indeed, he insisted upon the opposite.

Did she dare to hope that he meant to ask for her hand on this morning?

Did she dare to imagine that Alexander might agree?

Elizabeth dressed quietly and climbed to the chamber of Kinfairlie where Alexander was able to look inland over his holdings. The shadow of Kinfairlie's tower stretched like a dark finger across the land at this hour. She could hear the sea crashing against the shore and a few sea birds circled the tour, calling to each other. The sky was awash in hues of silver, blue and rose, and the wind from the east was crisp.

There would be a storm before the morrow.

Elizabeth's throat was tight. She pulled her fur-lined cloak more tightly around herself, unable to deny her sense that he had made a choice. She hoped it was one she favored. She eyed Ravensmuir's new tower, scarcely daring to blink.

No sooner had the sun cleared the horizon than a party on horseback cleared Ravensmuir's gates. Elizabeth narrowed her eyes, noting the size of the company, the number of the riders. She saw how the horses were burdened with belongings and how the men wore both their armor and their heavy cloaks.

They looked as if they took all of their belongings, as if they left for good.

Rafael had told her that the Sable League would ride out this day.

Elizabeth bit her lip as the rough party of departing mercenaries rode closer. She did not have to wonder whether Rafael was among them, for she could see the crimson ribbon that was bound to her own. It stretched across the sky, tugging slightly at hers, as if it would break free.

Surely it could not do that?

Elizabeth did not know. She followed the course of the ribbon, narrowing her eyes to see that the dark-haired man bound to it eschewed his helmet. He rode with confidence, tall in the saddle, and there was no doubt that his steed was the chestnut destrier with the white mark upon his brow.

Rafael Rodriguez.

She heard the hoof beats of the horses grow in volume and noted that the men rode in grim silence. She straightened, hungry for every detail about Rafael.

She hoped he would come for her, that he would drop to his knee in the hall and offer for her hand. She hoped that their ways could not be parted, that in some way they would be together for all time.

But Rafael did not slow his steed. He did not turn Rayo down the road that led to Kinfairlie's gates. Elizabeth's heart thundered as he rode directly past, without so much as a backward glance. The crimson ribbon that bound her fate to his was stretched so thin and taut that she could scarcely discern it.

He was leaving.

Elizabeth prayed with fervor, determined to believe that he meant to return. She would hope for that day. She would wait for it. She would not lose faith.

A man of honor.

Elizabeth gripped the sill as Rafael's figure faded from view, and the world itself began to grey around her. The color drained of all she could see and that chill permeated her body. She felt cold and apart from the world of men again, and she had forgotten how vigorous an impression it was.

Because she had been with Rafael.

She did not regret what she had done and she would not take another. She thought of the Douglas clan and their infernal lust for

Ravensmuir and knew she would see that plan foiled. It might be years before Rafael returned, if ever he did, but she would wait for him.

And if she had to let others know that she was a maiden no longer to protect her unmarried state, so be it. The sole man whose opinion mattered would not think less of her for it.

Whatever transpired, Elizabeth would not forget Rafael. She had finally found a man to whom she could surrender her heart, a man she believed could fulfill all of her desires and one with whom she would savor every day of her life—and he had thought himself unworthy of her. Elizabeth turned away from the view with tears in her eyes.

She descended to the chamber she occupied alone, all of her sisters now married with babes of their own. It was unthinkable that she could wed another man, for she would not be able to offer her heart to him. Elizabeth saw this as a fundamental basis for marriage, and she would not cheat any man who would think to wed her.

She would spend her life alone, if Rafael did not return.

Never seeing him again was a dour prospect and one that made her want to weep.

The mirror tugged at her thoughts, as if tempting her to dig it out of the trunk. On this day, Elizabeth could not deny the temptation. She locked the portal behind herself and fell to her knees before the trunk, her hands shaking as she retrieved the mirror. For a terrifying heartbeat, she feared it to be gone, then her fingers touched the cold silver of its handle. It was the only thing that seemed to glimmer with promise in all of her surroundings. There was a fierce enchantment upon it, to be sure. She brought it to light, caressed the strange leaves that formed its frame, then turned it over and looked within it.

She saw the realm of the Fae, in all its beauty and color, as surely as if she peered through a window to that realm. She was immediately charmed by the sight of their joy. She saw a thousand sprites, dancing in the sunlight, their wings glittering like jewels. She saw fountains of golden mead and platters of fruits she could not name. She heard their lilting music, that music that so coaxed a person to dance, and was certain there was no finer place to abide.

She tore her gaze away from the vision presented by the mirror with an effort and looked around herself. The mortal world was pale and grey in contrast to the splendor of the Fae court shown within the mirror. She could no longer see any Fae within the chamber and feared they had retreated to their own realm. Elizabeth went to the window, seeking some sign that all was as it had been, but found none. The Fae appeared to be gone, but it was more of a shock that the air over Kinfairlie village was no longer filled with the tangling ribbons of those who loved. She twisted her head and looked skyward, noting that the ribbons that had been over Kinfairlie's tower were also gone. There were no ribbons to be seen.

She could not believe that her gift was gone. Nay, it must be that the Fae had retreated, taking their tokens and treasures with them.

Either that, or there was no love left in the mortal realm at all.

The thought struck a chill in her heart. Elizabeth looked again into the mirror, and was relieved to see similar ribbons there in abundance. Indeed, the sprites danced through them, used them as slides and knotted them for lovers who stared adoringly into each other's eyes. Elizabeth smiled and peered deeper, leaning so close to the mirror that the tip of her nose nearly touched its surface.

She did not realize that she could not longer avert her gaze. If she had realized as much, she might not have cared.

Rafael, after all, was gone, and until he returned, she had only to wait.

Elizabeth also did not notice that a deep blue vine appeared on her flesh, sprouting from beneath her breast, where her heart's beat could be most strongly felt. It twined, silently spreading over her skin, snaring Elizabeth in a tracery of blue leaves and vines.

It was not unlike the silver setting of the mirror Finvarra had dropped, except that it grew with steady persistence, unchecked and unnoted.

For no one else in Kinfairlie's hall had ever been able to see the Fae or their signs.

Claire Delacroix

Sunday, October 31, 1428

Feast Day of the martyr Saint Quintinus and of Saint Wolfgang, Bishop of Regensburg.

All Saints' Eve.

Claire Delacroix

Chapter Sixteen

Outside Orléans

It had been comparatively simple for Rafael to return to his familiar trade. Despite Malcolm's warnings, passage across the Channel had been easy to arrange, though more than one man who remained in the Sable League jested that it was because the English wished to be rid of them. They had word of Rodrigo Villandrando immediately in Calais and rode to seek him out. *L'Écorcheur* was where he had been reputed to be, though newly established as a nobleman with a title to his name.

Rafael had been struck by the change in the man he had known for years. Rodrigo was jovial where once he had been calculating. It seemed that service to Charles the VI suited him well. He had welcomed the Sable League with gusto, hiring them all at a fair price on the spot. Within days, Rafael and his men had been dispatched to reconnoiter the situation at Orléans. The city had been surrounded by the English in their ongoing quest to lay claim — or reclaim — much of the territory of France.

Orléans was besieged, but the English troops were stretched thin to surround the city. Rodrigo believed that the siege could be broken, and the Sable League had been dispatched to discover the means to do so.

It was labor that paid well enough, but unlikely to yield the results Rafael sought. He was impatient to win a holding and return to Elizabeth, mindful of the dark king and the closing of portals between the realms. He felt that time was short, but this was the test Rodrigo offered to him, and he was determined to succeed at it.

Rafael had divided the company into small parties and dispatched them to taverns and villages around the perimeter of Orléans. He charged them to listen in the taverns and buy ale for soldiers, then report regularly to him of whatever they learned. He was certain that some man would err and speak too loudly.

He had made preparations, in case all did not proceed well for his person.

Rafael had sought out a scribe in two different towns on his route south. He had no ability to write himself and wanted to guarantee that Elizabeth's future was assured, if he did not return. The gold was hers; the djinn in the trap hers to command. In his absence, both would give her choices. He chose cryptic wording that only Elizabeth would understand, committing his message to her in one missive and recording his will in the other.

Then he sought a third scribe to address the missives, to which he had already affixed his seal.

It was then that he recalled Elizabeth's assertion.

Trust is the most stable currency.

He had never traveled with a squire, for he had never wished to trust another being with his secrets or even his routines. If he meant to become the man Elizabeth might wed and, more importantly, the one who might make her happy, he needed to continue on the path of change that she had set him upon.

Rafael summoned Hans and Xavier to him, knowing his impulse was good. They came to him quickly, though with some trepidation, for Rafael never summoned any boy unless he had labor for him or a chastisement.

"I have need of a squire," Rafael told the boys, who both blinked in their surprise. Hans looked even more astonished than usual. "In fact, I would have two, because I would entrust to you as task to be done in the case of my demise. You each shall stand witness to the other, as well as serve me as squires."

"You will not die, sir!" Xavier exclaimed.

"All men die, and none can choose the day." Rafael showed them the two missives. "I carry these within my tabard. If I die, I would charge you both to see to their delivery."

"I cannot read, sir," protested Hans.

"Nor I," said Xavier.

"Nor I," Rafael admitted with a smile. "It is a skill for clerks not warriors, and so I must trust that these scribes wrote what I instructed them to write. In case they did not, you two shall stand witness to my desires." He waited until they both nodded. "I own little, save my armor and my steed. Should I die with both yet in my possession, I would have you take my coin and travel north to Scotland. I would have you take my sword and Rayo to Malcolm at Ravensmuir, along with this missive with the single seal." He held it up and they nodded. "Within this is my will, which grants both of these to him."

"And the other, sir?"

"The other you will deliver to the lady Elizabeth at neighboring Kinfairlie. You will entrust my dagger to her, as well." He sat back and considered the boys. "I also grant you the right to use whatsoever coin I possess at the time of my death for your travel expenses, and if any remains, you have the right to divide it equally as your own."

"Sir!" Hans gaped in wonder.

"Fear not," Rafael said, warning the boys with a smile. "I intend to live long and for you to labor hard before you lay claim to that coin."

The boys laughed, reassured, for this was the Rafael they knew.

And Rafael smiled, for he had created a legacy for the first time.

Now he would build upon that foundation.

☙

It was not long before Rafael's scheme bore fruit. A mercenary in the employ of the English and one stationed near a minor gate to the city took Eustache into his confidence. It seemed that he and his fellows were selling bread to the townspeople and delivering it under cover of darkness for a high fee. He offered to share the takings with Eustache, in exchange for that man's assistance in making the delivery.

Eustache was young and comparatively new to the trade of a mercenary. He was a handsome young man, born to advantage but sufficiently unlucky to be the youngest of four sons. There was not a *denier* that would fall to his hand from his family's modest estate, and so he—like so many others of his background—chose to become a mercenary, using the skills he had mastered in earning his knighthood. Like so many of his fellows, he had few other choices, for he knew naught else.

Rafael supposed Eustache could have gone on crusade, but that course would not have seen his belly filled.

Though Rafael had been young when he took up the trade, he had never been so guileless as Eustache. Teaching the younger man to be skeptical and to doubt the word of others oft put Rafael in mind of his insistence to Elizabeth that he had never been innocent. Eustache was quick to trust and slow to strike, a combination that Rafael feared would lead to his early demise.

Once he would have been disconcerted by this combination. Once he would have felt no responsibility to try to change Eustache's fate.

But Scotland—or a maiden resident there—had wrought a change in Rafael. He trained more with Eustache and tried to convince that man to be more skeptical. Though he made some progress, he saw that Eustache's soul would never be wary.

When this mercenary made his offer, Eustache was pleased.

Rafael thought it too good to be true.

"You are skeptical of all!" Eustache protested.

"And you are skeptical of naught," Rafael retorted. "Step back and look at yourself. You look French. You sound French. A man could be forgiven for believing that you had no love for the English."

"But any man can be bought."

"Aye, but you do not look like a man who can be bought so cheaply as this," Rafael said. He stood up with pride. "While I look like a man who will do any deed for a price."

Better you than me.

He heard Franz's mockery in his thoughts and recognized the counsel of his instincts. It was true that Eustache had made the wager. It was true that Rafael could let matters proceed as they would, even fearing that the younger man would be betrayed. It was true that none would hold it against him if his premonition proved to be right.

But Rafael could not do as much this time.

He borrowed Eustache's cloak, pulled up the hood, and—after some argument—took the younger man's place.

It was no consolation to learn that he *was* right.

Rafael had a stronger sense of deceit as he drew close to the arranged meeting spot. He spied a pair of shadows ahead and gave a whistle, the arranged signal. Even though he drew his dagger, keeping it hidden beneath his cloak, he was surprised.

He was ambushed from behind by at least two other men. One jumped upon his back and fitted his hands around Rafael's neck. His grip was poor, though, and a solid jab of Rafael's elbow into his gut loosened it more. Rafael spun and kicked him in the crotch, flinging the man's weight aside. The other seized Rafael's shoulder and decked him so hard that he heard his nose crack as it broke. Blood gushed from his nostrils, but Rafael jabbed his dagger into that assailant's gut.

He was momentarily glad when the two ahead of him raced to join the fray—until he realized that they were allied with his assailants. One punched Rafael in the stomach, making him double over in pain.

The quiet fury of battle seized Rafael, along with a certitude that he had been deceived. He fought with deadly precision then. He stabbed the fourth, driving his dagger so deep that he could feel the man's blood on his hand. The first man leaped on him again, but Rafael spun and slashed at that man's face. When he fell back, his hands over his face, Rafael kicked him until he fell to the ground. He was satisfied when he felt his boot connect with bone. There was a crack and a moan that might have made him laugh aloud, had he not been tripped from behind.

Someone tried to seize his dagger and disarm him. Rafael gripped it tightly, unwilling to surrender the weapon, and his wrist was twisted so hard that it snapped. The dagger was wrenched from his hand, but there was naught he could do about it with his wrist broken. He felt the cold blade of a knife slide over his skin, grazing his side but not biting deep. Something hard collided with his temple and he staggered, dizzy from the blow.

In that moment of vulnerability, a cord was snapped around Rafael's throat and pulled tight. The garrote choked him and he sputtered, as helpless as a babe. He heard his attackers chortle as he tried to get his fingers beneath the lace. He kicked and fought, struggling to escape while he could.

Against his every effort, all faded around him as he gasped for air. He was dimly aware that he hit the ground and knew someone roughly pulled off his boots, then Rafael knew no more.

His last thought was regret, certain as he was that he would soon be in Hell.

An eternity with Franz would be a torment that could not be endured.

But Rafael would have no choice in that.

☙

Elizabeth was in her chamber, bent yet again over Finvarra's mirror. Eleanor was calling her to the hall for the evening meal, but she did not want to put the mirror aside.

She knew that on this night, All Hallows' Eve, the veil between the worlds was thin. It seemed that the shadows were full of ghosts to her, specters that whispered of peril and danger.

The notions of peril and danger turned Elizabeth's thoughts to Rafael.

He was always in her thoughts, but the memory of him was brighter on some days. She had wept bitterly when her courses had come in a timely fashion, hating that she would not have a babe as a memento of their night together. Still, she knew that Rafael would have preferred that she bear no outward mark that her maidenhead had been lost.

The first of the earl's candidates for her hand had come to the board at Kinfairlie, but Elizabeth had been able to dissuade him with her indifference. She heard tell that another was to come soon and had not yet decided whether to feign a pregnancy, just to repel his interest. It could be easily achieved, with a bundle of cloth beneath her kirtle, and once she would have done it without hesitation. In these days though, she was so cold that it was hard to care so much about any matter, much less expend any effort upon it.

Elizabeth looked into the mirror, wanting the reassurance of a glimpse of the realm of the Fae, where all was vital and vigorous, where the residents were merry, where the court was filled with dancing and music.

On this night, the mirror was dark.

Elizabeth peered more deeply into it, bending close at a flicker of movement. Her eyes widened as she saw a man assaulted by four other men. He was beset in darkness and though he fought with skill, he was quickly overwhelmed. She saw the leather lace snapped around his neck, the blood on his temple and more blood streaming from his nose. She saw his eyes widen in terror, she saw him grit his teeth and struggle to pull the lace free. She saw the cord dig deeper into his throat, saw him flail, then gasped when he suddenly stilled.

His eyes were wide open, his expression one of horror.

He did not move again.

And he was Rafael.

Elizabeth dropped the mirror from her shaking hands, unable to suppress her rising tears. Rafael! Surely it could not be so.

She looked again, only to see the men stripping her beloved of his clothes. Doubtless they would sell his cloak and boots. He was cast into a dirty little creek, his nude body discarded like so much rubbish.

He did not battle them.

He did not move.

Elizabeth knew she would never forget the sight of Rafael's broken and bloody corpse, motionless in the rushes, touched by moonlight but otherwise forgotten. She choked back a sob.

Rafael was dead.

A missive was flung into the water after him and Elizabeth saw that her own name was written upon it. The ink ran in the water, though, washing away and blending with Rafael's own blood. What word had he meant to send to her?

The very fact that he had carried a missive intended for her fed her conviction that he had meant to return to her.

But he was dead. She sat down, recalling his description of the Fae court, of the corpses and specters that had appeared to him each time he had been there. For him, the court of Finvarra was a vision of Hell.

Rafael would be trapped there.

He would be tormented and alone.

Elizabeth straightened with new purpose, for she knew precisely what she had to do. She and Rafael *would* be together, but not in the mortal realm.

She would follow him to Hell.

ة▲

Rafael dreamed of an unfamiliar court. He knew he had never sat in this hall, never even glimpsed it before, but the familiar man who presided over its high table told him where it must be.

Aye, it was Alexander Lammergeier in the place of honor, his wife, Eleanor, upon his left hand. There were children aplenty but Rafael knew this must be Kinfairlie. Rafael identified Malcolm and Catriona, also sharing the board at this particular meal, as well as Vera rocking Avery. He saw Elizabeth and was shocked by her pallor. He had thought her haunted when first he had seen her, but on this night, she looked to be in mourning. She toyed with her food and was so thin that she must have eaten little recently.

Had his departure done this to Elizabeth?

Rafael did not want to believe it. He had not wanted her to have false hope, but that would have been better than the complete lack of hope she seemed to have in this vision. He had never seen her in despair and did not wish to see it again.

Was this vision of the future? The present or the past?

The way Catriona's hand rested on her belly, just slightly rounded, indicated that it could not be the past. She must carry Malcolm's seed, and Rafael was glad for his former comrade.

But Elizabeth looked like a lost soul, and the sight made him ache with a longing to tempt her smile.

Or better yet, to bring color to her lips with an ardent kiss.

Catriona leaned forward, addressing Alexander. "Since we are at Kinfairlie, I should like to hear the tale of the red, red rose."

The red, red rose. The dark king had mentioned such a thing. Rafael listened avidly.

In his vision, Malcolm chuckled. "Aye, show us the mark upon the floor, Alexander."

"Nay, Alexander must *tell* the tale so that we know the full meaning of the mark," Eleanor said.

"You all know it as well as I do," that man protested, but a chorus of dissent greeted his words. Elizabeth's eldest brother raised a hand for the company to fall silent, laughing as he did so. Alexander straightened his tabard and rose to his feet, taking a last sip of his wine before he began. They had made merry on this night, Rafael could see, and he noted again their uncommon confidence in their security. "You must all be kind to me on this night, for I have not told this tale in years."

"Not since you encouraged a certain maiden to sleep in the highest chamber of this tower," Malcolm said. At Catriona's confusion, he smiled. "He induced our sister Vivienne to sleep in the high chamber with this tale."

"Do I sense that he had a scheme?" Catriona asked.

"A trick, more like," Eleanor said with a shake of her head. "Had I been in residence, it would never have occurred."

"It all ended well enough," Alexander said in his own defense and they laughed in easy agreement. "And so, a tale!" The company cheered and settled themselves in anticipation. Cups were topped up and the serving women darted between the tables to ensure that all had what they desired. Elizabeth glanced up for the first time, though still she looked pale and disinterested.

Had she been ill? Rafael's innards clenched at the notion.

Alexander raised his voice. "First I must regale you with a bit of family history. Most of you are aware that Kinfairlie was razed to the ground in our great-grandmother's youth." He lifted his cup in salute to Elizabeth. "And the youngest of my sisters was named for that lady, Mary Elise of Kinfairlie."

There was a patter of polite applause before he continued. "In time, the holding was returned by the crown to Ysabella, the daughter of Mary Elise for she had wed Merlyn Lammergeier, Laird of Ravensmuir. Roland, our father, was the son of Merlyn and Ysabella, as was Tynan, later Laird of Ravensmuir himself. Our grandfather Merlyn rebuilt Kinfairlie from the very ground, so that Roland could become its laird when he was of age. And so it was that Roland and Catherine came to Kinfairlie newly wedded. There were already tales told about this holding and about that chamber." He paused and surveyed the rapt company. "It was already whispered that Kinfairlie kissed the lips of the realm of the Fae."

A ripple of delight passed through the company, and Rafael shivered even as Alexander continued.

"The first castellan of Kinfairlie had a daughter, a lovely maiden who was most curious. Since there were only servants in the keep before Roland's arrival, this damsel was permitted to wander wheresoever she desired within the walls. And so it was that she explored the chamber at the top of the tower. There are three windows in that chamber and all of them look toward the sea.

"Though the view is fine, the chamber is cursed cold, for the openings were wrought too large for glass and the wooden shutters pose no barrier to the wind, especially when a storm is rising. That was why no one had spent much time in the room. This maiden, however, had done so and she had noted that one window did not grant the view that it should have done.

"Clouds crossed the sky in that window, but never were framed by the others. Uncommon birds could be spied only in the one window, and the sea never quite seemed to be the same viewed through that window as through the others. The difference was subtle, and a passing glance would not reveal any discrepancy, but the maiden became convinced that this third window was magical. She wondered whether it looked into the past, or into the future, or into the realm of the Fae, or into some other place altogether." Alexander paused and spared a pointed glance at Elizabeth. "And so, like so many intrepid maidens of my acquaintance, she resolved that she would discover the truth."

Elizabeth barely glanced her brother's way, and that man frowned as he sipped his wine. Rafael was relieved that he was not the sole one to have noticed the change in her.

"The maiden slept in the chamber for several nights and when she was asked what she had seen, she only smiled. She insisted that she had seen naught, but her smile...her smile hinted at a thousand mysteries." Alexander shrugged. "And then there was no opportunity to ask her, for on the morning after she had slept in that chamber for three nights, the damsel could not be found."

Vera shuddered in obvious disapproval at this detail, her gaze falling upon Elizabeth.

"I do not have to tell you that they searched every nook and cranny for the maiden. Though they fair tore Kinfairlie apart, there was no sign of her. In fact, she was never seen again."

"But..." someone in the company prompted.

"But—" Alexander acknowledged with a smile and a raised finger "—on the sill of one window—I suspect I know which one it was—on the morning of the maiden's disappearance, the castellan's wife found a single rose. It appeared to be red, as red as blood, but as soon as she lifted it in her hands, it began to pale. By the time she carried it to the hall, the rose was white, and no sooner had the castellan seen it, than it began to melt. It was wrought of ice, and in a matter of moments, it was no more than a puddle of water upon the floor."

Alexander left the high table and strode to the middle of the hall. The children squirmed from their seats and followed him. He had a few benches moved, then pointed to a spot on the floor. It shimmered beneath his finger, as if stained by some substance that none could have named.

"It was here that the water fell," Alexander said softly, his words carrying over the rapt silence of the company. "And when an old woman working in the kitchens spied the mark and heard the tale of the rose, she cried out in dismay. It seems that there is an old tale of Fae lovers claiming mortal brides, that the portal between their world and ours is at Kinfairlie. A Fae suitor can peer through the portal, though they all know they should not, and he could fall in love with a mortal maiden he glimpses there."

Finvarra, the dark king. Finvarra, who had his gaze locked upon Elizabeth and had crowed of his intent to claim her by Midwinter. Was Elizabeth's manner the result of some trickery of the dark king? She looked sepulchral, to be sure, as if she could easily take a place alongside Franz.

The notion troubled Rafael deeply. He had expected that he might die, with his quest unfulfilled, but had never believed Elizabeth to be in peril. Too late he understood that her confidence had done her disservice, for she had been sure the choice would be hers whether she went to Finvarra. Worse, her confidence had fed Rafael's own surety that she would be safe until his return.

Rafael eyed Elizabeth. He sensed that something had quickened within her at Alexander's reciting of this tale, though her pose had not changed. She kept her gaze locked on her hands, but he had the feeling that she paid closer attention than the others realized.

He recalled Finvarra's claim that the portals at Ravensmuir and Kinfairlie would close soon, and seal shut forever. He wished he was not so far away, for he felt a dreadful portent of doom.

Alexander smiled at the children as he continued with what he clearly believed to be a mere fable. "And the bride price a smitten Fae suitor leaves when he claims that bride for his own is a single red, red rose, a rose that is not truly a rose, but a Fae rose wrought of ice." He scuffed the floor with his toe. "Though its form does not endure, the mark of its magic is never truly lost."

There was a moment of silence at the end of the tale, then the company broke into applause. The children cheered and Alexander scooped up the youngest one, urging them all back to the high table. Discussion broke out in the hall, but Rafael noted how Elizabeth straightened with purpose. There was a gleam of determination in her eye, but she excused herself demurely and left the hall. Though the women watched her go with concern, not a one followed her.

That, Rafael feared, was an error of the greatest magnitude. Worse, he could do naught to set matters to rights.

*

There was naught in the realm of mortals for Elizabeth any longer, not with Rafael dead. She would be with him, as she could not be otherwise. She went to her own chamber and donned her fur-lined cloak, then took the mirror so it would not be discovered in her absence.

The prospect of being with Rafael again encouraged her as little else could have done, and she climbed the stairs to the top of Kinfairlie's tower with new purpose. She had a torch to light her way, though she could scarce feel the heat from it. The cold seemed to be more intense to her this winter.

She cast a glance behind herself, then bent to pick the lock with a pin from her hair. She was beyond glad that Rosamunde had taught her this skill, for none would discover what she did in time to intervene. She smiled when the tumblers rolled. There was some resistance to her attempt to push the door open, and Elizabeth was astonished to discover that the chamber was knee-deep in snow. The snow had drifted against the door, driven there by the wind, and though it was light and filled with sparkles, still it was deep enough to make a barrier.

She did not put a blade of steel in the threshold, nor even did she carry one, for Elizabeth had no plan to return. She would give Finvarra no easy way to expel her, either.

She strode through the snow, scattering it as she walked.

There were three windows facing the sea, just as in Alexander's tale, three large windows on the opposite side of the chamber. The outer two were shuttered, though the wind made a whistling noise as if blew between the wooden slats. The middle window, the one reputed to open to the realm of the Fae, had no shutters. It was a vast square opening in the stone wall, and one through which both the snow drifted and the starlight fell. The night sky beyond looked too dark to be a normal sky and the stars were too thick in its expanse.

There was something uncanny about the view through that window, and Elizabeth knew this to be a mark of the credence of Alexander's tale.

Finvarra sat before that middle window, his back to the night, the snow having drifted around his throne to swirl around his boots. His dark beard fairly flowed down his chest to his knees, and his garb was richly embroidered with silver and gold. A host of small Fae fluttered around him, a trio of them hovering in the air as they offered a golden chalice for his favor. His hands were braced on the arms of the regal dark chair, and his fingers were thick with jeweled rings. Those gemstones seemed to shimmer with the light of the stars, but their glitter could not compare with this king's eyes. They were dark, so dark that they might have been wrought of that midnight sky beyond the window, and his gaze was fixed upon Elizabeth.

"You have come," the king said, his voice deep and melodic. That tracery of blue remained on his skin, and when he offered his hand to Elizabeth, his sleeve pulled back to reveal more of it.

When Elizabeth stretched out her hand to take Finvarra's, her sleeve tugged in the same way and she saw the similar marks on her own skin. The sight relieved her, as if this course had been their destiny all along. She walked toward the king like a woman in a dream, then put her hand in his.

"Take me to Rafael," she said, only then noting how coy the king's smile became.

"And so it is as I foretold," Finvarra murmured with satisfaction. "And so it is that the first portal closes." He pursed his lips and blew. The flame burning on Elizabeth's torch was immediately extinguished, leaving the chamber illuminated only by starlight, moonlight, and their reflection on the snow.

*

In distant Kinfairlie, a woman who looked precisely like Elizabeth but was not that maiden descended from Kinfairlie's high tower. Outside of Elizabeth's chamber, this creature smiled at Eleanor, even as the Lady of Kinfairlie studied her in confusion.

"I thought to look out that window to the realm of the Fae," this false Elizabeth said with a meekness the real Elizabeth had seldom exhibited. Eleanor frowned at both impulse and tone. "But the portal was locked."

"You should not venture there," Eleanor chided softly, and a more keen observer would have noted her suspicion.

The changeling that had replaced Elizabeth was not aware of nuance, though. She laughed, which did little to dispel Eleanor's suspicion. "I will not do so again, to be sure. Good night!" Eleanor blinked, surprised by the change in the younger woman's manner. Elizabeth had been so saddened these past years that many had thought her ill, but suddenly, she seemed to be restored to her former self.

How could this be?

The children came running up the stairs then, calling for their mother, and Eleanor could not help but notice that Elizabeth showed little interest in them.

It was most strange. Usually, Elizabeth doted on the children, and Eleanor saw their disappointment that their aunt blithely passed them by.

Eleanor considered the portal of the chamber where Elizabeth slept alone, the one that was now securely closed, then glanced up the stairs to that high chamber. Once the children were nestled abed, she took Alexander's ring of keys and climbed the stairs. She unlocked that door and was relieved to find it as empty as ever.

Perhaps Elizabeth was smitten with a boy from the village, and Eleanor would need to intervene to ensure that Alexander allowed his sister to be happy, regardless of the status of her beloved. Perhaps a small holding could be found for that man, to satisfy both siblings and to deny the earl's increasing insistence.

Eleanor would have to find out more in the days ahead.

She locked the portal behind her, reassured that Elizabeth found some man to capture her heart and descended the stairs to the solar.

Had she noticed the red, red rose on the sill of the middle window, Eleanor would not have been so content.

Monday, November 1, 1428

All Saints' Day.

Claire Delacroix

Chapter Seventeen

Rafael dreamed of the King of the Dead. He was certain he dreamed of that hellish court because it was his fate, and he looked for Franz in the ranks of courtiers.

Instead he saw Elizabeth, her hand within that of the dark king.

The sight sent terror through Rafael and he tried to shout a warning.

But there was a loud sound, like something tearing in the core of the world. His view changed and he saw the last stall in Ravensmuir's stables, the one with the hole in the back wall that led to the realm of the Fae. Brilliant golden light spilled from the hole, but a dark mirror slid across it with lightning speed. When it slammed home, there was no music and no light, and the wall was no more than a wall in a stable.

A portal closed, just as the dark king had forecast.

And his Elizabeth was on the wrong side of the barrier.

≥●

Rafael awakened suddenly, uncertain where he was. He was on his back, his body aching, and stiffness in his bones. He could see sunlight coming through a tent overhead and smell the smoke of fires as well as the dampness of the ground.

To his relief, the bracelet of Elizabeth's braided hair was still around his wrist.

He was not dead.

Was Elizabeth lost?

"He should be dead twice over," a man whispered from close proximity, awe in his tone.

"You know what they say of Rafael," said another, his tone wry. "He would defy the very Devil to survive. The man might well be immortal."

The two men laughed quietly together. "Perhaps he has an angel watching over him," suggested the first.

An angel. His angel was lost in darkness.

"We should all have such good fortune as that."

The men mumbled agreement, then the first called to a third. "Send word that he stirs. He might awaken soon."

"Aye, sir."

Rafael heard the sound of running footsteps but he kept his eyes closed. *Mi piqueño ángel*. His first impression of Elizabeth had been the correct one. She had shown him truths he would never have faced without her and compelled him to change. But had it been too late? She was right that he had been afraid to claim her, for such a choice did make him vulnerable to loss.

But the matter was not done. Her fate was not sealed so long as the portal at Kinfairlie remained open. Though his head throbbed and his body ached, he recognized how fortunate he had been this day. The angel who watched over him had given him another chance.

Rafael was not fool enough to waste it. He would ride north as soon as he was able, ride with all haste for Kinfairlie, and win her hand, regardless of whether he had the right to do so or not.

❧

Elizabeth found herself in a Fae court adorned with silver. There was hoarfrost on the arches of the hall, on the table laden with refreshments, on the back of Finvarra's throne. There was snow underfoot, light snow that flew into the air with every step she took, and more snowflakes falling even in the shelter of the court. The Fae themselves were dressed in silver and shades of grey and white, even the marks upon their skin faded to the hue of charcoal. It seemed their world had been leeched of its color, that only shadow and light remained where once there had been all the colors of the rainbow. They still danced and sang, they still savored their mead—though it was silver now instead of golden—and they still made merry amongst themselves.

There was something amiss, something that made Elizabeth shiver even before she met the gaze of Finvarra.

"The portals close," he said softly, then beckoned to her. "The world grows dim, but we shall survive in starlight and shadow." He smiled, though his gaze remained dark and ominous. "And you have chosen to come to me, just as I foretold, and so you, too, will spend all of eternity in our court."

Elizabeth looked down to find herself similarly adorned in shades of grey. Her chemise was as white as ever it had been, but her kirtle had changed from blue to silver, and her red slippers had turned black. The gold embroidery on her hems was now silver and she saw now the tracery of dark whorls upon her pale flesh. She dared to glimpse into Finvarra's enchanted mirror and started at the sight of her wan reflection.

Her eyes, instead of being the clear green she knew them to be, were now as dark a grey as the soot on a hearth.

She looked up in alarm and scanned the company, but still she could not see the dead within their ranks. "Where is Rafael?" she demanded, realizing as soon as she had uttered the words that she should not have done so.

Finvarra laughed. "Alive, of course."

Elizabeth took a step back in horror. "But he said that he saw the dead in your court, and I saw him dead in the mirror..."

"The mirror shows what I desire it to display," Finvarra said, then put out his hand in obvious expectation. "It is a tool and one that has proven its usefulness."

Elizabeth was horrified. "He is only injured, then!"

Finvarra nodded, then snapped his fingers and extended his hand again.

"Then you deceived me!"

"I told you naught. You made your own conclusions based upon what you saw." Finvarra's eyes glittered. "And what is of greater import—you made your *choice*."

Elizabeth found herself newly fearful of his intent, for there was a cruelty in his manner that she had not noticed before. She stepped forward and hastily put the mirror in his hand, shivering when her fingertips brushed the chill of his skin.

He watched her, as a snake watches a mouse, his eyes glittering. "Mortals see their own truths in our court and in our company. The illusion shifts depending upon the viewer, as truth shifts depending upon the listener. This Rafael saw Hell when he stepped into my court, for in his heart, he fears his own judgment." Finvarra shrugged. "I have little interest in his soul, not any more."

He stood then, towering over her, the mirror disappearing into the folds of his robe as surely as if it had never been. He touched her chin with his frigid fingertip and Elizabeth struggled to keep from shivering, for she did not wish to earn his disfavor.

If she was trapped in his court forevermore, she would have need of his favor.

Finvarra studied her and she could not help but note that his lashes were less thick than Rafael's, his expression less sensual, his skin more pale, and the prospect of his kiss far less enticing. Indeed, she had been enticed by the peril both offered, but there was a world of difference between the two. Rafael would have always treated her with honor: Finvarra, however, would destroy her at a whim, if it would please him to do so.

She had erred by putting herself under his control.

And there was naught she could do to repair her mistake now. She had spoken aloud in the Fae circle, she had put herself in Finvarra's debt, and she had willingly come to him on this day. She was lost.

Unless some mortal saw fit to aid her.

Elizabeth knew who she hoped it might be, though the chances seemed remote. If ever she had need of a champion, it was on this day, but she did not know how badly Rafael was injured.

Finvarra shook his head slightly, as if seeing her dismay. "You *chose*," he reminded her, then bent to claim her with a kiss.

As soon as his mouth touched her own, Elizabeth felt a frisson of cold. It could have been a blizzard sweeping through her very veins, stealing the heat from her skin and slowing the beat of her heart. She could have sworn that she felt her innards turn to ice, even as her memories of Kinfairlie faded. Her family might have been ghosts, her recollections of them suddenly so ethereal that they might not have been even real.

Or they might have been the memories of another person, distant and irrelevant. She might have kissed a statue, one left outside for a hundred winters, one wrought of stone so cold that it could never be warmed.

Elizabeth gasped, certain that when he claimed her completely, she would be turned to stone. Finvarra lifted his head. His smile was menacing to her now.

She closed her eyes and summoned the memory of Rafael, the

fervor of his kiss, the passion of his argument, the heat of his fingers upon her breast. She felt Finvarra's influence recede and her heart beat more stridently, driving back the frost that he had conjured within her.

When she opened her eyes, Finvarra's gaze was assessing. "You defy me," he murmured, evidently both intrigued and displeased. "I have never seen the like." A storm gathered upon his brow and a ripple passed through the court as the Fae sensed their regent's pending wrath.

Elizabeth knew she had to find an explanation, and one he would find pleasing.

"It is because there is one thing I must do before I fully surrender to you," she said.

Finvarra's eyes narrowed slightly and the court stilled around them, listening avidly. "One thing?"

"I must tell you a story," Elizabeth said, her words falling in haste. "I must tell you a story to earn your good will, before I put my hand in yours for all time. I would see you entertained, my lord king, no more than that."

Finvarra appeared to be amused by the suggestion. He released her and strolled back to his throne, sweeping out his robes before he took his seat. "A story?" He chuckled under his breath and regarded her with indulgence. "We have all eternity, my beauteous Elizabeth, and it is said that any morsel is sweeter when anticipated. If you wish to build my anticipation with a story, I see no harm in it." He snapped his fingers and a stool was brought for Elizabeth, one upholstered in silver velvet with legs that seemed to be wrought of ice. It was set at his feet.

Elizabeth followed his gesture, seating herself upon it and arranging her skirts with care. Small Fae landed upon her shoulders and her hands, more hovering in the air before her, still others sitting cross-legged on the floor beside her. The music halted and the company pressed close, listening intently.

She cleared her throat and lifted her head, hoping that her ploy had some chance of success. Rafael had given her the tale she needed, and she would spin it for as long as she could, just as Scheherazade had done. "Once there was a king," she began, "a king in distant Persia, a king who loved his wife most ardently..."

Finvarra stifled a laugh and Elizabeth knew she had found the right tale.

&

"What is your name?"

The murmured Spanish question could have been from a dream. Rafael realized he had fallen into slumber again but the words awakened him. He had not heard that dialect of Spanish spoken in so many years, not since he had been a boy. It was the way they had spoken in Pamplona and he wondered if the dead greeted him again.

He stirred and frowned, but did not open his eyes.

"What is your name, my friend?" The querist persisted, and Rafael reasoned he would only fall silent when he had his reply.

"Rafael Rodriguez."

But no, the man persisted. "And your father?"

"Pedro Rodriguez."

"Your mother?"

"Iniga." Despite his inclination to sleep, Rafael felt himself being roused by this man's incessant demands.

"Have you siblings?"

"Four older sisters." Rafael continued impatiently, anticipating the question. "Constanza, Elvira, Domeca, Aldoncia. I have no other relations, so leave me be."

The man chuckled and there was something familiar about his voice.

Rafael's eyes flew open and he found himself supine in a tent, sunlight making the silk bright overhead. Rodrigo Villandrando himself sat beside him, his expression unusually benign.

Indeed, the commander of the mercenary force smiled.

Rafael was certain he had never seen *L'Écorcheur* smile so broadly before.

"Do you know what happened to you?" Rodrigo asked.

Rafael swallowed and found his throat to be sore. He raised a hand and touched his neck, wincing at how tender it was. "I was assaulted." His voice sounded hoarse and it hurt to talk.

"You kept the appointment in Eustache's stead."

"I did not trust them."

Rodrigo arched a brow. "Yet you went for Eustache."

Rafael shook his head. "He is too slow. I would give him the chance to learn better who is worthy of trust."

Rodrigo laughed. "Indeed. They nearly killed you—he would have been dead twice over." He braced his hands on his knees to regard Rafael. "They stripped you naked and left you for dead. We are lucky that Eustache has learned some measure of your suspicion, for he sought you out when you did not return. He found you before you *did* die."

"I shall see him compensated."

"I already have." Rodrigo studied Rafael, serious again. "But let me tell you a story, Rafael."

"A story, sir?"

"Once upon a time, there was a young man who earned his way with his sword."

Rafael's eyes drifted closed as the older man spoke. He could not imagine why the warrior would tell him a tale, but he strove to not be rude.

"He traveled far and wide, reliant upon no one and savoring all that life had to offer. One day, he arrived in a town where he had lived as a child, and he saw again a woman he had once loved with all his heart. Let us call her Iniga."

Rafael started so that his eyes flew open. "It is not that common a name."

Rodrigo held his gaze. "Nay, it is not." He paused for a moment, then continued. "She had been wed in his absence, though she recognized him as well. He thought the matter resolved between them and did not regret it, for he knew that he was no man to stay in one place with one woman and be happy. But one night, Iniga sought him out and begged for his help. It seemed that she had borne four daughters to her husband, and he was impatient for a son. She said she knew her husband's seed would not make a son— indeed, with four daughters, she had evidence aplenty—and she entreated the young man to lie with her, one time, for all they had meant to each other. She asked him to assure her future."

Rafael could not doze, not when he knew the woman in the tale bore such a resemblance to what he knew of his own mother.

"The young man understood then that her husband was unkind to her, and that much depended upon her bearing the son that man desired. He argued with her, but he knew as well as she how matters would be. He and Iniga were together not once but three times before he left the town behind. He thought of her often, though she could never be his woman, and he hoped that all had come right for her.

"A little over a year later, he had the opportunity to return to that same town. He was glad of the chance and he sought out Iniga. To his delight, she had borne a son. To his dismay, the boy was less than vigorous, for he had been born too early. She did not say and the young man did not ask, but he sensed that her husband's fists were the reason the boy had left her womb too early. There was little he could do for her, but she showed him the boy that was his son, and he gave her coin that she might go on pilgrimage to pray for the boy to be healed."

Rafael could not believe his ears. "To Compostela," he said softly. "With all her daughters."

Rodrigo nodded. "And so she went, but Fortune did not ride with Iniga. Plague came to Compostela while she was there and swept through the city. It was particularly virulent in the crowded accommodations used by pilgrims. Her youngest daughter succumbed first."

"Aldoncia," Rafael whispered.

"Perhaps so. They could not leave before she was buried, and while they awaited the priest's blessing, two more of the girls fell ill. By the time all of her daughters had been buried in Compostela, all dead of the plague, Iniga herself was ill. She begged her husband to leave her there to die, to take their son to safety and to ensure his own welfare as well." Rodrigo looked across the room, his lips in a grim line. "At least that was the version of the tale he recounted."

Rafael frowned, for it seemed that Rodrigo knew more than he shared.

"The young mercenary had returned to the village a year later, seeking Iniga, but could only learn that she had gone on pilgrimage and not returned. Her husband had once earned his way as a pirate and a thief, and the young mercenary feared the man had discovered Iniga's infidelity and abandoned her. It took him two years to find Iniga's husband, though he sought him with fervor. In the end, he found Iniga's husband by happenstance, spotting him in a tavern in La Rochelle. The husband vaguely recalled the young mercenary, and confided that he had returned to his trade, having lost his wife and children.

"He told of the pilgrimage, but insisted that he had been unable to leave his beloved wife, despite her entreaty, and that both she and the son had died shortly afterward. Though he wept into his wine, the young mercenary sensed that he told but half the tale. Perhaps Iniga's deed had been discovered. After leaving the husband, the young man traveled to Compostela in search of Iniga's grave and the place she had died. The woman who had rented rooms to the family confided not only that the infant boy had survived, but that the husband had taken the boy to his kin in Gijón. Hoping that his son might have been cast aside but still alive, the young mercenary hastened to Gijón in search of his son."

Rodrigo shook his head. "But if ever the boy had been there, he was in Gijón no longer. The year before, pirates from the north of Castile had attacked the town of Poole on the south coast of England. In retaliation, English pirates had sailed to Spain and attacked Gijón. All who had lived in that town were either dead or scattered to the four winds. Not a whisper could be found of one small boy who had been born too soon."

His gaze met Rafael's steadily. "And so, the young man continued with his life and his trade. Ultimately, when he had a title and wealth to his name, he wed a beautiful woman. It was God's grace that she should only bear him daughters, and he thought often of the boy who had been lost. He sought him still, dispatching men to seek some tidings of whether the boy had lived or died, and spent much coin on the quest for Iniga's son." Rodrigo smiled. "But as is so oft the case, he sought far and wide for what was right beneath his gaze."

"I do not understand."

"I was Iniga's lover." Rodrigo said with a conviction that could not be doubted. "Our son had a port wine mark on his buttock, the shape of an open hand on his right cheek. It was the only flaw upon him, and you bear the same mark."

Rafael nodded, amazed.

"I had heard comments about the Devil's hand being upon you, Rafael, but I had no notion that the men referred to a birthmark."

"You never bathe with the men, sir."

Rodrigo smiled. "And so I should have done. I do find it hard to believe that you, Rafael Rodriguez, were ever a sickly child born too soon, yet the mark tells no lie: you are my lost son." Rodrigo smiled. "And I could not be more pleased, for I have often thought that a man of such valor and skill as you would make his father proud." Rodrigo offered his hand and Rafael stared at it in surprise, before he placed his own within it.

Surely this could not be.

Then he smiled, for it was worthy of a tale, and that would make Elizabeth smile.

Rodrigo laughed and clapped Rafael's other shoulder in delight. "You are my son!" he repeated with joy. "And the best of it is that I have found you just when I have the means to ensure that you have the position in the world that you deserve." He nodded down at Rafael. "I will give you command of a company..."

"Nay," Rafael said, recognizing opportunity when it was before him.

"But you are a man of war..."

"And I would be a man with a holding." Rafael smiled at the older man. "I would be, like *Mío Cid*, a man with a citadel to defend."

Rodrigo smiled, understanding lighting his eyes. "If I give you a holding, you will have need of a bride, my son."

"I know just the one," Rafael said, for it was true.

He only hoped that he could arrive in Scotland in time.

Friday, December 24, 1428

Feast Day of Saints Thrasilla and Emiliana.
Vigil of the Nativity of Christ.

Christmas Eve.

Claire Delacroix

Chapter Eighteen

A ripple passed through the realm of the Fae, a whispering acknowledged by every leaf and spore and strand of hair. It felt to Elizabeth as if a million butterflies had fluttered their wings in the same instant, then stilled immediately afterward. There was no visible sign that anything had occurred, but she felt unsettled and anxious afterward.

It was clear that the Fae felt similarly, although they knew the reason for what they had felt. Elizabeth glanced up from her place at Finvarra's feet, realizing that the Fae stood at attention or bowed toward one end of the court. They were fairly humming in their anticipation, some excited and some tremulous, and she guessed that the sensation had indicated the arrival of some personage of importance.

When Finvarra cleared his throat, Elizabeth marveled. She turned to see a tall and exquisitely beautiful woman leading a procession into the court from the far end. She was garbed in rich brocade and jewels, her hair so long that it fell to her ankles. She was luminous but faded as well, like silvered sunlight.

She halted before Finvarra, who frowned, stroked his beard and did not rise from his throne. "My lady."

"Am I? Still?" she asked, her gaze sliding over Elizabeth with unconcealed disdain. "Is this the newest?"

"I owe you no explanation," Finvarra said. "And indeed, Una, I have a partner awaiting me for a game of chess."

She smiled. "I am sure the stakes are high, as you prefer."

"I am sure they are not your concern," Finvarra replied. He stood and bowed, his manner curt and somewhat impatient, then he strode from the court as if he could not leave it quickly enough. Elizabeth made to rise and follow him, for she was certain that was his desire, but she found the cool hand of the Fae Queen upon her shoulder.

"Stay," Una commanded. She slid into the place on the throne that her husband had vacated, as sinuous as a great cat, and stroked the arms as if to caress them. She smiled at Elizabeth, hunger in her eyes, then turned to the Elphine Queen. "Another mortal?"

"She came to him," the Elphine Queen replied, moonlight to the other monarch's sunshine.

Una laughed beneath her breath. "Not by choice, I am sure."

"Oh, but it was," the other insisted.

Una's smile broadened. "They all *believe* they make a choice. In truth, his sorcery is so strong that they have none." She arched a brow. "Was it the mirror this time? The one that snares the beloved with a single glance? Or was it the red, red rose wrought of ice, the bride price paid as if he were a suitor in truth?" Una pursed her lips. "I suppose it might have been the spindle that pricks the thumb of his intended and casts her into a dreamless sleep. He has not used that one for a while."

"A red, red rose wrought of ice?" the Elphine Queen echoed, her manner amused. "Of the tales?"

"The very one," Una said, her gaze fixed upon Elizabeth. "Do you know of it?"

"Aye, my lady. It is left for maidens who cross through the portal to the realm of the Fae in my home of Kinfairlie."

"Kinfairlie!" the Elphine Queen breathed. "I lost a mortal lover there."

"My husband has not shared your misfortune," Una said, uttering the last word with a bitterness that made Elizabeth wonder at her meaning. She kept her eyes downcast, knowing it would be more respectful, but she felt Una watching her closely, as if to dare her into defiance. "Indeed, he *hunts* frequently at Kinfairlie."

Elizabeth jumped when the Fae Queen seized her chin, compelling her to look up. Her eyes were like shards of mirrors, a thousand hues of silver and gold, melding and shifting so that Elizabeth was dizzied by the sight. "Do you know that you are only the latest, and that you will be the last?"

Elizabeth shook her head. "I know naught of King Finvarra's plans," she said, for it was true.

Una smiled and leaned back in the throne, beckoning for a cup of ale. "But he has no secrets from me, not any longer, for we have been wed since time immemorial."

"But he has never been faithful," the Elphine Queen observed.

"I am content to let him indulge his fondness for fine steeds and for a good match of chess. I am not content to share his other charms any longer, though."

"It seems you will not have to share him with mortals, not now that the portals close forever." The Elphine Queen was discontent. "The one at Ravensmuir is already barricaded against us."

"And so will be the one at Kinfairlie at Midwinter," said Una with satisfaction. "Then finally Avalon after that. The realms will be separated, the tithe for souls will no longer be due, and my husband will no longer be able to steal lovers from the world of men. I cannot wait." She seized the chalice offered to her and drank heartily of the mead. Elizabeth dared to glance up only to find the queen's malicious gaze locked upon her. "Do not imagine that you will survive in this court, mortal. I will not share my husband's charms any longer, and since he will not desist, I will remove all temptation. You are the last, but you will not live long."

"You should let her finish her tale," the Elphine Queen insisted. "It is quite excellent and I should not like to live forever without knowing its resolution."

"A tale?" Una held out her chalice for more mead. It flowed like quicksilver into her chalice. "*I* will tell you a tale, mortal, a tale of a maiden stolen from the high tower of Kinfairlie by her Fae lover. This Fae lover told her that he was a prince come to court her love and that he would wed her if she crossed the divide with her hand in his. He vowed to pay a bride price of a red, red rose, which was the last token her family ever had of her."

Una leaned closer to Elizabeth. "He *lied*. He was a king, not a prince, and he was wedded already." She turned the ring of pale gold upon her left hand. "He lied to his mortal maiden and he lied to his lady wife, and when they had both been despoiled, he turned his glance to the realm of men again, seeking another beauty to seduce. His appetite is endless, his charm abounds, and his heart, well, I fear he has no heart at all."

She sipped of her mead. "These maidens came always to the lady wife for solace afterward, in the hope that she could use some sorcery to turn matters to rights. All she could do was make them forget, and sometimes that was sufficient. His gaze would never light on the same maiden twice, after all. Once he has tasted, his appetite for that dish is satisfied, but never his hunger for more.

"And so it was that his lady wife tired of his infidelity, no less of the weeping maidens she had to console. She resolved that if she could not change her husband's ways, she would eliminate his opportunities. She knew he had an affection for the maidens at Kinfairlie, for he had claimed several before his desire for Rosamunde was thwarted by her lover true."

"Thwarted by a mortal?"

"With a little aid from a certain queen," Una said, prompting the Elphine Queen to laugh. "And so it was that the lady wife was inspired by the escape of Rosamunde from her husband's amorous intent, and so it was that she cast a spell."

The Elphine Queen chuckled. "This queen we shall not name was most talented at sorcery, I would wager."

"She was the *best*," Una said with fervor. "Better even than her husband. And she put her all into this spell, a spell that surrounded Kinfairlie as surely as a vine grows round a tower. Her spell was this: that from the casting, when three of the siblings of that family wed for true love, then the doom of the Fae would be sounded and there would be no other tithe due to Hell. The lives of mortal and Fae would be divided and each return to their own. In the following seven years, the portals that linked the realms would be sealed, beginning with the one at Ravensmuir and followed by the one at Kinfairlie. A portent of this she delivered to the Fae, though she did not admit to her own role in the casting of it."

"Ah!" said the Elphine Queen. "So, I have Finvarra to blame for the loss of my pleasures."

Una continued as if the other queen had not spoken. "And so it was that after the spell was cast and the portent delivered, the king himself chose to intervene in the matters of mortals to see his own ends achieved and his wife's scheme ruined. Was it an accident that the eye of the Elphine Queen fell upon Murdoch Seton? Nay, nay, but the queen's sorcery and the maiden's determination saw true love win the day."

Her voice rose even as Elizabeth's eyes widened. "Was it an accident that Garrett MacLachlan was driven nigh mad by visions, cast out by men and left to run in the wild? Nay, nay, it was the hand of the king, determined to protect his pleasures, but the power of the queen's spell and the vigor of the maiden's love saw that man healed and true love triumph."

Una got to her feet. "Was it an *accident* that the king chose to let Malcolm Lammergeier take his fellow's place, that he might be slaughtered to pay the tithe to Hell? Nay, nay, but the love he had kindled in the heart of his lady changed him so resolutely that the blade would not allow his life to be taken, for his soul was no longer the darkest to be found." Her voice rose to a shout. "True love thwarted the king *three* times in succession, and now the portals close."

She sat back down, sipped her mead, and studied Elizabeth. "And so the king ensured that the one maiden he desired most would be trapped within the realm of the Fae when the last portal was sealed. Do not imagine that he will love you forever. Your allure will be lost with your maidenhead, and you will be trapped here forever, in servitude."

"I know this, my lady," Elizabeth dared to whisper. "I was tricked by the mirror and would leave."

"You are snared," Una said flatly. "By your own choice to speak within the circle, you are bound to this place. Make peace with your situation, mortal, for it will not change."

Elizabeth frowned down at her lap. She of all her siblings had most desired to wed for love.

She knew she would never make her peace with that.

૨⁕

It was Christmas Eve when Rafael and his company of men galloped into the bailey of Kinfairlie, their shoulders dusted with newly fallen snow. Their destriers stamped with pride, their pennants snapped in the breeze, and their arrival had brought the villagers out to stare. It was just past noon and the sky was like a pewter bowl overhead. Rafael shivered as he dismounted, knowing that only his adoration of his lady could bring him back to this land.

He could not wait to see her grace his new home and hoped she still desired him as he desired her. He had thought long about his dreams and resolved that only the first one, of her at Kinfairlie, could be true. The second had been but a portent of what would happen if he did not return here by the Yule. Nay, Elizabeth lived, though she ailed, but Rafael would see her healed with his timely return.

He could not wait to see her reaction that he arrived like a champion, that he did so because she had prompted him to change his own course. That would put the sparkle back in her eyes, he was certain.

Rafael savored the mingled surprise and recognition in Alexander's expression when that man came to the bailey to greet his guests. It was evident he had expected someone else and his gaze roved over the party in amazement. A dozen men and as many boys rode with Rafael, all garbed in the black and gold of his new colors, all graced with his insignia. They were a fine and regal party, and Rafael stepped forward with pride to shake Alexander's hand.

"Rafael Rodriguez. I am surprised indeed to see you returned."

"It seems the fate of men who make their fortunes to come to Scotland," Rafael said, knowing his jovial manner mystified his host.

There was an echo of hoof beats and another party entered the bailey, a smaller group riding magnificent horses as black as night. Malcolm gave a cry of pleasure when he saw Rafael and the two of them shook hands and embraced.

"Dame Fortune has smiled upon you," Malcolm said with pride, admiring the party with a glance. "I did not realize matters went so well in France."

"Not for France, but for me," Rafael admitted. "It seems my father was not the man I believed him to be, but a baron in the service of the French king." He chose not to share his father's name just yet. "He has granted me a holding on the frontier to defend, for he would see it in the hands of one he can trust."

Malcolm appeared to be as pleased in this as Rafael and shook his hand again heartily. "And I see that you have tempted more of our former comrades to leave the mercenary's life behind." He greeted the men in the party each in turn, as Alexander looked on.

"Come into the hall and be warmed," the laird said stiffly, and Rafael did not doubt that Elizabeth's brother had guessed the reason for his arrival.

His men dismounted and he offered his hand to Catriona, who smiled at him. She was indeed rounding with Malcolm's son, just as in his dream, and Rafael bowed low after Malcolm lifted her from the saddle. The garrulous Vera was with them, chiding her new husband for some crime or another, then clucking over Avery who had grown much.

"I should have brought the others, had I known you would be here," Malcolm said. "You should have sent word."

"I preferred to ride in haste," Rafael said, prompting Malcolm and Catriona to exchange a smile. Alexander's manner remained grim.

"You must come to Ravensmuir to visit, then," Catriona said. "Before you depart."

"Do you mean to linger long?" Alexander asked politely.

Rafael smiled. "The decision, sir, is not mine to make."

Then he stepped into the great hall of Kinfairlie. It was precisely as his vision, although it was crowded with nobles who must be kin, children and servants. His gaze flew immediately to Elizabeth and he was struck by her unfamiliarity.

She did not look at all as she had in his vision.

She laughed gaily at some comment another member of the family made, and her manner was animated. But her gaze slid past him when he bowed before her as if she knew not who he was. He made a point of speaking directly to her, but there was no recognition in her eyes.

Elizabeth might have been a different woman altogether.

Rafael could not truly believe he was as forgettable as that.

The woman looked like Elizabeth. She sounded like Elizabeth, and she was dressed like Elizabeth, but there was something about her eyes and her manner that made Rafael think more of a doll than a woman.

When she left the hall, insisting that she would fetch one of the children, he followed her, lending chase as silently as a shadow. He felt Malcolm watching him, but Catriona touched her husband's arm.

"My lady!" Rafael called after her and Elizabeth turned to face him.

"Sir?" she said, as if she did not know his name.

Impatient with her manner, Rafael strode to her side and took her hand. He was stunned by its coldness, but bent to brush his lips across it. "My lady. I am most gladdened to see you again," he murmured, letting his lips linger on her flesh. She did not seem to notice and she certainly did not shiver with delight as he might have expected.

"Again?" she asked, her gaze seeming to pass right through him. "Have we met?"

"We have loved, my lady," Rafael confessed in a low voice. "And you have stolen my heart away."

She laughed, as if the idea were absurd, and her voice was high enough to make him wince. "You have had too much of the ale, sir. Let me fetch my niece while you return to the merriment in the hall." Her smile turned coy in a way that did not resemble Elizabeth in the least. "I will not tell my brother of your boldness, for we could not have a battle on this holy day."

Rafael frowned at this unexpected reply. "I will have a token from you first," he murmured, still expecting Elizabeth to reveal herself. He lifted a finger to her cheek, stroked its chill and leaned closer. She looked up at him as if unable to comprehend what he did.

"We stole away for a kiss, my lady," he whispered. "So that others might not witness our embrace."

"Oh!" she said and smiled at him. There was no heat in her eyes, no memory of the passionate unions that had left them both simmering. She might need a reminder that there was blood in her veins.

He kissed her, gently as if to coerce her participation. When she did not respond, he slanted his mouth across hers in a possessive kiss much like the ones they had shared before.

The lady neither responded nor moved away.

She seemed to endure his caress patiently.

Nay, she might have been made of wood for all the fervor of her response.

Rafael tried again to coax her reaction. He drew her closer, trailed kisses along her cheek and murmured in her ear, then captured her sweet mouth anew. When he lifted his head, she regarded him with disinterest, no flush on her cheeks or sparkle in her eyes.

"Are we done, then?" she asked lightly. "Shall we return to the hall now?"

"Of course," Rafael agreed. It seemed impossible to him, yet she acted as if they had only just met.

And as if she had no interest in him at all. The awareness that had snapped the two of them these past six months, the allure that had filled his dreams and the spark that had fairly leapt between them was dead and gone. She was not feigning disinterest. She truly was oblivious to him.

If she had been angry with him for his departure, there still would have been fire in her touch, not this indifference.

Rafael was more disappointed than he could have expressed. He had never thought Elizabeth fickle. Indeed, her determination to think well of him had been the one constant upon which he could rely.

He escorted her to the high table, well aware of how keenly the Laird of Kinfairlie watched him, then retreated to his place at the back of the hall, with nary a kiss upon her fingers. The lady did not seem to notice.

The laird, in contrast, was pleased.

Rafael called to have his cup filled and flicked back his cloak, settling at the board with newfound impatience. It was only when he lifted the cup to his lips that he became aware of a wound upon his finger.

It was the finger with which he had stroked Elizabeth's cheek, just moments past.

And there was a large sliver lodged within the flesh. He had touched nothing but the lady's soft skin.

How could he have gotten a sliver?

Could his other vision have been true as well?

If Elizabeth had been claimed by the dark king, then who was this woman?

More importantly, how could Elizabeth be saved?

※

Catriona's head was spinning with the introductions to all of Malcolm's gathered kin, although Vera had tried to prepare her in advance. Most of the siblings had returned to Kinfairlie this year, including Madeline and Rhys from Wales, with their three children, Dafydd, Rhiannon and Owain. Annelise and Garrett had traveled from the west of the Highlands with their three young children, the twins Aileen and Eva, and their youngest Gavin. En route, they had paused at Seton Manor, then carried on their journey with Isabella and Murdoch, along with their boys Duncan, Cameron and Murdoch. Alexander and Eleanor had four children of their own, Roland, Tynan, Eloise and Melissande, and the hall was noisy with children racing back and forth.

Vivienne and Erik had not come south from the Highlands after their return home the previous summer, for Vivienne was close to her time with their newest arrival. Catriona hoped they would visit the following summer, for she would like to see the children she had tended while in Vivienne's service. No doubt they had grown much taller and she hugged Avery close, wanting to savor every moment.

Catriona was surprised when Rafael came to sit beside her, though she was not displeased. She was glad to have an accord with the man who had been her husband's closest comrade and most heartened by the change in Rafael since Midsummer. He was less angry than once he had been, and truly, showed himself to possess a dangerous charm. There was a lock of hair at his temple that had turned as white as snow, but she dared not ask for details on that. Injury and shock prompted such changes, and she wondered what had happened to Rafael in his absence.

Other than his acquisition of a title and wealth.

Catriona asked after his adventures and of his newfound holding, though she sensed that he wished to speak of more than this.

His gaze strayed to Elizabeth time and again, his confusion echoing her own.

Elizabeth, after all, looked more odd each time she and Catriona met. Though the rest of the family insisted that Elizabeth had returned to her nature from years before, Catriona could not reconcile this cold and giddy girl with the one she had met the previous summer. Elizabeth had been downcast after Rafael's departure, to be sure, but Catriona had been able to understand that. This woman was so odd that Catriona could make no sense of such a large change in her nature at all.

She often did not even like Elizabeth, when once she had thought her likely to become a good friend. Catriona was reassured in a way that Rafael was so disgruntled, for it appeared that he too saw a difference in Elizabeth.

Catriona supposed it was because she was recalling the time

that she, Rafael and Elizabeth had joined forces against a Fae king's scheme that this tale rose in her thoughts.

When Alexander called for a tale, Catriona was quick to raise her voice.

"Once there was a maiden so beauteous that all exclaimed in wonder when they saw her," she began. "Her hair was long and golden, and her eyes were the clearest hue of blue." Malcolm squeezed Catriona's hand and she realized she had described her own coloring. "Her name was Ethna and she lived in Ireland. She was sweet and helpful, as well as lovely, and so it was that when her father gave her hand to the man who had won her heart, all were merry in the land. The lord she wed was young and handsome and possessed of a fine holding, and he adored Ethna more than any might have believed possible. His holding was near Knockma, the hill that covered the court of the Fae king Finvarra. He routinely took offerings of wine to Knockma and his respect ensured that their relations were cordial, as affairs between neighboring lords should be."

Catriona saw Rafael straighten slightly in his place and realized he had caught the reference to Finvarra.

"And so it was that the lord was so happy with his new bride, and his new bride so loved to dance, that the festivities celebrating the wedding lasted far longer than was typical. They went on, night after night, feasting and dancing, and Ethna wore a new dress each and every night of the celebration. On the night she wore her silver dress, the one that looked as if it had been wrought of moonbeams, she faltered in the dance then fell into a swoon and danced no more. All the company were distraught, her husband most of all, and she was carried to her chambers by the lord himself. He sat vigil beside her all the night long, but she did not stir until the sun had risen, and then she spoke only of the wondrous land she had visited the night before, and of her yearning to return.

"Now, the lord had been raised at the keep he held, the one located close beside Knockma, so he knew something of the Fae and their ways. He assumed his bride had been dancing at Finvarra's court, and he feared that she might have taken a sip of some golden wine or eaten a morsel from their feast. He set a watch upon her chambers when the sun began to sink low, and her old nurse sat beside Ethna and held her hand. One at a time, however, each person who sat vigil fell asleep, until the lord himself was the sole one awake. He was resolved to keep his eyes open until the dawn, but when the sun rose, he discovered that he, too, had slept. He saw immediately that Ethna was gone, and he guessed well enough where she was.

"He had his horse saddled immediately and rode with all haste to Knockma, certain his friend Finvarra would have some counsel for him and provide some means to retrieve his bride from whichever Fae had stolen her away. To his relief, as he climbed the hill, he heard two Fae discussing the abduction of Ethna: to his dismay, he learned that Finvarra himself was responsible. One declared that Finvarra was happy, for the most beautiful mortal woman in all the world was his captive forever. Though the lord knew that Finvarra adored mortal women of beauty, he had thought their friendship would ensure his lady wife's safety. He was sorrowful to learn that he had been mistaken and knew Finvarra would give him no good advice. But then he listened closely to the two Fae, for they might grant him some clue.

"And so they did. The first one was confident that Ethna's husband would never see her again. The other was not so, and the lord bent his ear close to the earth, that he not miss a word. 'He could yet gain her return,' declared the second. 'If he dug down into the hill and exposed the Fae court to the sunlight, she would be his again.' The lord did not need to be given this advice twice. He immediately summoned men from far and wide, and they dug with vigor into the hill that sheltered the Fae court. So great was their effort that when the sun set, they had dug a trench halfway to the Fae court. The lord was convinced that his bride would endure only one more night in Finvarra's kingdom before she was home again.

"But in the morning, he had a foul surprise. The hill was restored, the trench filled in and the green growth atop it looked as if it had never been disturbed. The men despaired but the lord was determined to save his lady love. He called for more men and he paid for them to dig faster, and by nightfall on the second day, they had dug two-thirds of the way to the Fae court.

"And yet on the third morning, the hill was restored once again. The lord nigh wailed with despair, for he could not see how he could find more men much less have more men digging in the same place. He feared all would be lost, but he heard a voice in his ear.

He could not see it, but a small Fae had landed upon his shoulder. He could hear its counsel, though, and it advised him to sprinkle salt upon their labor at the end of the day. And so the lord sent for salt, even as he set the men to digging the trench anew, and at nightfall, once again, they were three-quarters of the way to the Fae court. When he put his ear to the ground, he could even hear the music of the Fae beneath the hill and even that faint sound was enough to make his feet twitch. He knew better than to dance, or to let any of his men dance, and so he had the salt cast over the soil, then took the men back to his hall for the night.

"To his delight, the sun rose to reveal the trench as it had been the night before. The men cheered as one, then took their shovels to work even before the sun had warmed the earth. The lord knew that the iron of their spades would destroy the Fae court if even one breached its ceiling, but Finvarra had played him false. And so it was that they were very close when Finvarra's voice carried from inside the hill. 'Cease your digging,' he cried. 'And Ethna will be returned at nightfall to her lord husband.' The lord agreed, content with this compromise, for he truly had no desire to do ill to the Fae: he simply wished for the return of his wife. He paid the men and sent them on their way, and at sunset, he stood at Knockma waiting in the dusk. No sooner had the sun slipped below the horizon than his beloved Ethna came walking toward him in her silver dress, looking like a shaft of moonlight come back to him. He caught her up and rode back to his abode with her seated before him in the saddle, certain that all had come aright.

"By the time he reached his own abode, though, the lord had begun to fear that Finvarra had tricked him. Once he had seized Ethna, she had fallen into a sleep. He had assumed on their ride home that she had not slept these three days and nights and was tired as a result, but when they arrived at his hall, she did not awaken. Nor did she ever awaken again. Days and nights passed and she slept, growing more pale. The old women whispered that she must have eaten of the Fae feast. They said that a log with a Fae glamour upon it had been returned by Finvarra and that the lady herself was still trapped in the hill. The lord did not know what to think or what to do. He went to Knockma, but Finvarra would not receive him, and the hill seemed both still and dark, even at night. He feared he would never be with his lady love in truth again.

"He was mounting his horse at Knockma one night, after yet another failed appeal, when he once again heard a pair of Fae voices from beneath the hill. 'It has been a year and a day that Finvarra has held Ethna's soul and kept her from her husband,' said the first, and the lord realized it had indeed been that long. 'She is lost beneath the hill forever.' 'Nay, nay,' said the second, once again more optimistic for the lord's chances. 'He could win her back in a night if he but unfastened the girdle around her waist and removed the golden pin from it. If he burned the girdle and cast the ashes around her bed, and buried the pin deep in the earth, she would be his again.' The lord did not need to hear this counsel twice. He galloped home and did as the second Fae had advised. He unfastened the girdle around his wife's waist, though it took no small effort to do so. He pulled out the pin, though he had to wrench it free with all his might. He burned the girdle and cast the ashes around her bed, then buried the pin deeply in the earth."

Catriona paused to take a sip of her ale, well aware of how avidly the children listened.

"And?" prompted Madeline's daughter Rhiannon.

"And in the morning, Ethna awakened for the first time since he had brought her back to their abode. She smiled and embraced her lord husband, thanking him for freeing her from Finvarra's spell. She remembered all that had happened to her, but believed she had been gone but a single night. So it was that they were happy together, and had many sons, and lived long and well. The trench in Knockma hill remains, and it is called the Fairy Glen, and Finvarra never cast his eye upon Ethna the bride again."

The company applauded and stamped their feet, well pleased with the tale, and Catriona inclined her head at their pleasure. Her gaze danced over the hall and she was struck by the thoughtfulness of Rafael's expression.

Never mind that his gaze was fixed upon Elizabeth.

Chapter Nineteen

Elizabeth toyed with her cup, seemingly indifferent to the tale Catriona had told. Catriona felt herself frown, for it was unlike the Elizabeth she had met not to respond with great favor to a tale of a man saving his one true love from peril.

"A fine tale finely told," Rafael said with a smile, and Catriona nodded in acceptance of his compliment.

"I thank you."

"You tell tales like Papa tells," little Rhiannon declared from beside Catriona.

"Do I?"

"Aye, Papa tells us always of the Fae, though his Fae are Welsh like him."

"And like you," Rhys declared, scooping up his daughter from behind. He bowed to Catriona, the little girl on his hip. "I apologize for her interruption," he said, nodding at Rafael. "Doubtless you have matters to discuss that are not for little ears." Rhiannon shouted at one of her brothers, and Rhys put her down, shaking his head as she hastened back to play with the other children.

Rafael's gaze lifted to Rhys, and Catriona introduced the two again. "You tell tales of the Fae?" Rafael asked the other warrior, with some surprise.

"Indeed. Such tales carry truth at their root, as my lady wife will gladly tell you."

Rafael appeared to consider this. "A truth such as a Fae king seizing a mortal woman as his bride?" Rafael let his gaze slide to Elizabeth and back to Catriona. "You and I will both recall a risk she took but six months ago."

Catriona nodded and Rhys listened avidly.

"I wonder if there might have been a way that this dark king could have disguised his collection of what he saw as his due,"

Rafael said softly, his gaze meeting Catriona's. "So that none knew he had stolen a bride."

Catriona gasped, her fingers rising to her lips. "A changeling," she whispered, though it was clear by the way that Rafael frowned that he did not understand the word.

Rhys tapped Malcolm abruptly on the shoulder at that. The younger man moved along the bench, for he was talking to Eleanor, and Rhys perched on the bench in the newly made space.

"There are tales of the Fae replacing those mortals they capture with one called a changeling," Catriona confessed in an undertone.

"How can one tell the truth?" Rafael asked.

"There is a tale," Rhys said, keeping his voice low. "Of a Fae revealing her true nature in three ways." He touched his index finger. "She laughed at a funeral."

Catriona straightened. "Elizabeth laughed when Malcolm had word that some of the Sable League had been killed, though she had met those very men last summer. I was affronted, but Malcolm said to make naught of it."

"But she would not have done as much before?" Rafael said.

Catriona shook her head. "I do not think so."

Malcolm turned and Catriona realized he was listening to them, as was Eleanor. "She always wept the most," Malcolm confided. "I thought she but mourned some man's absence." He flicked a glance at Rafael.

"Though on this day she does not know me."

Rhys tapped a second finger. "That she wept at the birth of a child."

Eleanor leaned forward. "There were two christenings at the chapel this month, of babes born in the village," she confessed, keeping her voice low, "Never have I heard a woman lament as Elizabeth did. I was embarrassed, and the mothers most insulted."

They exchanged worried glances. Rhys tapped a third finger. "That she celebrated the untimely death of a child." He pursed his lips when no one spoke. "Madeline went to visit the grave of Madeline Arundel yesterday. That child died young here at Kinfairlie though they had played together. She always goes to the grave with Elizabeth, and she said that her sister's manner was most inappropriate." He lifted his gaze. "She said she could make no sense of Elizabeth's laughter."

They all sat back as one and tried to hide that they conferred. Fortunately, the hall was sufficiently crowded and busy that no one seemed to take note of them.

"But who is she, then?" Rafael demanded quietly.

"A changeling is usually an elderly Fae or even a log," Catriona said. "But it is disguised to mortal eyes by a spell and appears to be the missing person."

Rhys winced. "It is not simple to be rid of one, for she must be burned."

"You would not dare be wrong," Eleanor said.

"A log," Rafael echoed, and examined what appeared to be a sliver in his finger. Catriona frowned without understanding. "I stroked her cheek," he admitted, and she knew it had to be true.

"Still we must be certain," Eleanor said.

Rhys met Catriona's gaze and nodded once. "The children must be sent to bed," he said, then stepped away to summon them. Eleanor rose to do the same, encouraging Annelise and Isabella to send their children to their pallets as well.

"There must be a test before the burning. I will need your help, Rafael," Catriona whispered.

Without hesitation, Rafael leaned closer to hear more.

೭⚘

A year before, Rafael would never have given credit to Catriona's story.

Now he found himself her willing assistant. It was late and the children were abed. Many of the wives had retired as well, and servants had gone to the kitchens to prepare for the next day. Eleanor had deemed there should be few witnesses, in case matters went awry, though she had argued mightily with Isabella and Annelise as to why they should retire early.

It seemed that Isabella was one with a keen sense for a hidden truth.

That fire still blazed high on the hearth—Rafael complained mightily and regularly about the cold, while Rhys coaxed the blaze higher and higher. Elizabeth sat before the fire, doing her embroidery with such cheer that Rafael's belief in Catriona's scheme was buttressed anew. The castellan summoned Alexander away to confer on some detail and Malcolm spoke with some of the men on the far side of the hall.

Catriona gave Rafael a quick nod, then bent down before the fire. She had obtained some egg shells from the kitchens. She filled one half shell with wine and balanced it on the lip of the hearth. She filled a second with wine and set it alongside, nearly tipping the first in so doing.

Elizabeth watched with open fascination.

Catriona filled a third egg shell half with wine and balanced it beside the others with care.

Rhys brought her half a dozen more shells. "I confess I can find no more."

"We must somehow contrive to make it work," Catriona said.

Eleanor came to them, wringing her hands. "The vegetable cuttings and egg shells were already taken to the pigs," she said, her tone apologetic. "I did not realize you meant to do this, Catriona, or I would have saved them."

"I think I have enough. I thank you," Catriona said, setting the shells on the hearth with care. Rhys squatted beside her and straightened a few, knocking them over and spilling the wine in the process. He winced and set to straightening them.

"What is this you do?" Elizabeth demanded, dropping her embroidery in her curiosity.

"I would mull some wine, so that Malcolm and I are warmed for our journey home this night," Catriona said, as if this made perfect sense. She filled another shell and placed it carefully on the hearth.

"But you will need so many egg shells to mull two cups of wine," Elizabeth said with a laugh.

Rhys straightened and stood by the fire.

Rafael took a step forward, prepared to do what he must.

"You need not worry," Catriona said with complete calm. "They served eggs in the hall this day, so I have a goodly number." She displayed her paltry collection to Elizabeth, then filled another shell with care. As she placed it on the hearth, she knocked the one beside it and tipped it. The wine spilled onto the hearth and hissed.

Catriona heaved a sigh and filled the tipped shell again, persisting in her course.

Elizabeth laughed, a high cackling laugh that had no similarity to the warm laughter Rafael recalled. "I have never seen such folly in all my thousand years!" she cried, and laughed yet harder at Catriona.

At the confession of her age, which could not be that of Elizabeth, Rafael seized the changeling. She struggled with a strength beyond that of any human but he held fast. Rhys seized her other side and the two of them cast her into the fire. She screamed with fury to be so discovered, and a hag appeared for a moment in the smoke.

Then there was but another log on the fire, though it crackled loudly as the flames devoured it.

"Tales in truth," Rhys said. "I knew there was something amiss."

"I hoped there was not," Eleanor said. "But now I see that I ignored the signs."

Rafael offered his hand to Catriona that she could rise. "We make an intrepid pair," she whispered and Rafael smiled.

Malcolm joined them, then, his hand falling to the back of Catriona's waist. "You were right then," he said. "I thought she had but changed in my absence."

"But the task is only half done," Rafael noted.

Catriona nodded even as the others looked grim.

"What is it?" Rafael asked.

Catriona shook her head. "In all the tales of changelings that I know, the captive must be retrieved from Fae by a mortal."

"In those I know as well," Rhys agreed. "It is not small peril to our kind to enter that realm, for our chances of leaving alive are slim."

Malcolm smiled and nodded at Rafael's boots. "Rafael knows as much, as do I. I wager your new boots do not have holes in the soles."

Rafael smiled. "Nay, and I know better than to accept any invitation to dance."

Alexander came striding toward them in that moment, his brow dark with disapproval. Eleanor told him of what had transpired, and he turned his frown upon Rafael. "I will guess that you, being who and what you are, will perform this deed for a price."

Malcolm eyed his older brother.

"I am a mercenary no longer, but the son of a nobleman with a title of my own," Rafael said silkily.

Alexander's lips remained a taut line. "I do not doubt you have a price."

"I do," Rafael agreed. "A most fair price, in exchange for saving your sister's life."

Alexander folded his arms across his chest.

"I will take Elizabeth as my wife, should I succeed," Rafael said, then offered his hand to Alexander in expectation of agreement.

"I remember a man claiming a woman he rescued from harm as his bride," Eleanor said, but still Alexander eyed Rafael's outstretched hand.

"She must be returned hale, or there can be no wager," he said.

"Of course." Rafael understood that Alexander was protective of his siblings and could not fault him for that. "I did not ask before because I did not have a holding," he said, softening his tone. "I did not have the *right* to ask, for I had no ability to ensure her welfare and safety. That has changed. Elizabeth will be lady of a fine keep, and live, at the very least, in the style to which she has become accustomed."

Rhys smiled and braced his hands upon his hips, his gaze flicking between the two men in challenge.

Alexander met Rafael's gaze. "Do you love her?"

"With all my heart and soul."

Catriona smiled at that, leaning against Malcolm with her eyes shining.

Alexander considered them all so arrayed against him and sighed. "And I suspect that Elizabeth loves you." He gripped Rafael's hand in agreement. "I vowed to let her choose, and she told me that you were her choice. It is not the match I would have envisioned, and you surely recognize as much, but I think my sister might be right about you, Rafael Rodriguez."

And to Rafael's astonishment, Alexander smiled.

"God speed to you. I would know that she is well."

Rafael found himself surrounded by Elizabeth's family, as the men wished him well and the women kissed his cheeks. They stood clustered tightly together, taking solace in each other's presence, and he knew they would pray for his safe return. Rafael knew that he departed on this quest alone, but he felt as if all their good will rode with him.

It was a new sensation for a man who had always battled alone, and it was welcome indeed.

୨ଈ

The creature Darg was much more amenable to Rafael's plan than it had been before.

Indeed, the spriggan heaved a sigh of relief when it saw the earth being cleared from around the trap. Though it was immortal, it had little patience and these months had been long indeed.

Darg was almost glad to see the mercenary's face again.

"And so?" Rafael demanded, his anticipation clear.

"Your will be done, you need not gloat, freedom is what I desire most. Wishes three will I fulfill—but mind your demands do not serve me ill."

Rafael's smile flashed. "I will tell you of them now. Elizabeth has been captured by Finvarra, or perhaps she has surrendered to him. I have destroyed the changeling and now must retrieve the lady. In this you will help me."

Darg could not truly find any issues with that. *"I like the maid, that much is true, and I would see her love run true."*

Rafael held up one finger. "My first wish is that you will find a means for me to send her a message. Not a short message, but a tale, and it must remain secret from Finvarra."

Darg considered that. *"At least by me it can be done, though his oblivion is not easily won."*

Rafael nodded and held up another finger. "My second is that you deliver the missive directly to her. She must receive it or all will be lost."

Darg nodded. *"The Fae realm is not barred to me. Wherever she is hidden, I can be."*

"And thirdly, when I enter his court, you must speak for me."

Darg grinned. *"If you would have me beg your suit, of this quest you should abandon pursuit. The king has no fondness for me: should I speak, he will not hear thee."*

Rafael leaned closer to the glass, his gaze intent. "Which is why I will tell you in advance precisely what to say."

With that, Darg's curiosity was piqued. The small Fae had no fondness for Finvarra either and would have heartily enjoyed seeing the old king defeated.

Or at least thwarted.

The prospect, as well as its curiosity as to this mortal's scheme, meant that Darg was more than agreeable to the terms of release.

❧

Elizabeth did not know the day or the month any longer. Indeed, the seasons were unvarying in the realm of the Fae, and day did not even seem that distinct from night. All blended together so that time passed effortlessly and without note.

Truth be told, it was somewhat dull in Fae. After her time there—however long it might have been—Elizabeth could understand why the Fae meddled so often in the matters of men. There was no risk or danger in this realm, either, for all were immortal and all eternally young.

The dancing was beginning to grate for Elizabeth. She yearned for an argument, or an exciting event. The peril of Rafael's smile, certainly. The passion of his kiss. While she had once felt numb in the mortal realm, since meeting Rafael, she felt numb in the Fae realm.

She was strolling through a garden, a place she favored simply because it reminded her of the walled herb garden at Inverfyre, when a ball rolled out from beneath the undergrowth and came to a halt directly before her. It was reddish brown, apparently covered with leather. Elizabeth picked it up, thinking that some child had lost it, then recalled that there were no children in Fae.

Once she held it in her hand, though, she realized it was no ball. It was a fruit, a stem at one end and a star at the other, reminiscent of the last of the blossom on the bottom of an apple. She glanced around the garden, seeking the tree from which it had fallen, but could see no good candidates. Elizabeth looked down again, turning the fruit before she recalled where she had seen that shape before.

On Rafael's tabard, the embroidery that he had said was not an insignia.

It was a pomegranate.

How strange that she should have the opportunity to sample that fruit here, in Fae, when she feared she was destined to never see Rafael again, instead of having him bring her one as a gift. She had vowed to not let any morsel of Fae food cross her lips, lest there be absolutely no hope of departing from the Fae realm, but

The Warrior's Prize

this fruit did not look as if it were Fae. The rich color, for example, was in contrast to all the faded hues around her.

And it could not be a coincidence that it was a pomegranate.

Elizabeth turned the fruit, seeking a way to unpeel it. Sour yet sweet, he had said, and she would never forget his expression when he had uttered the words. There was a tear in the skin of the fruit, shaped like a V, and Elizabeth had the strange sense that it invited her exploration.

She pulled back the skin easily at that point and caught her breath at the gleaming beads arrayed within. They looked like round rubies, and she could smell a tantalizing mix of sour and sweet.

Just as Rafael had said.

He had promised honesty to her.

There was a plump bead darker than the others that invited her touch. Elizabeth plucked it from its bed, recalling Rafael's warning that each pearl of juice held a seed, and broke it against the roof of her mouth.

Her eyes widened at the flavor, pungent and wondrous, then she nearly gasped aloud as a vision formed in her mind.

Of Rafael.

He was garbed in black and white, as before, his attention fixed so surely upon her that he might have stood before her in the garden. His black boots had been buffed to a shine and his dark hair combed to order. His chausses looked to be new, for they were perfectly clean and trimly fitted. He wore a white chemise with full sleeves, and a black tabard thick with golden embroidery over it. The embroidery was that of three pomegranates with a braid encircling them and a crescent moon, its points downward, placed above. It was not the insignia he had worn before, and Elizabeth guessed this to be a vision of him since they had parted. His belt hung over his hips, both sword and dagger at the ready there, and he wore heavy red leather gloves that covered his arms to his elbows. His cloak was short and of the same vivid red, slung over one shoulder to hang down his back to the hips.

What was most remarkable was the shock of white hair over his left temple. Had he been injured? Did she see him dead? Elizabeth hoped it was not so, then Rafael scowled and cleared his throat, his gaze becoming more intense.

"I hope to Heaven that this sorcery works," he muttered, his tone so familiar and skeptical that Elizabeth smiled, her heart in her throat. He raised a finger. *"Mi piqueño ángel,* once you insisted that I was afraid, and I argued vehemently. In that time, I thought you were wrong, but I have learned that you were right. You saw to the heart of me, as no one ever has done, and I discarded the gift you offered."

He paused then, scowling at some small figure by his side. "This is madness. Such a ploy cannot possibly succeed."

To Elizabeth's delight, a familiar figure darted out from behind Rafael's boot. *"Trust in me and you will see, that more is possible than you believe,"* Darg said, the small fairy's tone scolding.

"To place memories in a pomegranate is a whimsical notion," Rafael argued. He seemed vexed with Darg, and Elizabeth found his exasperation endearing. He flung out a hand. "You ask me to believe in sorcery! You trick me solely to ensure that you have more ale to drink. This ploy is to your advantage alone!"

Darg now looked as vexed as Rafael, and Elizabeth had to admit they made unlikely allies. *"A plan it is, one that will succeed, but only if you trust in me."*

Rafael's lips tightened, and he looked as if he might have sworn with vigor. Instead he continued his appeal. "Once, you asked me to tell you of my past, and I declined. Once you asked me to grant your sole desire to you, and I declined. And so on this day, in this way, I would grant you the tale you desired that you might choose with full knowledge." He glanced downward for a moment, his brow furrowing. "I fear that you have chosen already, and perhaps the result suits you well. I chose once, thinking I was right, and wished later I might have had the opportunity to change my mind. I would give you that chance." He granted her one last intent look, one sufficient to make Elizabeth's heart flutter, then he disappeared.

His voice though, resonated in her thoughts, as reassuring and thrilling as a whisper in her ear. Elizabeth closed her eyes, easily imagining him beside her, his breath against her skin.

"This one tells me that dreams escape the bounds of the realm you occupy and that your thoughts and memories will yet be your own," Rafael murmured. Elizabeth took a seat in the garden, giving every appearance of simply savoring the fruit and her surroundings.

"It tells me, too, that it is imperative you give no hint of this communication between us, nor even of what you learn from me. The creature tells me it has filled the beads of the pomegranate with my memories and messages, and that those that are plumper and of a deeper hue of crimson contain these truths."

Elizabeth looked down at the pomegranate, noting that there were two more pips as fat and ruddy as the one she had eaten.

Rafael fell silent, though she sucked long upon the seed. Just to be certain that no Fae could conjure Rafael's message from it, Elizabeth swallowed it whole.

The kernel within the sweetness of life.

Elizabeth smiled.

Then she chose another bead from within the fruit.

※

Rafael climbed to the high tower of Kinfairlie after he returned from the cavern and had dispatched Darg with the pomegranate. Catriona hovered beside him, granting him advice.

"You must not speak in his court," she said for the twentieth time and he turned to her with a smile.

"I know as much as I can know, thanks to your assistance," he said. "Now it simply must be done." He shook Malcolm's hand, then that of Rhys, nodded to Alexander, then took the key to the high chamber. He could feel a cold wind blowing through the lock as he inserted the key.

It turned easily and the door swung open, seemingly of its own accord. They clustered together, peering into the room.

Three windows there were, just as Rafael had heard in that tale. The ones on either side were shuttered, the larger one in the middle open. Beyond them, the sea shone, reflecting the light of the stars and moon, and the air was cold. There was even a bit of snow on the floor, though it glittered with a light that seemed unholy.

"There is a rose," Alexander murmured.

"A red, red rose," Catriona agreed.

"Wrought of ice," Rhys said.

Catriona kissed Rafael's cheek in her concern and he pulled his dagger from his belt. He strode across the chamber and claimed the red, red rose.

It was cold, colder than the grave.

He pivoted to face them, noting their fear.

Rafael would show none. "I will return with Elizabeth, or not at all," he vowed, then bowed low.

Then Rafael buried the hilt of his knife into the mortar on the window sill. He leapt to stand upon that sill, feeling the wind from another realm lift his cloak. He glanced back, saluted the others, then strode over the threshold into the Fae realm.

❧

Elizabeth savored the second pomegranate seed, with its taste of mingled sour and sweet. She closed her eyes, letting Rafael's voice fill her mind.

"They tell me that I was born in Pamplona in Navarre, as I recounted to you already, and that I was born both early and in poor health. I told you of my four older sisters, and my responsibility for their death, but refused to tell you more of it. My mother was resolved that the entire family should pilgrimage to Compostela to pray for my improved health. It was because of me that they undertook the journey, and because of me that they contracted the plague. They were all lost there, lost to the plague, though my father and I survived. He returned to his former employ with the Castilian fleet, which attacked towns along the English coast at the behest of the French king. Men of our kind were known for our effectiveness in battle and for being relentless opponents." A note of humor lit his tone. "It could be said I come honestly by my trade and reputation."

Elizabeth gripped the fruit more tightly.

"He left me in the care of his unwed brother in Gijón, a man I remember as kindly. He was killed in the assault upon that town by pirates, protecting me. A stranger saw my uncle's care for me, and though he could do naught for my uncle, he carried me with him as he fled. He left me in the care of a monastery in the hills. He had no coin to donate along with the responsibility of me, and I remember the brothers were not pleased to have another mouth to feed. From the earliest age, I knew myself to be unwelcome. The labor was hard there and the rations small. There was one brother who saved bread for me and was kind." Rafael paused in his story for a moment and Elizabeth feared he would cease his confession. "I was with him when the monastery was attacked and burned. I do remember him being slaughtered before my eyes and the smell of the flames as all was razed. I had seen six summers."

Elizabeth could not imagine enduring such an attack or knowing so much of death at such a young age.

"Much happened quickly in subsequent years. I was captured by the raiders and put to work on one of their ships. One day, without warning, I was sold or perhaps even given to a ship commanded by Pero Niño, which departed shortly thereafter for the Mediterranean. The crew were Castilian and Basque, and I learned much in their company. As has become the mark of my days, though, I was not to savor that situation long. They entered a battle with Tunisian pirates once in the Mediterranean and lost. I was taken captive, along with the rest of the crew who were not killed. They were saved by another force. I was sold to Ibrahim."

Elizabeth felt her eyes widen in dismay.

"Ibrahim was not a bad man, I can see that now, although at the time I despised him. He thought me a heathen or an infidel, no better truly than an animal, though slightly more useful. I labored hard for him, because he beat me when he was dissatisfied, and in time I learned both his language and some of his trade. He would never have taught anything to me, given my origins, but I watched covertly and learned much. He bought and he sold goods, always at a profit, traveling ceaselessly in search of new wares. He would have sold anything to make a coin. He sold tales when he had no goods to sell." Rafael smiled sadly. "He told me often that he would have sold me, if he could have found a buyer for a child so lazy and ugly."

Elizabeth's heart clenched.

"He knew much of healing, too, for his father had been a physician and his mother knew much of herbs. He spoke seldom of them, but I believe he had been bastard-born, and his father denied him." Rafael expression turned intense. "Brutality is learned, Elizabeth. As Ibrahim had been treated, so he treated me. I remember being hungry with Ibrahim. I remember my gut aching with emptiness. I remember being bound in my corner, for he did not trust me not to flee him and he had paid good coin for me. I remember being compelled to watch him eat with leisure and satisfaction. He told me, in halting Castilian, that a man could not expect to have anything he could not afford to buy for himself. I had no coin. I had no prospect of gaining any. He told me I was no better than an animal, and he beat me like a donkey. And I despised that I was so hungry that I did eat like an animal when he deigned to cast me a morsel."

Rafael's voice dropped low. "I remember how much I hated him. It was fury that kept me alive, and a determination to survive simply to show Ibrahim that I was better than he believed. I wanted also to see myself avenged upon Ibrahim. And so it could be said that Ibrahim cast the die in making me what I am."

Again, Rafael paused, then cleared his throat. "You see that you have asked much of me, for I must confess my sins and condemn myself to you, when truly I would seek your favor above all others." His soft laughter sounded wry to Elizabeth. "I called it aright when I thought you an angel, for it is angels who compel us to admit the truth, and angels who may judge us for our faults. I pray you will not judge mine too harshly."

Elizabeth gripped the fruit and pressed yet more juice from the kernel.

"The day came, of course, when the tide turned against Ibrahim. He had aged, of course, and was no longer so strong as once he had been. I had seen sixteen summers then, and although thin, I was stronger than he knew. I let him beat me at the end, wanting to sustain his conviction that he had me utterly in his control. In truth, I awaited my moment, like a viper in the garden, and it came to be in Ceuta. Ibrahim had the misfortune of being in that town when the Portuguese attacked it, intent upon reclaiming it and control of the gate between the Mediterranean and the ocean."

Rafael sighed. "I had never seen the like. The slaughter was tremendous, the chaos nigh overwhelming. Ibrahim was called to assist the wounded, and to his credit or perhaps due to ignorance, he went. Perhaps he thought the fee would be worth the risk. But it was a trap, and though he was not the target, he was caught within the rout. Those snared in that square turned to flee, a great stamping mob that would not be halted in their frenzy. Ibrahim was pushed down hard and he fell, breaking his ankle and nearly trammeled to death. He rolled against the wall and put his arms over his head. His error was in appealing to me for help. It was the moment of opportunity I had awaited."

Rafael pursed his lips. "I acted on impulse at first, the slave determined to avoid a beating. I carried him from that square and returned him to his lodgings. He was shaking with his relief and declared he was in my debt." Rafael looked up. "I asked for the key to my fetters. When he declined, when he laughed, I was enraged."

He cleared his throat. "I am not proud of what I did that day, but I survived because of my choices. I took the key forcibly, careless of what injury I did to him. I took the best of what he had, his garb, his weapons, and I left him there to die. Indeed, as I stood on the threshold and he pleaded for my aid, I taunted him as he had so often taunted me. Better you than me." Rafael frowned. "Brutality is learned, and its lesson was not one I soon forgot. I fought alongside the Portuguese, earning their respect with my deeds. I had naught to lose and all to gain, and I was as merciless as my countrymen are reputed to be. I fought with vigor from that day forth, earning coin to buy what I desire and relying upon no man to ensure that I am fed, clothed and safe from harm."

Elizabeth turned the fruit in her hand, a tear on her cheek for what he had endured.

A smile touched Rafael's lips. "When first I heard the tale of *Mio Cid*, I thought it a fable to entertain those who knew naught of war. I believed no man could show both honor and fight to win. And then, about seven years ago, a knight joined our forces, a knight from far to the north, with steel in his gaze and a ferocious power in his sword. His name was Malcolm Lammergeier. He had barely joined our ranks when I saw him risk all for the sake of a stranger, a remarkable deed."

Rafael nodded in obvious recollection. "We had stormed a town, and there was looting and mayhem in the aftermath of triumph, as always there is. Several men had cornered a young woman, who was no whore, and meant to take her by force. I would not have been surprised if they left her dead or near to it by the time they were sated. Malcolm came to her defense, though he was sorely outnumbered, and when the tide turned against him, I could not let his choice cost his life." He grimaced. "It cost the noble line of his nose. Perhaps my understanding that a man could be both warrior and man of honor began on that night, though I did not guess as much at the time."

His voice dropped lower, his tone so intimate that she ached for him. "I believed myself doomed, Elizabeth. I believed this world was the only existence that mattered and that the only consequences would be my own survival or death. I believed that, until I saw an angel, and she reminded me that there is merit in my heart, until she compelled me to treat her with the honor she deserved and showed me fully what I had lost."

Elizabeth could have listened to Rafael's tales forever. It was so wondrous to hear his voice. Although she knew she should savor this prize, she could not keep herself from listening to just one more.

She took a third seed and closed her eyes, smiling at the sound and sight of Rafael in her mind.

Her smile broadened as he confided the tale of his father discovering him and endowing him with a legacy.

Elizabeth's eyes flew open. Rafael had the right to ask for her hand! He could leave his trade as a mercenary!

If only she could escape Finvarra's court.

That was the moment Elizabeth knew that Rafael would come for her.

Chapter Twenty

Elizabeth was at the board in Finvarra's hall, hoping with all her heart that the pomegranate was a portent. She glanced up when there as a fanfare and her heart stopped cold.

Rafael himself strode into the Fae court, so fearless that she was thrilled. His gaze was resolute, his stride determined, his expression as inscrutable as ever. He looked neither to the left nor to the right, but marched to stand before Finvarra's throne. He halted there, facing the Fae king but not looking into his eyes.

He looked precisely as he had in the visions granted to her by the pomegranate.

Elizabeth could not keep herself from scanning him greedily to note each and every detail. His garb was richer than it had been before and the small embroidered pomegranate on his tabard had been replaced by a larger emblem. Perhaps he was in service now to a great baron, instead of laboring as a mercenary. The most striking change in him was the shock of white hair at his temple, precisely where she had seen him struck.

Rafael was alive.

He had confided in her.

And he had come for her.

Elizabeth was both exultant to see him and terrified at the price he might pay for his valor. The Fae fell silent, their reveries stilled by the presence of the intruder.

Elizabeth could have reached out a finger to touch his boot.

Finvarra's grip tightened on the arm on his throne and Elizabeth imagined that the king knew why Rafael had come.

She hoped he would not do Rafael injury, but dropped her gaze as if more interested in her cup of mead. It was easy to recall Rafael's own words.

A man who means to survive does not reveal all he knows.

She felt Finvarra glance her way, then back at Rafael, who remained silent.

"What brings you to my court, mortal?" Finvarra demanded, his manner regal. "Have you the desire to dance again?" He waved a hand and the music began once more, a merry jig sufficient to set any toe to tapping. A group of Fae began to dance, sparkling as they frolicked toward Rafael. They joined hands in a circle and danced around him, creating a circle of gold around his knees.

He neither moved nor spoke. Elizabeth wondered how Rafael would save her if he could not speak, then he tucked his hand into his tabard. When he pulled out his hand, he brandished a red, red rose that glittered as if it had been wrought of ice. Rafael cast it on the floor of the hall, then ground it beneath the heel of his boot, his expression impassive. Finvarra caught his breath, and behind him, Una smiled.

"What travesty is this?" Finvarra demanded.

Rafael said naught. He reached into his tabard once more. When he pulled out his hand again, a small familiar creature was standing on his palm, her chest puffed with self-importance.

Darg! Elizabeth had to drop her gaze to hide her anticipation.

Darg bowed low to Finvarra. *"My king who left the red, red rose, bride price for the maiden who you chose, that boon is now restored to you, as untouched as the morning dew."*

Finvarra was discomfited by this, Elizabeth could see. Did the return of the rose ensure her freedom? She could not be certain, but Una's delight was undisguised.

"Your hold weakens over your prize," the queen whispered to her spouse, who did not deign to reply. "At the very least, this man should be granted one request."

"Not her," Finvarra growled.

"Surely your honor demands that you cannot keep a maiden without paying her bride price," Una murmured.

Finvarra turned on her with a flash of anger. "Surely, my honor is beyond rebuke, as I am king of his realm."

Una's eyes narrowed but she said no more. Finvarra settled back with satisfaction, his gaze fixed grimly upon Rafael.

Darg bowed again, clearing her throat. *"This mortal would not be so bold, as to demand the most valued prize you hold. Indeed, he would wager with you and exchange a riddle as his due. But should you not solve his rhyme, a boon he would claim of you this time."*

Finvarra made a sound of annoyance in his throat and drummed his fingers on the arm of his throne. Elizabeth knew he loved to match wits with others, for he dearly loved to win. She hoped Rafael had a good riddle, because she had a fair idea what he might ask if he did win.

Her heart filled with hope anew.

"I need not play your games," Finvarra said. "I know your desire and I would not relinquish her."

His wife Una leaned over his shoulder, her hand stroking his neck. "But surely, my love, you can defeat a mere mortal!" she said, laughter running beneath her tone. "You have lived thousands of years and know nigh every riddle there is!" She leaned down and lowered her voice. "Show him that you are master in this kingdom."

Her taunt worked, for Finvarra straightened. Una shot a triumphant glance at Elizabeth, and she realized that the Fae queen had also guessed Rafael's intent. "I take your wager," Finvarra said, then gestured to Darg. "But if I *can* answer it, then you will be my captive forever."

Darg glanced up at Rafael, saw the reply in his eyes, then turned to nod at Finvarra.

"Tell your riddle that this folly may quickly be behind us." Finvarra pretended to be dismissive but his eyes glinted with interest and he stroked his beard, unable to fully hide his anticipation of victory.

Darg straightened and clasped her hands behind her back. Her voice rang clearly through the Fae court.

"Splendid palaces and rich attire,
A love to set her heart afire,
Children to fill her days with joy,
Labor that she does enjoy,
A smooth young face for all her days,
Cause for laughter, come what may:
These gifts there are and more besides
But all women name the same one prized.
Cocks may strut and braggards boast:
But what does a woman want the most?"

Una laughed lightly, her laughter sounding of silver bells. "Surely you, my lord husband, with your great fondness for women, should solve this one easily." There was an edge to her voice and Elizabeth glimpsed again her jealousy. She could have named what Una wanted most, that was for certain, for it was clear the queen wished for her husband's faithfulness.

Finvarra hemmed. Finvarra hawed. Finvarra knitted his fingers together and furrowed his brow. He glowered at Rafael, who remained impassive, Darg standing on his outstretched palm. He glowered at Elizabeth, then at Una, then at the Elphine Queen—who appeared to be mightily amused by this exchange. Elizabeth supposed that he, like she, could not imagine what objectives they three women might hold in common value.

Darg cleared her throat again, this time more portentously. *"Your time cannot be infinite, a reply I need so answer quick."* Finvarra glared at the spriggan for her audacity, but Darg was not deterred. *"'Tis only just that kings show grace. Your reply must be made apace. Ten pulses of the mortal's heart, then I shall have your best retort."* Darg bent down to touch the pulse at Rafael's wrist and began to count aloud.

One, two, three.

Elizabeth was amazed that Rafael's heart beat so slowly, despite the moment before them. He was so composed that she might have feared he did not care for her, had he not sent the pomegranate. As it was, she knew he sought to have Finvarra underestimate him.

Elizabeth toyed with her mead, determined to feed the illusion, knowing that surprise was the best weapon. As ever, she did not drink the beverage, but simply let the Fae pour it for her.

Four, five, six.

Finvarra drummed his fingers on his knee, then snapped them, summoning a cloud of Fae advisors. They whispered to him, suggesting solutions, as he glared at Rafael.

Seven, eight, nine.

Elizabeth dared not breathe. She feared her agitation would be evident to any one who glanced her way.

"Ten!" the spriggan cried. *"Ten beats there were and ten is time. Your answer now shall be mine."*

Finvarra rose to his feet. He strode toward the spriggan and the warrior, his manner so forbidding that Elizabeth feared he would smite them both. Rafael did not move. The spriggan quivered a little but stood tall on Rafael's palm. Finvarra seemed to grow larger and his silhouette more ominous. The words burst from him with evident reluctance and no small measure of frustration.

"I do not know!" he declared and the court was all a-chatter.

Darg beamed. *"Then you have lost and he has won. His will in your court must now be done."*

"But what is the answer to the riddle?" Una demanded.

Darg glanced up at Rafael, then nodded at the king and queen. *"A lady would choose her own way, for choice is what brings joy to her day. And so it is my warrior's request, that you grant a choice to Elizabeth."*

Finvarra pivoted sharply, his gaze locking upon Elizabeth. He smiled slightly as she deliberately feigned indifference, then spun to face Rafael again. "You are a fool," he said softly. "You give a choice, but she will not choose to leave. Our marks are upon her skin; she has become one of us. You have wasted your victory."

Darg cleared her throat pointedly and Finvarra laughed.

"I shall keep my word, have no fear of that." The king spun then, his robes flaring out behind him as he strode to Elizabeth. He spoke softly, urgently, his voice pitched low in an evident attempt to beguile her. Elizabeth stared down at her mead, trembling inside. "And so, my Elizabeth, a choice lies before you," he murmured. "Will you stay in Fae, or will you leave with this rough warrior?"

Elizabeth dared to lift her gaze. She glanced at Rafael as if she did not know him, then surveyed the court with obvious admiration, letting Finvarra believe he had won.

The king smiled slowly, chuckling at his evident triumph, then Elizabeth straightened.

"I will go," she said, speaking loudly and with clarity so her decision could not be questioned. "I would have my own choice, and he is the one who gives it to me."

Una laughed merrily at that. Finvarra's brow grew dark as thunder and he raised a fist, but Darg clucked her tongue. Rafael bowed to the king and offered his hand to Elizabeth. She could not truly believe that they would be allowed to depart, but she was not going to surrender the opportunity to do so. She hastened to Rafael's side and put her hand in his, struck by how right his grip felt upon hers. She spared him a smile of gratitude, only to find his eyes narrowed.

And his gaze fixed upon Finvarra even as he backed away, retracing his steps out of the Fae court.

Finvarra smiled at them, his manner indulgent. He was so satisfied that Elizabeth could not explain his manner. Was he glad to see her gone, then? It made no sense. His wife Una came to stand behind his throne, her own pleasure in the result more than clear. It was impossible to Elizabeth that this pair should agree upon anything, but Una's hand stole over Finvarra's shoulder in a possessive gesture. The king glanced at her hand, then moved as if to shrug it off.

There was a sound then that seemed to come from deep in the earth, a sound that set the very court to vibrating. It could either have been a mountain moving or the sky tearing. Elizabeth could not say, but it was a sound that filled her with dread.

That Finvarra laughed heartily did naught to change her thinking. "You had best be quick," he murmured with obvious glee. "Soon this portal will be closed between the realms and you will be my captives forever."

Una, his wife, cursed like a fishwife. "Vermin!" she cried at her spouse. "You would seal your mistress in our realm when the way is barred. You tricked them and me, by stalling until it was too late for them to flee."

The portal closed!

Finvarra laughed and laughed, well pleased with what he had wrought.

※

Rafael spun on his heel and began to run, tugging Elizabeth behind him. His mouth was set to a firm line, evidently to keep him from swearing aloud, but his eyes blazed with anger. He clearly remembered the course he had taken, for he ran with all haste, never hesitating at a junction or a turn.

Elizabeth was running as quickly as she could, her breath coming in great gasps, even as the rending sound continued. She did not know how far they had to flee or even where they would emerge in the mortal realm. In truth, she did not care. She feared she was slowing Rafael's retreat but his grip was tight on her hand,

and she knew he would not leave her behind.

The tunnels reminded her of the ones that had once been beneath Ravensmuir, the ones that had fallen in years before. They were hewn from rock and would have been dark without the golden illumination of the Fae court far behind them. Their shadows were long and dark on the walls and the light grew ever more dim as they ran. But they were unfamiliar tunnels, and she had been beneath Ravensmuir enough in her life that some corner should have looked familiar.

As they ran, the sound of the realms being torn apart grew only more fearsome.

They climbed a pile of loose stone and Elizabeth stumbled, stubbing her toe on some of the rock. Rafael did not hesitate but swept her into his arms and continued to run. She clung to him, hoping they would survive.

Before them a great portal was suddenly revealed, a deeper shadow in the darkness ahead. It was more than two-thirds obscured, a door of mirrored obsidian drawing steadily across the gap. A light glimmered far beyond the opening, and Elizabeth was reminded of the flame atop an oil lantern. It seemed like a beacon and she was convinced that if they could reach it, they would be safe. The gap, though, grew smaller with every step they took. The dark mirror moved with convulsive jerks, closing the space on one great lunge. The flame was out of sight and Elizabeth gripped Rafael tightly.

The portal would be sealed before they passed through it!

Rafael evidently came to the same conclusion. He bared his teeth and leapt for the door, just as it rumbled again. The remaining gap was too narrow for Rafael and Elizabeth's heart clenched in fear.

But Rafael seized the lip of the mirror as if to halt its progress. He shoved Elizabeth through the space to the other side as he forcibly kept the portal from closing.

Nay! Not alone! Elizabeth tumbled to the ground from the force of his push, but was on her feet in a heartbeat.

The opening had already shrunk to half its width again.

"Rafael!" Elizabeth screamed, seeing that they would be parted forever. "I love you!" She saw the blood flowing from his fingers and knew the portal was as sharp as a blade. She gripped his hand

and he leaned to the gap so that she could see part of his face.

"*Mi pequeño ángel,*" he mouthed, still recalling the rules of Finvarra's court, still hoping for triumph. "*Better me than you,*" he added, to her horror, and blew her a kiss through the space.

Nay! She could not lose him.

Then the mirror shook and moved again. Rafael pulled back his hand and there was only his blood on the stone. Elizabeth beat at the barrier, wanting to be with him, but its course was relentless.

He would be trapped in his worse nightmare, snared with the dead in Finvarra's court and compelled to pay a price forevermore for seeing her free.

This could not be!

As Elizabeth shouted in frustration, a small figure leapt into the remaining gap and braced itself between portal and wall. The space was no bigger than the width of two of Elizabeth's fingers held together and the door shuddered to move. Whatever it was would be sliced in half!

To her amazement, Elizabeth recognized Darg, the Fae spriggan that had both befriended her and plagued her. She had no notion what to anticipate from the small creature, for its loyalties oft changed.

Darg granted her a sharp look, then drew herself up taller. "*A boon is owed from me to you, and on this day all debts are due. The fourth of true loves bound to each other, this portal will not cleave asunder.*"

Before Elizabeth could make sense of that, the spriggan took a deep breath, then screamed.

"*Aiiiiiii!*" was her bellow, the sound loud enough to pierce Elizabeth's ears. In the same moment that Darg roared, the spriggan became a large phantom of furious, pulsing red. In the blink of an eye, she was taller than Elizabeth, wider than the corridor, and Elizabeth was thrown backward by her sudden and growing presence.

She shielded her eyes as the stone of the corridor began to crack, overhead and on all sides, the rock strained by the spriggan's need for space at all costs. She heard a rumble and a groan and feared that she would be trapped beneath a mound of rubble, just as her uncle Tynan had been.

Then she saw a jagged line erupt across the smooth black

obsidian that created a barrier between the worlds.

The dark mirror cracked.

Darg screamed again and the rock shivered. Elizabeth heard another crack and then a third. Rafael's boot appeared as he kicked at the mirror from the other side. The portal shattered and broke, creating an opening into darkness.

Rafael did not hesitate but lunged through the space, landing in a tumble and rolling to his feet. Elizabeth was already on her feet by the time he reached her and he urged her away from the portal.

She heard a bellow from far below, a roar that made the earth rumble and the ground shake beneath their feet. They held hands and ran toward that flickering light. Elizabeth did not know precisely where they were, for it was dark on all sides, but Rafael ran with confidence.

There was the sound of crumbling behind them, the echo of rock falling and tunnels collapsing. She looked back to find a cloud of dust rolling in pursuit, a roiling cloud filled with debris and undoubtedly ill will. It gathered speed, approaching so quickly that she feared they could not outrun it, but Rafael tugged her onward.

They were panting when they reached a threshold of stone. It made no sense that there should be a lip of fitted masonry in this cave, but there was no time for questions.

Rafael pulled out a dagger that was wedged into the mortar, and Elizabeth had time to recognize it as his own. Then he swept her into his arms and jumped over that sill, catching her close as he fell down into some space beyond. He turned his back to the onslaught of debris, holding her tightly against him. Elizabeth buried her face in the warmth of his throat, glad beyond all to be in his embrace.

The dust and stone erupted beside them, and she fully expected it to follow them. But the gap had become a barrier, a clear barrier that halted the assault of the debris.

Elizabeth felt the floor beneath their feet shake, but Rafael held fast to her. She clung to him, reassured by the steady pound of his heart beneath her ear and the strength of his arms wrapped around her.

With Rafael, she would always be defended.

She would tell him later that his rescue of her from Finvarra's court was fitting of a troubadour's tale. She would tell him later that he was a champion beyond her wildest dreams.

But first she would show him how glad she was of his return.

Saturday, December 25, 1428

Feast Day of Saints Anastasia and Eugenia.

Christmas Day.

Claire Delacroix

Chapter Twenty-One

When the tumult was passed, Elizabeth dared to open her eyes. They were in a chamber and she realized with a start that it was the one in Kinfairlie's tower, the one with three windows looking out to sea.

The middle window no longer offered a different view than the other two.

The portal to Fae was closed, and they were on the right side of it. Elizabeth could see the sea in the moonlight, its surface glittering as if it were studded with gems. The moon rode high and silver in a sky as dark as velvet and there were few clouds. A slight wind blew and it was chilly, but she found it invigorating. She took a deep breath, well pleased with where she stood.

There was no sign of Darg.

The flame flickered atop the lantern left on the floor beside the door, and Rafael went to check the level of the oil. "I thought we might have need of a beacon," he said, heaved a sigh of satisfaction, then returned to face her with a smile.

Elizabeth smiled back at him, letting her pleasure show. She had no chance to express her thanks, for Rafael cupped her face in his hand, then bent to kiss her thoroughly.

"I suppose there is one good way to celebrate your return," she said when she could speak again.

Rafael grinned. "I would think it a fitting deed for a lady to meet her legal husband abed."

Elizabeth took a step back to consider him, pretending to be more surprised than she was. "You said you would never wed."

"I had not the right to wed. I left to win that right." Rafael gestured to his tabard. "I have a holding, now, our own little Valencia, if you will have me as your own." His eyes twinkled in a way that made her chest tight. "A man of honor."

Elizabeth smiled in turn. "I fear you will never become as tedious as others we have met." She bit her lip. "But I suppose you will have to ask Alexander for his permission."

"He has given it," Rafael said. "In exchange for my quest to save you." His dark brows quirked, giving him the wicked expression she so loved. "But let us ensure that he cannot change his choice."

"How so?"

Rafael took off his cloak and spread it on the floor, then beckoned to her with a dangerous smile. "Come here, *mi piqueño ángel*, for it is time we had a son."

Elizabeth laughed and went to him, for he offered everything she had ever desired.

And more.

There was no possibility that Rafael could lose Elizabeth now.

He spread his cloak on the floor of the chamber, humbled by her confession of love. He was not a man who uttered such pretty words readily, but he would show her the fullness of his heart with his deeds.

She came to him, eyes alight, and touched one hand to his cheek. She looked into his eyes then brushed her lips across his, her touch fleeting and achingly sweet. "You gave me the right to choose," she whispered, sliding her lips over his once more. Rafael closed his eyes, savoring the sweet softness of her, the feel of her breath against his skin. "And I chose you, Rafael Rodriguez. I care not where we live or how. I would be with you."

Rafael smiled and slanted his mouth over hers, claiming her lips for a kiss that made his heart thunder.

When they parted, she examined his hand, wiping the blood from the cuts across each finger. "They will heal well enough," he murmured, dismissive of such details. Elizabeth was safe, she was in his arms, and he wanted to taste every increment of her skin to reassure himself after so nearly losing her. She seemed to feel similarly, for she pressed herself against him and ran her hands over him repeatedly.

"You might have lost your fingertips," she chided.

"I would have lost more if you had been trapped there for all time," he said with heat, earning himself another passionate kiss. Rafael found himself backed into the wall of the chamber, the object of her amorous assault.

He had no complaints but caught her around the waist and lifted her against himself, kissing her so deeply that they both were out of breath when he lifted his head.

Then Rafael smiled. "The marks upon your flesh are fading before my eyes," he whispered, well pleased that the dark king's hold over his beloved was broken.

Elizabeth smiled up at him, appearing to be equally pleased. "Because my champion saved me, just as I knew he would."

"You do not ask of my insignia," Rafael murmured, bending to kiss beneath her ear. He unbound the lace in her hair and spread her hair over her shoulders, spearing his fingers through its silken length.

"You told me you did not have one."

"I did not, not then."

She drew back slightly, wonder in her eyes. "You went to claim our Valencia," she whispered, echoing his words and only now understanding them. She seized his tabard, examining the symbols upon it. "You are in the service of some lord! Where is this?"

"Guess."

"Three pomegranates."

"Three potent seeds," he confirmed and she smiled up at him.

"And an encircling braid." She frowned at him, as she traced the circle on his tabard, mystified.

Rafael lifted his left wrist, showing her the bracelet he had made of her hair. "A mark of my lady's favor."

"You did pull my hair! I thought I had dreamed as much" Elizabeth laughed, then eyed his tabard again as she nibbled her lip. "A crescent moon, with its opening downward. I do not know its meaning."

"It is the symbol used by Rodrigo de Villandrando, who is now in the service of Charles VI of France."

"Your father?," she guessed and Rafael nodded. He enjoyed watching her decipher the puzzle. "If he is in service to the French king, it must be a border territory, perhaps in Normandy or Burgogne." She glanced up. "Close to Navarre?"

He could not disguise his pride, nor did he want to. "Very close to Navarre. The pilgrim's road to Compostela passes through it, and one could follow that road to the pass of Roland as well."

Elizabeth smiled at him, well pleased. "And your lord has granted you the right to wed. Have you a home in his abode?"

"I have a holding to mine own name, Elizabeth. I would offer you no less."

She laughed and kissed him in such delight that he wondered at his own doubt in her reaction. "Oh, Rafael, I am so proud of you."

"You will be far from your family..." he began but she interrupted him.

"My aunt journeys to Sicily regularly." She rolled her eyes. "If there is a port and the weather is warm, we will be plagued by guests."

"There is a port," Rafael admitted. "And they press fine wine in this land."

"We shall never be rid of them," she said then laughed again. She sobered as her fingers rose to the shock of white hair at his temple. "I thought you dead," she admitted, her voice uneven. "I thought you snared with the dead you had seen in Finvarra's hall. That was why I went to his court, in the hope that I might at least see you."

"Elizabeth," he murmured, overwhelmed at these tidings. He framed her face in his hands and kissed her deeply, pouring all the emotion into his touch that he did not know how to express. She pulled him down to the cloak and he was glad he had brought the fur-lined one. Her hands were on his belt, but he lifted her fingers away, pressing a kiss into each palm. "Let me, *mi piqueño ángel*."

She smiled and complied. Rafael set aside his scabbards, then unfastened his belt. He removed his boots, then tugged his tabard over his head. Elizabeth took it from him and folded it with care, caressing the embroidery on the front of it with evident pride. He unlaced his chemise and pulled it over his head, letting her look upon him to her own contentment. She rose then and came to his side, running her finger over the wound she had stitched closed. She smiled impishly at him, then bent and touched her lips to the scar.

It was the first wound of his she had healed, but he knew it would not be the last.

She ran her fingertips up his arm and over his shoulder, and he was content to let her explore him. She eased her fingers into his hair and stroked the back of his neck. "Our children will have dark hair," she whispered.

"I shall pray that the girls have the alluring green eyes of their mother," he murmured and she smiled again.

"I shall pray that they all have the thick lashes of their father," she whispered, brushing his eyelids with her fingertips. "I am quite jealous of yours."

Rafael chuckled and unlaced the sides of her kirtle. He slid his hands beneath the embroidered cloth, locking them around her waist. He tugged her against his chest and kissed her slowly, savoring the way she responded to his touch. She wanted to experience passion, but she offered it as well, and Elizabeth was a feast of which Rafael knew he would never tire. When her kirtle was set aside, he caught his breath at the shadows of her curves beneath the sheer linen of her chemise.

Never bashful, she pulled off the chemise and dropped it, standing before him in only her stockings. Rafael dropped to one knee to unfasten her garters, unable to resist the opportunity to kiss the inside of her knees. He smoothed the stocking from her leg, then did the same with the other. Still on his knees, he kissed the inside of her thigh, trailing kisses to the sweet pearl he had touched once before. Elizabeth gasped and her knees trembled, prompting Rafael to sweep her into his arms. He stretched her out on the fur and kissed her intimately, summoning the storm within her so that she writhed beneath him. Her fingers dug into his shoulders, and her skin flushed, the pulse of her heart against his very lips.

"Not alone," she gasped.

Rafael rolled to one hip and unlaced his chausses with haste. Elizabeth's fingers were on him, her kisses and caresses making him fear it would be too quick. She urged him onward though and, wanting to surprise his bold maiden, he pulled her astride him. She spared a glance at his erection, her eyes shining, then smiled down at him.

"Show me," she invited, her trust so complete that his chest was tight.

Rafael guided her hips so that their union was complete. She was tight and slick, as heavenly as he recalled and more willing than he could have dreamed. This time, she began to move with him and as he suggested, her cheek against his, her breasts on his chest, her buttocks filling his hands. He tried to hold out, to move slowly, but she was too tight and too ardent, too sweet after he had waited so long. He gritted his teeth as the passion rose and he felt her smile as she pressed a kiss to his ear.

"I still wonder that married couples ever leave their beds," she whispered wickedly and Rafael laughed.

"Perhaps we will not leave ours."

She laughed and he resolved to show her yet more. He rolled her over to her back, remaining buried inside her and drew back slightly so that he could ease one hand between them. He caressed her again, watching her passion rise and her flesh tinge pink. He teased her even as he moved within her, loving how she moaned with pleasure and yet continued to demand more. There was naught in all the world save the pleasure in her smile and the heat in her eyes and Rafael knew he would do whatever was necessary to ensure the happiness of his beloved.

He pinched that tight pearl between his finger and thumb, casting her over the edge of pleasure. She shouted in her release and gripped his shoulders, even as he buried himself deep within her and found his own release with a roar.

"I love you, my own angel," he whispered into her ear and she cast him a sleepy smile of contentment.

"I know," she said, running her fingertips over his jaw. "Destiny cannot be thwarted."

Rafael braced his weight on his elbows, looking down at her in satisfaction. "We shall make a home, Elizabeth, for you will teach me how that is to be done."

"And you will tell me all of your stories," she countered. "Each and every one."

"Perhaps we will be too occupied in living an adventure fit for an old tale."

She laughed then, laughed with a pleasure that could not be feigned and one that lightened his own heart. "What did you write to me?" she asked suddenly. "There was a missive in the vision, one that fell in the river after you were attacked. It was addressed to me."

"So, the scribe did not lie," Rafael mused.

"What was it?"

He smiled down at her. "A confession that all that was mine was yours. I bade you go to the cave and dig, for I left all my wealth there for you."

"You did not!"

"I did. We will gather it on our return." Rafael sobered. "I feared that you might conceive a child and I wished you to have choices."

"I choose to conceive one now," she said with delight.

Rafael put a finger on her lips to halt her kiss, for he knew that once she embraced him, he would be lost all over again. "There was also a copper vessel with a small djinn trapped inside, one that had been told it must grant three wishes to whosoever released it."

Elizabeth frowned at him. "But wait. You always insisted that you could not see the Fae. How did you trap one then?"

Rafael smiled, caught in his own tale. "A man who means to survive does not reveal all he knows," he reminded her and Elizabeth laughed.

"And that Fae was Darg!" she breathed. "*She* brought the pomegranate."

Rafael pulled back slightly. "That being is female?"

"I have always thought so, though I do not know."

"I have my doubts," he murmured. "But in the end, it fulfilled the three wishes I requested."

"Which were?"

"The first was the tales put within the fruit, the second the delivery of it to you, the third its speaking for me in Finvarra's court."

Elizabeth bit her lip. "But I believe Darg sacrificed herself to see you saved."

Rafael kissed her temple. "Then that was done by the creature's own choice, perhaps because it too loved you."

Elizabeth pulled him closer and kissed him again, a potent kiss that made him think they might linger a while to celebrate their triumph. Rafael had gained all he had ever aspired to hold within his own hand, as well as a greater prize in his bride than he had ever dared to hope might be his own.

He could not think of a better thing to celebrate, or a better way to celebrate it than by pleasing his lady repeatedly.

They would have need of many sons, after all.

And it would be hours yet before the sun rose.

※

Father Malachy awakened to the sound of someone rapping upon the door to his cottage. It was a commanding knock, one that brooked no delay in his responding. His first thought was that he had overslept and not rung the bells early enough for the first mass of Christmas morning. There was more than one resident of Kinfairlie village who would find fault with that, and truly, Father Malachy did not have any desire to be remiss in his duties.

It was darker than he had expected and he opened his portal cautiously, though he could not recall the last time there had been brigands in Kinfairlie village. He anticipated mischief more than anything else.

He certainly did not expect to find that comrade of Malcolm's on his threshold, his garb uncommonly fine, with Lady Elizabeth in his arms. The lady herself was disheveled, to say the least, her hair unbound and her feet bare. A fur-lined cloak was wrapped around her and he had to wonder whether she was fully garbed beneath it.

She was, however, so radiantly happy that Father Malachy could not make sense of it.

He recalled events at the keep well enough and knew this man's name to be Rafael Rodriguez.

The one who had sworn to retrieve Lady Elizabeth from the realm of the Fae and had demanded the right to wed her as his reward.

"Good morning, Father Malachy," Lady Elizabeth said, as if there was naught untoward in their presence on his porch at this hour, or her own state. "We have come to be wed, if you please."

"I have coin for your services," said the warrior and strove to reach for his purse without putting down the lady. This made Elizabeth laugh as Father Malachy had not heard her laugh in years.

"Later," she chided her companion. "Father Malachy will trust us for the duration of the service itself."

"Indeed," the priest said. "But I think it would be wise for me to confirm with the laird that this match is to his satisfaction..."

"He gave me his pledge last night," the warrior said, his manner grim.

"Aye, but..."

"Do you suggest that he will not stand by his word?"

"Nay, but matters may have changed..."

"Aye, they have," the man said with confidence. "The match has already been celebrated."

Father Malachy felt his mouth open, but no sound came out. He hoped he had misunderstood but suddenly the lady's state of dress made sense.

As did the shine in her eyes.

There was truly no choice, then. Laird Alexander would have to keep his word, and the match—whether pledged in a church or not—could not be annulled, not if both parties agreed it had been consummated. "But I must don my cassock," he managed to say, feeling flustered. "I will meet you at the chapel."

"In all haste, if you please," the warrior growled. "I will come to fetch you if you linger overlong in my estimation."

The lady smiled and kicked her feet with pleasure. "Are you in the habit of threatening priests?" she demanded of the man she would wed, clearly unafraid of him.

"If they have not the wits or the inclination to perform their duties, I see no issue with some *encouragement*," he countered, earning himself a kiss of such enthusiasm that Father Malachy retreated inside his cottage. It took him a moment to catch his breath, then he donned his cassock and his shoes, prayed he was choosing aright, and hastened to the chapel.

Lady Elizabeth had rebraided her hair and stood upon her own two feet, her hands clasped in those of her intended. That man handed Father Malachy a gold coin so large that the priest blinked in wonder.

Then he considered. "The banns have not been called."

The warrior handed him another coin.

"And I should confer with my patron."

A third coin joined the other two. Father Malachy looked down at them in wonder. "You spare no expense in taking this bride."

"I will expend my coin in York to claim her if matters do not proceed promptly." The warrior reached for the coins, but Father Malachy tucked them hastily into his purse.

He raised his hand in blessing over the pair, just as the first light of the morning sun peeked over the horizon. Kinfairlie village looked to be touched with silver, and the bit of snow that had fallen during the night glittered as if lit by inner fire. He could find no issue with the fervor evident in their exchange of their vows, nor in the satisfied smile of the warrior as he took a gold ring from his own hand to slide it onto that of Lady Elizabeth.

"*Mi piqueño ángel*," he murmured, looking like a man much smitten with his bride.

"*Mío Cid*," she replied, her expression no less adoring than his. "*Il Campeador*."

Father Malachy had no idea what they confessed to each other, but it was clear they were both well pleased. The warrior actually laughed, his voice rich with merriment, and Lady Elizabeth threw her arms around him with delight. He swung her high in his arms then kissed her so thoroughly that Father Malachy felt obliged to avert his gaze.

It was time he rang the bells for mass, after all.

The pair led the way to the altar for that mass and dropped to their knees together, their hands clasped tightly. Father Malachy stood on the porch to await his flock, unable to stifle a sense that this particular morning seemed filled with promise. Perhaps it was because the last of the daughters of the house of Kinfairlie was wedded now. Indeed, all the siblings were married, save Ross, the son who was in service at Inverfyre. Perhaps it was the marvel of this day of days, a day that filled his heart with joy every year.

Father Malachy decided he would light a candle for Ross, in the hope that boy—who must have become a man these recent years—did well in the year ahead.

He caught a glimpse of Kinfairlie's smith, Bertrand, and waved. It was not uncommon to see Bertrand awake early, for that man labored long and hard. He would come later to mass with his family, as was his custom. On this morn, though, Bertrand stood outside his smithy without a chemise. He surveyed his own bare skin with apparent astonishment, then gave a hoot of joy. He then danced around the yard of the smithy, seizing his astonished neighbor and dancing with her until she laughed aloud.

It was rather chilly for such antics, in Father Malachy's opinion, but on this day of days, he could judge no man.

It was Christmas in Kinfairlie and all was right beneath the sun and the moon. Father Malachy could only pray it would always be so.

The Warrior's Prize

Claire Delacroix

Ready for more medieval romance?

Read on for an excerpt from

The Crusader's Bride

A company of Templar knights, chosen by the Grand Master of the Temple in Jerusalem to deliver a sealed trunk to the Temple in Paris. A group of pilgrims seeking the protection of the Templars to return home as the Muslims prepare to besiege the city. A mysterious treasure that someone will even kill to possess...

Gaston has had his fill of war and the Latin Kingdoms when he learns that he has inherited his father's estate in France. He accepts one last quest for the Templars, the order he has served for fifteen years, and agrees to deliver a package to Paris on his way home. A practical man, Gaston knows he now has need of a wife and an heir, so when a lovely widowed noblewoman on pilgrimage catches his eye, he believes he can see matters solved to their mutual convenience.

But Ysmaine is more than a pilgrim enduring bad luck. She has buried two husbands in rapid succession, both of whom died on her nuptial night, and believes herself cursed. Accepting the offer of this gruff knight seems doomed to result in his demise, but Gaston is dismissive of her warnings and Ysmaine finds herself quickly wed again—this time to a man who is not only vital, but determined to remain alive.

Neither of them realize that Gaston's errand is one of peril, for the package contains the treasure of the Templars—and some soul, either in their party or pursuing it, is intent upon claiming the prize for his or her own, regardless of the cost. In a company of strangers with secrets, do they dare to trust each other and the love that dawns between them?

The Crusader's Bride

Excerpt from THE CRUSADER'S BRIDE © 2014 Deborah A. Cooke.

Jerusalem—May 15, 1187

Gaston de Châmont-sur-Maine read the missive from his brother's wife again, unable to believe that he had understood the words correctly the first time. That Raymond should have died so suddenly and at such a young age was incomprehensible to Gaston.

That his older brother was not laughing as he rode to hunt was beyond belief.

But Marie's meaning could not be doubted. It was there, before his own eyes. Raymond was dead, and he, Gaston, was now Baron de Châmont-sur-Maine. He touched the red wax seal, embedded with the mark of his family's house, impressed with the signet ring that he had only to ride home to claim.

Châmont-sur-Maine was his.

He would have preferred that Raymond yet lived. His older brother had taken the responsibility of Châmont-sur-Maine with an ease and grace that Gaston did not possess. Gaston was a fighting man, a man accustomed to a simple life. He looked around the stables of the Knights Templar, situated in the Temple in the Holy City itself. He leaned against the wall of the stall assigned to his own destrier, Bon Chance, even as that steed nuzzled in the hay. His squires had been dispatched to take a meal in the kitchens, and he had come to this place to read his unexpected letter.

He ached that he would never hear Raymond's bold laughter again.

As always, the extensive stables were bustling with activity. Knights returned from errands and from duty, their horses slick with perspiration. Others were preparing to ride out, their steeds stamping with impatience to run. Some great destriers were being brushed down while others were saddled up. The floor was thick with squires, hastening to do the bidding of their knights, and the air was filled with jokes and commands. He could smell the hay in the stables and hear the clang of anvil on steel from the smithy as repairs were made to armor and armament. Bon Chance nibbled Gaston's hair playfully from behind, and he rubbed the beast's nose with affection.

Gaston had pledged to the Templars fifteen years before and had never expected to leave the order. Raymond was only two years older than him. He was hale and vigorous.

But Raymond had only daughters. His will decreed that Châmont-sur-Maine pass to Gaston instead of his own children.

It was sensible, more sensible than Gaston would have expected from his older brother, but he could not deny the practicality of the choice.

All the same, Gaston was accustomed to war and battle, to the company of men and the good care of horses. He knew little of running an estate, although he had witnessed his fair share of politics and intrigue. He fingered the letter again, astounded at the opportunity, knowing he could not deny it, yet strangely uncertain of what lay ahead.

He would need a wife.

He would need to father children to ensure Châmont-sur-Maine's future.

He would be a baron. He would ride to hunt at whim, feast in his own hall upon fine fare, and sleep in the same bed each and every night for the rest of his life. It was impossible to associate his brother's life with himself, and Gaston doubted he would accustom himself readily to the change.

There was no choice, though.

He tucked the missive into his tabard, eyeing the activity that surrounded him. Responsibility could not be denied, and Raymond's clear thinking could not be undermined. Gaston would return to France and his legacy.

He would find a bride with all haste and embark upon the task of making sons. He had seen six and thirty summers, and Raymond's death made him taste his own mortality. There was not a moment to waste in securing the future.

Although he would choose the moment he shared these tidings with the Grand Master of the Temple with care. Gerard de Ridfort was passionate and unpredictable, and truly Gaston could not regret that he would no longer have to follow that man's command. Gaston instinctively distrusted those who followed their impulse and were impetuous as Gerard tended to be. The astonishing losses of Templar knights at Cresson this same month showed the merit of that man's leadership, and Gaston did not imagine for a moment that Saladin meant to leave matters as they stood.

Gaston straightened with purpose. If he meant to return alive to Châmont-sur-Maine and ensure the future of his family holding—as was now his responsibility above all others—he had best tell the Grand Master the news as soon as possible.

A Templar could not disobey an order from the Grand Master. Gaston had to ensure that Gerard had as little time as possible to grant him one.

Then he would find a wife, with all haste. Christian women on pilgrimage oft prayed at the Church of the Holy Sepulchre. It seemed reasonable to Gaston to begin his search there. His expectations were minimal. She would have to be of noble blood, unwed, and both young and vigorous enough to bear him multiple sons. It would not be all bad if he found her attractive, for that would make rendering the marital debt more pleasant.

Beyond that, Gaston expected little of a wife. He hoped to find a practical woman, for he knew naught of courtship or even of conversing with women. He imagined that his inheritance would offer sufficient inducement to the kind of woman he sought.

Gaston de Châmont-sur-Maine left the stables with a whistle upon his lips, certain that all could be arranged sensibly and quickly.

This optimism was only possible because Gaston knew so little of women in general, and of Ysmaine de Valeroy in particular.

That situation would not last.

The Crusader's Bride
is the first book in Claire Delacroix's new
Champions of Saint Euphemia series.

Available May 15, 2015!

Bestselling author Deborah Cooke sold her first romance novel in 1992 – that medieval romance, **The Romance of the Rose**, was published by Harlequin Historicals in 1993 under the pseudonym Claire Delacroix. Since then, she has published more than fifty romance novels and numerous novellas in a wide variety of sub-genres under the names Claire Delacroix, Claire Cross and Deborah Cooke. **The Beauty** by Claire Delacroix, part of her successful Bride Quest series, was her first novel to land on the New York Times' List of Bestselling Books. In 2009, Deborah was the writer in residence at the Toronto Public Library, the first time they have hosted a residency focused on the romance genre. In 2012, she was honored with RWA's Mentor of the Year Award.

In addition to writing the **Champions of Saint Euphemia Series** of medieval romances as Claire Delacroix, Deborah is currently continuing her **Dragonfire** series of contemporary paranormal romances which feature dragon shape shifter heroes. She lives in Canada with her husband and far too many books.

Learn more about Deborah's books at her websites:
• http://www.delacroix.net
• http://deborahcooke.com

Deborah's monthly newsletter includes additional contests and news for subscribers:
• http://eepurl.com/UCUdf

Catch the latest news and reviews on her Facebook page:
• http://www.facebook.com/AuthorClaireDelacroix

Printed in Great Britain
by Amazon